SARA ALLERTON

MAKING SHORE

Saraband

FOR *Brian and Edith*
AND FOR *Mum and Dad*

This novel was inspired by incidents that took place in 1942 following the torpedo strike on the SS *Sithonia*, but all the characters, including that of Brian Clarke's namesake, are fictional. Any resemblance to real persons living or dead is purely coincidental. The story and the actions and words of its characters are based on a blend of the author's interpretations of Brian Clarke's reminiscences and the author's own imagination and invention of events that did not actually occur.

Saraband

Suite 202, 98 Woodlands Road
Glasgow, G3 6HB, Scotland
www.saraband.net

FIFE COUNCIL LIBRARIES	
HJ287266	
ASKEWS & HOLT	04-Apr-2012
AF	£8.99
GEN	CA

ISBN 13: 978-1-887354-74-5

Printed in the EU on environmentally friendly paper.
3 4 5   14 13 12

'This is a brilliantly conceived story of endurance and romance, in which Sara Allerton's mastery of detail and sympathy with her characters fully engage the reader. It held me enthralled until the last sentence.'
LORD BUTLER OF BROCKWELL

'Sara Allerton's novel is a remarkable imaginative achievement – she takes you every inch of the way on this extraordinary journey across the Atlantic; it is a compelling story of both shame and heroism.'
EDWARD STOURTON

'This breathtaking debut novel deals with man's harrowing struggle for survival in a hostile sea, but this book is so much more – a life-affirming account of love, camaraderie, anguish and coming of age, played out against a backdrop of the Atlantic swell. *Making Shore* is destined to become a true maritime classic.'
ANGUS KONSTAM, AUTHOR OF *Sovereigns of the Sea*, *Piracy* AND *Naval Miscellany*

'Sara Allerton's debut novel is an impressive and affecting war story ... truly memorable. ... Written with poetry and lyricism, but with the feeling of authenticity added by the real-life Brian Clarke's involvement, this is an impressive and enjoyable debut novel, and a reminder, if one were needed, that behind the bald statistics of Allied shipping losses during the Second World War lie the stories of many, many thousands of brave merchant seamen. This novel is a fitting testament to their sacrifice.'
SIMON APPLEBY, BOOKGEEKS.COM

'The profoundly moving story of a brotherly bond forged in unimaginable wartime suffering, of the bitterness of a terrible promise honoured, and, above all, of the hope-giving, life-sustaining selflessness of true love. *Making Shore* is a powerful and remarkable novel.'
CLARE GIBSON, THE ARMY CHILDREN ARCHIVE

'I don't cry much over books, but this one brought a great lump to my throat. It is an extraordinary story – the grim face of war, chirpy unassuming courage, and running through, the need to keep faith whatever the cost. In the end, I did weep, but not from sorrow or despair.
ANDREW WHEATCROFT, AUTHOR OF *The Enemy at the Gate*

'The best book I have read for a very, very long time.'
PEOPLE'S BOOK PRIZE VOTER

The People's Book Prize is a national competition aimed at discovering new authors; the winning titles are chosen by reader votes rather than a panel of judges.
Making Shore won the 2011 annual prize for fiction.
www.peoplesbookprize.com

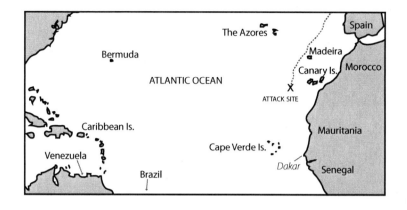

HISTORICAL NOTE

The Battle of the Atlantic was the longest continuous military campaign of World War II, pitting German warships against Allied convoys from 1939 through to 1945, and was at its height from mid-1940 through to the end of 1943. Convoys of merchant ships between North America and the South Atlantic and Europe were protected by British and Canadian forces, aided from 1941 by US ships and aircraft.

Some of the incidents described in this novel are based on one survivor's recollections of serving on the British merchant ship SS *Sithonia* on such a crossing in July 1942, and of the ship's sinking after a torpedo strike roughly at the site shown on the map above. The story of how some of her crew managed to reach safety is rooted in actual events, although all the characters and their interactions and dialogue (including Brian Clarke's) are fictional.

It was widely rumoured throughout the war that merchant seamen would be gunned down, or their lifeboats destroyed, in the event of their surviving a torpedo attack. The historical record has shown that on 14 May 1942, two months before the *Sithonia* was struck, Hitler ordered his submarine commander-in-chief, Admiral Karl Dönitz, to 'reduce the number' of survivors of strikes on merchant ships by whatever means.

'Human speech is like a cracked cauldron on which we bang out tunes that make bears dance, when what we want is to move the stars to pity.'
GUSTAVE FLAUBERT

CHAPTER 1

THE MEETING

I had imagined that she would already be there, waiting for me. She was not, and it unsettled me completely. Paralysed by the prospect of such a meeting – its most probable course, its outcome – my mind had clung to the only version of events it could afford to contemplate and that could go no further than finding her waiting there and blurting out what I would have to say. I had allowed myself to consider only what was necessary and it had not included any of the finer detail: not my reception, not her reaction and not her initial, if temporary, absence.

I sat down heavily and felt the certainty of my resolve break up and seep away. Closing my eyes, I leant my elbows on the table and covered my face. The tips of my fingers sought the sunken sockets around my eyes and began to press their way along the grainy irregularities of bone beneath the fleshless skin.

Perhaps it would not matter. Only I would ever know. I pressed my fingers hard against my eyeballs until they bulged, patterning with pain, and once again indulged the thought that I had fought so hard against, but which alone soothed and slowed the endless circular motion of my mind's distress. Perhaps I would be forgiven for saying nothing. For seeking and admitting clemency. Had he had the chance, perhaps he would have granted that the spirit of such a promise given might be more important, after all, than the absolute adherence to the dictate of its letter.

Either way, it had made a coward out of me. I had pushed it away, staved it off. It had been weeks since her letter had arrived, too many weeks, but still it was too soon. I was not ready. I had told myself that I needed time to muster strength, but what I meant was courage. I had dreaded it. After all the horror, even after all the horror, I dreaded it.

I blamed Joe for having left me with this graceless legacy. I had been brave, everybody said so. And hadn't I learned after everything that real courage is not, after all, the absence of fear so much as the refusal to give it rein? Complacently perhaps, I told myself that I had done with fear. I had run its gauntlet, parried its every thrust. I had feared the stealth of U-boats, stalking, far out to sea. Feared the maverick ocean. Her moods and whims. The unrelenting heat in the dawn and the black lapping of the night. Inexorable thirst. Slow starvation. I had feared for my sanity, for that of the others. For my life. And for Joe's.

It hadn't killed me. I was still here, fiddling with the doily in this calm, cool café. There were normal people all about me here, and as I had gained weight and begun gingerly to bask in rudimentary relief, I saw that I might become one of them again. Fear could not touch me now. Except within my dreams.

And yet I sat in the café, waiting for her, fighting the leaden lurching of my guts every time the door swung open.

I tried not to look up too jerkily, willing my eyes and fingers to keep steady on the stiff paper lace and fell to cursing Joe for making me swear, and to remembering.

Remembering. How could I ever forget?

I felt the quiet reproach of her presence not two feet from the table long before I could bring myself to look up at her. Sweat, unexpectedly cold, prickled along my hairline and, in bringing a trembling hand up quickly to dispense with it, I sought to cover, just for one moment longer, the shame in my disarray. I watched from beneath the slow, deliberate rhythm of my hand across my brow, the hem of her coat rising and falling almost imperceptibly at her knee.

'Mr Clarke? Cubby Clarke?' My own name, as she said it, with such eager, sharp-edged clarity, surprised me somehow and I flinched. I had not heard his name for me since I had got off the *Barneveldt* in Barrow. The fingers of my free hand clenched involuntarily around the remnants of the doily, and the fork at my elbow clanked obtrusively to the floor as I half rose, sweaty-palmed and stomachless, to greet her.

'Maggie.' I gestured towards the chair opposite mine and waited for her to sit. She edged her way onto a quarter of the seat and put her hands, which clutched and unclutched her gloves, on the table in front of her. I sat down again awkwardly and, unable still to look right at her, I watched her restless hands.

'Why did you say…'

'Tea?' My voice, overloud, jutted out across hers.

She nodded and waited quietly while I beckoned the waitress over. Clutching and unclutching. Having ordered, we sat, apparently with nothing to say. The tea came and I busied myself with the pouring and the fussing.

'Sugar?'

'No. No, thank you.'

Tea. What I wouldn't have done for a cup of tea then. It was unimaginable.

As I stirred and stirred with inordinate interest, I chanced a glance at her. She wasn't at all what I had been expecting.

The windswept desperation of the figure I had encountered so briefly on the dockside had pursued me ever since but I had taken in her mental anguish only and, crippled by my own, had been in no fit state to consider her physical presence much at all. Joe had talked to me of beauty, but then Joe had been in love.

There was a quiet earnestness in her bearing, which would make it easy for her to go unnoticed. She was older than me, by four or five years or so; but then Joe was older still. She no longer had that glow of confidence that girls my age exuded; that innate self-assurance in the invincibility of their youth.

She was dark-haired and olive-skinned. Her facial features, taken individually, could not have been described as pretty, or even sweet. Her brow was wide and her nose too flat while the large, oval shape of her face seemed overawed by the wayward waviness in her hair, strands of which refused doggedly to remain tucked behind her apparently tiny ears, wholly inadequate for the job. But these irregularities, far from undermining her personal appeal, seemed only to have added to it, for the overall impression she gave was one of a woman who, long used to viewing them as flaws, no longer saw them as important. This artless lack of vanity had imbued her with a physical ease, an ingenuousness that was mistaken, for her attributes taken as a whole made her unusually, if unobtrusively, engaging.

'Thank you for coming to meet me... um, Cub?' she tried it out, uncomfortable.

'Brian. Brian's fine,' I said, too quickly. 'Cub' was too raw, too close, and given the apparent impossibility now of avoiding that which still I might have done almost anything to avoid, I had to keep her distant.

But she had composed herself in the break for tea and her voice was now more even. I slid my eyes up to the middle distance beyond her, avoiding hers, and waited.

'You look a lot better than you did.'

'I am getting stronger... yes.' I nodded stiffly. 'It'll take a long time.'

My answer, only half-heard, faded with the smile of vague encouragement that had hovered briefly about her lips. She was already at her next question and those we both knew lay beyond it.

'Why did you say that at the docks? That you couldn't help me? When you knew?'

There was nothing that I could say to her. I could not explain it. There was no language in the world that would adequately translate the reasons for my reticence.

And so I did not answer, but like the coward I felt myself to be, I took refuge in a question, shrinking from the words I still did not actually know if, when it came to it, I would have the heart to say.

'Why were you there? When you knew he wouldn't be?'

She paused for one moment, contemplating my prevarication, but I kept my eyes away and conceded nothing. Then she said quietly, 'I just needed to see for myself. Just in case… you know.' She tutted. 'Silly, really. False hope.' Shrugging, she forced a little smile which subsided almost as soon as it had begun.

'False hope? I know a lot about that,' I said grimly. She didn't know what to say to that so she didn't say anything. She stared instead abstractedly at her hands as if they were not her own. They continued to work at the gloves.

'But how did you know? What ship we would be coming on?' I asked. 'It's classified.'

'My sister's husband is at the War Office. He is a good man.' I could feel her eyes upon me, intent, sizing me up.

And again, silence. It's curious, but people say that when two people are only interested in each other in a room, all other noise is soundless. Curious and true. The silence that fell between us was loud, weighty. I wasn't aware of the other diners, their conversations and the general clattering of crockery. It must have been going on. I was aware only that she, unsuspecting, was anxiously awaiting misinformation that I was ashamed to give.

'Billy Rawlins said you and Joe were close.'

'You know Billy?' I interrupted her, confused, but she shook her head.

'I saw him when you docked. Somebody called his name. After you… after, I remembered it. I looked him up and went to talk to him. He couldn't tell me much but he told me that I should speak to you.'

Billy Rawlins. The name sounded like one I might have heard years ago but couldn't quite place. An echo of someone. Yet not so very long ago I had been living in such close proximity with him that I could recall every single sinew on his skinny little carcass. I had come to know them all, maybe as intimately as their own mothers did. Their mothers perhaps could have forgiven them. I could not. And not least because we had been the ones who'd made it. We had survived.

Billy Rawlins was sharp-eyed, flinty. We had seen each other as men do not wish to be seen or remembered. I never wanted to see him – or any one of them – again.

'I wanted to know…' She stopped abruptly and I waited.

'You were with him when he died, weren't you? You were with him.' She repeated this last quietly, but not so quietly that I didn't hear the heightening of her voice.

It required an answer, and for the first time I looked right at her and saw in that moment all that Joe had loved.

An almost unnatural, unnerving beauty lit her up from beneath the depths of her astonishingly large, dark eyes. I saw who she was. She had been speaking of him and there it was, shining out at me: the glittering radiance that was her passion. All that she had expected was there, all that she had hoped for and all that she had left to dream, a silent charter of hopeless hope played out in the ever-darkening shades of brown. Water that had gathered but did not fall added a brittle brilliance to the strident, luminous intensity flickering within.

I could see with a clarity that physically shook me, how she had loved him. She would have loved him no matter how many days they had been afforded, she would have married him, borne his children and she would have loved him. She would have loved him into old age and she would have loved him until the day that she died. With an unflinching honesty that was almost crude, her eyes betrayed her very core. She was beautiful and I understood.

I am a terrible liar. I always have been. In fact, I am almost pathologically truthful and it got me into trouble a couple of times both on the lifeboat and in Sebikotane. Joe used to say don't ask Cub, he'll tell you. That's what he used to call me. Cubby Clarke. Cub. Because of McGrath. Because I was the youngest. It seemed like centuries ago. I used to worry that if I ever did end up being a prisoner of war, would I be able to lie convincingly enough not to give away things I shouldn't? Why then, oh why, Joe, did you leave me with this? I knew why. He knew that I would do it, that was why.

I became uncomfortably aware as I gazed at her, that she was waiting for me to say something. I looked down at my untouched tea.

'Yes,' I said. 'I was with him.' She breathed out softly and put her hands one on top of the other over her gloves.

'Was he... in pain?'

'Yes. It was painful, yes.' Her eyes, which I could feel were scanning my downturned face for the slightest scrap that might afford some insight, forbade me from trying to dissemble in this. I would stick to the truth as long as I could.

'Was he frightened?'

'Not then, no.' She drew herself up and tried to tuck some strands of thick, unruly hair away, swiftly, absently. They fell back into her face immediately. She rewrapped her coat around her, tight, and almost through gritted teeth she forced out what she had come for.

'Did he say anything? You know, for me?' The desperation in such a naked plea made me want to cry out to her.

'Say anything?' God, did I have to make her beg?

'A message. For me. Something.' Her voice was thin, alone. She too took refuge in staring at her unwanted tea, some hair still bobbing out in front of her eyes. I noticed that most of it had been mashed into a sort of makeshift bun at the back of her head, but there was far too much of it for her ever to have got it tidy. Having hurled the question into the air, I knew she was willing it with all her being to land the right side up.

I sat on my clenched fists, my legs and buttocks so tightly squeezed together that I felt the pain in my stomach.

'No.' I paused and suddenly, the strange, deeply sickening sensation of dislocation that comes with no food, dehydration and bludgeoned hope settled cold across my bowels. It is the chronic kind of fear that takes up residence inside you, quickening your mind and darkening your soul. You stop noticing it's there until the balance of your circumstance shifts again slightly, one way or another, and fear spurts out of every pore, corrupting your behaviour and drying up humanity. You are simply afraid in entirety and nothing, nothing can allay it. My mouth went slack, saliva-less. For a second, I felt his fingers tightening again around my forearm, as if he were here, pricking my conscience, steeling my resolve. The hair on the back of my neck prickled.

'I'm sorry.' I looked up at her bowed head. Her hair really was a mess. 'No, he didn't.'

There was silence. She shook her head quickly as though shaking off my lie, as though trying not to let it in.

Then: 'He must have talked to you. About me. On ship? On the lifeboat? You were his friend,' she coaxed. Somewhere, on some other airwave, every single nerve in her body was shrieking, high-pitched and searing, 'please!'

'Look,' I said, switching her off, looking away towards the waitress, the umbrella stand, the door. 'I don't quite know what it is you want to hear but…' I put my hands up and apart, attempting careless ignorance, affecting not to understand. Hesitating, I glanced back up towards her and winced at the raw, expectant hope inscribed on every muscle in her face. I tried to lick my lips.

'But I can't tell you… Joe…' Striving to swallow, I closed my eyes and the haggard image of his face, burnt onto the backdrop of my mind, appeared before me, forcing me to look once more into his eyes. Wide and bloodied, charged with all the fixed ferocity of passionate intent, they bore into me, they willed me on.

'He talked about a lot of people. He was popular… you must know that. But I'm sorry, I don't remember that he mentioned you… or any other girl…' My voice trailed away and, putting my elbow on the table, I covered my mouth with my hand that I might hide the next words from her. I tried to clear my throat. '… In particular,' I said.

It was the best that I could do.

For a minute, we both stared dumbly at the tiny, poisonous seed of doubt I'd cast down between us, a seed that, however obliquely, implied if not casual indifference then worse, whispered infidelity. It unfurled before our eyes and took root.

She looked up at me sharply and after a moment, sat back in her chair. She stared at me and as I watched her, I saw hurt catch fire and crackle across her features. Her mouth formed a little 'o' and, as her face flushed dark with heat, she turned it from me.

Then she laughed. A high, shallow laugh that had no truth behind it and I noticed that she shut her eyes in its delivery. 'Any other girl …? In particular? What does that mean?' She shook her head, 'What are you trying to say?'

'Look,' I said, stage quiet, trying to stifle the alarm her rising voice aroused in me. 'I can't tell you anything much more than…'

'He told me he loved me. When he left. I believed him.' Effectively her ace, she threw this across the table at me, interrupting, almost snarling. Protecting herself, protecting him.

Shrugging as carelessly as I could, I folded my arms. 'He said a lot of things. That's what I'm trying to tell you, he talked about a lot of… people.' I leaned towards her quickly. Get it said. Get it done. He said make sure. He told me to make sure.

'You know what he was like. Couldn't hardly ever shut him up most of the time. He'd been at sea a lot. And sailors… well, they get a reputation, don't they?' May God forgive me. I closed my eyes and my teeth involuntarily clenched. 'All I am saying is, don't waste your life using him as your yardstick. He wasn't worth it. Do you understand me? I haven't any message for you because… well, because from the way he talked… it just didn't seem to me that there was anyone… I just don't think that he could have been entirely…'

My gaze, which had become so assiduously preoccupied by every other minute detail of the room, the other diners and their tables, the plates of food arriving at them – everything in fact, other than that which most demanded it – inadvertently slid at that moment back towards her face, and my eyes were caught and inextricably held by the agony of understanding I saw hardening in hers.

Appalled, ashamed, disabled, I could not say it. The word, which would have unequivocally encompassed all that he had wanted me to say, started and then stalled at the back of my throat. Faithful. It would not come. I could not do it. I could not. To denounce as faithless and unworthy the man who I had found to be possibly the most faithful of all men and to do it before this woman with her huge and faithful eyes – it was worse than base. It was a violation from which my spirit recoiled.

But she had seen my struggle, and her puckered face, already so reduced and gaunt with grief, creasing every moment further with incredulity and with pain, crumpled suddenly with comprehension. Intuitively swift, she had glimpsed at what it was that I had meant to say and innocent still, quite probably ascribed my inability to speak to some misguided attempt at chivalry. I had not said it but what I did not say had been enough. Though I had not quite done what Joe had asked of me, I had clearly forced her up against the conclusion he had wanted her to make. I did not need to say any more. Had I struck her, it would have pained her less. She stared at me, her preposterously beautiful eyes fixed upon my face, stupefied.

At last, her hands were still.

How long we might have sat there was anybody's guess. Neither one of us could quite believe the implications of my silence and each, frozen in our separate grief, seemed incapable of ending it. We must have made a desolate tableau but since neither of us moved and the café was slowly emptying, the waitress took it upon herself to crash in and clear away our plates. She was big and clumsy and she clattered across us roughly. Nobody spoke, but all the while, without moving, Maggie held me in her great, dark gaze. Finally, the waitress lumbered off.

Abruptly, Maggie looked away, as if suddenly she could no longer bear to look at me.

'I don't believe you,' she said flatly.

But there is a fundamental, nonetheless self-destructive flaw in the makeup of many of us that can brook no such close assault. For no matter what we may know to be incontrovertibly true about a person, when another casts aspersions on that truth, self-doubt will settle itself around the edges of that knowledge and begin its insidious work. Gradually, so very gradually, its whispering tendrils weave their way in and around until even the purest supposition, undermined by suggestion, time and re-hashed memory, is strangled.

Even as she said 'I don't believe you,' I heard the uncertainty in her voice and saw the imprints of fleet-footed doubt make tracks across her face.

She got up to go and as she turned away I stumbled to my feet and, reaching out my hand towards her, blurted 'You have beautiful eyes. He said that about you. I remember now.' I had to give her something. Surely he would have allowed me that. I couldn't let her go and have her think him entirely without honour.

She stopped but did not turn back.

'Thank you,' she whispered, very gently, as if she were speaking from some far-off place. 'You have been kind.' There wasn't the slightest trace of irony in her voice.

My eyes misted over. I have trouble with that these days. That and sleep. By the time I had blinked it away, she was gone.

I sat back down. Her green gloves lay listless on the table. She had left them behind.

CHAPTER 2

KNOWLEDGE

At nineteen, I was sure about a lot of things. I knew that I was good-looking in a mischievous kind of way, and I knew that girls liked me. I could be funny. I knew that I was bright and that I was stubborn. I meant to learn. I was sure that there was more for me than Courtauld's nylon factory. I wanted more. And I knew that the sea was promise, it was graft but it was a multitude of places I had barely heard of. But most of all, without being wholly conscious of this thought, I knew that my body was strong, invincible, and I immortal. Death was not for me. Not yet at any rate. The sea and I, we had some parity – we were limitless, we were infinite. Its grace and charm enchanted me.

I began to long to be off. At fourteen, already desperate, I begged Father to come down to the docks with me to try to persuade some skipper, who had already told me *nay, I was but a bairn yet*, to take me on. Father had come but the captain had shaken his hoary head again and refused me even as a cabin boy. Father, secretly relieved, cuffed me affectionately and told me I'd best make myself into someone useful if I wanted to go with them. So to get me where I yearned to be, I went to the radio school on Friar Street.

I worked hard. Courtauld's became a means to my end rather than the end itself, and by taking the two-till-ten shift, I could be in Friar Street all morning. By seventeen, I had my Post Master General's Certificate, albeit The Special, which, attainable in less time, was the Merchant Navy's quick-fix response to the sudden dearth of young and qualified recruits. There was a war on, and above all they needed bodies.

I proudly presented myself at the Marconi Offices in Lime Street in Liverpool and was assigned aboard my first vessel. Third radio officer on the *Empire Tide*. I could scarcely contain myself.

My life became all I had wanted it to be. It didn't much matter to me where we were headed. The world was what I wanted. As far as I was concerned, Calcutta was as exotic as New York, Ceylon as fascinating as the southern tip of Africa, and I drank them in. Life aboard ship in the midst of war struck me only as a great adventure. And it struck me too that I had become a man. I was needed. The crews relied on me to decode the messages from across the airwaves that would keep them out of danger, that would keep them all alive. Had I stopped to think about it, those dangers were uncomfortably real. If I had been older, if I had known what I know now and if I had had any concept of the responsibility with which I had been entrusted, I might not have walked so tall, nor slept so soundly.

There was no doubt that the merchant navy was playing an important part in the war effort. For our island country, the cargoes we carried across the seas were not only crucial to the survival of those at home but enabled our armed forces to continue their objectives effectively in Europe. Packs of German U-boats patrolled the waters and torpedoed indiscriminately, their aim to create as much disruption to our purpose as they could. In consequence, radio officers were assigned listening watches only, as transmissions from our ships would certainly be picked up by the prowling wolfpacks and our convoys systematically destroyed.

My mother saw the danger, and her worn, worried face, forced into a taut smile, accompanied my thoughts at least until I reached the docks for each departure. Then excitement always took a hold of me and I forgot. Besides, it wouldn't ever be my ship.

As usual, there were a few men waiting in the Marconi offices when I arrived according to my summons in July 1942, and I sat down to join them. Behind the desk was a pudgy, self-important looking man of about forty whose top lip curled so emphatically upwards, it implied a constant attitude of supercilious disdain. He was balding and sweating and wholly unprepossessing, save for his piercing blue eyes, which held their object so fiercely in their sights that it was difficult not to find him intimidating. He looked like the kind of man whose own shortcomings compelled him to be harsher on those he scented in others. 'Colin McGrath' it said on the name plaque in front of him, and he radiated ill temper.

Clearly he was hot, and all his tasks that morning seemed to be demanding a great deal of extravagant concentration, the least disturbance to which resulted in an exaggerated display of annoyance. He glared and he huffed, he tutted and he squirmed. He seemed particularly incensed by the inordinate cheeriness of a big man wandering around at the back of the room, who was whistling with consummate unconcern. No amount of belligerent stares and emphatic sighing affected the whistler in the slightest and McGrath was becoming increasingly exasperated.

Sitting next to him was an uncommonly pretty blonde girl of about twenty-five. She really was quite beautiful. Her hair was arranged in dainty curls about the elfin arches of her flowerlike face, and sweet grey eyes framed with long, dark lashes challenged almost every man there to distinguish himself for their approval. Her lipstick was ruby red and she was lovely. I hoped I would be called up by her. She quite effortlessly commanded the attention of all of us except perhaps for the whistler, who was now reading the notices in the corner and who scarcely seemed aware of anything much at all.

Amused by McGrath's impotent fury and with the pretty blonde to distract my thoughts, I didn't notice Jamie come in until he sat down next to me. I had sailed with him on my last trip but one on the *City of Exeter*. We had shared the radio shifts and a cabin all the way to India and back. He was a lugubrious fellow, not given much to mirth or conversation. Though he was three years older than me, at twenty-two, he appeared much younger as he was so small and skinny. I suspected that he was more level-headed and certainly calmer than me and I suspected equally that the crew on the *Exeter* had thought so too. I liked him though.

'Jamie.'

'Brian,' he nodded.

'You just back?'

'Ten days.'

'Where'd you go?'

'Italy.'

'Anything?'

'Nope.' I couldn't remember getting much more out of Jamie all the way to India and back either and so, defeated by his monosyllables and knowing full well there wasn't much chance of, or inclination for, any meaningful conversation, we lapsed into silence. We listened to Colin McGrath deal brusquely with various sailors and kept our eyes on the beguiling blonde, though we pretended not to.

After half an hour or so, McGrath called out my name.

He didn't look up as I stood before him. I hesitated.

'Well?' he barked. As I didn't move, he thrust out a hand and snapped his fingers at me three or four times impatiently. 'Book, laddie! Book!' He still hadn't looked up. His pencil continued to scroll steadily down the lists.

'I'm sorry,' I began, 'but I don't have it.'

'You don't have it? Why not?'

'I've mislaid it.' He looked up sharply then, scenting an opportunity to flex some official muscle. 'Mislaid it?' he asked, too loudly.

'Lost it.' I said, helpfully.

'You have lost your discharge book?'

'So it would seem,' I said. This came out a little more flippantly than I had intended but it was a stupid game. How many ways were there of saying it? It irritated him. He would not be cheeked by a mere nineteen-year-old boy, and certainly not in front of such a pretty office junior and, by now, quite a crowded office. He threw his pencil down on the desk and eyed me narrowly.

'You do realise you need your discharge book to sign on?'

I said that I did.

'And you have come here without it?' He looked first at me and then at the blonde with mock incredulity, eyebrows raised, eyes wide.

'So it would seem,' I said again, my own hackles beginning to rise.

'Don't you take that tone with me, laddie,' he snipped quickly, his ice-blue eyes darkening with anger. Then he blinked purposefully and inhaling slowly through pursed lips, he tilted his head, regaining control. 'Well, I suggest now, boy, that you run along home and find it.'

Pointedly unpleasant, he glared at me for an instant longer, and then picked up his pencil and went back to his lists. I studied his balding pate for a moment or two but didn't move.

'I've told you,' I said. 'It's lost.'

I was suddenly aware that the waiting room had gone quiet behind me. Even the whistler had stopped. And with the thought that all eyes were now upon me, I felt myself beginning to blush. I could feel its spreading glow, racing up the back of my neck and making my armpits and ears hot. Anger gave way to embarrassment. Even the blonde, who to her credit had so far kept her face firmly averted, was now absolutely still.

'Sorry,' I said. He looked up again, sighing crossly and I tried for a winning smile. It was ill-judged. He took me for facetious and it infuriated him still further. His cheeks flushed pink and his face crystallised with dislike.

He smiled a feline, little sneer. 'Well, sorry isn't really good enough, is it? How old are you, Mr Clarke?'

'Nineteen.'

'Mmn. Nineteen.' Nodding slowly as if my answer afforded him all the enlightenment he needed, he folded his arms and sat back in his chair. 'Think you know everything, don't you, boy?'

I couldn't think of anything to say to this and, loath to incur further wrath, I just stood there. I am not by nature particularly deferential nor am I afraid of confrontation but I was more than a little taken aback by this man's unwarranted vitriol. It occurred to me that his determination to belittle me was not wholly unconnected to the presence of the beautiful blonde. Some men, I knew, seek to aggrandise themselves by disparaging others in front of girls but they are not generally men who know much about women. Perhaps he felt that by putting me so firmly in my place, he would impress her with his authority. Either that or he was trying to teach her how young upstart sailors should be dealt with. But to start returning fire at my employer, no matter how condescending he might be, at this moment, seemed just foolhardy.

'You have a Special I presume?' he went on. I nodded. 'How am I to know what you are or what you have done if you fail to bring your discharge book along with you, Mr Clarke? We at Marconi do have a reputation to consider, you know.' He smirked slyly along the counter at the blonde. 'Well, Miss Davies, what would you recommend we do with Mr Clarke here? Do we just issue him with another book and let him get away with such feckless behaviour or do we send him home to find it?' His eyes returned to me and he looked me up and down sourly. 'And bear in mind, Miss Davies, that some sort of discipline is necessary for a merchant sailor, no matter how unsuitable the raw material.' Directly appealed to thus, Miss Davies could no longer politely ignore my embarrassment and she tittered nervously in hers.

'Steady on, old man,' a cheerful voice came from the back of the room and to my enormous relief, all attention swung suddenly away from me and the unfortunate Miss Davies to its owner. 'Just give him another book, why don't you? No need for a row.' It was the whistler.

'I suggest you mind your own business,' McGrath snapped back. He shucked down his jacket sleeves with a shake of his arms, slowly and deliberately as if to re-establish just who was in control. 'Well, Clarke. You will go and sit down and wait. I will endeavour to rectify the administrative chaos your carelessness will no doubt have left in its wake.'

Jowls shaking, he got up from his chair, presumably to go and fetch me another book and moved to pass behind Miss Davies. As he did so, he leant down to mutter in her ear, but not so inaudibly that the rest of us didn't pick it up. 'Bloody insolent. Nothing but a cub! Won't last five minutes at sea.'

I had just reached my seat but had not yet sat down. I paused. I could have pointed out that I had been at sea since I was seventeen and that I had got along very well so far but given that all of this information was stored in my lost discharge book, I thought it imprudent to give him further ammunition. Especially since I assumed that he had got up to go and get me another book. But I was furious and must have looked it.

'Don't mind him, Mr Clarke,' came the jovial voice again from the back of the room. 'These officials. Spend a lot of time trying to impress,' here he tipped his head at Miss Davies, 'and not enough making any actual progress. They tend to be just so incredibly...' He spread his arms, wide apart, palms up, and raised them with exaggerated resignation, '... officious.' He pushed himself off the wall where he had been leaning and came over to me, hand extended. I took it and we shook. 'Like I said, Cub,' he winked, 'no need for a row.'

McGrath glowered at him from behind Miss Davies and then stalked off into the room behind. He reappeared a minute or two later and went back to his desk, tight-lipped and crimson still with rage. He began shuffling angrily at his papers once more and called the next name.

'Joseph Green.'

'Joe,' my ally said to me, loosing his grip and then louder to McGrath across the room, 'Joe Green' and he wandered over to the counter, taking his time. Wordlessly, McGrath took his discharge book and made a great show of looking it over. Finally, he gave it back and glanced down his list.

'The *Sithonia*. First Radio Officer. Hoskisson dock.'

'The *Snithonia*?' Joe repeated, laughter behind his voice.

'The *Sithonia*.' McGrath growled back at him, more loudly.

At this point there was a snort of derision from behind me and I turned to see a small wisp of a man with hair stuck up all over the place, doubled up with mirth.

'What?' I asked.

'Arh, 'tis nothing. Nothing at all,' he rasped, as Irish as they come. 'She's a real beautiful vessel.' He crossed his arms and tucked his hands up underneath each armpit, before adding gleefully, 'All kitted out and new, beautiful like. For sure, 't'll be the most comfortable trip the lad ever took.'

Joe, hearing this exchange, grinned cheerily.

'Snithers it is then,' he said, snapping up his discharge book and sauntering back to the seat next to mine. 'I might wait on here with you fellas for a while if you don't mind. We might all be going the same way. It isn't going to sail without me, now is it?' he said, directing the whole piece to McGrath who was now positively emanating fury at him from behind the counter.

Jamie wasn't called long after Joe and he too was assigned to the *Sithonia* as second radio officer. He didn't seem very inclined to leave me there either for he came away from the desk and sat back down on my other side.

For as long as he could bear the three of us patiently watching him, McGrath made us wait. Arms folded, the three of us, like the three wise monkeys. In the end though, I think he was finally defeated by Joe Green's absolute inability to remain quiet or still. He hummed. He whistled. He tapped his feet. He rapped out tunes on the chair rest. He fiddled with his shoes, his coat buttons. He emptied his pockets and chewed loudly on some hairy mint humbug he had recovered from within. Even Miss Davies' nerves were beginning to unravel; she began to look imploringly at her colleague and then carefully incline her head towards Joe.

'Right, Clarke. The *Sithonia*. Third radio officer. Let's hope you don't lose your way,' was all McGrath could muster.

The Irishman behind us, unable to contain himself, was still cackling and wheezing when we left.

'Can't stand a bully,' Joe said as he clattered down the stairs behind me. Out in the street, back in the sun and away from the stifling atmosphere of the office, I took a better look at him.

He was huge. Broad-shouldered and tall, he was a great big bear of a man with enormous forearms and spades for hands. I had always been considered tall but I was wiry and lithe. This bloke made me look like a reed. I guessed he was probably no less than thirty. He had large, open features, the most conspicuous being a wide, generous mouth that relaxed readily and often into a broad and easy grin. His eyes wrinkled at the temples and generally sparkled, giving the impression that he was about to embark on the telling of a particularly hilarious joke.

He wasn't good-looking, his face was weathered and lined, but he was striking, not only thanks to his size but also to his evidently irrepressible good humour. The favourable impression he gave was capped off by a wild, unruly thatch of hair, neither fair nor brown but somewhere in between the two. Slightly longer than most men would have considered tidy, it was unkempt but not, it would appear, for want of any attempts to try and tame it. There was a vague kind of parting on one side, though what purpose it might serve remained unclear.

At nineteen, I did not yet know that there are only two or maybe three people you meet over the course of your life with whom you recognise an instant bond, an inexplicable connection. Sometimes it is evident before either one of you has even spoken and yet both of you are intuitively aware that it exists between you. Man or woman, it is not sexual, though it may not be wholly beyond the physical. It may be chemical, though more likely it is spiritual. It could be perhaps that your two souls were moulded from the same mettle and somewhere beyond all reason, the two souls recognise in one another their original kin and dance with delight at their reunion. So it was with Joe. If we had met at any point in our lives, we would have been friends.

'What did you call me in there?' I asked. Somehow there was no need for preliminaries.

'When? Oh. McGrath coined it. Cub. Cubby Clarke,' he laughed. 'Suits him, don't you think?' and he appealed to Jamie who raised a quizzical eyebrow and, very unusually for Jamie, laughed.

We set off for the tram to Hoskisson dock together in inexplicably high spirits. The incident with McGrath had been distasteful but somehow Joe's intervention had trivialised it for me and my anger and embarrassment dissolved in the midday sun. Furthermore, his natural cheeriness was infectious, giving rise in me to a kind of skittish exuberance. It was hot and cloudless, I was off to sea again with like-minded men, our ship was apparently a real beauty and I was young and eager to get going. Even Jamie was more jovial than usual.

'We could always refuse to sail,' he said, 'just to annoy McGrath.' It was within our rights as merchant seamen to turn down up to three tours of duty if we felt the ship we'd been assigned was unsuitable.

'What, and give up the *Snithonia*?,' I said, bouncing along beside them when we got off the tram. 'Didn't you hear what the Irishman said?' I stopped and, throwing my arms out wide, brought my companions to an abrupt halt that they might more fully get the benefit of my best Irish brogue. 'All freshly kitted out and new like! A beautiful vessel for sure, he said. No chance!'

'You haven't sailed with that many Irishmen, have you, Cub?' Joe asked, eyes laughing.

'Some. Why?'

'Well, for a start your accent is God awful. Sounded like Welsh. Or Burmese. And . . . well, we'll see,' was all he would say.

The dock was humming when we got there and we wandered around a little, enjoying the general hubbub and the banter among the dockers in the bright morning sunlight. We examined other vessels and were even making jokes about the dilapidated state of some. Then I was brought up short by a laconic 'I see' from Jamie. He stopped suddenly just in front of me and I jostled in to him. My eyes followed his and there she was – the *Sithonia*. I saw too.

She was just about the cronkiest old boat I had ever laid eyes on. She looked like a salvaged wreck, cobbled back together with rusty steels and topped off with a hulking, concrete-encased bridge at the forrard end. The height of this was almost matched by a disproportionately huge counter-stern. The two seemed to be performing a precarious balancing act, plonked heavily upon the deck of a steamer whose bodywork was composed of little better than scrap metal.

The living accommodation, which evidently made up the after superstructure, was dismal, sea-stained and yellowing. The windows on the bridge and all the portholes I could see dripped greeny-brown semi-circles of corroded rust beneath them, giving the impression of extremely sad, tired eyes. At the waterline, these sagging bags of brown gave way to a general swathe of oxidisation along the whole side of the ship.

Grey and miserable, she looked anything but seaworthy and she was filthy. She was loading coal alongside and the coal dust that covered almost every inch of her could actually have been instrumental in holding her together. I could make out the tiny radio shack at the highest point above the cabins at the stern. Shack was the right word.

I turned to Joe, incredulous, but Joe was beside himself with laughter. Shaking and gulping, he was laughing like an eight-year-old whose brother has just farted in church. 'Your face, Cub! Your face!' was just about all he could get out and then, 'Yep, a beauty. A real beauty!' Despite his helpless hilarity, I noted somewhat ruefully that he had absolutely no trouble at all in capturing almost perfectly the lilting intonation of the Irishman's amusement. He pulled himself together a bit and by way of apology, he slapped me amiably on the back and rocked my shoulder to and fro. 'Snithers it is then, boys,' he said again.

CHAPTER 3

JOE, SNITHERS AND ME

Even the gangway has planks missing, I grumbled inwardly as I reported for duty two days later and made my way along the corroding companionways to find my cabin. It was a two-bunk cupboard just above the waterline, in the forrard superstructure below the bridge, and there I found Jamie.

'Jamie,' I said, bundling my bag in through the narrow door and back-kicking it shut behind me. He was sitting on the bottom bunk polishing his shoes. He nodded, raising his eyebrows in greeting.

Taking in at a glance the limited proportions of the room, I reached to dump my stuff on the berth above him. The top bunk was the privilege of the most junior officer and that would be me. I put my hands on my hips and, addressing the top of his head, added wryly, 'Well, you could just about swing a cat in here, I reckon.'

'Only if it had a very short tail,' Jamie sniffed, not missing a beat.

Without warning, the door then flew open again with such force that its hinges rattled and it clattered up against the battered old locker behind it. One of its doors was already missing but a panel in the other teetered and then dropped to the floor.

Stooping to enter, Joe Green crashed in. He looked huge in the confines of the tiny, shed-like space, which barely exceeded his arm span in either direction. As usual, he was grinning from ear to ear.

He gazed about vaguely to see what he had broken and then he laughed. 'Ah, well. The skipper said she was old. What do you make of her then lads?'

'Pretty ancient,' I said. 'But sound. What else did he say?'

'Said she was an old tramp steamer from Tyneside. Been brought out of retirement. All five thousand tons of her. Mind you, same could be said about the captain.'

'He's that big?' I asked, leaning back against the bunks and folding my arms.

Joe guffawed, eyes disappearing behind his sunburnt wrinkles. A big, hearty laugh of a man, I thought.

'No, but just as knackered. He's an old steamer from Tyneside too. Him and his first mate. All three of them, dragged out of retirement. Need all hands on deck, just now, I reckon.' He manoeuvred his arm around the back of the door and picked up the broken bit of locker panel. He turned it over in his enormous hands and then tucked it under his arm and made to go. 'On second thoughts, old bugger probably couldn't wait to get back to sea after five minutes at home.'

'With the wife,' put in Jamie glumly and we both looked at him. I laughed but glancing towards Joe, thought I caught him looking slightly puzzled.

'C'mon,' he said. 'I'll show you where we work.'

He set off at his natural pace, which was fast, and we hurried along behind him through the labyrinth of dingy companionways and then up on to the crusty deck. He whistled blithely all the way, greeting everybody we came across as if they were old friends. Some looked rather taken aback by his familiar cheeriness and stopped to wonder if they had possibly sailed with him before but some of the older sailors did not even bother to reply. Joe was unabashed. He expected to like people and didn't much consider whether the feeling was returned.

The radio shack was in the stern. Joe threw the door open and stepped aside to let us go in first. It lived up to expectations: that is to say, it was dank and musty and almost as small as our cabin. It was crammed to bursting with old bits of kit. On the desk a bulky, antiquated radio receiver vied with the transmitter and the dusty direction-finding gear for space. The Morse key was in among them somewhere, but there were so many wires and leads apparently coming from and going to nowhere that it was difficult at first to locate. Two or three sets of chewed-up looking earphones had been slung carelessly on top of all the chaos.

I put my hands on the back of the chair and attempted to swivel it casually. It moved half an inch stiffly and rocked a little on its base. The small table provided for our code tables slanted drunkenly against the bulkhead.

I was flummoxed. I had been used to much more sophisticated equipment both at the Radio School and on my previous tours of duty. I hardly recognised any of this stuff and I said so.

Joe grinned, 'Came straight off the ark apparently. Don't look so worried, Cub. You'll soon pick it up. Can't be any harder.' I didn't really share his optimism but there was nothing else for it.

We spent the rest of the day finding our bearings on board and getting to grips with all the old girl's idiosyncrasies. On the bridge we came across the skipper and the first mate. Captain Edwards did indeed look his age and more, though he was probably just the wrong side of sixty-five. Facially he was creased and wrinkled but his body, though small, was fit and strong-looking, with a deftness of movement that made him appear sprightly, if not young. His first officer, Walter Henderson, was much bigger than him and broader too, with a deep, naturally resonant voice. He might have overshadowed his senior officer had it not been for the evident high regard in which they held one another. They were laughing together as we approached.

Joe introduced me as Cubby Clarke and, seasoned seamen both, neither of them raised an eyebrow. From that moment on, as far as all the crew on the *Sithonia* were concerned, Cubby Clarke was my name. I did not mind. I liked it. It immediately made me one of them.

We finished loading that evening and, having battened down the hatches and hosed off what was possible of the ubiquitous coal dust, we were joined by the pilot. It was his unenviable task to navigate our plodding progress down the river where we were to fall in with the rest of our convoy at the mouth of the Mersey estuary. We chugged on through the increasingly congested and relatively choppy waters to our mustering point outside the Bar lightship, pausing to give the pilot time to disembark just before we reached it.

The dim lights, port and starboard side, of the clustered ships winked red and green their welcome, beckoning us on as we approached to join their number in the gathering dusk. There must have been forty ships or more, each bearing a national flag from countries far and wide and all similarly daubed in camouflage or grey. Against the gloomy skyline, which was fading in the onset of the evening and blurred by misty sea spray, their varying shapes and sizes were ill-defined, meshed and intertwined, a two-dimensional collage in swathes of grey. Save for their guiding lights. Smaller than many, we huddled among them, seeking refuge from the roughening sea.

As always, the sight of such a gathering of ships, their weighty frames hustling and jockeying for position, yet apparently moving with such grace and ease in a strangely seamless, slow dance, filled me with excitement. The familiar sounds of engines humming with anticipation, horns insisting on attention and of halyards flapping and cleats shinkling in the wind: to me, they signified the calling of the ocean. I stood on the deck, eyes bright, revelling in it.

It was windy and in the waning light, the task of our escorts in getting us into order was not an easy one. Rounded up like recalcitrant sheep by three ferocious frigates and a couple of determined corvettes, each ponderous vessel had to be bullied and badgered into line, to make up the requisite five lanes of eight. Though hampered by an equally unruly sea they finally achieved what had seemed impossible, and with the raising of the Commodore's flag the convoy began to move off.

Our ship was abuzz with anticipation. After supper, sneaking a quick smoke on the bridge, we had taken bets as to where we might be heading. Tomas Resendes, a stocky, flat-faced quarter-master from Portugal had opted for Gibraltar. It was close enough to home, he said. But Clarence Belson, the third mate, had reckoned it would be further. He put a packet of fags on the Suez Canal and then the Far East. Joe was having none of it and pushed for South America. He'd never been in all his time and basing his faith on the laws of probability, with reckless hilarity, he raised the stakes to two. Clarie reluctantly agreed.

I genuinely did not care. The places I had been sent to so far had dazzled me with their difference. Across the world, each country I had seen wore its own distinctive clothes, the like of which had been beyond all my experience. Exotic colours, sounds and smells thrilled my whetted appetite. To return to any one of them would be exciting: to be sent somewhere new, so much the better.

Our sailing orders were top secret until they were opened by our skipper, according to protocol, at the raising of the Commodore's flag, and then the news of our destination would spread like wild fire through the ship. I saw the flag go up and immediately left my viewing point, hurrying down towards the saloon and guessing that the first person I came across would probably already know.

It was Calhoun, the second officer and he was terse at the best of times.

'Where is it to be then?' I asked, screeching to a halt.

'Slow down, lad,' he put out a hand, palm down. 'Montevideo.'

'Montevideo?'

'On the Plate estuary. Uruguay. South America.' Joe would be whooping and Clarie Belson short on smokes for the remainder of the trip.

'In convoy to Gibraltar. Then peel off and sail single ship across the Atlantic,' he went on. 'Pernambuco first. Down the coast to the mouth of the Plate. Montevideo.'

'That's fantastic!' I beamed at him.

'If you don't mind the heat. And the mozzies,' he returned sourly. 'Better get yourself up to the bridge and fetch the code tables down to the radio shack.'

The code tables for the radio officers came in the same lead-weighted bag as the sailing orders and they were changed three-monthly as it was feared that, should they fall into enemy hands, they would prove a boon of inestimable value to any German U-boat commander. The cat would have the means to presuppose the whereabouts of a myriad of mice.

Calhoun stalked off and I took to my heels again, arriving on the well deck just in time to hear Joe crowing mercilessly at poor Clarie, 'Well, Claribelle, I hope you're not a sore loser. Cough 'em up!' Clarie dug deeply into his pocket, glum resignation written all over his face, and slammed a packet of cigarettes into Joe's outstretched hand. They stared at one another for a second, Joe's eyebrows raised comically and Clarie looking rueful. Joe stuffed the fags into his pocket with a flourish and then put out his palm again, fingers beckoning up and down. 'There's more,' he said. 'Come on, Claribelle. You can do it.' He started whistling *South American Way* cheerily.

Clarie began to pat his pockets, feigning ignorance but eventually he grudgingly produced the second packet from his top pocket.

I laughed as I passed them and carried on up towards the bridge. From then on, Joe would start up whistling that song whenever Clarie was in earshot and Clarie would thump him on the arm and tax him for a cigarette.

My shift that night in the radio shack was less alarming than I had imagined. The archaic equipment was not so difficult to master after all, for though it was clumsy and slow to react, the principles were similar to those in kit I'd come across on other ships. I found I could generally work out what I did not know. Joe, Jamie and I would take four-hourly shifts twice in twenty-four hours, leaving us each with eight hours off between our watches. Joe gratefully allotted me the midnight to four slot because I offered. I liked the relative peace and calm of the small hours, the silence, save for the drumming of the engine and the steady swish of the sea as the old *Sithonia* purposefully sliced on through. I liked the unwatched liberty in being awake while others slept.

Joe did not. He'd crash in at 4 a.m, banging the door and clattering about, face folded still in sleep. Invariably, he'd knock the code tables to the floor and stumble around demanding coffee. Being a night owl, I'd sit with him for a while, at first because I wasn't quite sure it was safe to leave him, half-asleep and jerky, in care of all our lives, but then I began to look forward to him coming. Sometimes, I fetched him coffee from the galley and I stood and smoked in the doorway of the shack. He'd sling his headphones sideways, holding one against his ear, and we talked. Of other journeys, of near misses and the war, of our families and of home. He spoke to me of Maggie, this girl who'd brought him from the wildness of his youth and given him a purpose, given him the self he'd thought that he might be but had been struggling to uncover. It struck me that he spoke of her with almost wistful reverence, as if he could not quite believe his luck.

I had known some girls, thought myself in love at times but had never yet felt what he was trying to describe. I thought his fondness due to leaving her behind, to the loneliness of men on ship. At nineteen, I had not yet been made to understand the measure of such a bond.

Sometimes I sat with him until five or so and then headed off, finally wanting sleep, to bed. Quite often, woken by Jamie's morning rituals, I went back up there for the start of Jamie's watch and collecting Joe, sauntered down with him to the saloon for breakfast.

Joe would start by hounding big Sam Tate about his cooking and Sam, a massive African and possibly the only man on board to compete with Joe in size, would laugh him off and grab him round the neck, pulling his head down low, and drub his crazy hair.

'Say you're sorry, you great thick oaf,' Sam would holler. 'Can't go round abusin' a man's food and expect to get away with it.' Joe would howl and scrabble to no avail and Sam would laugh his great deep laugh and eventually let him go. It didn't take long for Sam to become Big Sam Cook to all on board. Joe, it seemed, had a name for everyone. And Sam, the only person on the ship who could pull it off with any credibility, returned the favour from time to time by calling him Little Joe.

Big Sam, as it turned out, had been far and wide, heading up the teams of cooks for numerous crews to every distant corner of the globe, and though he could hardly have been that much over thirty, he'd apparently been everywhere. And so one morning, soon after we'd left the Irish Sea, Joe asked him what he'd made of South America.

'You two're gonna love it,' he boomed. 'Went to Rio. It's a beautiful city. Great food, nice bars. Beautiful women,' he winked at me and then raised an eyebrow. 'Willin' too.'

'Sounds bloody great,' I enthused and, grinning at the prospect, turned to Joe to share it. He laughed too a little but without much real conviction and his eyes, as he shook his head, slid away from mine and found instead the floor. The direction of his thoughts was not too difficult to follow and his discomfort equally transparent.

'Oarr, don't tell me… Maggie!' I scoffed, jerking out an elbow to jab him in the ribs, unable yet to quite believe there was a man alive who would pass up the chance of many women for the sake of one.

'Maggie?' You couldn't get anything much past Big Sam Cook. Down in the galley, he heard it all. Within days of sailing, he'd managed to establish a reputation among the crew as being the ears and eyes of the whole ship. But, though affable and easy-going, he was neither discerning nor discreet. He listened but he also talked. You wanted personal information, you went to see Big Sam.

Joe looked up and, shrugging slightly, smiled almost shyly.

'The love of his life,' I said, not serious, tutting towards Joe and raising my eyes up to the heavens.

'Well now, Cub, it's funny you should say that,' Joe laughed, his own sparkling with delight. 'It's very funny you should say that!'

As we steamed further south, the weather warmed and the seas calmed and we settled down to largely uneventful days, punctuated only by our duties and the usual scaremongering among the crew. As with all the ships I had sailed on, the men were jumpy and easily spooked. It didn't help that one balmy evening, quite soon after making the open ocean, we saw a swift corvette, capable of thirty knots or more, inexplicably shoot past the convoy and steam off station. As a result, someone was always claiming to have spotted a periscope or the hull of a U-boat and Joe began to keep a running tally. Tomas, who was particularly excitable, took the lead early on with about four 'sightings' in the first few days. Mick, the ginger, curly-haired bosun from Ireland, ran a close second. He was always swearing on God's honour that he had seen a shiny pin-prick in the far distance. To ensure I won, I took to leaning over the ship's side, apparently scanning the waters and then jumping up, pointing and yelling wildly, 'There, over there! There's one!' The first few times, deckhands from all sides would immediately drop what they were doing and rush harum-scarum to investigate.

'Arh now, Cub,' Mick would shake his head when he saw my twitching mouth and Joe's laughing eyes, 'would you pack it in, for pity's sake!' It was better not to risk it when the volatile Pat Murack was around, still less before Jim Mackingtosh. Known as Mac throughout the ship, his thick-set brawn denoted perfectly his bullish mind and he was as ignorant as he was humourless. Incurring the wrath of Calhoun was also something we felt best avoided. It was a foolish game but we reckoned it was worth it just to see Tomas, typically hot-blooded, hopping from foot to foot in sheer exasperation at our childishness.

I spent a lot of time with Joe and the more I did, the more I liked him. Everyone did. From the moment he had stepped aboard the ship, he had seemed to know everybody. He had a genuine word for and a ready laugh with all of them and he treated all with level-ling good humour and open-hearted faith. From the deckhands to the cooks, officers to engineers, he made each one feel as if their presence was important to his contentment. The light of his atten-tion beamed persistent warmth, persuading even the most awk-ward individuals to unfurl and to contribute. His real interest in, and predisposal to enjoy, the company of others was difficult to rebuff: people, despite themselves, wanted him to like them. Even hardened souls like Mac saw themselves more favourably reflected through Joe's eyes and behaved less harshly in return. And once, one night in the saloon, I even witnessed Fraser, the remote and taciturn chief engineer, moved to laughter when Joe had chanced an arm and taken to imitating his distinctly Scottish burr.

This natural and unspoken understanding of others' characters, his propensity to seek out the best in them, granted him a rare indulgence. As with a favourite child, people didn't care to take offence if it had been Joe who'd crossed them. They'd tut and raise their eyes and grin his name. He got away with murder with his genial smile and easy grace. This was fortunate given that he displayed absolutely no capacity for quiet. He sang, he talked, he hummed, he joked, he hollered, he mimicked and he whistled. I could have killed him sometimes. Wherever he happened to be, at one time or another, one of his companions would end up shouting out, half laughing with exasperation, 'For Christsake, Joe, shut up! Will someone shut him up?'

His presence was impossible to ignore for if he was loud, he was also restless. He could not keep still. Not only was he big, his enormous frame both broad and tall seemed to fill the room, but he was always on the move. It was as if his burly body could not contain his overactive spirit, which leapt up and out unbidden, producing in his physical being nothing short of constant motion. It was just unfortunate that the agility of his mind, manifest in this commotion of his person, was in direct conflict with his heavy, bearlike build. It wasn't that he was clumsy, he just thought himself as fleet-footed as his thoughts, and failed to take into account the greatness of his size. Quite simply, he was larger, louder and more lively than life itself.

We sought each other out. I appreciated his interest in my well-being, which turned out to be typical of his generous nature, and I made him laugh.

One Saturday morning though, I could not find him. I had slept through Jamie's early wake-up call and had gone down to breakfast slightly late, finishing dressing hastily as I hurried down to the saloon. Joe had not come down to breakfast after his watch, which was unusual because his appetite was huge. I took my tea and went to look for him.

He was alone, sitting in the sun, with his back against the wall of the radio shack, oblivious to the burgeoning beauty of the day and the vast expanse of blue stretching out for miles behind.

Head down, he was thoughtfully turning something over in his hand. It was a small, gold disc. Twice he stopped the turning and stroked the smooth surface of it with his thumb. When he heard me approach, he looked up and slipped it into his pocket. Sniffing, he picked up his tea and began swirling it gently around in its mug, both enormous hands knitted around it.

'I was thinking about Maggie,' he said. I slid down the wall next to him but didn't say anything. If he wanted to tell me, he would.

I contemplated the frothing wake the ship spewed up behind her. Two long white furrows churned up in time to the constant hum of the engines and for a while we were silent.

'She gave me this. When I left.' He reached in his pocket and brought out the disc for me to see. It looked small, marooned in the palm of his hand. 'Her father's compass,' he said, putting it away again.

'I was going to ask her if she would marry me. But I didn't. She was waiting for me to ask her. But somehow I couldn't get it right. I couldn't get the right words,' he smiled wistfully. 'Never can in front of her.' He didn't seem to need me to say anything, so I didn't.

'It's her eyes, I think. They…' he cast about for a suitable word, one apparently big enough, as if reduced by the very thought of them to the confusion of which he spoke. He moved his hands quickly in frustration, slopping his tea over them. 'Orf!' he exclaimed, shaking one and then the other. 'It's not hot.'

'Anyway,' he continued with a sigh. 'I will do it when I get back. She's all I want. From the first time I ever saw her. All I want.'

He stood up, stiffly, stretching out his great, long legs. 'God, I can't believe I made such a muck of it! Not doing it. What an idiot!'

I squinted up, shielding my eyes from the sun behind him. 'She will wait,' I offered uncertainly.

'I know she will,' he said. I sat on a while after he had gone, impressed by his unqualified confidence.

Later that morning, we were one of five ships to peel away from the main convoy and set a solitary course across the Atlantic for South America. I went down to the radio shack for my watch at midday and, by now at ease with our equipment, I took my book. The news bulletin came in at one as it always did and, having typed it up, I settled down for a quiet afternoon. I was relieved by Joe at four. After posting my notices in the mess rooms, I took the chance to find a deckchair up on the flat deck near the fo'c'sle, thinking that I might just have a kip. It was a hot afternoon, after five, and lulled by the steady droning of the engines and the sapping heat, it was not long before I fell asleep.

A change of rhythm in the humming of the ship brought me vaguely back to consciousness. I started awake. Looking at the sun, I could tell that we had changed direction too. Something must be wrong. I left my chair and began to make my way back towards the bridge, and as I did so, the prow turned again, almost at a right angle with the way we had just been heading. Zigzagging. The skipper was taking evasive action.

I met Jamie by the wheelhouse.

'What's up?' I asked him.

'Joe got a four-S signal. Real strong. From one of the ships up ahead of us.'

'We can't out-steam a sub. We only manage about ten knots at best!' I hoped he might know better.

'That's why we're zigzagging. If it's just one, we might avoid it.'

'And if it's a pack?'

'Well then,' said Jamie dourly, 'we're doomed.'

In the early hours of Sunday morning during my watch, I picked up another four-S message. A faster ship than ours, maybe four or five hours ahead, had had another sighting of a submarine and so, determining the position of the ship in front on the direction finder, we took a wide detour of her co-ordinates, hoping that it would be enough.

By mid-morning, fears were running high. Everyone was on the watch, squinting out at mile on mile of glistening blue. It was another beautiful day, bright and clear, the sea and sky reflecting and admiring each other's glory. It seemed impossible that something so threatening, so destructive should be prowling deep beneath us. But it was highly likely that we were steaming into a hunting pack of U-boats and, mid-Atlantic and painfully slow, we must have looked an easy target.

The third four-S message, which came at lunchtime, confirmed our fears. The hunting pack was down there somewhere, in all probability closing in. We steamed on, changing course at irregular intervals, the whole ship's crew screwed up with tension. Waiting. Barely daring to look.

As darkness fell, we only had good fortune to rely on. That, and the dubious hope that whichever beady-eyed commander spied our darkened hulk had had an overly successful week and had exhausted his torpedo supply.

'Get some kip,' Joe said, unusually serious. 'You need your wits about you come midnight.' So I turned in and slept, the last time for many years, the sleep of the unhaunted.

CHAPTER 4

HIT

Asleep.

Flung, flailing from my bed. Hit the deck. And again. Smashing my elbow against the bunk end. My body. Sliding. Shaking. Hit? Me or us? Wet. Water. Salty water. The taste of it. Hands and knees in it. Vibrating. Sound. Deafening, crushing, ringing. Hissing. Palpable black. A sharp list to the left. Slam against the wall. Catching hold of the bed side. Staggering up. I am not hurt.

God, I am not hurt. We must have been hit.

I held my hands up before me to see if I could see them but I could not. I grabbed hold of the bunk end again, my only point of reference, and one hand above the other, felt my way up to the top of the bunk. My hurry bag. I always hung it, like we all did, on the bulkhead above where I slept. It had my essentials in it. Spare trousers, socks, a pullover, some chocolate. I couldn't find it. It wasn't there. I tried to steady myself. It must be there. I felt again where I thought it should be. It wasn't there.

The cabin continued to tip and I couldn't keep my balance. It would stop momentarily and then jerk sharply further left, causing something I couldn't see to smash against me, knocking me sideways again. My ears didn't seem to be hearing properly. They were throbbing painfully but below that I could make out water gushing; also wood breaking apart and the muffled shouting of men.

It must have been a hell of a hit.

The door. Scrambling along the side of what I took to be the wall, I made for the door. Or at least where I thought the door should be, but at first I could not find it. I clambered my hands up, around, feeling frantically out in front of me. It was not there. Unable to comprehend the disappearance of my only escape route and disorientated by the tangible darkness pressing in against my eyes, I opened them more widely to see if I really could not see. Black. Only black.

My throat began to constrict and my limbs began to lighten. The creeping, sickening spreading of an old childhood fear revisited me, not consciously but up through my guts, leadening my lungs. It was the same cold, gripping fear of my infancy, of being shut in a small, dark room when all the people and the light were downstairs. Panic throttled my thought and my mind stuck stubbornly to the knowledge that the door had been here. Just here.

My hands compulsively covered the same ground over and over as if by willing it to be so, the door would suddenly appear. I stifled the screaming that was already overwhelming me inside and forced myself to think. Think.

I was knee-deep in water now and could barely keep my feet. I am not going to die here, I thought. I know I am not.

Another sharp lurch of the boat to the left caused my arm to fling out above me to the right and as it did so my hand got caught up in what felt like material. My pyjama top. In the heat of the confined cabin space on hot nights, I hung it on the back of the door. Bizarrely, it seemed to be hanging from somewhere above me. I grabbed at it again, sliding sideways all the while and luckily, this time, I found it. I clasped the reassuring folds with both hands and with it as a guide, I was able to grope to the door handle. Relief flooded through me for just that split second and as I pulled, my body relaxed into the shaky giddiness that comes with liberation. For just that one split second.

But then the door would not budge. I twisted the handle, pulled, yanked. Pushed my feet up against the bulkhead below it to try for greater purchase. In vain. Splashing and kicking, I yelled furiously in my frustration, flinging my head from side to side as if in childish petulance. My arms exhausted quickly and just when I thought that I could not do it, the hinges gave. The force with which the door flew back surprised me off my feet again. But I could get out. I scrambled through the hole and into the companionway leading to the well deck.

My station in an emergency was the radio shack and so, doing what I could to remain upright and reaching the steps, I clambered up on to the deck. The ship was tilting forty-five degrees or more, hard to port, and though the swell was fairly gentle, the seas were already swamping her. There was little doubt that she was going down.

I clung to the canvas of the hatch covers, precariously scrabbling from one to the next, refusing to allow myself to slip undetected into the enveloping water. The noise was overwhelming. Escaping steam kept up a steady, shrieking hiss, spars crashed, glass shattered. Timbers, splintering, bowed and snapped, while concrete and steel crumpled all around me into heaps. My whole body, not just my mind, absorbed it, reverberated with it. Shook.

Barefooted, I scurried over fallen wood and broken metal, canvas and rope until I was brought up short by a huge, jagged edge of timber. On this side at any rate, the *Sithonia* had clearly been spliced in two. There was no way that I could get to the stern of the ship across this growing, watery ravine, dark and deep and terrifying.

I darted for the bridge companionway and started up it, making for the port lifeboat. I was somehow not afraid by now, just determined. I was quick and I was strong – there would be some way out. I do not think I was even that alarmed to find the port lifeboat useless. It had been stoved in, crushed by a fall of shattered concrete from the bridge reinforcements.

I took to the railings and started to pull myself along the length of the bridge. As far as I could tell it was still intact, and if I could just make my way across it, the starboard deck might yet afford me access to the stern. If it had not already been blown apart. The list of the ship was growing more pronounced now, and every now and then a sudden lurch downwards loosened my grip. My hands, wet and grimy, often slipped and I swung out, dangerously close a couple of times to losing hold altogether. I was immensely encouraged though by the fact that the further along I got, the louder the shouts and cries of men became, and when I finally reached the starboard lifeboat, to my utter relief, it seemed that the whole ship's company was already there.

I saw Joe, crazy-haired and quick, but calmly trying to stay Mick's arm. Mick was wielding an axe. The lifeboat was dancing free at the forrard end but had snagged on something in the stern. Regardless, men were surging forward, from all directions, shoving and falling over and across one another in their determination to make the boat. Mick, wide-eyed and panting, was hacking away at the falls, swinging his axe wildly, willy-nilly and in grave danger of laying out flat anyone foolish enough to get too close to his heedless backswing.

Men were crowding in on them, panicky, barging to get past and into the boat. Joe, using his bulk, was patiently pushing them back, around and away from Mick's lethal slashing. Captain Edwards was among them, bleating ineffectually, in a vain attempt to establish some kind of order.

On catching sight of me, he hurried over.

'Got the emergency radio, Cub?' he yelled. Another huge crash behind him made us both wince.

'No, sir.'

'Fetch it up. Down at the bottom of my companionway.'

'Sir.'

I struggled, fighting against the list, desperately clinging to whatever I could manage to grab on to, along the deck to the ten steps leading below to the Captain's quarters. Looking down the hatch, I saw that only two or three steps at the top were now visible. Gurgling, swaying water was rising rapidly from below and I hesitated. Surely he couldn't mean it. Who would ever know? But then we were going to need it. And I would know. Taking a deep breath, I quickly started down the ladder. The water was cold, black, entombing. I clung to the steps, counting them as I went down, and at seven I was forced to go under completely.

The tumult above me abruptly ceased. Aside from the pounding of my heart in my ears, there was the strange, echoing soundlessness of the water. There was the vague muffled clunking of the ship's body as it creaked further, slowly into the gloom. The sea pushed and pulled me, forcing my body this way and that as, eyes closed, I thumped about with my free arm and my legs, desperately trying to locate the small suitcase-sized radio transmitter. It was hopeless. Blind, weightless and powerless, I floundered around in vain. My temples began to throb, my heart to race, louder still, and the air that I had been holding bubbled uncontrollably from my lungs and mouth. A few more seconds, just a few more. After one final, useless grope, I kicked with all my might, up and out. I broke through the surface, shaking and gasping, heaving in air as if it were my last. I clung weakly for a second to the steps and then slowly clambered out, light-limbed and grateful. Stumbling, half crawling, I made my way back towards the mêlée at the lifeboat.

By now, Joe was shouting and pointing, trying to make Mick hear, to show him that the boat was caught by the after falls which, stiffened by old paint, held it fast. Finally, Mick understood. Switching his aim he smashed the axe on target and with two or three swift, decisive blows he got the boat away. It slid onto the water. The drop now was not a great one, for while Mick had been struggling, the after end of the ship had been sinking fast and dark water was beginning to swirl up and over the tops of the hatches.

Men jostled and blundered into me, crashing against one another, shouting, swearing, crying out but impervious to all except the one primeval objective of getting in the boat. It mattered little that others were knocked down or trampled over in the fray and as men fell, jumped and scrambled in, the little boat was fast becoming overloaded. Built for twenty-three, at least that and more were now already thrashing about within. And the deck was not yet empty.

Big Sam Cook had got himself on board. So had Mac and Tomas. Clarie. Fraser, the chief engineer, was there. I stopped, suddenly struck with the realisation that Jamie was not with them. I had not seen him since supper the night before. He had been heading off to the radio shack to take the eight 'til midnight watch, the one before mine. I grabbed at someone skittering past me.

'Jamie. Jamie Robinson. Seen him?' He looked at me blankly and shirked me off.

'Jamie! Jamie!' I yelled at the top of my voice, but it was useless. I couldn't even hear my own cry. My shouting was then whipped away in a sudden crushing crescendo of splitting and splintering timber, which culminated finally in a resounding crack. I cringed, half expecting to be flattened by whatever it was that had caused it, but on turning saw that the forrard half of the ship had upended. I could do nothing but look on, horrified, as, with a terrifying quickening of motion, its fast-shrinking hulk vanished, hissing and grumbling into the black, glistening quicksand of water.

Time was running out.

'Jamie!' Frantic, I began to dash about, grabbing at the last of those still passing me and squinting about at the faces of the men on board already. The deck was emptying. As the lifeboat slowly began to bob away, I saw the captain take a jump for it and, as he landed heavily across numerous others, he fought in vain to keep his balance. 'Wait!' he screamed in the futile hope that those now scrabbling at the oars might hear him and somehow prevent the gap between the boat and ship from widening. Stricken with the knowledge that anyone who did not take their chance immediately would surely now be lost, he twisted his head to look back up at those of us still on the deck and, throwing up his arms, he bellowed hoarsely: 'Jump!' And then his legs gave way and he fell among the mass of struggling bodies around him.

The last of the men were now leaping in, on top of one another, batting and kicking and shoving as our half of the ship continued to slide into the grasping sea. I was sure Jamie had not got in.

I peered helplessly up the sloping deck towards the stern and then towards the lifeboat. I could not decide. The lifeboat. My friend. I could not decide. I put my hands up to my head, desperate to cut out the incessant, confounding roar around me.

Then, a heavy paw upon my shoulder. He turned me round to face him. 'Brian,' Joe said. Strangely, in spite of the noise, the constant, brain-numbing noise, I could hear him. He spoke calmly, almost quietly. 'Brian. It's time. There's no one else.'

'But Joe. Jamie!' I shrieked.

'There's no one else,' he said. He propelled me towards the rapidly widening gap between the ship and the boat and shoved me hard. I jumped too late and landed half in, half out, on top of Mac, who swore and then heaved me over. The boat rocked again as Joe leapt behind me, knocking over one of the others who was standing, struggling to get an oar into the rowlocks. Domino-style, he fell backwards on to those behind, sending them sprawling. The scrapping for space, increasingly aggressive, intensified.

Panting, Joe scrambled across to me.

'Probably made another boat,' he yelled, nudging down in front of me. 'Jamie.' We were huddled towards the back end of the lifeboat, next to the water. I had been afforded a little space on one of the wooden seats while Joe hunched down on the floor in front of me.

'Another got away. I saw her,' shouted Tomas, over my shoulder. 'Port side, by the radio shack.'

'Bloody hell!' Mac, who had remained the other side of me, suddenly jumped up and, clambering roughly across me, snatched up one of the life jackets stowed down by my feet beneath the boat's rim. Without a second's pause, he leapt up onto the ledge, standing painfully on my hand as he did so, and astonished all of us by diving headlong into the sea. He made off away from the boat into the darkness as quickly as he could. There was a sudden resurgence of frantic panic and several other men piled in and swam off after him.

'Don't look now,' Joe said, looking up and over my head, 'but things aren't looking too clever behind you.' Startled by his expression, I glanced quickly back over my shoulder. Our boat, so overcrowded, had been impossible to steer. No one had had the room to get the oars into the rowlocks, let alone row with them, and so our safe haven had begun to drift uncontrollably, drawn towards the pull of the water under the heavy counter-stern. Due to the swell and the angle the ship's end now had, like a weighty hammer, it was slapping up and down on the surface, sucking our boat in beneath it with each mighty blow.

'The oars! Get the bloody oars!' Calhoun was on his feet, yelling and gesticulating wildly. Two or three more men to his right hastily took to the sea. Thankfully, some of the more nimble-minded among our crew leapt into action and were able to take quick advantage of the space created by the bailing lemmings. Mick virtually ran across a number of bodies and seized one of the oars, yelling to Big Sam Cook to grab another. Given suddenly more space, others pitched in and, with a supreme effort, hollering until hoarse, they managed to coordinate the rowing and force the boat around, away from the smashing stern.

I became aware during this desperate frenzy of activity that Joe was holding on to my pyjama trouser leg, pinning it with a firm fist to the wooden bench where I sat. I realised that having witnessed my reluctance to get into the boat just minutes before, he didn't trust me not to decide injudiciously to leave it. In fact, I had no intention of leaping out of the frying pan and into the fire, but Joe wasn't taking any chances.

We rowed a little distance away until Captain Edwards called a stop. Mick and Sam and the others hunched over their oars, sweating and breathless while the rest of us, with all the excited exhilaration that comes with such a close call, took to slapping the oarsmen on their backs and crowing at those who were beginning to swim over to clamber back in.

I turned around to watch. There wasn't much of the *Sithonia* left to see: she had become a small island, diminishing by the minute. The dense, greedy waters were claiming her more readily now, sucking her in. It was almost an anticlimax when at last she gave up a final, furious, protesting hiss of steam and the last of her shuddering shell slithered effortlessly beneath the undulating surface. She was gone. There was an appalling, soundless pause and then the gentle lapping of the waves against the few pieces of wreckage left behind, the only evidence that she had ever been there at all.

For the first time on the lifeboat, we fell silent. I saw Fraser make the sign of the cross and realised that he surely had lost men. The torpedo must have ripped through the hull of the ship, right through the engine room. There would have been no time for anyone to get out before the seas smashed in, had they even survived the blast. There could have been no one left alive down there.

Somehow, oddly, it was only then that I fully began to appreciate that this wasn't just an exciting interlude that had relieved the boredom of our otherwise uneventful voyage. We had lost our ship, our belongings and we had lost some men. Men with real lives, thoughts and feelings, aspirations. Men with families at home. Men I had worked alongside, greeted in the companionways and shared jokes with. They were dead.

The magnitude of what had just happened settled upon us and we were quiet.

'Hey lads, give us a hand!' It was Mac, slowly making his way back towards us through the blackness. It spurred us into action and we began manoeuvring a weaving course through the deck covers, wooden spars and bits of old flag lockers to pick up those who had preferred to take their chances in the water. Most had managed to don a lifejacket before their flight, and as each had a tiny light attached they were not difficult to locate. Only Billy Rawlins and Moses had not had the time to take any such precaution, and we heard Billy long before we could actually see him, swearing and cursing. We found him clinging to what looked remarkably like my old bit of locker panel, but I could not be sure. The sea was relatively calm and Moses a capable swimmer. He managed to make his own way in. We heaved them aboard, cracking jokes at the lightness and ease of our load without them, how their absences had saved us and how much better off we'd been without them.

The mood lightened further still when Tomas jumped excitedly to his feet, pointing away off to the right, shouting, 'The other boat! Over there! See the lights?'

We turned slowly, awkwardly, as having recovered all of those who had leapt from the boat in peril, we were once again heavily overladen. The oars were difficult to manage and we were low, dangerously low in the water. There were too many people in the way for those trying to row to get any rhythm going and Mick was having a hard time making himself heard over the whistles and catcalls aimed at attracting the attention of the other boat.

It made greater speed and when it hove more clearly into view, some twenty yards off, Joe unfurled his great frame from the bottom of the boat and bellowed, 'How many are you?'

No answer that we could hear, but the figures of two men standing in the prow were now discernible and the fact that at least four of the boat's oars were working quickly, smoothly and in time, was reassuring. It seemed interminable but by the time they got within shouting distance I could make out six, perhaps seven bodies. They were few.

She finally came alongside, nudging and bumping in the gentle swell and we roped together, starboard to port. Joe and I were hunkered in on the furthest side from her, so I had difficulty in seeing exactly who made up their number. I stood up, craning to see over the heads of the other men in our boat who had also risen, shouting and laughing, jubilant at the reunion. It was as if the presence of these other men meant that we were not alone. Two was better than one, and other survivors – in the same boat as it were – were an enormous relief. Such ebullient joy was ludicrous given that we were a couple of cockle shells, lost in the night, somewhere, anywhere, in the middle of the vast Atlantic Ocean. But in the circumstances, it was equally natural. There is comfort to be had from company.

I scanned the faces of the men in the other boat anxiously. And finally, glimpsing through the heads and bodies of the crowd, I spied Jamie. The only member of their crew of seven still seated, he held sombrely on to his oar. Clearly, he didn't feel there was anything much to celebrate.

I flopped back on to my seat and breathed out emphatically. Joe, still standing, ruffled the top of my head with delight. The responsibility of having left Jamie behind was something that I knew would have burdened me for the rest of my life. That is the way it is with me: I hold on to things. And seeing him sitting there, as gloomily as ever, immediately alleviated the misgiving that had already begun to plague me.

As the occupants of both boats settled down a little, Henderson, standing in the bow of the other boat, began to call some order. His voice was stronger and carried more weight than that of Captain Edwards, so it seemed quite natural that he should be the one to take control. Certainly on board ship he had been able to command as much, if not slightly more respect among the men. He had treated Edwards as an equal and Edwards seemed not only to accept this but actively to encourage it, seeking out Henderson's advice and intervention when he required it. There had been no rivalry between them; the two were friends. Besides, Henderson was a canny seaman who had survived a torpedoing before, and Edwards was no fool. He recognised and rewarded ability. He must have been highly relieved to see that Henderson had made it.

'We need to distribute men more equally. I'll take Calhoun. And Roberts. You and you. And a couple more. Right, yes. You two. All right with you, Captain Edwards?' he queried, as men clumsily began to stumble across others to take their places in the other boat, causing ours, weighty and unstable, to rock disconcertingly. I was sorry to see Calhoun leave. He might be tough and uncommunicative, but he was stalwart. He could be relied upon to make the right decision, which perhaps explained why Henderson wanted him.

'We should maybe go over with 'em. Could ask to,' Joe whispered, nudging me in the ribs. 'Calhoun's good in trouble. And Jamie's there.' And when I didn't answer, he pushed me on it. 'Should we?'

I hesitated. To follow Calhoun was tempting; he was twenty years or more younger than the skipper and therefore appeared much stronger. Of the two, physically, he looked the more likely captain, and he and Henderson together had both confidence and capability. But Captain Edwards, with his gnarled and knotted hands and slightly stooping body, exuded quiet experience, a steady thoughtfulness which resisted rashness. He had led on ship, not from out in front but by taking his cue from in among the crowd, listening to opinion and then acting accordingly. His inclination was apparently for moderation, and his lenience, which could sometimes look like weakness, made him the more likeable. Besides, Jamie was no company. He'd have the lot of us hopelessly forsaken and forgotten before we'd even sat down next to him.

'I'll keep Fraser if you don't mind,' Captain Edwards returned to Henderson, holding on to Fraser's shoulder and pushing him back into his seat. 'I need an engineer this side. And Mick. You stay this side, please. You two,' he pointed at two of the firemen a couple of places in front of Joe and me, 'you two move across. How many've you got, Walter?'

There was a short pause as the men settled themselves and Henderson weighed it up. I shook my head at Joe. It would suit us both to stay with Mick. Though radio officers fell outside his jurisdiction, he had been as industrious as he was cheerful as the bosun, and much more tolerant of the younger members of his deckhand crew than were the older ones among them. An able and experienced seaman, he was keen for them to learn and thus had been patient in imparting knowledge. But being neither lazy nor incompetent, to find these traits in others astounded and annoyed him and his intolerance of both was well known. Fortunately, once provoked, he forgot offence almost as soon as it was taken and Joe and I, in teasing him, had made the most of it. And his readiness to laugh away our cheek, coupled with the evident playfulness with which he mocked the sedentary nature of our work, had made me think he liked us. I suspected he'd be glad of our company.

I didn't know that much of Fraser. The chief engineer had kept largely to his engine room where he was reputed to have maintained a strict but judicial order. Tight-lipped and stern, he was reserved, but, I had it from Big Sam, intelligent and resourceful too. 'Let's stick with Mick,' I murmured quietly back at Joe. 'Besides, I don't think they even have an engine.'

'Fifteen now,' Henderson said, surveying his new crew. 'Could do with some oarsmen. You've an engine, haven't you? We're just oars and sail.' I tilted my head triumphantly at Joe, certain now I'd made the right decision while Henderson picked out two more deckhands and signalled for them to come over. Their mate jumped to his feet as they got up, 'Me too, sir. Can I go with them?'

'Fine. Eighteen, I've got. That about do it?' he asked, and Captain Edwards nodded.

'We are twenty,' he said, after a swift head count. 'Given that we've the engine, I think the best thing for us to do would be to tow you, Walter. Mick, what do you think? We should do our best to remain together if possible?'

'It'll be a better use of resources, sir, if we stick together,' Mick nodded his agreement.

'Speaking of which – Cub? Where's Cubby Clarke? Is he here?'

'Sir?' I rose, but he signalled for me to sit.

'Did you get the emergency radio?'

'Couldn't locate it, sir. Sorry.' There was a murmur of disappointment among the men. 'It wasn't there.' I shrugged, trying not to mind.

'Ought to take a roll call.' Captain Edwards had regained composure and reverted to procedure. 'Sit down men. All of you.'

Our boat, relieved of eleven extra bodies, was now much more comfortable. I was able to budge up and Joe could sit down for the first time. We listened in relative silence to the list of names called, answering when appropriate and avoiding each other's eyes when no answer came.

CHAPTER 5

KILL ME WITH KINDNESS

'Never seen that Jim Mackingtosh move so fast as when he took to the water,' laughed Mick, standing up to stretch and daring more than most in crowing down the boat at Mac. 'Except maybe for his food.' Mac looked up quickly but, perceiving nothing other than exuberant relief on Mick's face, began to smile despite himself.

'He don't ever move that fast for my food,' grumbled Big Sam, feigning indignation. To produce fine fare from the ingredients he had generally been expected to work with would have required the kind of culinary wizardry Sam clearly did not possess. He knew as well as we did that his food was sometimes awful and on ship he'd responded to our merciless ribbing by revelling in and even courting it. His huge, broad shoulders would shake with low, good-natured laughter, as he brushed away our mockery with flagrant disregard.

'Well, nobody does that, now, Big Man, do they?' Joe queried, grinning widely. Sam made a vague attempt to swat him roughly across the top of his head but Joe ducked down and Big Sam swiped at air.

'Anything to avoid his cooking,' Mac pulled a face. 'Never had such punishing muck! Christ, can't hardly wait to see what he does with... wait,' he opened one of the lockers nearest to his feet, which contained some of the lifeboat's food supplies and he shone his torch inside, '... a couple of ship's biscuits and a tin of pemmican!' Some of us groaned but Big Sam just threw back his massive head and, dispensing with all insult roundly, laughed his generous, throaty laugh.

The roll call complete, the excited chatter of men, relishing their apparent deliverance from a fate that at times had looked worse than catastrophic, rose in volume accordingly. Spirits were high. We had made it to an albeit relative safety and we were alive. The banter crisscrossed between the boats and our voices must have carried in the comparative silence and darkness. Apart from two or three hastily snatched-up torches, the stars afforded us our only light. They shone as a concession in an otherwise indifferent sky whilst the vast tracts of the Atlantic rolled out immeasurably beyond us, equally unmoved by our ordeal and by our premature celebration. We had no expectations as yet for our future; we were merely rejoicing noisily in our salvation.

Without warning, we were stunned into an abrupt, spine-stiffening silence by a cavernous voice, booming out across the darkness, through a crackling megaphone.

'What ship are you?' We froze. Absolutely still, every one of us.

Again, 'What ship are you?' and again there was silence, broken only by the gentle breaking of the waves against our softly bumping boats. About thirty yards off, silhouetted against the sky-line, I could just about make out the shadowy malevolence of a submarine hull, and as my eyes adjusted to the murky middle distance, the 4-inch gun mounted on its deck. The ship had stolen up almost right beside us, unnoticed.

There was some sudden, silent movement in the bow of our boat. Captain Edwards had risen quietly and crouching, he began picking his way through the men, slowly and gingerly, down the length of the boat. Nothing was said but all eyes were upon him and men bowed and bent sideways to let him pass. About half-way down, he stopped and signalled to Calhoun in the other boat. Calhoun immediately stood up. On reaching the stern sheets,

Edwards ducked down and out of sight. We were all aware that the captain and quite possibly the first mate of any vessel seized would, in all likelihood, be taken aboard an enemy submarine and interrogated – that, or worse.

The submarine, silkily smooth, had lessened the distance between us now and was almost on top of us.

'Jesus Christ. He's gonna shoot us. Gonna shoot us all outta the water. Christ,' muttered Mac, panicky, in my ear.

'Shut up, Mac,' I breathed.

'Got through all that… for this. Jesus Christ,' he murmured.

'For Christsakes, shut up, Mac,' Joe leant across me. 'Leave it to Calhoun.'

The voice, in impeccable English, tried for a third time, 'What ship are you? An answer please.'

Calhoun cleared his throat. 'SS *Sithonia*. Bound for South America.'

'Thank you. Your cargo?'

'Coal.'

'And you are the captain?'

'No, I am not. The captain went down with the ship.'

'And you are?'

'Second Officer Calhoun.' Calhoun's voice was steely, impressive. He was a brave man.

'Tell him not to shoot us. Tell him we're not armed,' Rawlins hissed up at him. 'Go on!' Some people, I noticed were beginning to edge themselves down, between and even under the wooden seats. Moses, one of the younger firemen on our boat and his friend, Jack Parnell, had almost disappeared altogether.

Calhoun ignored them all.

'How many ships in your convoy?'

'About fifteen.' Calhoun's ability to lie under pressure struck me as tremendous. He was so calm. Had it been me, I felt sure I'd have blurted out the truth and thrown in that the skipper was alive and well and hiding in the stern sheets for good measure. I couldn't have helped myself. I doubted even that the captain would have made so good a job of it. Weathered by long years at sea and no longer young nor daring, his inclinations erred on cautious. But Calhoun: he was undaunted.

'He'll know he's bloody lying, for Christsakes. Bastard's gonna shoot us now for sure. Bloody hell, Calhoun,' Mac kept up a running commentary in my ear, which made me sweat. By now, I could just about discern a figure, visible from the shoulders up, in the conning tower of the sub. Occasionally, a sliver of light glinted from the edges of his loudspeaker as he moved it up to speak and down again to listen.

'Mac, will you shut up. You're scaring the kids,' Joe whispered fiercely across me, nodding towards Moses and Jack and some of the other deckhands who were now huddling together, curled up with fear, as far down in the bottom of the boat as they could slide. 'He isn't gonna kill us. He'd've done it by now.'

'Are there any injured men among you?' This next inquiry, which showed such surprising consideration for our welfare, seemed an unlikely preamble for murder and so, breathing out slowly, I began to relax, though Mac did not let up. 'Wha' the fuck does he care?' he muttered incredulously, pausing for one second before racing to his own conclusion. 'Fuckin' damn sight easier to shoot if he reckons he'd just be doin' us a favour.'

Calhoun answered that there were none.

'Did you get a distress signal away?' Even Calhoun was not expecting this and for a moment, he looked confused. He looked down at his feet and then half turned around, looking for a radio officer among his crew. He found Jamie.

'Did you, Jamie? Were you in the shack?'

'No, sir. I mean yes. Yes, sir. I was in the shack but the kit was damaged. In the blast. So I didn't get a signal out.'

Calhoun turned back to his faceless inquisitor and looked up, clearing his throat again.

'No. No, we didn't,' he shouted.

'I will send one for you. Give me your call sign. You will be picked up sooner.'

'Ahh, for pity's sake. Don't go and give 'im it!' Mac's voice was getting too loud and Calhoun, distracted a moment, glanced across at us, annoyed. But Mac, garrulous in his fear, was apparently oblivious to Calhoun's displeasure. 'He's only wanting to make sure we're not lyin' about the ship. He's jus' toyin' with us. Bastard.'

Joe, losing patience, slapped his hands down on his knees and shot up, stepping roughly over me and sandwiching himself down heavily in front of Mac, effectively cutting him off from the cluster of cowering figures in middle section of the boat. His huge frame formed an invaluable barricade. He didn't say any more and neither did Mac.

My blood began to run more freely through my veins and I found that I could breathe.

Offering to send a distress signal out for the survivors of a ship you had just destroyed in an effort to help conclude their suffering was not an act of animosity. The man was clearly doing what he could to make some amends within the confines prescribed by his nationality and loyalties. Calhoun obviously agreed with me, for he gave the call sign over.

More solicitous still, the next enquiry proved Mac's fearful apprehensions groundless.

'Do you know your exact position?'

Calhoun replied that we did not. There was a short pause. The figure vanished momentarily, only a tiny slice of light from the rim of his megaphone still visible and then he was back.

'25 north, 24 west. You are about 350 miles from the Canary Islands. Do you have enough blankets? Cigarettes?'

Surprise registered even on Jim Mackingtosh's face. Calhoun looked vaguely about him. 'Cigarettes. Get cigarettes,' someone muttered hoarsely from somewhere behind in the other boat.

As we were just north of the equator, the nights were warm and blankets seemed superfluous. We knew nothing of what was to come – how skinny bones and wasted muscle would shiver with the cold and how those burning up with fever might cry out for the comfort of some extra layers. Calhoun turned the blankets down.

'We are a little short on cigarettes though,' he wavered.

Again the figure disappeared, megaphone and all. He was gone for longer this time, minutes maybe, and when he returned, he sounded rueful.

'I am sorry. We too are a little short. Well, good luck.' He gave a cheery wave. 'Bon voyage,' and he was gone.

We watched, speechless, as the submarine glided off into the darkness, effortlessly folding back the black and yielding water.

Joe gave a long, low whistle. 'What a guy!' he hooted. 'Kill me with kindness, why don't ya?'

The collective exhalation on our two little boats was almost visible. It was as if we had all been sitting tightly upright, fists and stomachs clenched, rigid with fear, and as the U-boat moved off and out of sight, everyone expanded and relaxed. Moses, Jack and the others reappeared and I heard Jack, wide-eyed and breathy with relief, yabber to his friend, 'Did you think we was gonna die? I thought we was definitely gonna die.'

'We weren't never gonna die,' Billy Rawlins butted in, all nonchalant now. 'Should've known Calhoun'd nail it, eh Calhoun? Shame about the fags though.'

Calhoun didn't answer him. He was sitting down, looking out into the darkness after the U-boat. I saw Henderson go over to him and shake his hand and when Captain Edwards, who had re-emerged from his hiding place, had made his way back up to the prow of our boat, he saluted him. I have never seen that done by anyone within the Merchant Navy before or since.

Talk gradually dwindled out as people began to drowse. It had been a long night and both physically and mentally we had taken a battering. Nevertheless, it was hard to find a comfortable position to settle in. There wasn't enough room to lie down and the upper half of my body, pyjama topless, chafed against the rough and splintery wood of the boat's lining. Sleep seemed barely possible. Some men had managed to bring along their hurry bags, Joe included, and so they were able to use them as rough pillows but I had nothing. I must have squirmed and fidgeted and tried to readjust my long body and legs so many times that Joe eventually sat up, huffing, and rummaged furiously in his bag.

'Here,' he said, thrusting a pullover at me. 'Use that.'

I folded it up and tucked it on the rim of the boat side and there I laid my head. I knew that I was tired, my body ached, but still I could not sleep. My thoughts would not allow it. Image after image of the night's proceedings swept before me, tangling me in their confusion and on the black, blank canvas of the quiet night, they came to me more vividly and I saw and heard again their lurid horror. Despite my fierce attempts to keep it straight, my contrary mind insisted on examining each precarious twist of our recent fate, forcing me to contemplate, in grotesquely garish detail, alternatives I would rather not have witnessed. My body, thick and bloated, swayed within the waters of my tiny, doorless cabin. I watched, powerless, as our boat was drawn inexorably beneath the savage stern. Jamie was not on the other boat, and ours, pock-marked, floated aimlessly in the darkness, a chilling graveyard for twenty men butchered by a U-boat gun.

I don't think anyone among us slept that much. Shock, delayed by the nervous energy expended in our escape and subsequent exhilaration, slowly took its turn and bedded in. It confounded sleep. Wakeful eyes watched the passing of the night, wrestling with the rising sense of loss that sought refuge in disbelief. And every time my body sought passage to slide and shift towards the margins of benumbing sleep, I was wrenched awake again, sweating and appalled. Several times I looked across at Joe. His arms were tightly folded across his chest, his fists were clenched and his eyes remained wide open.

I must have dozed eventually though, for at least a little while, as when I roused, the grey light of dawn was making its way over the horizon. Before long, the molten oranges of the approaching sun had tinged the purple sky with swathes of pink and pastel blue and lined the early morning clouds with silver. Dawn at sea. I had always loved it, and that morning its gentle and familiar tones soothed and calmed my chattering nerves and threw the livid colours of my imaginings into sharp relief.

Others began to sit up, stretch and rub their faces. People stood to relieve their stiffened limbs and most made their way, at some point or another, to take a pee over the side.

Captain Edwards called Henderson and Calhoun up for a conference and they stood together where the two boats met. Mick and Fraser got up to join them. With the information the U-boat commander had given us, they calculated that we were about 350 miles south-west of the Canaries, and so they set our course for north north-east.

'With a good breeze and favourable currents, I reckon we could make it in three or four days,' Henderson said. 'Does anyone have a compass?' He looked around at the upturned faces in the two boats hopefully and I looked at Joe. He hesitated just a fraction of a second and then stood up.

'Here.' He put his hand in his pocket and drew out Maggie's small, gold disc. It looked minuscule, insignificant in his massive palm. He leaned forward, across the heads of Moses and Jack, holding it out towards Henderson's outstretched hand. Something of its consequence must have shown in his face though, for Henderson looked at him and then at the compass and said, 'Good. Right then, thank you. You hold on to it, Joe. We're going to need it.' And he turned back towards the captain.

'We need to share some stuff out, is what I think,' Billy Rawlins spoke up gruffly. 'Some of us are better off than others.' He hadn't come away with his hurry bag either.

'Quite right, Billy,' the captain smiled politely and cleared his throat. 'All of you, keep your clothes but everything else, food, cigarettes, we'll need to share… we'll make a pile here.' He pointed to the space where the middle seat met the ledge above the lockers. There was murmuring and shuffling down the length of each boat as men mumbled their dissent and reluctantly began opening up their bags and taking out precious supplies.

'I'm not giving up my smokes,' Pat Murack growled. 'I'm not bloody goin' without.' He opened up a packet and took the majority out, stuffing them in his top pocket before getting up to throw the packet, now containing one or maybe two cigarettes, across to the pile.

'I bloody saw that, Murack,' Billy spat, jumping up from his seat. 'You bloody selfish bastard!'

Murack flicked back up too and the two glared at one another across the boat. There were perhaps six or seven heads between them. 'Who the fuck are you calling a bastard?' he shouted.

'Sit down, Pat. Billy.' Captain Edwards put his arms out, though he could not have reached out far enough to stop either of them. 'Sit down.' Neither of them moved.

Joe, still standing with his hands in his pockets, suddenly stepped across the seats and leaned down to pick up the packet. He threw it back to Pat who caught it at his chest.

'If you don't want to share… don't,' Joe said. Billy, behind him, sat back down, smirking, and everyone looked at Pat in silence. He had no dignified alternative but to reach into his pocket and return the cigarettes to their box. He flung them back onto the pile and sat down again, furious and embarrassed.

'If that bloody Jerry'd've given us some fags, we wouldn't've had this bloody problem,' he muttered resentfully, turning to hide his face in the cover of the night's retreat. 'Didn't have any! Probably had fuckin' boxes of 'em stashed down there.'

'If that bloody Jerry hadn't blown us out of the water, we wouldn't have this bloody problem either,' Mick piped up, smiling and indicating with one expansive arc of his arm the boat and the mass of ocean beyond it. 'And this bloody problem's slightly bigger!' A few men laughed, relieved by Mick's attempt to loosen the tension, so few heard Moses quietly murmur, 'Just be glad that he didn't finish us off with that bloody great gun.' His body shuddered quickly. I was amazed. Reputedly a mute, Moses never spoke at all, at least not to my knowledge, and to risk drawing himself to the attention of the likes of Pat Murack, a malcontent twice his age and quick to take offence, would in most circumstances have been considered dangerous. But Murack did not hear. He was still sulking in his corner.

It turned out that only about a dozen or so among us had their bags. Each man came forward, most with thin-lipped bad grace, to drop his offerings down, but even so the pile was not much more than meagre when the desultory procession finished. There was chocolate, some biscuits, a few crumpled packets of cigarettes. Joe threw in his hat too. He said with his hair and the heat down here, he wouldn't have much call for it. Edwards, handing roughly half of the loot to Henderson, asked him then how his men were fixed for torches. They had one between the lot of them so Edwards appealed for volunteers among our crew to give a couple over. All eyes looked down, away. Sighing, the skipper took one from Billy and another from Big Sam, much to the silent consternation of them both. He shared the cigarettes out between us. Six each. The chocolate he put in the locker near his seat.

'Not enough to last a bloody day,' Pat grumbled, ungraciously taking his quota of fags while everyone watched the passing packets, sly-eyed, checking that the next man did not get more.

One of the deckhands, Fred Watson, got Joe's turrie. He was bald save for three or four salt and pepper-coloured strands of hair that sprouted from just above his left ear. After what must have been years of careful cultivation, they were now long enough for him to paste up and over the top of his freckled scalp so that they almost reached his right ear. Any sudden movement or energetic activity saw them flop back down so that they dangled scraggily around his left shoulder.

'Here, Fred,' Mick laughed, picking it up and flinging it at him, 'you'll need this in this sun. Otherwise the top of your head's gonna burn and you'll look like a bleeding zebra.' Although it was still very early, the sun was already strong. Its restorative rays sloped across the glittering ocean from just above the horizon, warming our faces and helping to dispel the lurking shadows of the night.

Fred grimaced and put it on. It was a small, thin, wool hat, the kind that had to stretch to fit. 'He looks like a flaming peanut now!' Clarie exclaimed, to cackles of increasingly infectious laughter.

Breakfast added to the better humour, though it was less than appetising. Food and water, no matter how unpleasant, numbed the edgy irritation of our minds and instilled calm. The ship's biscuits, kept in canisters, proved too hard to bite apart but doused with the water from the barrel, they softened up. Once broken open, to some they were immediately inedible as weevils riddled out from almost every crumbling pore. Tomas threw his down, disgusted, but I am not so squeamish with my food and I was hungry.

The fast-receding horrors of the night, coupled with the effects of fitful sleep, had made my head feel thick and slow, disconnected from the workings of my body, and I knew that food would set me straight. I began to pick the weevils out. They squirmed and writhed between my fingers but one by one, I flicked them overboard. Some pemmican in a tin was being passed around and, borrowing Joe's knife, I took a liberal scooping and mashed it on the biscuit. It was foul: meaty and bitter. I forced it down, trying not to touch it with my tongue, trying not to taste. By swilling it around my mouth with water, I could work it into smaller pieces, small enough to swallow. We each got a Horlicks tablet too, which, though more palatable, had a fine, powdery consistency. It dissolved too thickly, its chalky particles clagging up behind my gums and in between my teeth. The biggest remnant clung resolutely to the roof of my mouth, and only a tablespoonful of condensed milk followed by great swigs of water served finally to dislodge it. A single square of chocolate handed out by Captain Edwards felt like a well-deserved reward.

With the towrope in place, we started up our engine and, taking our bearings from Joe's compass and the sun, we set off northeasterly. It was not windy and the sea was relatively calm, but still the waves were challenging, buffeting the boats between them, pushing one away and down and raising up the other, so that the engine struggled with the weight of both and the towrope broke and broke again. Swearing and sweating in the beating sun, we tried to keep the boats together and on line but the sea, dispassionate, threw and skewed them sideways and apart. And the towrope broke again. Our precious fuel supplies would soon run out if the engine had to work so fiercely and besides, we were getting nowhere. Knowing that we might need some fuel to get the boats up through breakers when we reached the shore, it seemed unnecessarily reckless to squander it without restraint.

By midday, the skipper called a halt. He and Henderson agreed to separate the boats and put up sail. The air was thick, barely stirring, so there was little breeze to offer us much impetus but the sail at least would help to curb the influence of any adverse currents and, having struggled so fruitlessly in the uncompromising heat, we needed respite to recover water and recoup our misspent energies.

We ate again – a repeat of breakfast, which some attempted with more fortitude than others – and then set to, preparing the ropes and readying the canvas. It did not look as if it had ever been unleashed before, not since the old *Sithonia* had been built, for, grimed and greasy, its folds stuck together and screeched at their unbinding. As we hoisted it up the ageing mast, it snagged a quarter of the way from the top and no amount of twisting and jerking on the ropes or at the sail itself could loosen it.

'We can't do it from down here,' Mick cried in frustration. 'Someone'll have to go up and unhook 'er.' The propect of climbing up the spindly mast as our little boat lurched from side to side in the persistent swell was not attractive and several men spoke up disclaiming their suitability for the job. Tutting and shaking his head, Mick himself started forward then to make the climb but Fraser stopped him, pointing at the rickety mast and then laughingly alluding to the size of the Irishman's girth. Mick smiled too then. He was impetuous and he was brave but he would listen to good reason and he trusted Fraser's judgement. Fraser was more phlegmatic. He was not much given to wasting words and was well respected for it. As a result, greater store was set by what he did say and a few choice words from him to any man among us would be taken as rather more than just a friendly piece of advice.

Joe and I cocked an eyebrow at one another, nodding up towards the mast, each encouraging the other to have a crack at it. We both knew that neither one of us was right to try it and so were hardly serious. He was far too huge and I, too long and lanky.

But Tomas got up and said he'd go. He was small but broad-shouldered and his body, though slim, had a wiry strength. He proved agile and set on up at an energetic pace, making it look easy, and the rest of us called up to him, pushing him on with encouraging updates on his progress and a plethora of other helpful tips and pointless observations.

He had almost made it when the boat, cresting the top of a particularly hefty wave, plunged downwards suddenly, twisting sideways as it careened towards the bottom of the trough. Tomas cried out. Before the boat could right itself, a resounding and decisive snap appalled us all and then there came a thud, as Tomas hit the side of the boat and smashed into the water, half of the mast crashing down behind him.

He bobbed up, shaken, and grabbed on to the floating piece of useless wood beside him. We hauled him in and he sat, breathlessly swearing, half in English, half in Portuguese, while Fraser looked him over. He'd gashed his hip where he'd skimmed the boat but otherwise he was unhurt.

'Couldn't take his weight, I don't reckon,' Mac sniffed. 'Should've sent someone lighter. Moses mebbe. Them darkies climb like friggin' monkeys.'

Mac's prejudice against any man with skin a different colour from his own had been something I had heard Big Sam complain about on board ship, but I had not, until now, heard or had to witness first-hand his crude contempt.

And as he spoke, from my viewpoint in the stern, a sudden movement in the middle of the boat caught my eye. Moses had flinched bodily at the insult that Mac had muttered loud enough for half the boat to hear, and as he digested its obscenity, his face contorted sharply with uncharacteristic anger and he started to his feet. With one quick, barely perceptible movement, Wallace, a broad West African who had worked with Moses in the engine room and who sat close enough behind to see his reaction, jerked him down again. Moses spun round to question it and as he did so, Wallace flashed at him a sharp look of warning, hissing up into his downturned face, 'Leave it, Moses. Bastard ain't worth the fucking fight. Sit down.'

Mac, Mick and most of the rest of the crew were too busily taken up with the mast to even notice what had taken place. None of them had turned a hair at Mac's casual abuse, and though quite aware from previous voyages on other ships of the existence of the insidious order ingrained within our culture, I felt uneasy. Misfortune had been no leveller and it was evident that some among us would clearly be at a disadvantage for, by virtue of their nationality, language and the colour of their skin, they would be marginalised by some, and worse, by others, totally disregarded.

'Moses is a bloody fireman. What the hell would he know about the frigging sails?' snapped Murack. 'Anyways, ain't no use now. Look at it!'

The mast had broken a little more than halfway up. Even what was left slanted slightly, its jagged tip crowned with spiky, splintered wood.

Fraser was leaning over the side of the boat, trying to bat the broken mast top towards us so that he could get a better look. 'Give us a hand here, lads!' he called over his shoulder at Joe and me. We helped him paddle at the water until he could reach a hand to it. 'Bloody thing was rotten through. Look at this,' he cried, standing up to show the others what looked like a pitted piece of broken driftwood, about a foot long, which had come away in his hand. That it was wet did not explain that it was so soft and crumbly. He made to pull a bit off and there was no resistance; inch-thick shafts fell away between his fingers.

'Bloody hell, Tomas, you did well to get that far.' Captain Edwards, trying to be consoling, shook Tomas' hunched shoulder. 'We can still use half the mast. Mick? Get the sail up as far as possible. It's not disastrous.'

But looking at the other boat, it was difficult not to disagree. Its sail, unfurled and white and brilliant against the glinting blue beyond, was catching at the gentle undulations in the air with easy elegance, while ours hung down, disconsolate, its crumpled skirts lying listless at its feet. With only half of it exposed, it was only half efficient and making do was all there was on offer.

So severed from stability and shaken by the absence of all familiarity, we immediately sought solace by establishing security in new habits. It did not take long for each of us to stake a claim on a half-square-metre piece of territory within the boat. From that very first morning, the skipper took his place up in the prow with Fraser. Clarie and Mick occupied opposite seats behind them and Big

Sam tried hard to squeeze his great, hefty body along the wooden bench between. Fred stayed up towards that end too, with Billy Rawlins and his deckhand mates. There were two of them, Cunningham and Butler, though Joe had dubbed them Billy's boys. On ship Billy was rarely to be seen without them, and they deferred to him as if afraid.

Moses, Jack and Wallace settled themselves into the middle section of the boat with Li, a stocky-looking fireman from China whom I barely knew, and two greasers, Moley Wells and Slim Jackson. These two had lost particular friends in the engine room when the ship went down, so they, though not as young as their immediate neighbours, were edgy, still reeling with the shock. They sat along the middle seat, cocooned on every side by other men.

Joe and I fixed our position on the stern side of the last seat across the boat, near Mac and Pat Murack, with Tomas close behind. And at dusk that night Joe began his notches. Whistling carelessly, he made a groove, carving out a thin wedge from the wooden rim of the boat, just behind the rowlock for the last port side oar. I watched him slowly working it away, smoothing it off with his thumb after every second gouge and blowing off the wood dust when he'd finished.

'We'll need to know how long we've done. When we get there,' he said by way of explanation. 'What's to make tomorrow any different from today? Down here the sea's the same, the sky's the same. The sun. The days will be the same, and the nights. They'll probably get longer. We'll lose count. Unless there's a storm or we get picked up.' He began to hum and, snapping up his knife, he put it away. 'Gotta keep a record, so we know.'

In the short term, he was wrong. The following day was different, proving harder still upon our spirits, already lowered by the inadequacy of our sail, when we discovered that we had much less water than we supposed. The day before, we'd watered well assuming that the two metal tanks stored in the lifeboat were full and we had taken as much as we had needed, in the scorching sun, from the barrel. This was now three quarters empty and when Mick had gone to fill it from the tanks, his venomous expletives brought the true state of our supply to our horrified attention. One contained about two thirds of what it should, the other less than half.

Moreover, yesterday it had seemed hard to cut the cord and separate from the other boat but Henderson had planned to stay close by us. Neither crew had seemed too eager to be alone, a tiny, speck-like insignificance at the mercy of the infinite ocean. But it was harder still to watch his boat tacking effortlessly away on into the distance while we wallowed fretfully behind, a whining child clasping vainly at its brother's shirt tail. A couple of times, we cranked the engine up and sped to catch them, but the skipper, with an anxious eye on our fast diminishing levels of fuel, declared that next time we would have to row. It was immediately obvious that such physical exertion was untenable during the day, for it was just too hot even to move, so Clarie drew up a rota to be implemented as soon as darkness fell. Dividing us up into crews of six with two to bail, he tried to distribute strength as equally as possible, though eventually, and with increasing exasperation, he was cajoled into conceding that mates should row together. We worked hard throughout the night, changing hourly, to make up for our deficiency, steering by the North Star and by torch light on Joe's compass. We started up at dusk and pushed on through, till as far as we could bear into the morning. But to no avail. By the dawn on the third day, the other boat had gone.

'Bastards,' Billy griped. 'Flamin' bastards. Might've known Henderson'd leave us here for dead. Always was a sly bastard, that one.'

'You'll keep quiet, Rawlins, if you know what's good for you. Don't talk like that about Walter Henderson. He's a friend of mine,' Captain Edwards, small and birdlike in the prow, was still peering out in to the far distance, clinging to the fast-fading hope of catching sight of the small, white triangle.

'Some fuckin' friend,' Billy muttered, turning away from him.

'We'd've done the same,' Joe sat down, giving it up. 'Besides, we're not dead yet, Billy boy,' he added, slapping his knees and grinning through cracking lips. 'Be picked up today, I reckon. And if not, another day or two, be sunning it up in the Canaries.'

'Forget sunning it up,' I smiled too. 'Watering down'll do for me.' Jack and a few others around him tried to raise a concurring laugh but shrinking skin, starting to crack and itch with unwelcome stubble, prevented much enthusiasm. I was not yet quite frightened. That we were now alone was disconcerting, but I never for one moment considered that we would not make it. It might take us longer than the other crew, but they would greet us on the islands with water tins held high, joyfully exclaiming at our tardiness. Or we would be picked up. It would not be long. Even the knowledge that our water supply was lower than expected did not alarm me greatly. There was enough, if we rationed, to last us the two, at worst, three days that it would take us. I was irritable and disgruntled, physically discomforted by the ache of clawing hunger and fatigue, that of plaguing thirst, but it was not yet irreparable. And so I was not yet afraid.

But morale upon the boat was already getting low. Billy's sentiments, though unfair, reflected a general feeling of abandonment. We could hardly blame Henderson's crew for pressing on, and yet somehow, we did.

More unnerving still for me was the persistent, nagging worry that I may have inadvertently prolonged not only my own suffering, but also that of Joe. The disappearance of the other boat, its obvious progress and thus seemingly more imminent salvation meant that I, unwittingly, had made the poorer choice. Joe's suggestion that we should follow Calhoun onto the other boat had been, perhaps, an oblique request, reflecting his intuitive faith in Calhoun's proficiency. He'd wanted us to take our chances with Henderson and Calhoun, sensing instinctively that they might be the better bet. That he had not even thought, at my refusal, to move across without me struck me now as loyal, and although I could not possibly have predicted what had happened to our mast, I felt vaguely responsible. Sorry I had not listened with more care to the implication of his question.

I knew the thought that we could have been among them, that we could probably have almost made land by now, must have crossed his mind. How could it have failed to cross his mind, cramped upon our limping lifeboat, bored and hungry, dehydrating by the minute and seeking only to while away the blanching hours for the next meagre insufficiency of water? My only consolation lay in the speculative hope that it might not be too long.

Being Joe and generous, he would never say it. But it did not stop the awkwardness I felt for my decision from bothering me and I spent most of the day wondering how best to broach it with him. Knowing well that he would brook no apology for something he would not in the least consider necessary, I tried to lighten it by making it a joke. 'Bloody hell, Joe,' I said eventually, crouching down next to him that evening, 'I told you we should've gone with Jamie! We'd've probably bloody been there by now!'

He was on his knees, working at his notch but when I spoke, he turned around to look at me and then with a derisive snort, he shoved me lightly at the shoulder. I tipped backwards, guilt dismissed, and fell giddily onto Mac. He was half sitting, half lying across the bottom of the boat, his arms up on the last seat, taking in the cool and ease of evening, the chance to get some rest. My ungainly landing doused him liberally with the bilgy water that pooled constantly along the belly of the boat and in which he, in his efforts to stretch his body out, was forced to lie. His legs and feet were already half submerged but my intrusive splashing irritated him. 'Jesus, Cub!' Mac glowered at me and then at Joe. 'Don't know what the fuck you two are sniggering about. Ain't too funny – any of this fucking crap.'

Joe shrugged at Mac and then grinned at me, 'Always pick the wrong 'un, I do,' he said, offering me a hand to yank me back.

'Sorry, Mac,' I said breathlessly, over my shoulder as I struggled to right myself. 'Wouldn't let Maggie hear you say that, Joe.' As soon as the words had left my mouth, I was sorry that I'd said it. I knew him to be misguidedly susceptible to thinking himself unworthy as far as Maggie was concerned and by bringing her up before his eyes, just as he'd maligned his judgements, I felt I'd somehow blunderingly implied that he was right. His face clouded for an instant and he looked down. Then he shook his head slowly and passed a hand across his grizzled chin, scraping thoughtfully back and forth. 'Yeah, well… she must be the exception to the rule,' he said. He cleared his throat after a moment and throwing it off, he glanced back up at me and with laughter behind his voice, he added, 'But you, Cub, on the other hand! You're a bleeding disaster! Look at the state of you… you look as if you've slept behind a hedge… or on a lifeboat. And…' he adjusted his fictitious spectacles and peered in an exaggerated manner at my scraggy pyjama bottoms, 'am I right in thinking that those are your pyjamas?' I looked down at the bleached and thinning material that covered my bottom half and both of us began to laugh.

That night I was not cold but for the first time, I wanted covering. The nights with their still and balmy breath were warm and so far had offered only singular relief from the bleak, ill-tempered raging of the sun during the daylight hours. But that night, my shoulders and my back craved the comfort of a wrapping. As I lay awake, forced to listen to the rhythmic dipping of the oars and the fluctuation of the waters, my eyes were drawn to the infinities above, the endless blackness of the sky, the stars, unperturbed by our predicament, and the cold-eyed, fixed attention of an impassive, glacial moon.

I fought against the sly, gradually pervading suspicion of my insignificance, wanting to hide from it, shut it out, to bury my head beneath blankets and lose it in the sweet oblivion of unfettered sleep. But wakefulness, like thirst, like hunger, would not let me be.

'Hey, Resendes!' Mick's voice rang out across the rower's heads, behind me, from the prow. His irritated tone snapped me back sharply from the isolation of my thoughts. 'You're taking us off course. Jesus! You wanna be goin' east from the North Star. Right. Bloody hell. Are you asleep?…' He was suddenly on his feet, incredulous and angry. 'Is he a-fucking-sleep?' he shouted, appealing to anyone awake near Tomas whose turn it was apparently to man the rudder. Most of us by this point had been long enough in Mick's company to recognise that the extent of his annoyance at any given moment could be measured almost exactly by the increased intensity of his natural accent. The more agitated Mick ever became, the more pronounced his native tongue and, as he stood now railing down the boat at Tomas, it was obvious even in the darkness, from the inflection of his words, that he was furious.

'No. Jesus Christ, Mick. Of course I am not sleeping,' Tomas, affronted by the accusation, sounded indignant. He shot up from his seat, one hand still on the tiller, as if to verify his consciousness. 'I am on the bloody course. North north-east.'

'Well, it don't look much like it from up here.' Mick snapped testily. Tomas' quick reaction was apparently enough to pacify Mick to a degree, for his voice lost a little of its spleen, though he was clearly still annoyed. 'You're too far to port. Well, ain't he, Captain?'

There was a moment's pause as the Captain rose and turned to follow the line of Mick's pointing finger. His answer when it came was measured and without censure, 'Yes, I think you're right there, Mick. A point to starboard, then, Tomas. Please.'

Mick spun round. 'Joe? Where the hell is Joe?'

Joe, hunched up near me behind the last seat, lifted up an arm and waved it cheerily, 'Here, Mick. I'm down here.'

'Get that bleedin' compass out and show it to Tomas, would you? Otherwise he'll have us all in bloody Timbuktu before we know it.'

'Better there than here I'd say,' laughed Joe, unfolding his cramped-up legs and getting to his feet. He caught the torch that Jack threw up at him and whistling through his teeth, went down to sit by Tomas. Mollified slightly, Mick followed the skipper's cue and sat back down, settling himself at the head of the prow and allaying his own anxieties every now and then by calling back, 'A little more. Right. More. OK!'

I listened to the murmurings of Joe and Tomas talking for a little while and, comforted by their company, I must have dozed.

I was woken by Joe's clumsy attempts at quietness on his return. He stood upon my foot as he tried to step into his place. 'Ooph! Sorry, Cub. Sorry,' he whispered loudly, stumbling and almost falling over the seat in front of me. He manoeuvred his way past my body and hunkering down, leant back against the far side of the boat but did not, as I was expecting, start to shuffle about in his habitually noisy but nonetheless ever-unproductive attempt to find a comfortable position for sleep. Instead, I saw him lift his knees so that they folded up against his chest. He brought his hands up to rest upon them and then I saw that he still held his compass. The sheen of its gold-coloured casing gleamed softly in the moonlight. He gazed at it, immersed, turning it over and smoothing it just as I had seen him do that morning by the radio shack. He sat there, with his thoughts of her, oblivious to it all.

Eventually, coming to, he glanced across at me and saw that I was now awake again and, for want of any other occupation, was watching him.

Craving a little perhaps of the immunity her proximity clearly afforded, I propped myself up on one elbow and ventured softly, 'So it's true then, Joe. How people say it is?'

His eyes found their way back to his hands and the physical embodiment of his dreams which lay between them. He continued to work his thumb steadily across the muted lustre of its surface but made no attempt at first to answer. I began to wonder if perhaps I had not spoken my thoughts out loud, but then he shook his head slowly, thoughtfully. 'I don't know. Who can ever say what it must be like for someone else?'

'But how do you know?' I asked, young enough and eager still to believe that there had to be some kind of formula, some useful code of understanding to which, through Maggie, he had miraculously gained access. Something that he could at least communicate that would ensure that if and when love should ever come to me, I would not be fool enough to mistake it. 'What makes it any different? With Maggie, I mean?'

'I don't know,' he murmured, the words barely coming audibly above the heavy sigh accompanying them. 'I don't know if I ever could explain.' He let his head drop within the circle his arms made with his knees and, left only with the ragged outline of his hair to look at, I waited. But just as I thought that he had probably given up, that he must, albeit unconsciously, have accepted that there are certain aspects within the emotional spectrum of humanity for which there are no words, his voice came again, more thickly now and muffled. 'It's just that somehow Cub, she is inside me. As if she always has been. And when I met her, she simply stepped back into her place. As if she already knew me. Knew that she belonged. As if she always had.' He paused and then he breathed more quietly still, 'And so had I.'

Though I had pushed him to it, somehow I had not expected so close-hearted an admission. It shook me and, unsteadied before that which suddenly seemed so sacred, I scrabbled to shield us both from a disquieting sense of sensibility stripped bare. Covering it hastily with an appeal to his more tangible memory, I asked abruptly, 'Where did you meet?'

'Hmm?' He lifted his head.

'You and Maggie. Where did you meet?'

'On a tram. She was with her sister and her sister's husband. Maggie looked at me. She looked into me. And I knew then who she was.'

Neither of us said any more for a while and, as his eyes returned once more to the small, gold object in his hand, his attention wandered back towards the peace and consolation of her presence.

Folding myself back down, I tried to shuffle my body into a position that might better preface sleep. I closed my eyes but I knew it was no good. My most pressing discomfort now came so much more profoundly from within. For in attempting to make plain his own, Joe had shown me Maggie's heart, and in so doing, had unintentionally given me a glimpse of the immeasurable depth of their connection. What he had been struggling to convey had brought before me so strong an image of two separate souls as one single entity, as so inextricably combined, that I had been left with the distinct impression that until the moment of their convergence, their lives, though independent, had been nonetheless incomplete. The loss of either one of them could do nothing then but condemn the other to the hollow half-existence of a being rent in two; bereft and broken, left to limp across the unrelenting winter of a life that could only ever be half lived.

I had been made to understand, for the first time, her stake in his safe and punctual return. And that Joe had thrown his lot so conclusively and, it had proved, somewhat ill-advisedly in with mine, meant that the consciousness of responsibility I had begun to feel towards him now extended further and encompassed her.

And as I curled up against the boat's side and fought to shut them out, the dark and shifting shadows of misgiving, laying siege to the somnolence of the night, repeated to me softly that Joe had relied upon my judgement. This boat had been my choice. Should his and Maggie's mutual reliance in consequence be threatened or, unthinkably, severed absolutely, then would I not in part bear blame for the devastation such a separation implied?

Unconscious of the icy shackles of anxiety chafing at the edges of my mind, Joe suddenly brought me up short with the pressure of his foot against my shin.

'Cub,' he whispered and, pressing more insistently, he jabbed his toe sharply into my leg so that I was forced to open my eyes again and look at him.

He was grinning. Tossing the compass lightly from one hand to the other, he caught it up in one enormous fist, which enfolded it completely. He held this clenched hand up for me to see and waved it slightly as if proving his resolve. 'I'll do it when I get home,' he said. 'I'll do it when I get home.'

CHAPTER 6

SMALL CANARIES

'Jesus Christ! I can't bloody last till midday on that!' Billy cried incredulously, swilling the meagre contents of his tin around and then looking back up at Clarie as if the latter's expectation simply beggared all belief. It was Billy's turn. He had reached the head of a dishevelled and unruly line of impatient, increasingly irritated, dehydrated men, which had formed at the middle of the boat and which, trailing down along one side, extended on around the stern. Skin, creased with dirt and grime, itched. Clothing, hardened with salt and already oversized, chafed at every turn and matted hair on heads and faces seemed to crawl. Dawn again and we queued for water.

The captain and Clarie had come to the conclusion that two tablespoonfuls of water at every meal would see us safely to the Canaries if we could make it in five days or less. And so they stood up by the barrel three times a day and dispensed it carefully. For a couple of days this rationing had seemed reasonable: we were thirsty, hot and dry, but it must be borne. Then, with the blurring of the days, our skin and muscles began to shrivel, shrieking out against the tyranny of rationed water, and the good sense of the decision palled. All rational thought fell victim to our bodies' craving. Water. Two tablespoons were not enough. They couldn't be. Thirst: appalling, unremitting thirst. It clung to us, it clawed at us, it started to consume us. Almost from the first dread moment of the sun's appearance every day, the blasting heat commenced its torture, stealing moisture from the air, our mouths, our skin. Sucking our very beings dry, in the purity of its conviction that each could finally be reclaimed as dust.

'You'll have to give me more! You bloody gave 'im more than that,' Billy jabbed a finger at the retreating figure of Bob Cunningham, his mate who'd gone before him. Cunningham held his tin above his mouth, his head thrown back and his lips gaping wide as they sought to catch the last tiny droplet of water still clinging to its rim. He was close enough for me, near the back end of the line, to see the final, hesitant drip suspended, enshrined in silver by the early morning sun. I licked the peeling slivers on my lips with the dry, rough slab that had once felt like my tongue. My impatience mounted.

'Ah, for crying out loud, Billy. Come on!' Murack called out, two or three places behind him. 'It's the same for all of us.'

'Get a fuckin' move on, Rawlins.' Mac, little known for tolerance, could bear the wait no longer.

'No, it ain't.' Billy snarled. 'He gave 'im more than what he's given me.'

'Jesus, Billy. You've got the same as everyone else,' Clarie snapped in irritation. Usually so calm and diplomatic, Clarie was not easily riled, but Billy's insistence on Cunningham's preferential treatment, coupled with the thought of yet another day stuck in stifling temperatures, was enough to try even Clarie's patience. 'You're not getting any more.'

'Well, it bloody ain't enough,' Billy leaned in towards him, his face screwed up with scorn. He jabbed his tin forwards, up at Clarie's face.

'We damn well know it isn't, Billy... but it's all we've bloody got!' The skipper's voice rose in sudden anger, silencing the rest of us who'd begun to heckle at the hold up. He leant across and, surprising possibly himself and certainly Billy, pushed him lightly at the chest, forcing him back away from Clarie. 'Now, move it on!'

Billy took just one step back, his body stiffening at the touch. There was a split second's pause as the implication of the action struck him. 'You ain't got no fucking right to touch me!' he seethed through gritted teeth, his voice quivering at the scent of insult.

'Jesus Christ!' Big Sam, immediately behind him, suddenly exploded. He grabbed Billy by the scruff of his shirt with a swift, decisive hand and more or less flung him to one side. 'We're all of us fucking waiting, Rawlins. He's your bloody captain. You fucking well move on when he fucking tells you!'

Billy rounded and they faced each other. The smaller, leaner man crouched slightly, set to spring while the massive, burly frame of Big Sam towered above him, fists out front, rigid with impatient rage. I had never before even considered that Big Sam should have a temper, but now, denied water, hungry and inflamed, it seemed he'd reached the limits of his physical equilibrium. For the first time, his size implied violence and he menaced.

Billy Rawlins was not stupid and suddenly he straightened up. Bodily, there was no contest; Big Sam would finish him with a single blow and Billy must have thought the better of it. He laughed instead, low and laced with insolence. 'The captain? Some captain,' he sneered, glancing from Big Sam towards the skipper and back again. He swigged the paltry contents of his cup, swallowed and then made to spit but again reconsidered. He wiped his mouth across his shirtsleeve and began to slink away. As he turned his back on Sam, he threw out across his shoulder, 'Tell me, what exactly is he the fucking captain of?'

Big Sam, heavy fists still high, looked immediately towards the skipper, expecting the swift and merciless response required, and if not, then at least a tacitly conveyed permission. But none came and no one spoke.

The captain winced momentarily, stinging at the verbal slap and then swung round to look at Clarie, questioning, hoping vainly that he had perhaps misheard. But Clarie, further incensed by the disrespect, gazed back at him with angry confidence, certain that Billy would at last be dealt with for the insidious, now glaring, disregard of rank that had become increasingly more evident in his behaviour since we had left the ship. At the confirmation in Clarie's countenance, the captain's features hardened briefly as if he had determined in that moment to take Billy on, but as we waited, he suddenly seemed to lose conviction. His face drained of all assurance and his eyes came to rest, transfixed on Billy's words, somewhere in the middle distance in front of Big Sam's huge fists. He looked appalled, winded almost, and for the first time since I'd sailed with him, I saw him for what he really was: a small, old man, who, for all his toughness and experience, had already had his day. Until that point, my youth had ascribed his captaincy with kudos, with due respect, but now, I saw him frail and worried. Before my eyes, he assumed the emotional credibility of a man. From him, my eyes travelled slowly down the line of men, to Mick, to Fraser, Fred and Tomas. To Joe. They might be older but I could not rely on their maturity to exempt them from the same concerns as mine, the same all-eclipsing, demoralising thirst, the same attendant hunger. The same fear.

And Billy Rawlins, for all the expedience of his words, had a point. Much as I disliked and instinctively distrusted him, I could see that he was right. Our boat was old and shabby, her peeling paint and crumbling wood providing little confidence that she would be any match for a crueller sea. With her broken mast and half-hearted sail, she was not much more than forsaken driftwood. And the captain's crew, no longer a band of strong, fit sailors, had been reduced in just a few long days of shock and hardship to a bedraggled and disheartened group of vulnerable men. The skipper clearly could not save us, and with that knowledge the hierarchy of command looked tenuous and slowly began to fall apart. The captain, Clarie, even Fraser: they no longer seemed to want to wield dominion. They had become simply men among us, tried and sorely tested. At a loss.

Summarily robbed of the chance to vent his anger, Big Sam stooped to snatch up his tin from where he'd dropped it, glaring still at Billy's back. Hunching his shoulders and keeping his head down low, he lumbered back then towards the barrel, unable to look either Captain Edwards or Clarie in the eye. It may have been that he felt ashamed at his sudden and unwonted burst of temper but somehow he didn't look ashamed. He looked confused, or worse, let down.

The rest of us were silent. Vaguely embarrassed that the authority of the captain had been so publicly flouted and certainly disordered by the lack of his reaction, the queue shuffled slowly forward. Either not wishing or not knowing how to show support, each man accepted the couple of splashes to his tin without a word and quickly moved away.

Billy had just regained his seat between Butler and Cunningham as Tomas and I, almost at the rear end of the queue, drew level with them. Eyes slit and glinting with frustrated spite, Billy shucked back his shoulders in an effort to reassert control, to reassure himself, if not his sycophantic mates, of his authority. Out of the corner of his mouth, he snarled in a low undertone at Cunningham, 'Did you seen that? Big, black bastard fucking threw me! He needs a lesson that one. A good dousin' one night mebbe?' He elbowed Cunningham who smirked complicitly back and Billy, evidently satisfied, glanced up again in Big Sam's direction, 'He's gonna get what's comin' to 'im, in't he, though. Fucking nigger!'

Evidently secure in the knowledge that Big Sam, back up in the prow, was too far away to hear him, Billy had felt confident enough to spit his venom but he had not bargained on the proximity of Wallace, behind us, who heard every vicious word. Wallace, no longer capable nor inclined to endure the outrage of such basic provocation, moved stealthily, and Billy remained completely unaware of his presence until he felt the sharp edge of Wallace's knife pressing carefully just below his Adam's apple, hard enough to cause the sagging skin above to pucker and to prevent him swallowing. Wallace slithered a restraining arm over Billy's chest and, pushing his mouth up close to his captive's ear, rasped in it hoarsely, 'You call one of us nigger one more time and I swear I'll have you for it, Rawlins.' He paused for a moment and then leaning his knee in at the base of Billy's spine, jerked him backwards suddenly, yanking

Billy's rigid body tightly up against his own chest. Billy yelped. 'You understand me? I'm watchin' you,' Wallace breathed. Billy could barely move his head to nod before his body flopped forward, sagging with relief at sudden release.

By the time I looked back up to see how much longer it would be before I got to the water, Joe had already reached the barrel. Only he, refusing to be swayed by the likes of Billy Rawlins, was able to approach Clarie and the captain as openly as ever. He grinned as widely as he could manage, first at Clarie. 'Don't you be going too wild now, Claribelle. Just a dash'll do it!' he said, crashing his tin up under the tap.

Coming upright then and sobering, he tilted his head almost imperceptibly and nodded at the captain. 'Captain,' he said affably. Captain Edwards looked slightly startled but seeing that it was Joe, he smiled, relieved. 'Joe,' he nodded back to return the greeting.

'Shall we see to breakfast then now, Captain?' Joe asked. Despite my own discomfort, I smiled involuntarily. It took me back to the Marconi offices not so very long ago. Joe could not help but wade in for the underdog. The captain was as well aware as Joe was, that there was no real need for the rationing of food now but grateful for the courtesy, he clapped Clarie gently on the back and left him at the barrel. He went slowly down with Joe to get out the canisters.

We'd been struggling with food increasingly for days and by this time, after nearly five days at sea, it was not necessary to supervise its sharing. No one could really swallow it. The desiccated nature of what we had, even with water to swill it down, made it scarcely edible. Now, for spitless mouths, parched and panting in the hot, reductive air, food became barely possible. We had to drag the ship's biscuits in the sea to moisten them enough to break them open. Picked free of weevils, they were sharply salty. They made me retch. With no water spare to help dissolve them, the Horlicks tablets were an equal trial, thick and clarty, and a greasy, cloying tablespoonful of warm condensed milk held scant attraction in the blazing heat. It was at least a fluid though, and therefore manageable, but the twelve cans we'd discovered in the boat's supplies had only stretched a little short of the first three days. Even chocolate had lost its appeal for, though by far the most pleasant tasting, it sapped away saliva and left us dry. Besides, a piece each after every attempt at food meant that the skipper's cache had soon depleted and by sundown on the fourth evening, we had run out. We tried to eat. We knew we had to keep up strength but water, breaks for water, punctuating the seamless hours, became the focus of our existence.

So sudden an inability to take in regular and proper food, the paucity of water and its quality, stale with age, and our enforced exposure to the throbbing sun, brought on in some, at first, violent bouts of diarrhoea. If there was time, the afflicted got up quickly, battling with their trousers to get them off, and leapt into the water to relieve their griping bowels. But more than once, particularly as we began to weaken, they couldn't make it. Stumbling to the boat's rim, unable to control it, and increasingly unaffected by the audience, they stuck their backsides overboard and spurted painfully until they bled. I developed the opposite problem. The dryness of the food I forced myself to swallow bound me up, packing my insides and causing me at first discomfort and then a kind of heavy, nagging nausea that did not let up. It made eating all the harder but still, I could not go.

In desperation, some men began to drink water from the sea. One morning towards the latter end of that first distorted week, Moley Wells, tin in hand, got up and began to make his way down the boat, incurring disgruntled insults from the left and right. When he got to us, he flopped down against the stern and scooped to fill the tin. He placed it on the gunnel and sat there watching it.

'What the bloody hell are you doing now?' Mac asked, staring at him, incredulous, before rounding on Joe irritably, 'Will you cut that out, for Christsakes, Joe?' Joe stopped whistling through his teeth and Mac, satisfied, turned back to Moley. 'Well?'

'Getting a drink. All this flamin' water…'

'You're not gonna drink that, are you? It'll make you sick if you drink that,' Mac warned.

'Nah. The sun'll burn the bad bits out of it. Sterilise it, like. If I leave it there an hour or two, it'll be fine to drink. Ain't that right, Sam?' Moley turned and hollered up the boat.

'What's that?' Big Sam propped himself up on an elbow.

'That ain't right,' Mac shook his head. 'You drink that, you'll get sick. You'd be better off drinking your own piss.' He looked up the boat to where Big Sam was half sitting now. 'He reckons if he leaves 'is tin out full of sea water, the sun'll clean it and make it fit to drink.'

Sam looked dubious. 'Might be all right. Feels bloody hot enough. Worth a try, ain't it?'

'I wouldn't.' Captain Edwards said. 'Never heard that before.'

But Big Sam had rooted out his tin and passed it down the boat to Moley. A few others did the same, Murack and Fred among them, eager at almost any cost to rid themselves of the increasingly intolerable need to quench their thirst.

The ones that drank it did get sick. Some, like Murack, drank, at first, less than the others, but growing confident in the lack of ill effect and feeling themselves perhaps immune, continued taking it, so that days went by before the disintegration of their faculties became apparent. Big Sam too, seemed early on to have escaped its side effects and tried to persuade Joe and me to drink it, assuring us sincerely of its benefit. 'It's not that easy swallowing,' he told us carefully, 'but it keeps your mind off thirst a while.'

But Joe, smiling, shook his head and spread his hands apart, 'But it's salty, Sam. That can't be right.'

'I'm tellin' you, it's fine,' Big Sam shrugged apathetically. 'It's your loss.' Dull-witted now in the heavy heat, he couldn't be bothered to argue. His eyes, blank and lustreless, blinked slow, uncharacteristic disinterest.

Others among them, who had slugged great mouthfuls quickly, either to get by the taste or in their impatience to rid themselves of longing, fell ill within the day. Their eyes glazed over as feverishness caught hold, and shaking uncontrollably, their bodies collapsed, relinquishing all control of mind, limbs and bowels. Unresponsive and disorientated, they lay where they fell, quivering against each pulsing tremor, rambling and then shrieking out, blindly thrashing in the face of new imagined fears.

Fred had glugged the salty water greedily, all too eager to give Moley's theory credence. Late that afternoon, in the early stages of his sickness and therefore still able to control his thoughts at least, he tried to make the boat side to release the urgent pressure in his bowels. He fell on Billy and, unable to contain himself for longer, unleashed a fetid torrent of watery excrement, possibly the last his body could afford, which spewed out and downwards, clamping his trousers to his legs. He groaned.

'Jesus Christ,' howled Billy, shoving him off so roughly that he rolled into the bottom of the boat, becoming wetter still in the inch or so of dirty water which ran along it. The sour stench of diarrhoea reached us, three yards down, on the wind. Tomas retched.

'You fucking bastard. You shat on me!' Billy, shaking with fury, was suddenly crouching over the keening Fred, his knife against his face. 'You fucking shat on me!' Mick and Fraser, who sat up that end of the boat, quite near to Billy, were on top of him in seconds and wrenched him up and off, but not before he had managed to deliver a vicious kick to Fred's hunched up body, causing him to cry out again, this time in startled agony.

Joe, already on his feet, pulled me by the shoulder. I followed him. We picked our way swiftly up the boat towards them. 'Gerroff me. I said geroff!' Billy yelled furiously into Fraser's face, thrashing against his grasp. Fraser's steeliness impressed me, for tall and ordinarily thin, he appeared no match for Billy's whippet strength, but he held on, scarcely ruffled, and effectively restrained him. Finally, clearly disgusted, he shoved him to the side and down. Mick threw Billy back his knife and turned away.

Joe reached Fred and, leaning down between the seats, helped him to sit up. Murmuring to him gently, he pulled him to his feet. I took his other arm, trying hard to dissuade my rising gorge, concentrating on showing no disgust. I could not help but try to close my mouth and nostrils so as not to take in air.

We made faltering progress back towards the stern. The others turned away their faces but did their best to move aside to let us through. Fred was weeping quietly but, compliant, he was not heavy. The difficulty lay in the three of us, stumbling across the others, getting a path wide enough to enable Joe and me to keep Fred upright. He finally fell, face forward, across the half a seat that we had made our own, but Joe pulled him up again and turned him round so that he looked out towards the ocean. Joe walked him then, his hands upon his shoulders, to the ledge of seating at the rim of the boat and helped him to sit down, his legs from the knee below dangling over the outside of the boat. Fred sat there pitifully, shivering in the blistering heat.

'Get him under the armpit, right?' Joe told me. 'A good grip. Ready?' Taking his other arm, we started to lift and lower him over. As soon as I began to take Fred's weight, I felt unbalanced. Dizzied by sudden blotting colours behind my eyes and light-headed in bending forward, I cried out, 'I can't hold him!' Joe yanked him back on to the ledge and Fred, sweating and mumbling, sagged between us. I sat down next to him, his stench forgotten in the psychedelic blindness I could not hold down and the strange swaying hollowness in my head. I sat a minute, head in hands, as Joe cast about. The broken bit of towrope lying in the stern sheets caught his eye. 'We could tie that round him, and hold him over. D'you think you can help me hold him?'

We tied it round his torso and up under his armpits and then pushed him in, despite his plaintive cries. We dragged him a little way, straining, through gritted teeth, to hold him at that angle from above. Tomas got up to help us hold the rope. 'Okay, enough!' Joe grimaced, just as I thought I could not stand it any longer, and we heaved him back up and in. We were exhausted. Dehydrated and weak from lack of food, we dropped down, panting with the effort. He was wet but he was cleaner. We left him in his clothes, which we knew would dry out quickly, and let him lie there, covering him with Joe's old pullover, talking across him quietly until he fell fretfully to sleep.

The days passed more silently now within the boat. The lethargy brought on by lack of water and therefore food was multiplied a hundredfold beneath the sun's perpetually unblinking gaze. From dawn to dusk, she held us in her vicious thrall, pushing us beyond endurance, petrifying our withering bodies in her blank and scathing fire. Various odd items of clothing swathed about our heads and the meagre shadow cast by our stunted sail gave no relief. The little shade the sail afforded moved by the hour around the boat, and tempers flared when some men tried to shuffle round a little more, for just that fraction longer underneath it. The boundaries we had almost unconsciously drawn up around tiny individual territories had become completely unnegotiable; there was no changing them. Every man protected and defended his with narrow eyes and mouths slit with savagery, with threatened fists and, if necessary, with a knife. Through the night, though, forced into forbearance, people had to shift to let the rowers work. This was done with slightly better grace for as the sun went down, relinquished from the grip of the tormenting heat, petty irritations abated and rationality gained ground.

It was short-lived. Bad-tempered irascibility, brought on by lack of sustenance and raw fatigue, exacerbated by unbearable temperatures in the close constraint imposed by the limitations of each space, simmered dangerously, constantly, just below the surface, erupting, quick and vicious, over the least suggestion of a slight or the most innocuous provocation. And so we lay about, holding on in desperation, wrung dry, as the callous pounding of the sun leeched the very last from us in sweat and breath and animation.

The glassy-eyed, featureless face of the ocean conceded nothing. I spent hours with my head upon my arms along the boat rim, burning, limp and listless, watching for the slightest change in her expression, trying to glean some small significance that might imply the time and nature of our redemption. I saw the slate grey turbulence of her waking, her broiling blues in acknowledgement of the midday sun and I watched the silver sleekness of her evening robes slither rippling into the heart of night. In my mind, I spoke to her, bargained with and beseeched her that she might give us up, show mercy and deliver us before too long to the safe haven of the shore. She gazed back at me, reflective but incurious.

From the outset of our misadventure, we had taken to the water from time to time, swimming close, keeping company with the boat, simply to relieve the heat, the petty irritation, the perpetual, grinding boredom. The sea had then offered cold, refreshing comfort and some small relief snatched from our close confinement. But the last time – and I would not try again – I had lost my nerve. Though venturing not much further than I ever had, the boat suddenly seemed an awesome distance at ten yards. The waves loomed up, larger than I remembered, pushing me back, insisting on carrying my body off, away from the tenuous thread of my existence. My heart lurched in sudden panic as I felt my body falter in a weakness I had only just begun to recognise, while the torpid languor of my mind and limbs struggled, working in slow motion as I flailed to make up ground. Once, I tried to cry out for help but the rush of water to my mouth prevented any sounding. Effectively, it gagged me. I made it back, shaking and unnerved, and I did not mention it. But the oblique sense I'd always had of my affinity with the ocean had been damaged and, no longer feeling able either to read or understand her, I shrank from trusting her.

The incident stripped me further of a confidence I'd scarcely been aware of, the presumptive faith I'd always taken in the reliability of my mind and of my body. As the strength of each exhausted, their symbiotic marriage failed and I lost control of both. Physically incapable of doing any more during the day than lying prone, suffering, stupefied by the sun, my mind began to shift and slide around the blurry edges of reality. Hallucinations began to harass me. The boat would spin, the faces of my companions distort and blur in garish colour while their voices varied in extremes of volume, startling and discordant. I saw land just off the boat side, long grasses flattening and bobbing at the wind's command. I heard and smelt the rain. But most disturbingly of all, and I could not shake it off, I sometimes saw the disembodied head of Colin McGrath. He leered at me, smirking, shining beads of sweat dripping down his forehead. Quivering with soundless laughter, he would whisper words I could not at first make out. Gradually, very gradually, as his appearances became more frequent, his voice became more strident and I heard the self-congratulation in his tone: 'Won't last five minutes at sea,' he said.

Too many days went by. Seven or eight. Seven by Joe's notches. Seven tortured days of battling with the blatantly uncompromising sun and seven dispiriting nights, taking turns to row through the blank, negating darkness to find, at dawn, the same. The same unyielding skyline, the same endless chasm of rolling water.

'We missed them! We've bloody missed them.' Mick finally said it. He turned away, grim-faced, from the brittle glimmer of the cold morning sun that crept up slowly, setting the eastern rim alight. He was brave enough to verbalise the fears we'd all been nursing for a day or more. The rowers stopped one by one and turned to look at him. No one spoke. In the half-light, the sun's pale rays caught each face, anxiously peering eastwards, and painted them a lifeless white. Except for Mick's. He stood with the rising sun behind him, his face still bathed in shadow. Others stood too then, cold and cramped, but startled up by Mick's bald statement of a suspected truth that none of us had been willing to concede. By our earlier reckoning, we should have landed on the Canary Islands two days ago. 'It's been too long. We've missed them,' he repeated, looking from one face to the next as if he hoped one of us might contradict him. A cold clutch of familiar fear stole shadowlike across me, lightening my insides and tightening hard within my throat. I had been determined not to think it, to ignore its possibility, and now Mick had let it out.

'How the fuck can we have missed 'em? We can't have bloody missed 'em.' Billy threw down his oar in exasperation and got up. 'We've kept our course. We've used the stars. Fucking hell, we've used the bloody compass.'

'I don't know how we've bloody well done it, but we have,' snapped Mick. 'We'll just have to turn around and go back to find 'em.'

'It's that bastard in the U-boat. He told us wrong,' Murack, gruff and bleary-eyed in the stern, still had not forgiven our enigmatic benefactor for the unforthcoming cigarettes.

'He did not. Of course he didn't. What the fuck would be the point of that? We've just gone past them. If we turn round now, it won't take us long to find 'em.' Mick tried again, this time looking to the captain for his support. 'We must be fairly close.'

Billy, casting round to place the blame, then turned angrily and, jerking his head towards the skipper and Clarie in the prow, shouted down the boat at Joe, 'Give them the bloody compass, will you? At least they'll know how to bloody use it.'

Joe had been standing quietly by his oar listening to the struggle between panic and persuasion rising in Mick's voice. At Billy's challenge, his face, stark in the white light of dawn, registered anger for one second, though he recovered quickly; he replaced it with a raised eyebrow and, putting his hands into his pockets, he smiled wryly and shook his head. 'Not sure it'll be that much use to 'em at this point, Bill. Seems we don't actually know where the bloody hell we are.'

'We're close, I'm telling you, I know we are. We must be. We can't be bloody that far off,' Mick insisted. 'Captain? We should stay round here to find 'em?'

'All we know, Mick, is that we're fucking well not where we should be,' Billy yelled, frustration at Mick's unwarranted conviction compounding his fury. 'In fact, we could be bloody anywhere! Fuck knows how far we've bloody drifted. There's been no wind. We make fuck all progress in the night. The bloody currents've probably taken us miles off where we bloody should be. Jesus! We probably haven't even reached the bastards yet.' Suddenly struck by the implications of his own analysis, Billy flung himself heavily back down onto his seat and, cradling his forehead in his hands, he rubbed his eyes with the heels of his palms. 'All we actually know, you stupid bastard, is that we're fucked!'

The captain sighed and shook his head slowly, 'I'm sorry, Mick, but Billy's got a point. We've no idea how close we are, if at all. Could well have drifted while we've not been rowing and who knows how far we could be from them now. There's no way of telling. But whether we've actually gone right past them or not, we've no other choice but to push on now for Africa.'

'What?' Mick exploded. 'You're joking, aren't you? You can't mean it! You said yourself we've no idea how close we are! Africa? It could be fucking miles! You must be out of your friggin' mind!'

Captain Edwards eyed him apprehensively. 'Mick, we might row around in the middle of this little bit of ocean for days, weeks, and never find the Canaries now. For a start, the bloody boat's so low in the water, we could pass within ten miles of one of them and still not bloody see it. But if we head east for Africa, we're sure to hit the coast at some point. We can't miss that.'

'We'll never make it!' Mick shrieked. 'We haven't got the water. We haven't got the strength. It could take us days. You've no idea how long. You're fucking mad. We haven't got a hope in hell. Look at us!' He waved a frantic arm towards the ghostly faces staring at him through the fading remnants of the night. 'We'll all be dead before we get there.'

'With all due respect, sir, he's right.' It was unlike Clarie to speak out against the skipper but he looked aghast, as much by Mick's assessment as by the captain's new proposal. 'We haven't got enough water. We can last two, maybe three more days on what we've got. If we stick around by here, we might strike lucky and happen upon one of the islands before we run out. But Africa?' He shook his head and glanced up across at Mick. 'Even if Mick's right and we've gone past the islands, then the water we've got left might just last us till we get there. If we're lucky. But if we haven't even reached 'em yet, if we've been drifting, and we turn east,' he clicked his tongue and looking down, folded his arms. 'It's gonna be one helluva lot longer than a couple of days. We'll never make it.'

'Then we'll have to cut the ration and pray that Mick is right,' the captain shrugged impatiently. Frowning, he began to work the knuckle of his wrist across his brow. 'One tablespoon of water at every meal. It will keep us all alive. Just. The inner Canaries are less than a hundred miles from the coast, and if we're in the right vicinity we'll have enough. But if we stay here we could go round and round in circles and never find the land we're after. There's an awful lot of ocean and they're very small Canaries. We just can't risk, with what we've got left, missing them again. Hell, we can't even assume that we've actually got anywhere near them!' He shook his head and throwing up his hands, appealed from one face to the next, 'No. We have to head east now towards the coast. It's the only chance we've got. Fraser, what do you say?'

Fraser's vote would swing it, we all knew. And he would carry Mick. But he was slow to answer. He was prudent and he was shrewd: he could not be rushed. He knew, probably as well as we did, that he was about to decide our fate one way or the other. As he deliberated, I looked around the faces that were watching him expectantly.

The sun's light was good enough now to show up every hideous detail. A week's worth of wasting had taken its toll. Layer upon layer of sunburn had darkened every feature, and scorched by overexposure, noses, brows and ears had blistered into crusted, yellowing sores. Leathery skin racked taut and painful over protruding bones before collapsing, flaccid, into sunken eye sockets and hollowed-out crêpe-paper cheeks. Lips, no longer lips, but merely fraying, puckered slits around gaping holes, had cracked and split and cracked again, ensuring any movement of the mouth was a stinging torment. Scratchy hair cropped up in scrappy patches and skinny necks showed every sinew. And their eyes. Their eyes looked wider, hounded. Ringed in red, they strained. They strained with hope and hatred, with horror and also with despair.

If Fraser chooses Africa, I thought, not all of these will make it home with Joe and me. Some are old, some are weaker. We would not all survive it. Some won't live much longer on such little water. And it looked more than likely now that our water would run out before we reached the land, a land that, given that we no longer had any real idea of our position, could turn out to be hundreds of miles away. Which of them, I wondered, would not be with us? Obtusely taking refuge in the complacency of youth, my mind refused to countenance the possibility that it would be Joe or me, or both of us, who did not make it. That I had influenced his decision to stay upon this lifeboat was undeniable: the other had most probably made land by now. And I knew the secret solace that alone sustained his spirit, the imperative that demanded his survival: Maggie's heart depended on it. The recurrence of these burdening thoughts, if we were to face an even greater journey, unsettled me entirely. It bound him to me further, and the idea that he was more at risk because of me made the loss of him unendurable. We would suffer with the rest of them, but somehow we had to be exempt from the most obvious conclusion to our increasingly perilous situation.

'Skipper's right,' Fraser said eventually. 'Might never find 'em if we stay round here. Can't miss the coast of Africa. We should go east.' Mick started swearing, Clarie too. Others waded in, voices shrill with fear and panic at the prospect of a journey which might take us to the very edge of life, to death. Yet risking the alternative seemed almost certain to do just that, and Fraser had decided. 'We should go east,' he said again, more firmly.

Later, under the tortuous misery of the midday sun, Moley threw down his tin of water in demented anguish. He shouted. For days he had been drinking from the sea and feverish now, his mind, seeping at the edges, misgave under the pressure of our change in circumstance.

He stood up, alarmed, and raved at Fraser and then the captain, 'We ain't never gonna make it. Of course we ain't. We ain't never. Canaries are round here somewhere, they can't be fucking that far off. Africa! You're fucking mad. We ain't never gonna make it.' Before any of us could stop him, he started lurching, making towards the back end of the boat. In the stern, he got unsteadily up on the ledge. Without warning or a backward glance, he threw himself into the water. He began to swim away.

Slow in the heavy heat, half-awake and uncertain for some seconds that what we had just witnessed had actually taken place, we all sat staring at the empty space where Moley had been standing.

Mac, the nearest to his point of exit and the quickest to react, stood up and, swaying to the rhythm of the boat, started shouting after him, 'You stupid bastard. You stupid fucking bastard! Get back here.' Moley took no notice and kept on flailing forwards, taken on the waves in bursts and falls away from us. Tomas, Joe and I staggered to our feet, squinting blindly after him into the glaring sun. From prone to standing in such hammering heat, it took some effort and some moments after to feel steady.

'Moley, what's the use? Come back! Moley! You'll die. You'll never make it!' Joe yelled after him.

'Ah, let him die,' Mac said, suddenly impatient, sitting down again. 'Let him go if he wants to. Stupid fucker.'

'We can't just leave him. Turn the boat around,' I shouted, not daring to take my eyes away from Moley's slowly receding head and shoulders, which as he crested each wave would disappear from view until the next one brought him up, into our sights again. I stood, hesitating, appealing to those behind me, those nearer to the oars, without actually looking at them. Eventually though, their lack of action forced my attention away from Moley and back into the boat.

Some, still seated, were watching Moley's progress with detached disinterest while others had lain down again and closed their eyes. Unmoved.

'We've gotta help him. Look at him! He'll drown,' I yelled. 'Turn the boat around!' I began to move frantically up towards the centre of the boat, stepping on and over others, trying to seek out Captain Edwards' eye. He at least, standing next to Clarie in the prow, was watching Moley's struggle with the sea. He saw me come stumbling towards him and held my gaze just long enough for me to register his resignation of the responsibility for Moley's fate. And then he dropped his eyes and also sat back down. No one had the energy, the inclination even, to exercise concern or care.

'Mick! Mick?' I swung around, beseeching, to the right, to where Mick usually could be found. I felt desperate. I could feel the pricking behind my eyes that as a child had come to me with panic or with anger, even fear. As if the abandonment of Moley somehow meant the abandonment of our humanity; the people we had been, stripped bare and to the bone, surrendering to those we'd now become, self-preserving, cold-eyed and pitiless. I was not ready to let it go.

'Mick!' I cried again. But Mick was sitting bolt upright, looking out determinedly across the ocean, away from me, away from Moley. He would not hear me.

I turned back, winded by their indifference, by the heartless lethargy that had settled over them, transforming them into lesser men.

By this time, Moley was twenty, maybe thirty yards away. He disappeared between the drop and sway of the waves for longer and we could not now hear his intermittent cries. I scrambled back towards the stern, ready to try alone, but Joe, reading the intention in my eyes, stepped across in front of me. He did not try to stop me but he looked into my face. Impossible to ignore, his was fraught with all the agony of thwarted courage. His eyes, grief-stricken by unaccustomed impotence, decried the striking weakness in his body that prevented him from doing that which he felt, with all his spirit, compelled to do.

'You are not strong enough!' he cried. 'Look at you.' But instead I looked at him. He was not yet quite thin but he was shrunken, bowed and stiff. His mighty body sagged. Muscles, sucked dry, flapped loosely from their wiry sinews, concave against the starkly prominent lines of smooth, flat bone. Parched veins stuck up from under crisped and scaly skin, at his temples, on his forearms, down his legs, throbbing their thirst. His mad, wild hair had overtaken half his face but it could not hide the exhausted, staring tension of eyes forced open in almost constant wakefulness. It could not hide the strain of keeping hope and heart alive when both were dwindling down to glowing embers. He stood before me, a much older, careworn version of himself.

'And neither am I,' he groaned. 'We neither of us could get to him and bring him back. He'd fight us all the way.' His half-bent hand hovered around his eyes as he shook his head with reluctant disbelief. 'And if you go in, I don't think I could get to you,' he added more vehemently. We gazed at one another, at the shocking truth. I couldn't speak.

I looked from him back up and out across the unrelenting waves which rocked us with merciless monotony. We no longer even noticed the peaceless sway. I scanned, eyes darting over and all around the area I thought that I'd seen him last, waiting to decide, half hoping still. But Moley was no longer to be found.

I don't know why it was. Perhaps burnt and shrivelled lips, a spitless mouth and tightened skin made it unfeasible but looking back, from that time on, I don't remember that Joe whistled any more.

CHAPTER 7

THE WATER MEN

On the evening of the ninth day, I could not sleep. I knew it was the ninth night because I reached up to the rowlock beside me and felt my way down on to the wood below it, finding the notches that Joe had started. My fingers found the first and worked their way slowly down the row. Nine. The soothing cool of nightfall had closed in around us and as ever brought relief. The agitated drowsiness enforced upon us in the hideous heat of day gave way at dusk to the chance for real rest. Until the early hours, when cold came in to wake us.

The sounds of other men struggling to sleep around me, the deep drawing and letting of breath, restless shuffling and the occasional mumbling had, at other times, been comforting, but that night it was irritating. The rhythmic stroking of the rowers, Big Sam and Mick, the others and their murmured conversation distracted me. I needed quiet to think. For once, it was not anxiety for my situation, cold discomfort or the nagging want for water that kept me wide awake. It was the clear and constant call of an idea that would not be silenced. It had been pulsing intermittently but with increasing clarity from the corners of my mind all day, but when I tried to hide in sleep, it had begun to sound with such insistence that I knew that I would have to speak, despite the bitter arguments that would undoubtedly ensue.

'Hey!' I poked Joe in the lower back. He was trying to lie still, head on the seat, hunched body in the bowels of the boat. 'Hey, Joe... Joe!' I pushed his shoulder.

'Gerroff. Asleep,' he mumbled, shucking me off. I waited.

'Joe.' I shoved him again.

'Bloody hell, Cub. What?' he said, raising his head and turning, not to look at me but up towards the stars above us. I could see just a dim profile of his face working on being awake. His wiry thatch of hair stuck out at every angle.

'I've got an idea,' I whispered.

'What about our rowing shift? Can't it wait till then?' he grouched, exasperated that having almost reached the hard-won refuge of numbing sleep, he had been woken up again to our collective nightmare.

'No.' I insisted.

'Well, it better be a bloody good one. I was this close to being asleep for once,' he muttered and he grumbled, all the while manoeuvring his great body, mashed in between the benches and hampered by other men's limbs, round so that he could face me. His legs were particularly problematic as he had to bring up his knees from under the bench in front of us and squash them painfully past it to release them again beneath on my side. He swore crossly.

'Well?' he huffed, finally.

'It's water. I think maybe we could make some.'

He was rubbing his big hand back and forth across his eyes but he stopped abruptly when he registered what I had said. 'Make some? How?'

'If we could boil up sea water, we could drink it. It would be clean.' I could see it plainly and was eager.

'Brilliant, Cub, quite brilliant. And how the bloody hell are we gonna do that? Boil it? And anyway, the water would burn off. You'd be left with salt.'

'Like a kettle,' I said. 'You know. The steam condenses back to water when it hits something cold. If we could boil some sea water and cool the steam that comes off it, the water would be okay.' There was silence. 'Well, wouldn't it?' I pushed.

'Very good, Cub. But there's one slight drawback to your otherwise quite excellent plan. We don't have a bleeding kettle,' he pointed out, good temper, as always with Joe, resurfacing.

'No, but we have the fuel tanks in the engine. We could use one. We could use the fuel pipe as the spout. If we could boil sea water in the tank and douse the pipe all along with cold water while it was boiling. Well, surely fresh water would drip out of the end?'

He regarded me quietly for a few moments.

'Would mean dismantling the engine. Getting rid of it.' This wasn't a question but I nodded.

'Might need the engine again. When we get to land, we're gonna need the engine to get us in to shore.'

I nodded again. His objection was one I had battled with all day, racking my brains for some alternative but I was sure now that there wasn't one. I had my answer ready.

'We've hardly any fuel. And anyway, if we don't get some water soon, we'll never even get to see if we're ever gonna need the engine again.'

'Skipper reckoned on making land tomorrow. Or the day after. Be taking apart the engine just when we might want it most. Mayn't be any need.'

'And if we don't? What if we never even got as far as the Canaries? You heard Clarie – could be one helluva lot longer than a couple of days.' I swallowed and for a moment, both of us shrank away from the spectre of protracted suffering that loomed huge and dark before us. 'We're almost out of water, Joe.'

He scratched behind his ear and, screwing up his eyes, considered for a moment.

'What the hell could we burn, though, to make a fire?' he asked slowly, his voice thick with thought and I knew then, with a sharp surge of unexpected relief, that he had seen it. My arms, which had unconsciously encircled and gripped my knees up tight, suddenly relaxed and each hand, clasping either forearm, let go, sliding down my shins to rest loose about my ankles. I realised how much I had been pinning on his opinion. That he had stopped throwing up the rational objections I had fought alone all day, and had already begun to see the plan as viable, soothed the anxious isolation I'd felt at its conception. It was not, after all, the madcap idea I'd begun to fear it might be, with glaring flaws that, in absurd naivety, I had been all too eager to overlook. As it was, Joe, with typically open-minded and pragmatic optimism, had given it credit, had grabbed it with both hands and was busy now, wrestling with the questions of how the two of us might actually achieve it.

'That's the only thing I can't work out,' I admitted ruefully. Frowning, I let my forehead fall heavily forward onto my knees and, knuckling the sockets of my eyes hard into their bend, I rocked my head rhythmically across them, frustrated. 'I think it's the only real problem. That's why I woke you up. See what you reckoned to it.'

For a minute or two, he didn't say anything and, raising my head, I had to wait for the blotching yellows behind my eyelids to fade before I could find the outline of his face again in the shadows not two feet from me. He was wide awake now, alert and thinking, casting around up the boat, weighing up and rejecting possibilities. 'Sail maybe? Nah, burn too quick. The mast?'

I shook my head. 'Be madness, wouldn't it? To take apart the engine and then burn the mast as well. Would leave us with nothing but the oars to get us anywhere.'

'That's just about all that's getting us anywhere anyway, isn't it? The engine's not much better than dead weight. Propeller's just dragging back there in the water. Making it harder if anything. And what use has the bloody mast been so far? Even if there was a bit more wind to get us going, the sail's never gonna catch much like it is.'

In the moonlight, I followed the direction of his eyes, which rested thoughtfully on the broken shaft in front of us. Reduced in the darkness to little more than a spindly sliver and a little less than three-quarters of its original length, it seemed unlikely that it would afford us much in the way of firewood.

'Wouldn't last us long enough,' I concluded doubtfully. 'Even if we could chop it up. A knife isn't gonna do it.'

'We've Mick's axe, haven't we, in the kit box?' he countered, his confidence growing by the minute as enthusiasm took hold. 'Anyway, you saw the way it fell apart in Fraser's hands. So rotted it'd break up pretty easy. Not sure many of the others'd have it though, even if we can persuade them to dump the engine.' He paused, contemplating for the first time the prospect of their reaction, before adding grimly, 'Gonna have enough of a job convincing some of 'em to do just that much.'

'I know,' I breathed apprehensively, 'but I'm about as sure as I can be that it's worth a shot.'

He turned his head to look at me then and, seeing in my face what the dim light must have only half concealed, he suddenly reached out to place an amiable paw upon my shoulder and he shook me gently. 'Some of 'em are gonna make a helluva fuss,' he said quietly. And then he smiled: a great wide grin. I knew he was smiling because I could see the flash of whiteness of his teeth and I could hear it in his voice when he said, 'But bloody hell, Cub, I think you might have cracked it!'

Joe was the first up in the morning and just as grey light began to steal across the shivering bodies and scanty belongings of the crumpled men, he began to rouse them. He was excited and therefore, much to their annoyance, he was loud.

'Get up. You've gotta listen to this. Come on, wake up. Cub's got an idea.' He wandered around the boat, rocking it at the edges, stepping over people and leaning down to shake them awake.

'Sir. You've gotta listen to this. Cub's got an idea about how we can make some water.' If he had been my father, I don't think he could have been more proud, though I was slightly disconcerted as the rowers stopped and the rest of the crew were suddenly wide awake, sitting up at the mention of water, rubbing their faces and looking down the boat, expectantly, at me.

'It's just an idea,' I said, hesitating. 'It might not work.'

'Course it's gonna work,' enthused Joe, beaming around the boat and nodding encouragingly. 'Of course it is.'

'Come on, lad. Out with it then,' the skipper, wispy-haired and weary, sighed. Clearly, I wasn't inspiring him with very much confidence.

'We could make a kind of kettle,' I said, all too aware of doubting eyes around me ready to dismiss before I had begun. Any kind of tipping of the balance, to some, was worse than lying back and waiting here to die. Some, I knew, had staked their all on the certainty that today, tomorrow, there would be land. That the skipper and Mick between them had been right, that the Canaries were behind us and that by bearing east from where we'd been, the African coast could not be far away. Failing that, we were sure to be picked up, our signal had been sent and somewhere, just beyond the ever-moving circumference of thin-lined blue, someone was surely looking for us. And if not, well then, at least we knew our fate. Change, to them, no matter how desperate our present situation, could only bring us worse. But then I thought, what could possibly be more harrowing than dying like this? Disintegrating beneath a spiteful sun, starving apathetically through an inability to eat, degrading slowly in vicious and corrosive thirst.

'Out of the fuel tank in the engine,' I went on. 'If we could boil up sea water in the fuel tank, if we could make a fire beneath it and boil it up, we could collect clean water that comes off it. The steam.' I finished in a rush as all about me voices rose in protest.

'Christ, the cub's a flaming physicist now,' Mac crowed. 'The bloody fuel tank! He'll have us drinking fucking petrol next!'

'You can't be taking apart the engine now, now can you? How're we to get to land if you take the bloody fuel tank! Jesus!' Mick, incredulous, turned to Clarie for support and Clarie, shrugging, shook his head, as though sorry to have to call into question the stability of my mind.

'You've had too much sun, Cub. Sit down,' he said, before turning dismissively on Joe. 'You're bloody mad, the both of you.'

'How're you planning on catching steam? Got a fucking net?' Mac raised his eyes to Billy, hoping to bring him in on the sarcasm and add his voice to the resounding denunciation but Billy's head was down, thinking. If nothing else, Billy Rawlins was never one to miss an opportunity.

'Wait, wait!' Joe cried. 'You need to hear him out. Listen!'

'We need the fuel pipe. Boil the water in the tank and have the pipe lead off it but keep it cold, really cold. The steam would turn to water in the pipe. If we bent it down, collected it in something, it would be clean enough. We could drink it.' I was sure of it.

'And what are we without the engine? Bloody dead is what we are. We won't ever get to land if we take apart the engine,' Mick would not let up. 'And we must be close. Should be any day now.'

'Ah, for Christsakes, Mick. There ain't no land and we're out of fucking water,' Billy spat out suddenly. 'If we don't get some water some'ow, we're bloody dead anyway. Fuck the engine. We need the water. You've no way of knowin' how long it's gonna be. We don't know where we are, for fuck's sake! It could be bloody days. So if we don't try something, anything, now, we're gonna bloody die.'

'Jesus Christ, fellas, will you let Cub finish?' It was Fraser. He had got up onto his feet slowly and was standing with a hand up to his chin, his other arm folded across his chest.

'How do you propose to make a fire?' he said, looking directly at me.

'I'm not sure,' I started to reply. 'We thought maybe the mast might...'

'The mast! Jesus Christ! First the engine, now the bloody mast!' Mick, throwing up his arms, erupted. There was no mistaking the country of his origin now for his tone, fast, furious, increasingly Irish, left none of us in any doubt as to the strength of his objection. 'I've bloody heard it all now.'

'Mick, wait!' Joe put out a placating hand towards him. 'Just listen, would you? The engine, that propeller, they've been holding us back anyway. And what use has the mast been to us so far? There's hardly any wind, for cryin' out loud. We make far more progress rowing.'

'Jesus, Joe! For fuck's sake. Would you just listen to yourself?' interrupted Mac. 'You've fucking lost it. You think we'll ever make it out of here alive without an engine? Without an engine or a sail? Hellfire. Of all the fucking hairbrained schemes…' He looked round for backing and found it most immediately in Clarie who stood behind him, hands on hips, and eyes and mouth working in soundless disbelief that there were some among us who could even begin to entertain this lunacy. That we might consider chucking out more or less all that was left to us in terms of serviceable equipment was, to him, utterly incomprehensible, and he could do little more than nod with speechless vehemence his wholehearted agreement with Mac's dissent.

Joe put his head on one side and, looking Mac directly in the eye, replied as calmly as he could manage, 'Mac, all I know is that we're not going to make it out of here alive without any water.'

Clarie suddenly found his voice, 'And if it doesn't bloody work, we still won't have any water, Joe, but we won't have a bloody engine either. Or a mast. It's bloody madness!'

'For pity's sake, will you give the boy a chance?' And again Fraser turned to me. 'Cub?'

'If we could shift the engine and leave the metal plate, on the bottom there, we could burn something on it. Put the tank a bit above it. I don't know… need to burn up something.'

'If you're gonna smash up the engine and burn the bleedin' mast, how about the bloody oars as well?' yelled Mick, sarcastically. 'Or why not the bleedin' life jackets. If you're gonna get rid of the bloody engine and the mast, you may as well burn the bloody life jackets too! Let's get rid of all our assets!'

There was a moment's silence and Joe looked across at me and then at Fraser, eyes alight and dancing at the answer having been so unexpectedly given. The captain, Fraser, even Billy, stared at Mick, arrested by the obvious, if inadvertent, brilliance of his suggestion.

'Arh, now, no, I didn't mean it!' he cried, understanding suddenly our appraising attitude and staring wildly round from one thought-struck face to the next.

'It's a good idea, Mick! I'd rather have a sail if we've no engine to fall back on. Kapok'd do much better,' Fraser congratulated him, nodding slowly as if having come to his decision.

'What's he on about?' I hissed at Joe.

'Kapok. It's what's inside the life jackets,' he answered, hushing me with a flapping hand, as he leaned forward, straining to hear what Fraser was saying to the skipper.

'Cub is right. We've got a chance. It could work. In theory, it should work,' we heard him say.

'Kapok'd burn even better if we soaked it in the rest of the fuel. Though we've not much left of that either. Or in Calzer oil,' the skipper replied, his tired, puckered face lighting up as the idea caught hold and spread. There was a plentiful stock of Calzer oil still in the lifeboat's stores. It was supplied by the Merchant Navy for use in the event of shipwreck in the extremes of cold in the far North Atlantic. Rubbed on to exposed skin, it prevented frostbite, so we had disregarded it in the first instance as not much use to us. Until our feet and lower limbs began to shrivel up and blacken, mouldering in the water which, no matter how we bailed, seeped in continually and swilled about along the bottom of the boat. Mick told Joe and me then to use the Calzer oil on our feet, to massage it in, to try to fend off further, perhaps irreparable, deterioration. He recommended at the same time, without a hint of irony, that we should keep our legs up as much as possible, out of the persistent swash. This struck me, given the paucity of space, as a resoundingly unhelpful, if not entirely fatuous, piece of advice. But the Calzer oil had helped a little, providing a layer of waterproof grease on our extremities, though it could not arrest the decomposition of spongy, putrid skin that had already set in.

'That engine's massive,' Captain Edwards went on. 'Be a job to shift it. It'll need unbolting from the underneath. Think we can do it?'

Fraser shrugged. 'Worth a try. What've we got by way of tools? In the kit box?' he raised his voice towards us.

Tomas leant down behind me and opened up one of the lockers in the stern sheets. He found the tool box and yanked it out. He rummaged around a bit, raking over odds and ends of rusty equipment and finally pulled out a large, adjustable spanner. 'There's this!' he said, brandishing it triumphantly in one hand. 'Would this do it?'

'May do,' said Fraser. 'Someone'll have to go and take a recce.'

'Jesus Christ! I don't believe this!' Mick, fuelled with fear, was furious. He could hardly get his words out and he stood, wide-eyed, hands held out in front of him, beseeching the rest of us to see his sense. 'We can't throw out the engine. It's all we've got! What happens when we really need it? How'll we ever get through breakers to get to shore without the fuckin' engine? You're tossing away the only thing we've got to get us out of trouble.'

'Wouldn't you call running out of water trouble?' Joe asked him. 'And anyway, we've hardly any fuel left. You heard the skipper. Not enough to be of any use even if we do need the engine now.'

But Mac waded in with Mick. 'It won't bloody work. What the fuck does he know?' he jerked his hand towards me. 'He's just a kid. Ain't never heard of anyone tryin' this before. People've been stuck on lifeboats before us and no one's ever been so fucking stupid as to take apart the engine to try and make a friggin' kettle.'

'You haven't heard of it,' said Joe equably, his ridiculously unruly hair belying the calmness in his voice, 'because maybe none of those poor bastards dared to do it. Maybe none of them had the balls to try it and so they did not make it. Well, Mac,' Joe moved towards him, deliberately seeking out his eyes, 'we've got a chance here to make a difference, to help ourselves. And I, for one, am willing to take it.' He turned back to the rest of us, 'We can die here without water. Give it up. Lie back down and hope for land. Hope to be picked up. And while we lie here quietly hoping, one by one, we're going to die. Or we can bloody well try to save ourselves. We need more water and here,' he waved a vague hand towards the engine, encompassing me within its sweep, 'here's our chance to make it.'

'I'll go,' said Moses. Unaccustomed to his voice, it took me a second or two to recognise the speaker. 'I'm a good swimmer,' he added shyly, awkward at his sudden impulse to be heard.

We took him at his word and sent him over to take a look. He returned, breathless and shivering, from underneath the boat. He reckoned we could unbolt the engine with the spanner but it would be hard. The nuts, six of them in all, were crusted, rigid with rust and large, but the spanner could be made to fit. It could be done. He went down again, this time with the spanner tied – at Clarie's insistence – with a bit of rigging to his wrist. When he finally re-surfaced, panting and so enfeebled physically by his body's lack of sustenance, we had to grab at him and haul him in.

It would be dangerous. Already reduced in size and strength, severely dehydrated and half-starved, we were further debilitated by the resulting, throbbing dizziness that swayed up unexpectedly and closed in, bringing frightening seconds of blotting darkness. We would have to work away at the rust-encrusted fastenings in short, sharp shifts. They needed hacking first to unloose the claws of sea and salt and age. Only then would we be able to work on their unscrewing.

Mick alone remained vociferously opposed to the ditching of the engine but he was disregarded, outnumbered as the rest of us began to concentrate our scant energies on the newfound common aim. Even Mac had quietened and was now offering to swim some shifts, converted maybe by our infectious hope. Either that, or in extremity, he was not quite strong enough to foreswear the crowd.

Work began. The tablespoon of water for our breakfast marked, as usual, the beginning of the day. Some of us tried still to eat a little but mouths without saliva can make only token progress and our fare had steadily become more difficult to swallow. Appetite fell away. The water, that one bewitching tablespoon of water, drawn out between three tortuous intervals, was all that stoked us into bothering to endure the endless blur of hours.

I offered to go in first. The responsibility of it being my idea overrode, before the others, the sickening dread I felt at having to get into the water once again. But the sun was up and blazing and so initially, there was some small relief to slink beneath the cool, encapsulating waves and be separate momentarily from the existence of the boat, those men, this purgatory. I kept one hand on the underside of the boat for reassurance and kicked my way beneath the stern, salt slapping my eyes and stinging my skin, which all over me had been sliced apart into a million tiny cuts by the shards of a slivering sun. I found a bolt but, flagging already, could barely manage two blows with the spanner's side against its uncompromising edges before black dizziness shuttered down before my eyes and blind with sudden, gripping terror, I had to kick out and up again to find release and air. The upward thrust was long, too long, and I surfaced, gasping, flailing my arms in panicky exhaustion until Joe reached down to heave me out. It was cold. None of us would be able to last long down there.

We took it in turns. The better swimmers among us – Moses, Tomas and Fraser, Jack and I, even Billy – went down more often and tried to force ourselves to stay under longer. But we were weak and wasted, and it was gruelling work. We hacked away, fighting against the obstructive water, over and over, clanging and striking at the rigid nuts until our lungs, bursting with the effort, would force us to abandon, just before that one last strike that surely would have been the one to unloose its clasp. Joe went down, and Big Sam, to try their strength but neither one had now the stamina and both returned, shaky and unsteadied by the claustrophobic limitations of their weakened bodies. Only the skipper and Fred Watson did not swim. The captain was more than ready to take his turn but he had fifteen years on even the oldest ones among us. His shrivelling frame was folding in upon itself, hunching in his shoulders and bowing down his back. He looked small and wizened. Old. So Mick, who could hardly bear to sit by and watch our desperate labours without the benefit of his wisdom and advice, against his better judgement, offered to swim for him. As for Fred, he had not recovered from his bout of sickness as some others had. He had withered into the bottom of the boat, unresponsive and incapable. We forced him to take his ration of water with the rest of us but as he lay there, by the seat where Joe and I had left him, he let it trickle from between his slackened lips.

The unbolting of the engine gave us purpose and despite its difficulty and our fatigue, we could not give it up. The task had occupied our minds and given us a smaller, more manageable objective. If we looked at that, at solely that, we did not have to confront more menacing questions which, while so engrossed, we did not have to try to answer. It galvanised us. For a short time again, we were a crew, not separate individuals, self-preserving at all costs and jealously guarding against each other's primacy.

And slowly but surely, we were rewarded. By the morning after, we had got rid of two of the bolts and loosened up the remaining four. It took the rest of the day, one by one, for us to screw each one laboriously round and off. And that evening, we lugged the massive engine up and off its plate, dismantling what we could to get at the fuel tanks and the copper pipe and salvaging other useful-looking bits and pieces under Fraser's frugal eye. Then we heaved it overboard. It thunked and disappeared. Not one of us, at that moment, was sorry to see it go. Even Mac clapped me on the back and said, quite cheerfully, 'Now, let's see you get to work.' It was not without effect.

I was appalled. He stumbled off, and eyes fixed upon his scrawny back, I suddenly felt the weight of what I'd done. I stared back down into the water, into the layered depths that had closed behind our engine just minutes before, and felt my confidence ebb away from me, drawn down towards the darkness in the engine's murky wake. What if I was wrong? What if this plan, this ridiculous, rudimentary scheme did not work? I felt as if I had laid down all my cards, and had bet with the lives of all of us, on one rash stake. In recompense for two whole days of intolerable physical labour in more extreme conditions than any of us had ever imagined we might endure, I had promised them water. And all of them were watching me. Waiting for me to perform some kind of impossible magician's trick. I could not do it. It would not work. I might as well go in after Moley.

'Cub, I need your help,' Fraser called. He was squatting down beside the metal plate where the engine had stood, balancing one of the fuel tanks on one corner beneath his hand, trying to find its best position. The copper pipe that I'd earmarked for our spout stuck out rigidly from it at a right angle. Its length, three feet or more, made it difficult for one person to manage alone, and Fraser was trying to turn the whole thing round so that the pipe fed up the boat towards the prow. I helped him turn it, swinging the pipe around and almost whacking Slim, who happened to be lying in its path, across the head. We took it up and over him and brought it down to rest upon the seat next to him.

'If we could prop the tank up, say half a foot both sides, above the metal plate, we can start the fire beneath. What've we got? Anything in the lockers?' Thinking out loud, Fraser was absorbed. His instincts as an engineer had latched on eagerly to the idea of constructing the water purifier, allowing him to lose himself in practicalities. It soothed and reassured me that he, a thoughtful and intelligent man, believed in it.

'There's these,' I said, picking out two or three of the larger bits of scrap from the small heap of metal pieces we'd taken off the engine. A couple, shaped like angle irons, were good enough to make a reasonable cradle for the fire and so we set about position-ing them so as to balance the fuel tank on their upturned ends.

Thus preoccupied, we had not really been aware of the angry voices rising at the centre of the boat until Jack came sprawling back towards us, just missing falling on, and therefore most prob-ably breaking, our precious pipe by inches.

'Jack!' I cried, concerned only in that instant with preserving the equipment that had been so hard-won.

Jack tried to scramble up, but Pat Murack, enraged and threat-ening, knife in hand, thrust him down again and bent down low with one foot either side of Jack's curling body to grab his hair. Taking a fistful, he jerked his head back and held the knife up to his throat. 'Tell them what you're eating, you little bastard,' he shout-ed, his mouth so close to Jack's flinching face, it almost touched it. I could see Jack's eyes, flicking and darting, pleading help from any quarter, as his hands sought to clench the cloth of Pat's shirt, which hung loose about his attacker's chest. Stung somehow into immobility, we all just stood there.

'Fucking chocolate! Snivelling little bastard kept it back. Been eating it on the quiet.' Pat looked up, from one face to the next until he found Joe's. 'Joe? So much for fucking sharing, Joe,' he spat. He turned back to Jack, leaning closer, viciously triumphant. 'It's each man for himself, ain't that so, you little shit?' Jack half nodded, half whimpered his agreement and Pat, satisfied, shoved his head back roughly and let him go.

I rowed much of the night that night. I was fretful and could not rest. Fraser and I had had to stop our efforts at construction at sundown though we sat on for longer, slitting up the life jackets and cutting out the Kapok by the light of the stars. Joe sat with us, humming intermittently as he worked, and talking to anyone who'd listen, while Slim crouched by his side, slicing silently. Their company distracted me from brooding on the gamble we were taking. Somehow, it was a job to be undertaken under the cover of darkness; the destruction of our emergency aids without the help of which, at the turn of fortune, would mean more certain death.

We made a pile of Kapok and flung the material from the jackets to one side, until Fraser suddenly held up a strip and looked at me. 'We could use this! It's useful. Look. If we wrap it round the pipe, along the length of it, we can soak it all the while with cold water. It'll keep the pipe much cooler longer.' He was right. I had thought we could just pour cold water straight on to the copper, but the soaked material would make it more efficient.

Joe smiled across at me, 'You know, Cub, if this works, you will probably have saved us all.'

'And if it doesn't?' my voice wavered. He shrugged and shook his head, as though the actual outcome of the attempt was almost immaterial.

'Then you were brave enough to try,' he said. There was a note of new respect in his voice and, in the warmth and light of his admiration, my misgivings momentarily receded.

We took our shift late on. I rowed with Joe and Tomas, Billy, Cunningham and Butler but when the skipper called for the changeover, I rowed on. Fred had long since been incapable of doing anything and Jack, I knew, had only just succumbed to sleep. The spasmodic heaving of his shoulders had only just subsided and I didn't want to rob him of the relief sleep brought him from his embarrassment at weeping. Besides, responsibility weighed heavily on me and I needed to do something to assuage my nagging doubts.

I need not have worried. At daybreak, Fraser was up and brandishing an empty Horlicks tin in front of me. 'We'll collect it in this,' he said, placing it below the end of the fuel pipe carefully. We filled the tank with sea water and set the fire, dousing the Kapok with the last of our fuel and some Calzer oil and then lighting up. It wasn't long before steam was dancing hazily from the copper spout but, given that the fuel tank still contained a residue of petrol, we let it boil away. We filled it several times and let the steam evaporate until we thought we'd done enough to rid the tank of all the traces of its fuel. We soaked the cloth from the life jackets then in the sea and wound them tightly all along the copper pipe and started again. Fraser and I sat either side and poured cold water continuously along the spout. Most of the others came to watch, sitting and standing, arms folded in an attitude of silent but very palpable prayer.

I concentrated with all my will on pouring, hardly daring to wrench my eyes away from the piece of pipe in front of me to its end, where all our hopes hung in the balance. I knew their eyes were all upon us, waiting, hoping, not quite ready to believe. The skin along my hairline began to prickle and my wrists went weak and light. It was taking just too long and disconcertingly, out of the corner of my eye, I could see that steam was still busily escaping from the end of our spout.

'It's never gonna work. It's been far too long already.' Mick, tutting angry vindication, flung his arms down against his sides impatiently, releasing his chest from the tight anxiety of their embrace. He was standing up almost behind me and the shadow of his doubt cast an unwelcome covering over the back of my neck and shoulders. 'All that fucking work. For nothing! Jesus. We never should've listened to them.'

The words, now actually out, were nothing more than the spoken fears every man present had been struggling to smother. They were thrown out harshly across my head and landed heavily in the centre of the concentrated silence the watchful company had been keeping, opening the floodgates and engendering a murmured and then increasingly more voluble wave of aggressive scepticism.

'Should've thrown them two overboard, never mind the bleedin' engine,' I heard Butler say, turning his head to Billy, who shrugged a scarcely perceptible, thin-lipped agreement.

'Fucking done for, now,' he muttered back.

'They shouldn't be allowed any water from now on in,' Murack said, slapping his hands down decisively on his knees and getting to his feet. He nodded at those around him, enlisting support before wheeling round to face the captain, 'We're so much fucking worse off now. You should never've let them do it. Them who thought of it should fucking well have to go without.'

'That's right,' Mac cried. 'They've lost their fucking right to water rations surely. I say the rest of us poor bastards should get their share!'

There were several audible murmurings of affirmation from various quarters around us and as the cold fear of failure and its consequence crept into my stomach and settled, I glanced up uneasily across at Joe, who, perching on the rim of the boat, had been hanging on to one of the mast-ropes and humming cheerfully as he leant out to refill our tins with cold water before passing them in to Fraser. He stood up slowly and balancing on the ledge, put his hands upon his hips.

'Give it time, give it time. It isn't over yet. Just have a bit of patience.'

'Patience! Jesus, Joe!' yelled Mick. 'Need the patience of bleedin' Job for this. Patience doesn't get you nowhere. We were patient with your clever feller who thought it might be a good idea to throw out the engine. And now look at us. No fucking water. No fucking engine. No bleedin' life jackets. Jesus. And you're asking me for patience?'

'The engine was just weighing us down. You know it was, Mick. There wasn't even fuel enough to get us far. We've not lost anything yet.' But even Joe's defence was beginning to sound a little more like dubious prevarication. 'Just wait. It isn't over yet.'

'Course it bloody is. Look at 'im,' Mac waved a scornful hand in my direction. 'Look at 'is face. He's bloody frightened. Even *he* doesn't think it's gonna work.'

Everyone looked at me and, fully conscious that my expression might easily betray the victory of deepening doubt, I struggled for inscrutability, forcing my eyes to concentrate firmly on the pipe in front of me.

There was a short silence before Mac, sensing weakness, pressed home his point.

'Well? Ask him. You ask him if he thinks his stupid fucking idea was any good. Go on. Bloody ask him!'

I was aware suddenly that even Fraser had stopped pouring on the other side of the pipe and that he too was watching me, waiting for my answer.

'Cub? Well, do you Cub?' It was Big Sam's voice, cracked and low, almost pleading with me to keep his fading hope alive.

'Course he bloody does. So does Fraser. So do I. Just hold your horses.'

'Shut the fuck up, Joe. We were asking him. Well?' Mac yelled.

'I thought it would. I think we need to give it longer... I can't be sure...'

'Jesus Christ!' Mick howled, turning roughly away towards Jack and Cunningham and barging his way furiously between them.

'You can't ask him,' Joe cried at Mick's retreating back. 'He'll always tell you exactly what he bloody well thinks and at this moment, course he thinks he's gonna fail. You're all breathing down his neck, threatening him with God knows what if it doesn't bloody work. But I'm tellin' you, he's as near as dammit worked it out. It isn't over yet. Give it time to come through.'

But, determined by Mick's disgust, most of the others, cursing us and swearing bitterly, began to follow suit, getting up and shambling slowly and resentfully away, shaking their heads as they went and casting cold-eyed backward glances at both the hard work and the worthless hope they'd wasted at our bidding. Some found their places and slumped down, defeated and exhausted, surrendering their disappointment to the soporific lethargy induced by the impenitent sun. But I saw Mac head purposefully across to Murack and Billy who, with Butler and Cunningham, formed a huddle by the mast where they remained, talking in low voices and stealing sidelong looks from time to time, down the boat at Fraser, Joe and me, who remained doggedly working on the fire and dousing down the pipe with water.

Fraser, taking care to make no comment, had picked up his tin and started pouring again while Joe, rolling his eyes, had squatted back down on the ledge and put out his hand ready to receive the next empty tin. He had stopped humming.

Another five, perhaps ten minutes slunk slowly by, until, all of a sudden, Fraser leapt to his feet, making me jump. 'Look, look, it's coming!' he cried, 'it's coming through. Would you look at that! Water! We've done it. Cub! Joe! We've bloody done it!' He hopped from foot to foot, pointing and laughing at the slow but steady dripping water plopping into the Horlicks tin below. I struggled to my feet, almost crying with relief and Joe grabbed me round the shoulders and shook me tightly, 'You bloody did it, Cub! You really bloody did it!' Everyone was suddenly back up in the stern, crowding round us, slapping me on the back and ruffling my hair.

'Calls for an extra ration of water all round, I reckon,' the captain said, shaking me by the hand. 'And you deserve it more than most!'

We stoked up the fire and left it burning with a gleeful Mick in charge of soaking the rag-clad pipe, while Clarie went to dispense the last of the water from our original supply. An extra tablespoonful each had never tasted sweeter. Joe took Fred's down to him presuming that Fred, who had remained motionless and apparently unmoved by the excitement going on around him, was not yet quite aware of the reason for our jubilation. It took me a while to notice that Joe had crumpled down next to him, head in hands.

By the time I got to them, he had covered up Fred's face.

'He's dead.' He swallowed thickly and looked up at me, his horrified face cast in ghastly disbelief, as if he hoped against all hope that I might be able to refute it. I sank down heavily opposite, landing on the seat around the boat's rim and all I could think of was that we had been too late. We had found a way to make fresh water but it was just too late for Fred.

We dropped him overboard. We wrapped him in a piece of canvas ripped away from the redundant piece of sail. We filled the other fuel tank from the engine with sea water and tied him to it. Captain Edwards said a prayer and then we let him fall.

I went back to making water. What else was there that I could do? I spent the day with Fraser and with Joe, pouring cold water along the pipe and emptying the Horlicks tin into our water tanks and barrel. We did not talk about it. We hid behind the immediacy of the work in hand, closing our minds deliberately to the shadows of cold, encroaching darkness that whispered their incessant fears of futility and of death.

By the early afternoon we had used up all the Calzer oil, and the little Kapok we had left did not burn so well without it. The thin but steady trickle of water coming from the end of our spout was just again beginning to slow and falter when Fraser, suddenly breaking the silent isolation in which we'd been absorbed, put down his tin abruptly and sighed, apparently in frustration. Surprised into looking up at him across the pipe, I watched his eyes as they travelled down its length to the fuel tank and came to rest on the now dwindling fire beneath it. Unconsciously, his hand went up to rub the back of his neck and then came round to work his grizzled jaw.

'I just can't see that it's gonna be enough,' he said slowly, more to himself than to me. 'Thing is, if we'd've been that close to the Canaries when we turned east, we'd've surely made the land by now. Easy, I would've thought.' He shook his head as if unable quite to fathom it. 'All I can think is that we must've still been well below them. Or still due west.'

'So?' I said, holding my empty tin up and out behind me for Joe to take, but keeping my eyes still firmly fixed on Fraser. He looked quickly across at me then, conscious perhaps for the first time that he had been thinking out loud and, reading the apprehension in my face, he frowned at his indiscretion. Sighing again, he let his hand fall heavily back onto his lap. 'So it's gonna be a damn sight further to the coast,' he said.

Joe, who had just returned from the boat's rim behind me as Fraser spoke, held out a slopping tin of water over the pipe for him to take. As Fraser took it, Joe straightened up and paused, putting one hand on his hip and taking with the other the empty tin I'd been holding out for him. He waited then, staring quietly down at Fraser as though expecting him to add something more but Fraser, intent on ignoring both of us, began to pour again.

'How long? How long d'you think it's gonna be then, Fraser?' Joe asked him softly.

Refusing to look up, Fraser kept his eyes stubbornly on the pipe in front of him, all his attention apparently focused on the water as it fell, soaking the material and then dripping down beneath to join again the water curling at our knees. We waited, watching for some silent clue to show itself within the grim lines of his face while he struggled to blank his features in a vain attempt to hide what was really on his mind. For several minutes he did not reply but the words he would not say made clear enough his answer.

I shot a helpless look up at Joe and glancing down at me, he raised an eyebrow.

'Fraser?' he tried again. 'How long?'

Fraser brought the tin down on to his lap and studied it for a moment. Then he squinted up to look at Joe.

'Who can tell? Trouble is, can't even tell how fast we're goin'. Or how far.' He put down a hand to steady himself as he unfurled his legs, stiff and sore, and grunting with the effort, he levered himself up onto his feet.

'But we need to make as much as we possibly can while we've got the strength. While we've still got will to do it. We still need more. We're gonna have to find something else to burn.'

Joe stood for a moment, regarding Fraser thoughtfully and then, nodding slowly his understanding, he looked down at me. Banging the empty tin I'd given him up against my shoulder, he put out his other hand to haul me up, saying as I took it,

'Right then Cub, you heard the man. Let's get this fire blazing up again. How about that mast?'

But Frazer shook his head, 'Too difficult. It'd take too long. We need to keep the fire burning. Hard to set again with no fuel to get it going.'

We cast about vaguely for some chance idea, any idea, knowing full well that there was nothing, and before I had given myself the time to properly consider what I was about to say, the words formed in my mouth and they were out. 'Could burn this,' I offered doubtfully, stamping my heel heavily against the boat's side, just above the point where the planks began to curve clear of seeping water. 'The inner skin, I mean.'

The lifeboat had originally been well built. It was solid enough, with the outer shell of the boat protecting an inner lining also made of wood.

Joe looked quizzically across at Fraser and Fraser, looking down at my feet, hesitated and then began to nod. 'We could. Bloody hell, I think we bloody could.'

'Won't it wreck the boat? Make it weak?' I asked, scrabbling suddenly to take the suggestion back. Taken seriously, it looked appalling.

'Not if we take it carefully. From the sides where it's driest and alternately across the bottom. I don't think so,' he weighed it up. 'Preferable to taking down the mast, I reckon. When we've no strength left, sail'll be all we got.'

We asked the skipper and he agreed with Fraser that it should not compromise the safety of the boat too greatly if we did not take too much. Mick, of course, had his own ideas. He exploded. 'You must be out of your fucking heads! What do you think you're doing? Would you look at this! Would you just think on?' Appealing to the others to join him in warranted astonishment, he jigged around behind, as Fraser got down upon his knees in the middle section of the boat and began to smooth his hands across the planks beneath the wash of dirty water.

'We need it, Mick. We need more water. Don't start again now,' warned Fraser. 'We won't take it all.'

'If there's a storm,' Big Sam's low tones, full of foreboding, took us by surprise. He had generally been, up to this point, a voice of optimism. 'Bad weather, the boat won't stand it if you weaken it like this. She'll break to pieces.'

'Well, let's just hope there isn't a bloody storm then, shall we? We need more water,' snapped Fraser. He was losing patience with the constant carping. Fighting it at every turn served only to compound our own doubts and chip away at the confidence we were struggling to maintain. He sat back on his haunches and turned to me, 'Look in the tool box, Cub. Need something we can use as a lever. Chisel or something.'

I turned to pull the box out from its locker and began to rake through its weathered contents. Nearing the bottom, I came across a small, blunt-looking chisel and pulling it up, I held it out to Fraser. 'Any good?'

He took it from me, nodding, and leaning down again, began to work its rusted tip in between the join of two short, central planks running across the bottom of the boat.

'If I start down by here,' he muttered, clenching his teeth with effort, 'these can be drying out while we work round the sides.' But by the time he had caught hold of and wrenched away the first one, Mick, beyond capable of calm, could contain himself no longer. Features fixed in rigid fear, panic quivered in his voice as he whirled round in the frantic hope of securing some sort of veto from the skipper, 'Captain? Jesus, Captain, this can't be right!'

But the captain, having already agreed to our proposal, had moved up the boat to sit down on the seat across the prow and, though weak and trembling, had taken up a Horlicks tin, and was slowly, with shaking hands, beginning to bail. 'He's the engineer. He knows what he's doing, Mick,' he said, sighing wearily.

'What he's doing is chopping up the bloody boat from beneath our feet. There's already far too much water coming in. Hey! Murack. Resendes!' Mick began to cast about wildly, his accent broadening as his desperation to enlist some other voice of similar reason became increasingly more shrill. 'Clarie, for Christsakes! You just gonna sit there, are you, and let them take up half the bloody boat?'

Some of the others, many of them drifting on the outer reaches of rippling semi-consciousness and seeking only to take whatever refuge they could find from the sun's virulence, had gone back to lying low, curled or hunched down in a futile effort to reduce the exposure of their bodies to the murderous heat. Largely unaware of the new dispute erupting in the stern until the heightened tones of Mick's distraction roused them, they were slow to react.

But Mick, impetuous and frightened, was determined not to let Fraser do any more damage to the boat before at least attaining further consensus. He made the mistake of leaning down and catching at Fraser's arm to stop him and though he failed to take hold, the swipe succeeded in jerking Fraser back momentarily, keeling him over slightly and throwing him off balance. In that moment, Fraser's composure deserted him completely and he was up and on him before Mick had even had the chance to move.

Grabbing at Mick's shirt front and twisting it up by his throat with one hand, Fraser forced the chisel up beneath his jaw with the other, and rushed him backwards to the boat's side. Finding Fraser's face so close and seething with sudden rage, Mick, though broad and stoutly built, was electrified by the unexpected ferocity of the attack and cried out in terror as the taller, thinner man shoved him back, bearing down on him with eyes that flashed a dangerous lack of all control. Averting his face, Mick put his hands up to clutch at Fraser's forearms, but his startled reflex could be no match for the whipped-up strength of Fraser's latent fury.

'I'm trying to save your fucking neck,' Fraser hissed at him through gritted teeth, jolting Mick's cowering frame at every separate word. 'Interfere again and I'll have you over,' he jerked his head up and out at the water's sway beyond. 'I promise you that much, Mick.'

In the seconds of silence that followed, Mick somehow screwed up the courage to glance upwards, askance and petrified into Fraser's face, and Fraser saw for the first time the naked terror in his tormentor's eyes and felt the quivering rack of Mick's body in his grasp. Suddenly appalled, he saw what he had done. He let Mick go and stepping back, stood staring at the chisel in his hand, which remained transfixed in the midair at the height of Mick's chest. Mick, still shaking and working to swallow, slowly stood up straight. He waited, watching Fraser warily and apparently unsure of how to move for fear of provoking further unpredicted violence.

Finally, Fraser's hands fell to his sides and his eyes crept up in search of Mick's. Wreathed in shame, his words came soft and low, 'We just need the water, Mick.'

He turned away and without raising his eyes again to any of us as he passed, he went back to kneel down in the pooling water and began to work on levering out the second plank to burn.

For the rest of the day, we kept the fire going and while Tomas and Jack continued to pour water along the pipe, Joe and I helped Fraser take up the inner lining of the boat. It was not as compact as the Kapok and it burned quickly and inefficiently, almost as quickly as we could take it up.

And as we did so, the bilge water seeping in through the outer casing became more visible and, whether we imagined it or not, the boat seemed to creak more loudly, more plaintively. Just as the sun began to roll up the last of its insipid rays, Fraser called to us that we had taken up enough. The skipper and Big Sam were still slowly bailing.

'If we take any more, she won't be seaworthy. Let's hope we've made enough,' grunted Fraser, his exuberance at our success that morning extinguished altogether. He was cheered a little though when we measured our achievement.

'Seven gallons!' Joe split his lips again, grinning at us. 'Seven bloody glorious gallons. It's enough, however long it takes, to get us all the way to Africa. We should have a toast.'

He stood up and lifted up his tin with his evening's ration of fresh water pitifully sloshing around the bottom of it. He cleared his throat and those closest to us near the stern fell silent and looked up at him. He looked ridiculous. His tattered shirt was torn and filthy and his trousers hung loosely at his hips. His neck and shoulders bowed over slightly as though he were slowly being crushed beneath the weight of some invisibly oppressive force. Physically, he was half the man he'd been in Liverpool. His skin was burnt, layer on layer scorched brown to flaking black, and his eyes, though still laughing, were raw and bloodshot. Only his hair had thrived in the heat and light. The shaggy, matted nest stuck out all over, enveloping ears, neck and nearly half his face.

'To Brain Clarke – the brians behind this outfit!' He tipped his tin towards me and then swigged, but I was the only one who tried to laugh.

For darkness, closing in, could obscure the very best of reasoned judgements, and as the boat groaned and whined more volubly in the fading light, dark anxieties swirled, cold and dispiriting, around our feet and lower limbs, dampening any earlier sense of triumph. As the rowers took to oar to work the boat, it became increasingly clear that bailing water was now a constant necessity if we were simply just to stay afloat. Not one among us now, staring down the tunnel of the night, could fail to remain unshaken by the shrill stridence of Mick's objections. Not only did they now look valid, but more alarmingly, absolutely justified. What use water, if the boat could not make the journey? And given that we had not already reached the coast, that journey now looked more than likely to be one of many days. The water we had made, even rationed, would not last indefinitely.

And more insidiously unsettling still was the fact that *in extremis* even the level-headed Fraser could no longer be relied upon to retain his self-control.

Besides, no one else seemed quite able to catch the drift of Joe's joke. After all, I was not even sure that any of the others knew my real name.

CHAPTER 8

PORTENT

Morning after morning, there was the sea, there was the sky and that was all. Unbroken. Except for where they met at the horizon. A thin, blue misty line in a perfect circle whose boundaries bobbed and shifted with us so that we were always at its heart. With all the properties of a mirage, it shimmered in the hazy heat, beckoning, promising, flirting with our straining eyes – yielding nothing.

There was no comfort. The sun, with all the spiteful fury of hell's fires, consumed us, reducing us to little more than bones of men. Pinioned, like insects to a piece of wood, scarcely still alive, we writhed beneath her unforgiving glare. And in stripping us of flesh, she robbed us of the appetite for life. We had food but could no longer eat; our bodies, waterless, baulked at it and then buckled for its want. We had company, but neither energy nor the will to talk and we had the blood still running within our veins but for what purpose, beneath the sun, we no longer cared.

By sundown, we were limp, weak with relief at temporary respite from the rack. And then we had to row. It had been shared. In teams of six, one man per oar, we'd taken turns working through the blackness of the night but whether we made progress, and at what rate, was difficult to discern. As time went on, our wasted muscles wrestled vainly with the labour, skinny buttocks and stringy thighs rubbed and blistered on the uncompromising seats and it was cold. We lacked the strength to build up heat with work and so, exhausted and lean-limbed, we shivered through the small hours, praying for and dreading the first warming rays of dawn.

One night, Big Sam, who rowed up in the prow along from the skipper, suddenly pulled up, staying his oar to watch the faltering rhythm of those in front. He stood up slowly and put his hands upon his hips.

'You boys ain't pullin'. You ain't pullin' your weight!' He looked down upon the skipper, whose crooked form jerked and jumped with effort, and said with irritation, 'And you ain't neither. You white bastards are leaving it all to me and Moses. We're the only ones doing any work!'

'Jesus Christ, would you shut your bleedin' trap? I am pullin' my bloody weight and more,' cried Mick, panting from a middle oar. 'It's you what's been bloody slacking. Jesus! Been pullin' this side on my own half the bleedin' shift! Thought you'd bloody gone to sleep.' Muttering furiously, he kept on rowing as if to try and prove his vigour, but the skipper did ease up and sat back to watch. Jack and Slim, who with Moses made up the rowing six, were clearly galled by Big Sam's slander, and though swearing, tried to compensate, pulling deep. Their scrawny backs warped under the weight of two or three great thrusts but, unable to sustain it, they fell back quickly, despite themselves, to faint, erratic strokes. Silently, one by one, they stopped. Mick and Slim hunched forward while Jack laid his head down against the boat's side.

'We none of us bloody are, for Christsakes!' Mick burst out, 'None of us are bloody up to it. Pull your weight? Jesus! What weight is that? Next to bloody nothing.'

'We have to bloody row. The sail ain't gonna fucking well get us there.' Billy's voice came from low down somewhere in the middle of the boat. Most of the crew, it seemed, were still awake.

'Don't you think I bloody know that,' Mick shouted, 'All I'm saying is we bloody can't. None of us have the bleedin' strength!'

'All right, all right. Keep your shirt on Mick!' Fraser spoke up calmly from behind Big Sam. 'We'll have to row in pairs, that's all. Two men per oar. Sir?'

The captain sighed, 'We won't be able to row as long. Twelve men rowing, then resting all at once. Bound to take us longer.'

'Not at the rate we're going now it won't. We're not getting anywhere like this,' Fraser replied, decision taken.

'Well, I ain't rowing with any bastard who doesn't fucking pull. You got that Mick?' Billy, sitting up, lit the touch paper. He disliked Mick, more so since Mick had yanked his knife off him when he'd taken it to Fred's face, and he directed his words specifically to aggravate. Incandescent with rage, Mick was off his seat in seconds, 'You callin' me a slacking bastard?'

Billy shrugged his shoulders carelessly, implying yes.

'Well, are you?' Mick made a move towards him, fists already up.

'Well, Big Sam said it. We all heard.' Billy, as clever as he was snide, fell back on Big Sam's reproach for cover. He got to his feet and snarled at Mick, 'You ain't been pulling as hard as you fucking might be.' This kind of slur to Mick was tantamount to a stinging slap. His impetuous nature sometimes caused his judgement to be faulty but it made him otherwise wholehearted in every sense. He could not do things by half and took pride in it.

He bellowed as he flung himself at Billy, and those around them, knocked and jostled by their falling bodies, were soon embroiled within the scrapping fray. Cries of anger and of pain filled the darkness, as, swearing and scrabbling, the scrum of men surged over and beneath the seats, from one side to the other, unsteadying the boat with their shifting and uneven weight.

'Stop! Stop. Shut up! Shut up and listen!' Joe, beside me, scrambled to his feet and stood stock-still, arms out straight, palms down. Craning. 'Shut the fuck up!' he roared. 'Shut up and listen!'

The dishevelled knot of men in the middle of the boat abruptly stopped the fighting, mid-swing, and faces turned, slightly startled, towards Joe. 'Listen!' he almost whispered. 'Can you hear it?'

There. There above the silky slapping of the waves and the gentle creaking of the boat, we could just about make out the distant but familiar hum of an aircraft engine. Mick got up, roughly yanking out his limbs from under other men's, and the rest of them, remorseless but suddenly distracted, disentangled. In twos and threes, everyone got on their feet to listen.

'Bloody hell. Quick. Get the sail up!' the captain shouted. 'Mick, the storm lamp!' The fight forgotten in common purpose, there was a sudden frenzied rush to action. We leapt towards the sail and hitched it up as far as it could go. Mick lit the storm lamp and jerked it up to rest by the craggy stump at the top of the mast. Its light beamed down and in against the whiteness of the sail, which, reflecting, gave it further cast.

The droning of the aircraft engine was louder now. We could not see it but its increasing volume told us it was nearing. It must have seen us. We stood, all eyes blaring at the blackness of the sky, searching. The hum grew louder, louder still, and our hearts, as one, beat faster. This could be it. We had been found. Surely, we had been found. The thrumming of the engine was still way off but we stared unblinking at the stars, straining in all directions to catch the instant of swift, dark shadow passing over them. The low rumbling reached a mild peak and then, then it began to die away.

'Ah, fuck!' Mac cried. 'It's going. Bastard's missed us.'

'Shut up!' hissed Joe, 'Listen.' We stood, barely breathing, ears screwed up to the slightest suspicion of a waver in the sound but the aeroplane was moving off and the comfort its throbbing engine had fleetingly provided dwindled with its noise.

'Mayn't have been one of ours,' Big Sam sniffed, wiping his arm across his face.

'Must've seen us. In all this blackness. Couldn't have missed the lamp against the sail, surely?' Jack appealed to Joe.

'They'll have seen us,' Joe looked at him, peeling his eyes unwillingly away from the faded promise in the sky. 'They'll report it. We'll be picked up tomorrow, I betcha.'

'They didn't see us,' Mac shook his head. 'They'd've circled. Jesus, how could they've bloody missed us?'

'For Christsakes, Mac. We don't know that they did! We're the only light in all this godforsaken ocean…' A startled shriek from

Slim cut Joe off mid-sentence. As he'd started speaking, there was a sudden, sharp slap against the middle of the sail and a heavy thud as something fell back from it into the boat. Those nearest to it leapt away.

'What the fuck was that?' Slim cried.

'It hit me. It bleeding hit me. Landed on my legs,' Jack knelt down and after a short scuffle, brought up in both hands to show us, a twisting, squirming fish. It was quite a big one, fourteen inches, maybe more. Still thrashing, it jerked its way out of his grasp and landed, flopping again, in the bottom of the boat.

'Must've been attracted by the light,' Clarie said, watching it in wonder.

'Shame the frigging plane wasn't,' muttered Mac, crouching down to look at it. 'It's a big 'un though.'

'Kill it, Jack. Here!' Billy pushed Jack aside eagerly and leant down, grabbing at it with one hand, pinning it to the floor and then he delivered a swift, decisive blow to the top of its head with the handle of his knife. He held it up, chuckling. ''S a flyin' fish. Supper tonight then, lads.'

We ate it raw. The captain cut it up into as equal shares as he could manage and we fell upon it. 'Don't leave me the fucking tail end,' Bob Cunningham cried as people jostled down over one another to grab their piece. 'Ain't got so much meat on it!' Hands darted in from under the dark edges of our huddled group, grasping at the bits of fish that lay, entrails exposed, within a small, circular pool of light. The captain, Joe and I were just about the last to get to it. There was a morsel each and it was salty but it was succulent. I sucked and sucked at it, draining up its moisture, and then savoured its soft and juicy flesh for as long as I could keep it in my mouth. It was sublime.

We lit the storm lamp for as much time as we dared in the nights that followed, in the hope that we might catch another, but it turned out that our fish had been a singular stroke of bizarre good fortune and luck spurned the chance of being so kind to us again.

The morning after, encouraged by the thought that we'd probably been sighted, Billy helped himself to a couple of splashes more than his allotted quota of clean water from the barrel and Pat Murack saw him. Since we'd made our seven gallons, we had stuck rigidly to our regime of rationing, fearing to make the same mistake we'd made on our first day. We could make no more water as the boat already weaved and twisted in protest at the heavier waves and, not knowing when, if at all, we might make land, we could afford no slackening.

Pat lurched at Billy drunkenly, weaving oddly up towards him before trying and failing twice to grab his shoulder and spin him round. Eventually, he grasped at Billy's arm and jerked him backwards, causing him to tip his tin and splash the ill-gotten water around and over its sides.

'Wha' the fuck…?' Billy, startled, pulled away but Murack stuck his face up close, raging eyes and snarling mouth working with an incoherent fury, 'Water, fucking water. Seen you.' He could barely get his words out through his gritted teeth and he brought two shaking fingers up, jabbing them at Billy's eyes. ''Sh'our water! 'Sh'our water!' he cried, breathing heavily and grunting with the effort to take in air. He rubbed the heel of his palm into one eye confusedly as if to try and regain focus. Then he swayed and, placing his other hand on Billy's chest to steady himself, he leaned his face closer still, almost into Billy's neck. Still too surprised to act, Billy wrenched his face away, disgusted at the other man's hot blast of breath. 'Fucking thief!' Murack shouted rawly, with all the poisonous anger he had left in him. Billy threw him off sharply then, shoving him at both shoulders and Murack, arms up and flailing, fell backwards, landing heavily on the seat behind. He hunched down, one arm across his stomach and his head nodding just above his knees. He toppled then, slowly, on to his side and lay there mumbling, 'Thief. You fucking thief,' over and over to himself.

Billy put his hands up in the air in an attitude of innocent surrender and said defensively to all of us quietly looking on, 'I didn't do a fucking thing. I swear it. You all saw 'im. He fucking well attacked me!'

Clarie, who'd been standing next to Billy, bent down low to peer into Murack's seething face. 'He's sick,' he said, drawing up.

'Look at him. He's really sick.' Murack's body twitched and shuddered along the seat and he muttered on, seemingly oblivious, in a voice that rose and fell according to the virulence of his rambling, the most of which only he could possibly have understood.

'Hey!' A sudden cry from Big Sam cut across the general contemplation of Murack's state and we turned to see the big man teetering on the ledge of seating, leaning out but keeping himself on board with one hand on a mast-line. He was pointing skywards with the other. 'Look! There's birds!' he cried excitedly. He was right. Looking up, I could make out one, no, there were two, small, dark coloured forms, wheeling and swirling in the air, a little more than a hundred yards away from us. 'Must mean there's land about here somewhere!' Big Sam yelled impatiently, not waiting for comprehension to dawn upon his frustratingly slow-witted audience. 'They've gotta live some place, haven't they?'

'Bloody hell. He's bloody right. We must be close!' Mick leapt up behind Sam and leaned a hand upon Sam's shoulder to steady himself. The rest of us moved closer, lining the port side of the boat, screwing up our eyes to watch with envy, the glorious freedom of their flight, swooping and dipping, from the cloudless to the shimmering blue and back again. Our spirits soared in hope at their every rising. Surely these birds nested somewhere, returned to land to rest and breed. It could not be so very far. Excitement spread among us and we began to squint at the horizon expectantly.

The captain did not spare us long though and shattered our barely savoured joy with wizened sagacity. Shielding his eyes with a trembling hand, he began to shake his head. 'No, lads. Those are Mother Carey's chickens. They don't mean a thing.' He turned away in disappointment, letting his hand fall limply to his side.

'What the hell does that mean?' Mac asked sharply, stepping into his path to stop him moving off. The captain looked tiny, what was left of him, a flimsy, bearded whisper of humanity. Mac glared down at him accusingly, frustrated at the inconvenience of his knowledge. 'And what the fuck's a Mother Carey's chicken?'

'They're storm petrels. Old seamen call them Mother Carey's chickens.' The captain looked up wearily into Mac's furrowed face.

'They live on the wing.' He paused a moment, waiting for this information to grant passage past Mac's obstructive body, but Mac continued to glower at him, demanding further explanation. 'They survive by feeding off the water. They live miles and miles out from the shore.' He had to spell it out. 'They don't need the land.'

'Ahh, for fuck's sake,' Mick, suddenly punctured, slumped down to sit upon the ledge.

'Why Mother Carey's chickens then? Who the flaming hell is Mother Carey?' cried Big Sam angrily, irked more particularly at having been robbed of the kudos of discovery. He grasped the rope with both hands now and, leaning inwards, brought his face to rest against it.

The captain hesitated, looking down the line of now attentive faces and then he sighed. 'It's a legend. She's an old crone. She's responsible for bad weather out at sea.' He stopped, unwilling to say more.

'And they're her birds.' Clarie finished for him, casting a glance back up towards the skimming birds behind us. 'They mean bad weather, don't they?'

'No kidding, Sherlock. Storm petrels. Kinda obvious, ain't it?' Mac snarled.

The captain shook his head but Fraser stepped in for him, 'Superstitious nonsense. They don't mean anything.'

But it was too late. A disquieting sense of deep unease had wreathed its way around us, its mists settling about the margins of our fragile minds. Men began to shamble away, eager to throw off the unwelcome omen. Mac moved aside begrudgingly to let the skipper pass and Clarie went back to look at Murack. Big Sam slunk down, muttering to himself, and wandered off. But I could barely move. I stood transfixed, staring at the graceful arcing of the birds. A spasm of panic swept across me, seizing my insides and twisting. It must have registered in my face, for Joe, suddenly conscious of my immobility, looked startled and then rearranged his face to try for calm assurance.

'For Christsakes, Joe, I made them hack the bleeding boat up. If there's a storm...' I babbled until I had to stop to swallow painfully.

'There isn't gonna be a storm. It's rubbish, Cub! You can't believe that old sailor's yarn. Hell, just look at the bloody sky! Not a frigging cloud… Cub!' He tapped me lightly on the furthest cheek, pulling my face around and forcing me to peel my eyes away from the flitting spectres and look up at him. 'You didn't make anyone hack up the frigging boat. We needed water. Half of them'd be dead by now if it weren't for you. And one day, they'll be grateful for it.' His tone lightened suddenly. 'Except for Mac. Oh, and maybe Billy. But then those two are prob'ly Mother Carey's bleeding brothers!' I laughed despite myself, despite the pain it caused my throat and lips, and turned my back upon the birds.

'Think Murack'll make it?' Joe asked Clarie in the evening. As the day had gone on, Murack gradually had quietened down. The constant stream of his invective against Billy had ceased abruptly but his incessant mumbling took longer, fading with the light. His body slowly stilled. He lay where we had left him since that morning, across the middle bench, and despite his stark exposure to the sunlight he had barely moved. We were getting ready to take up the oars for nightly rowing and so we were going to have to shift him, though all of us were reluctant to disturb what looked like more peaceful rest. Clarie shrugged. 'Depends what's up with him.'

'He's been drinking sea water,' I said. It seemed obvious to me.

'So've others. Big Sam's all right. So is Bob. Slim. They got better.' Clarie sighed. 'Mayn't be the sea water. I dunno. Could be anything. Could be the heat. Maybe some of us just aren't as strong as others. Some blokes' bodies don't cope so well without water. Without food. Who knows?' He looked around, from side to side and then beckoned us in conspiratorially. Joe and I leaned towards him and he whispered quietly, 'Between you and me lads, I've been having a go at drinking my own water.' He tried to grin at me, the corners of his mouth slitting with the movement as he fixed me with his rheumy eyes. 'Tastes like bloody piss!' he said, rasping with amusement at his own joke. He wandered off, still choking dryly and shaking his head. Alarmed, I looked across at Joe but found only my own fears for the reliability now of even Clarie's mind reflected in his face.

That night we rowed in pairs. We laid Murack by the stern sheets and though he moaned a little as we lifted him, he hardly roused. I took an oar with Tomas, Joe with Mac, the four of us cramped in along the last, long seat towards the stern. The skipper organised two other groups of four to row along the middle one and up by the prow, and we forced ourselves to work, pulling rhythmically against the heavy darkness. All the time, it seemed to push us backwards, taunting us to labour on, to make it through another never-ending night and greet again the disappointing dawn. Mick and four of the others were not rowing and would take over later and as they were quiet, I assumed that they were sleeping. The rowers did not talk much either. It took all our strength and concentration to keep in time, to keep on heaving against the weighty blackness of the sea. The only sounds, above the drop and swish of water, were the steady thud and chink of oars as they were pushed and pulled against the rowlocks and the low, pained grunts of struggling men.

'Stop! Stop a minute! Stop!' Mick was suddenly up and on his feet, waving his arms about and hollering down the boat at all of us. 'Stop your oars! Can you hear them? I hear breakers. I swear I can hear breakers!' In an instant, we were still, trying to hold back our panting breath and stay the blood which still pounded in our ears after such an effort rowing. Some of us stood up as if the added height might improve our hearing and transfixed, we waited, staring out into the layers of darkness.

'I don't hear 'em,' Big Sam whispered, after several minutes. 'You imagined it.'

'Shhh!' snapped Mick. And again we waited, listening so intently that I began to think I could hear the minutes, on wisps of shadow, passing softly by. 'There. There, you hear it?' breathed Mick.

'Yes! Bloody hell, yes! I thought I did. Just then,' Captain Edwards broke the spell and moved excitedly across to Mick.

'Shh! Wait. Listen... listen.' Fraser murmured and again we stopped, stock-still, concentrating all our thoughts on picking up the long desired sound of waters somersaulting in the shallows and racing up the shore to land.

'I can hear it!' yelped Billy suddenly. 'You? You must've heard it then?' He turned to Clarie beside him and Clarie began to nod thoughtfully, as if wanting to agree but still considering.

'We should stop here,' Billy cried, grasping Captain Edwards' arm and shaking it. 'We can't risk going on, surely! We must have made it!' He turned towards the rest of us, already celebrating. 'We must have fucking made it!'

'Now just hold on. Just wait a second,' Fraser's voice came calmly from the prow. 'I haven't heard anything yet.' He looked towards the skipper. 'Are you sure?'

'I thought I did… before. I can't hear it now,' the captain said, less certain.

'I can,' insisted Mick, 'just above the breeze. It's not just the waves, it's different. I'm sure of it.'

'I think I can,' Clarie said slowly, tilting his head to one side, face screwed up in concentration.

I looked at Joe and eyebrows raised, nodded the question at him. He made a wry face and shrugged uncertainly.

'We should put down the sea anchor. Sit it out here tonight. We can't risk drifting off away from it, if there's land.' There was doubt behind the captain's voice, and this was more of an appeal directed towards Fraser than a decision.

'If there's land. We'll lose time.' Fraser, sighing, looked up towards the noncommittal stars as if they might, by some unlikely act of graciousness, provide the answer. 'We're so low on water,' he said as if to himself as he rubbed a slow hand across the roughness of his jaw.

'We won't need the fucking water if there's land,' pushed Mick, convinced. 'And there was those birds. Maybe they weren't frigging Carey chickens. C'mon!' he looked around from one face to the next, willing all of us to take a chance and believe in it. 'We must stop here!'

The prospect was too tantalising to ignore. We pulled up the oars, threw the sea anchor over and then lay awake. Initially, I was all too relieved to give up rowing and flop down beside my seat to sleep, but night is cruel and darkness is a fiend that feeds on fear.

Could Mick really hear the breakers or had he been beguiled by the cold, sardonic sea? I tried to hear it, the all-elusive sound of curling water, hurrying forward towards the sands before finally flicking over in a frenzied crush of foam. I thought I could, but then I couldn't and then I heard it once again.

Lying there in the swaying blackness, the only constant the silent stars, I could imagine that I might hear so many things: the clattering of breakfast plates muffled by my pillow, Father calling out my name to rouse me, my mother's bright but tuneless hum. Could I really hear the breakers?

I must have dozed, for when I opened my eyes again the light was coming. Joe was not lying across from me as he usually did and so sitting up, shivering and numb, I looked around. He was up in the prow, standing in the shadow of the dawn, next to Mick. They were not talking. They were looking out across the miles of undulating grey before them, no longer scouring, but in an attitude of contemplation. Joe's hand was on Mick's back, high up between his shoulder blades, so that his fingers curled a little at Mick's neck. It conveyed a calm and simple understanding. And so I knew there was no land.

Murack was already dead. Tomas woke and found him, stiff and staring, and so he screamed, long and hard and raw, beyond control. All the wretched anguish of his soul, at that which every one of us was being forced to suffer, struck me in that scream, sounding through the depths beneath my being and thrusting me up close to share his horror. The hairs on the back of my neck and on my forearms stood on end and I sat still, sickened with the fear of it. He screamed until Mac grabbed and shook him angrily, pushing him away from Murack's corpse. Unnerved, none of us knew how to help him and so we busied ourselves with the morning's water and kept away. Tomas sat alone, by the mast, wide-eyed and yet unseeing, until Joe, hands in pockets, ambled over and tried to talk. Getting no response, he leaned against the mast-shaft and in his own discomfort began to hum softly to himself.

There was nothing left on the boat that we could use to weigh Murack's body down and so we dropped it over and watched it float away. With limbs splayed out upon the shifting waters, it rocked aimlessly behind the boat, shifting on the waves one way, then another. As the boat began to move away, his body lurched and rolled at the disturbance of the water in our wake. I turned away. It was too hard and I did not want to see.

Forced to persist in an existence so abhorrent, so beyond all that I could bear to comprehend, I felt my mind begin to fray. I struggled to maintain the sequence of my thoughts that fractured and fragmented, and for short periods in the daylight hours, I lost all sense of time, perspective and even purpose. Unsteadied by such harsh reality, the foundations of my being faltered and I found myself doubting my ability to endure. I feared for it, I feared that I would give up wanting it.

But Joe was there and he insisted on it. Twice, he brought my water ration to me, when I, half-delirious in the heat and soused in sleepy semi-consciousness, failed to notice that it was time. Sometimes, slipping under would have been so very easy but he refused to let me go. He talked to me; he made me listen. He talked of getting home, of who was waiting. He painted pictures with his words of the life we both had yet to live. He talked to me about his marriage and he smiled at Maggie's pleasure in my acquaintance. And when his mouth became too dry to talk, he sat on by me, humming quietly. He insisted that I took an interest, that I believed with him in the beauty of what seemed scarcely possible out here, in this barely floating boat on the timeless and unending ocean. And it was Joe who got me up to watch the porpoises.

'C'mon,' he said, 'get up. You should see them. You wouldn't believe, so close to us, that they could be so energetic, so full of life. They're playing, Cub! Remember that?'

For two long days, they came and danced and dived around us, leaping out between the waves, turning and spinning in the gleaming pearls of lustrous spray, before racing off ahead to double back and best us once again. They seemed to revel in their athletic bodies, glory in the sun and sea, take delight even in our lifeless company.

Big Sam knelt down by the boat's side and leaned out, as far as he could manage, waggling a ship's biscuit to and fro in his hand. He began to tut and click encouragingly.

'Jesus, what the fuck d'you think you're doin'?' Billy, thick with heat, had woken up and, turning to try to find a more comfortable position, had noticed Big Sam's efforts.

'If we could get one near enough, we could kill it. One of us could stab it. Or what about that spanner? Mebbe bash it.' Sam's eyes were wild, fervent with the thought of it. He gurgled manically. 'We could eat it.'

'It's a flaming porpoise, not a fucking dog! They eat fish, you fucking moron!' snarled Billy. He rolled back over and, hunching up, closed his eyes. Big Sam, however, was not to be discouraged but the porpoises just laughed at him, leaping and diving before his hand, rejoicing in their liberty, a yard or so beyond his reach.

'You know, people think that they are mermaids,' Joe said to me, as we cramped up by the boat's edge, our heads cradled sideways along thin and shrivelled arms. 'That old sailors, desperate for a woman's company, saw them in the distance and thought they'd seen a mermaid.' He sounded wistful and I looked at him. He was sitting quietly. Still. I had realised that his capacity for movement, so previously irrepressible, had gradually declined and I had reassured myself with the thought that it was only to be expected. But I had never seen him so absolutely still; in body, so defeated.

I did not reply. I did not tell him that he had reminded me of a story that my mother used to tell me when I was small. About the mermaids who came before a storm. How they swam before a ship about to wreck and how they sang so sweetly of delights beneath the fathomless deep. Their singing bade the ill-fated seamen on, seducing them, consoling them with promises of the pleasures they were now destined to enjoy.

I closed my eyes and waited for the evening and the lifting of the sun's relentless scourge. Then I hoped I might find more comfort in the revival of my more rational self.

That night, while we were rowing, I was distracted from the steady thrust and slacking of the oars, by a slight scuffle from behind. In the darkness, intent only on the rhythm of the rowers, their heaving breath and the mild slapping of the waves protesting at our inoffensive progress, I was deliberately oblivious to all else. It meant I did not have to think.

So I was slow to turn. But as I did, Jack's voice broke out hoarsely, cutting across the boat's hypnotic motion, and rousing me from the numbness of my mental isolation. 'Moses. Hey, Moses! Whatcha doin'? Moses?' His tone began to rise in panic, 'Where the fuck d'you think you're…? Moses! Don't!'

I glanced over my shoulder quickly and in that single instant caught the fleeting impression of Moses' arcing body, black and crescent-shaped, emblazoned momentarily across the shining, perfect circle of the moon. She was full and low and luminous, the shattered shafts of her reflection densely scattered on the water, breaking up the blackness with an ever-shifting constancy of light.

Moses had dived, soundlessly, into the sea. He slipped between the welcoming waves without disturbance to the surface; no noise, no ripple, no change. The waters welcomed and enveloped him, closed above him as if he had returned where he belonged and should never have been away. Jack scrambled up and clamoured after him, scrabbling at the ledge to get up on to it, screaming out his name into the silence and the darkness. 'Moses!' he shrieked, high and raw and hollow. Joe, still seated, turned around and grasped at him, catching on and pulling at his trouser leg, but Mick was quicker, getting him by the shoulders and pulling him back, forcing him to stay down. 'Moses!' Jack, struggling to free himself and desperate, howled again. The name carried far across the watery wastes, echoing into nothing. There was no answer save for the soulless lapping of the night.

When I closed my eyes to sleep in the months and years that followed, sometimes I felt the ceaseless rocking of the boat; smelt again the sickening, salty smell of fear and heard the whisperings of the waters. But always, always, when I closed my eyes, I saw Moses' body, its graceful arc, slashed dark across the beauty of the moon.

Jack suddenly gave it up and fell into Mick who tried to hold him up but could not bear his weight. He dropped him down and Jack crumpled into the bottom of the boat. He began to cry. This time, uninhibited, thick, dry sobs, which caught in his throat and stopped him breathing so that the scarcely intelligible words of his grief came out between each clutch at breath: 'He saw things… said he saw things… the playin' fields at home… his father callin' him… he weren't right, he weren't himself… should've stopped him… should've known he weren't right.' His voice broke up and he folded in upon himself, tucking his arms in across his chest and doubling over, head tilted inwards so that he rocked upon his knees, to and fro, in the cold, filthy water, which continued to seep constantly through the wooden floor.

The rest of us listened in relative silence to the outpouring of Jack's misery. We all knew too well now that the confusion brought on by hallucination was utterly disorientating but as the explanation for Moses' suicide, it made such involuntary lapses of control all the more terrifying. If Moses' mind had been so thoroughly addled that it had persuaded him to jump from the boat in the belief that he was doing something completely unconnected with his physical presence, then who knew what any one of us might do similarly, at the next bout of mental vulnerability.

Mick sat wearily down on the seat at Jack's side and then leaned forward with his elbows resting on his knees and his hands clasped together so that they almost touched Jack's hair each time his head came forward.

'Don't take it so hard now, lad,' he murmured. 'If he didn't know what he was doing, he couldn't've been too frightened, could he?'

Jack either could not hear or would not, for he continued on in his private ululation, rhythmically sobbing out the blackness of his sorrow and in doing so, pulling all of us frighteningly close to the gaping emptiness at its heart.

'Don't take on so, Jack. Think that he was thinking he was home,' pleaded Mick, the soothing softness in his voice struggling to defy his own crushing awareness of the pointlessness of words in the face of such inconsolable anguish. 'He weren't afraid. Perhaps he's better off. Come on, now, Jack, shush now. Shush…'

Mac, who rowed by Joe in the stern, jerked round suddenly, angrily, unable any longer to bear the raking torment of Jack's grief across his taut, thinly flaying nerves.

'Shut up. Just shut the fuck up, the pair of you!' he yelled. 'He was just a fuckin' nigger, for God's sake! He knew what he was doing. 'Course he did! No fuckin' strength of mind them darkies. Couldn't face it, that we mayn't make it. So he jumped. Easy way out. Typical nigger thinking. Now stop your friggin' wailing. I've had about enough.'

There was a sudden, massive roar from the seat by the first oar, which clattered heavily on its rowlock as Big Sam shot up onto his feet. Arms bent and out in front, ready for the fight, he began to move towards the centre of the boat and I saw, in the silver line of light reflected down the length of blade, that he held his knife. Despite his loss in body weight and though now stooping slightly, his size was still formidable and as his enormous frame towered in the darkness, the boat bobbed gently at the jerky impetuosity of his action. His heavy head swung slowly from side to side so that at intervals, from where I sat, I could see the enormous whites of his eyes, caught in the moonlight, rolling in apoplectic fury. 'I'm gonna fucking kill you Mackingtosh! I'm gonna slit your scrawny little throat. I swear I will. I'm gonna fucking kill you, you filthy piece of fucking shit, and then I'm gonna throw your bastard little body overboard.'

Provoked to a pitch beyond conscious control, he began to sway down the centre of the boat, paying no heed to whoever he knocked and stamped on in the process.

Fortunately for Mac, Big Sam had to make his way over two rows of seats and the bodies of most of the crew before he could get at him. It slowed his progress. Time enough for Joe to get to his feet and turn around, putting himself in front of Mac who cowered willingly behind him, crouching, ready to dive into the stern sheets or if necessary, judging by the stricken look of horror on his face, into the sea. I took a deep breath and, swallowing my reluctance but not my fear, got up slowly too and took my place a shoulder's width from Joe, though he was swift to put out an arm to ward me back as Big Sam, storming onwards, was joined by Wallace, who got up to follow in his wake. Sam came to an abrupt, aggressive halt a foot away from Joe.

'Get out the way, Joe.'

'No.'

'I'm fucking warning you. You get out my way.'

'No.'

'You think us fucking worthless niggers too?' The steely-edged warning in Sam's low tone promised predetermined violence. 'Thought better of you, Joe.'

'No.'

'Did you hear what he said? I don't want to kill you too, you bastard. But I will. For what he said. For the last time, you get out my way.'

The two of them, still easily the biggest men on the boat, stood for a minute, eyeball to eyeball, the furious menace in one counterbalanced by the relatively calm regard of the other. Joe, just the shorter of the two and certainly the thinner, looked easily the weaker man, for somehow his debilitation seemed more apparent. The fury evident in Big Sam's stance had drawn him up considerably, for now he held his shoulders back and stood squarely, bearing down on Joe. Joe, in contrast, looked shrivelled, physically spent. His shoulders bent forward and the bowing in his back and legs meant that he was forced to look up into Big Sam's face. He did not, at any point, look down at the knife tip that Big Sam held threateningly, a few inches from his jaw.

'Sam,' Joe said quietly. He held his hands out, wide apart, palms up in simple supplication.

'I won't forget it Joe. If you try an' protect that bastard after what he said about Moses. About us. If you don't move aside, you ain't no fucking friend of mine.'

'I am your friend. It's you I'm bloody trying to protect. If you kill him, Sam, what then?' I noticed for the first time as Joe spoke that his breath came slightly raggedly and he had to pause to catch it before he could continue. He swallowed with difficulty and winced. Then, indicating the rest of the crew, most of whom were, by this time, on their feet in ready accedence for a fight, he said again, 'What then, Sam? One of them'd have you for it. You'll be the black who killed a white because he lost control. As it is, Jim

Mackingtosh is just an ignorant low life who should have learnt by now to keep his stupid, bloody mouth shut.' He paused again to catch at breath, struggling for the words. 'It isn't about your colour, Sam. Or his. It's about respect. Humanity. His has gone, if he ever bloody had any, which I doubt. What about yours?'

In the quietness and the darkness, we waited, scarcely breathing. We waited for Big Sam to weigh it up. Either way. My eyes, transfixed upon his knife, could clearly make out the four massive bones of his knuckles that protruded as he clenched it tight.

'Ain't about colour? It's all right for you to say,' he sneered, leaning his face in, right up close to Joe's so that his knife point caught and pinned the baggy material of Joe's shirt fast against his chest. 'You're one of them.'

He looked up and around then, deliberately taking time to stare down each one of the startled faces which watched him through the darkness. 'You white bastards. You've been holdin' all the fucking cards, haven't you? Leavin' the weight of all the rowing down to us. Rationing the water. Extra if you happen to be white, eh, Clarie?' His low-voiced fury thickened and expanded, rising in volume as he lost possession of his rage. 'No wonder Moses chose to take his chances in the sea. You fuckers'll probably have us overboard anyway in the end to keep yourselves for longer.' He turned his face back to Joe and through clenched teeth, spat finally, 'Can't trust any of you fucking bastards after all.'

Then, leaning in once more and swallowing tightly, his face twisted up with hatred and he hissed, 'Don't you even talk to me again, Joe. Don't you fucking well come near me. You keep out my way. You ain't no fucking friend of mine.' He tapped his knife blade twice, lightly just below Joe's collarbone and then he turned away, throwing out over his shoulder as he did so, 'I'll have you, Mac, you fucking coward, another time.'

I exhaled deeply at Sam's retreating back and then looked at Joe. He was rubbing his face with both hands, passing the tips of his fingers in and out of the sockets of his eyes. Mac suddenly barged into him, knocking his hands from his face roughly as he pushed between us. Joe staggered slightly down and sideways, his knees buckling beneath him, and for a moment I thought that he would fall but somehow he did not. 'Ignorant low life. That about right?' Mac snarled as he moved past. 'You just wanna watch yourself, Joe.'

Staggered by the base ingratitude, I shot out an arm to make a grab at him though Joe's, just quicker, flicked up again to stop me.

'Leave it… don't take him on,' he whispered and he moved away to sit down heavily on the ledge. My face must have registered my frustration and surprise, for looking up at me, he said suddenly, in a voice so low and thin that I had to lean down to hear him, 'Thing is, Cub, we none of us are who we were. None of us can be sure of what we're gonna do. No one's safe. Like Murack said, it's each man for himself. Won't be long before someone gets killed. For water. For arguing. For anything. As dangerous in the boat as out of it.' He folded his arms and, hunching forward, leant his elbows on his knees. 'You need to keep your head down and your mouth shut from now on. Share my knife. We need to watch each other's back. Take it in turns to sleep. Seems there's nothing left.'

I sat down next to him but he continued to stare ahead, fixed on nothing. My eyes moved slowly up the boat, over the dark forms of our companions. Some men were still standing up, whispering to one another. Others had gone back to their oars and were waiting to resume. Big Sam had returned up to the prow and was sitting down, though Wallace stood before him and seemed to be talking at him earnestly. When it came to it, I wasn't sure of any of them. Extremes of thirst and hunger, fear and pain, had brought some of us to abject weakness, to instability. Others had turned aggressive, selfish, uncompassionate. And now, some would go as far as bloody murder.

Slowly, I nodded my understanding but Joe, if he saw, did not acknowledge it. He got up stiffly and looked down at me, 'Come on,' he said flatly. 'We're meant to row.'

'Were you scared – just then?' I asked him, as I got up. Somehow, it was important to me that I had not been the only one to respond to Sam's fury and the prospect of such a fight with the spine-knotting pitch of fear I had felt.

'I was bloody petrified,' Joe replied grimly.

Looking back, I know now that by this time, he had understood instinctively that we were close to the end. Any end. Whichever one it was, he knew it to be near. On the very cusp, it could not now be much longer before we tipped and fell. Dried to death, starved, drowned, stabbed, saved. One of them lingered close at hand.

He was trying to tell me that the threadbare bonds of our humanity, snagging only slightly still, had all but worn through. They would hem us in no longer. He knew that there would be murder. Someone would be stabbed or thrown overboard and there would be retribution. And there was nothing that he or I could do about it. He was preparing me.

If not that, then our bodies and our minds would no longer be supported by the tiny drops of water afforded to them. They would shrivel up and die. They would fail. And if not tomorrow, then it would be the day after.

Or we would, by some final quirk of unreliable fortune, chance to make a landfall in the tiny slit of time we might have left. It would be close. There was little margin now for error. The edges of the narrow gap between an unacceptable life and a horrific death had almost closed. And it had to be tonight. Tomorrow. Because there were not going to be any more tomorrows thereafter. It could not be borne, physically, mentally. At all. We had almost done.

And so when finally the land came into view, it was quite literally not a day too soon.

I did not understand what it meant at first and yet I was the first to see it. The boat was silent at the bidding of the sun's savagery. Our bodies lay disordered, transfixed beneath her steady, unremitting stare. It was better not to move. Once in a while, a limb jerked in reflex, flinching from her searing brand. My head rested on the boat's rim on Joe's old pullover, but I was awake, open-eyed and staring into nothing. Half-dead but taking unconscious comfort from the somnolent rocking of the swell, I lay unblinking and unseeing.

Eventually, my eyelids closed involuntarily, seeking once again to sooth the irritation that raged beneath, but waterless, they worked in vain. When I opened them again, I had found some focus. My eyes, by force of habit, petitioned the horizon. And then, then I saw it. A thin, grey line; short, but thicker than the blue. I gazed at it, uncomprehending. I did not even try to move my head. A thin, grey line: surely thicker than the blue. I watched it waver with the boat, rising and falling in my eye line, and with every gentle undulation my thoughts settled slowly to coaxing out a meaning. Land.

I sat up straight and squinted. There it was. I put my hands up to shield my eyes and winced into the blaring blue. A thin, grey line. I struggled to my feet, my head spinning with the effort. I stared at it, to see if it would shift within the corrugated shimmerings of the heat. It did not move. We must have reached the land.

'Land,' I whispered, 'land.' As if the word would make it definite. I passed my tongue across my lips in a pointless attempt at lubrication. 'There's land.' My disaccustomed voice broke and, quavering, rose, throwing off its arid inhibition and getting louder and more strident with every effort. 'Joe. Mick! Jesus Christ! I see the bloody land!'

Mick was first beside me. I pointed with a trembling arm out across the miles of water, willing him to see what I could see. I watched his eyes, scanning, darting, eager and impatient. They stopped and fixed. The muscles in his face relaxed. He'd seen it. There was land.

'Sweet Jesus,' he whispered. 'Sweet Jesus. Cub. It's land. It's the bleeding land.' He grasped me round my skinny shoulders and shook me, hollering hoarsely and laughing, shouting to the others that there was land, that we were saved, that it was over now. Disorientated, men got up and, squinting, blindly stumbled to the port side. Mick grabbed on to them and shoved them forwards, directing their heads and eyes towards the tiny slit of hope, then danced along the line behind them, unable to contain his joy. Some got up upon the seats and stared and stared, unable to believe that there, at last, lay the thin, grey point of our deliverance. They couldn't tear their eyes away for fear of losing sight of it. Some knelt, some laughed, some, tearless, wept at our relief. I saw

Fraser raise his fists up to the skies, as though declaring us victorious. Clarie took the skipper's hand and pumped it, before yanking the vestige of his body forwards and enfolding it in an exuberant embrace.

I looked around for Joe. Slow, too slow, he was the last to join us. He had made it to his feet and coughing hard to catch his breath, he was shuffling towards me. Head and shoulders bent, he staggered slightly just before he reached me and put a hand out to steady himself. I caught him at the elbow and, taking his forearm in my other hand, I shook him jubilantly, far too eager and excited to take much note of the pain it seemed to cause him. His body tensed but then he caught my eye and smiled. 'We bloody made it, Cub. Always knew we would!'

Later, in the cool of evening, the skipper granted us a double ration of water each to celebrate. It would not now be long and finally reprieved, we felt we could afford extravagance. There was talk and laughter among us now, enmity forgotten for the moment and an eagerness to start the rowing. But what I most remember of that night, bubbling up and frothing over, was the gloriously enlivening, intoxicating sense of imminent release.

I pointed to Joe's notches. 'Nineteen days!' I said to him, barely able to keep my splitting lips from stretching wide. 'There's only eighteen here. One more now and tomorrow, there'll be no need. Nineteen notches. You were right. We'd never have kept count.'

He didn't answer me but, flipping out his knife and still shaking slightly, he knelt to carve it out.

CHAPTER 9

JOE. OF ALL PEOPLE.

The next morning, Joe was quiet. Around him, there was laughter. The first tinted glimmering of the sun had brought relief; separate, secret sighs. We had not dreamt it.

The long, thin slash of grey separating sky and sea had fattened slightly overnight and men, old friends again, with sudden strength, attacked the rowing. The tantalising thought of fresh, clear water trickling between our fingers, over crevassed faces, between crusty lips and on to soothe our tiny, aching splits of throats, spurred us on. Water. It was unimaginable and yet surely, it was within our reach. We would try to row today despite the throbbing heat and we would talk of how we'd drink when we got to shore. But Joe was quiet.

The gradual reduction of his movement had not alarmed me greatly. For days now, though not inactive, he had been slow and more latterly, at rest, I had seen him still. Unconsciously perhaps, I had begun to measure our collective weakness by the lessening of his physical activity. As his body slowly stalled, I had begun to recognise the fading likelihood of our general survival, though somehow not my own. Not his. And, I told myself, it was only natural. Our bodies, now withered husks, had been sapped, sucked dry. Movement was a painful luxury.

His silence though. It stunned me.

'You OK?' I sat down beside him.

There was no warning. 'Cub, if you get back. If I don't. I need you to go see Maggie.'

I started to interrupt him but he stopped me with a heavy hand held up between us. He sat up and leant towards me. He was trembling.

'You need to tell her that I did not love her. Tell her she was one of many. She knows what I was like before. Tell her I was not worth the waiting for.'

'Jesus, Joe!' I stared at him, swallowing hard against the lightning shaft of panic that rose up suddenly, widening and tightening across my chest. 'Why the hell would I do that?' I asked, absolutely incredulous.

'Because I love her. Because I want her to have her life. I want her to be angry, not broken altogether. Anger fades and when it does, she'll teach herself that she should not have cared. I want her to survive it. Better that than be bereft, than have to mourn.'

I felt annoyed with him. It was ridiculous. The land was there before us. We were saved and he chose now to doubt that he could make it. His sudden misgiving rubbed me at the quick, chafed against my reignited hope.

'You're very sure of her,' I said. 'Or of yourself.'

He looked away from me a moment, away across the brightening water to the land and then came back to me.

'I believe her,' he answered quietly.

'Joe, you're mad.' I began to talk too fast. 'What are you talking about? She won't believe me. Why would she believe me?'

'Because she's honest. She thinks other people are like her. So you will do it?'

'No. I won't.' I sought for words. 'I can't. It's wrong. Anyway, it's nonsense. We'll both get back...' I tried to lighten it, to push it from me but he cut me off.

'Promise me you'll do it, Cub.' He was frightening me now. He'd felt a sneaking coldness steal across his soul and it had scared him into speaking. It scared me too. I searched his face, looking for his reassuring grin but it was gone. His skin was taut across protruding bones, cracked all ways like clay baked in the sun. His eyes were on me, pleading but determined. He would not let it go.

I tried to laugh. 'Joe...'

'Swear you'll do it. I need you to swear to me you'll do it.'

'All right, all right, I swear, but it's ridiculous. We've made it, look,' I gabbled, pointing at the widening line, increasingly apparent on the horizon. 'Almost. And when we're home, you can ask her and I can meet her and we won't have to remember this.'

But he had stopped listening to me. The minute that I said that I would do it, he pushed himself back away from me, slumping down against the boat's side, his head lolling at its rim and he had closed his eyes.

By mid-morning, he had begun to mumble. I thought at first that he was humming and, given that he had got up on his feet, I felt relieved. This morning's gravity had been an aberration. A delayed reaction to what we had been suffering, which had surfaced now that we were almost safe. He had been unruffled up till then but such a horror-ridden journey was bound to take its toll on even the strongest ones among us. But humming, he was Joe again.

But then he called her name, loud, as if in fear. It stopped us all and all eyes turned upon him. Body shaking, oblivious, he went back to his heedless muttering. I left my oar despite protests from Tomas and went towards him. He backed away from me, fending me off at first with flailing arms. Then he tripped, stumbling backwards over the side of the fuel tank, and gave way to me, slumping down in the water on the bottom of the boat. I put my hands upon his shoulders and shook him slightly. Called his name. His eyes, raw and rolling, could not focus. I called his name again and put my hand up to his face. He batted me back, flinching, but not before I'd felt the angry heat pulsing, almost an inch away from his flushed cheek and jaw.

My chest constricted. I had seen this all before in Pat Murack. Joe lay inert now, where he had fallen, though as I leant down to try to help him, he convulsed away from me, curling up his body tightly, bringing his knees up towards his chest and bending his arms about his head. He looked as he had never looked to me before: small. He could have been a child. As I stood above him, the fever suddenly grasped at his body, clenching it, forcing it to twitch and twist, each painful spasm that passed across it causing him to breathe in sharply, interrupting momentarily the garbled flow of words.

I tried to make him comfortable. I wet his old pullover in the sea and tried to lay it on his head but he snatched at it impatiently, throwing it aside. I tried to talk to him but he would not hear me, so I sat with him in the pooling water, my arms around my knees and watched him. I watched him, rigid-backed and straining, terrified to take my eyes even for an instant from the pain clawing at his face, lest I should miss some change, should miss some significant moment of lucidity, which might preface his return.

'For fuck's sake! I can't row on all day like this, on me own.' I became aware that Mac was starting to complain. 'It's too fucking hot. Can't we stop and start again this evening. Jesus! It's gonna take us longer than we thought and we're two men down again now!' I felt him glance at me and the other rowers, grateful that someone else had been the first to voice his objection to rowing under the brutal scrutiny of the sun, let up willingly. They sagged over their oars, unspeaking and exhausted, thankful for the chance of any meagre respite.

'I'll bloody row for Joe then!' Mick, up in the prow, shambled slowly to his feet. He and the skipper along with Fraser and Slim had been part of the crew rowing in the early morning and it had been their turn to take some rest. Joe and I had rowed in the small hours until first light, rested, and then been recalled at the changeover. Joe had failed to take his place with Mac but I had just assumed that he was slow in getting himself together.

'No, Mick. Sit down.' The captain sat up too then. 'Mac's right. It's too blasted hard. Give it up. We start again at sundown. Doesn't really matter. By the look of it, we'll still be there by morning.'

No one took issue. Pulling up the oars, each man ambled to his own unsatisfactory refuge and collapsed. All were beyond desperate to push towards the land but energy and even enthusiasm blanched before the physical impossibility. Not one among us had the strength to row against the glowering heat.

As Mac made to step over Joe, he stopped and, peering down at him, shook his head. 'Poor bastard. Goin' the same way as Murack, isn't he?' He didn't even bother to lower his voice and oddly, this discourtesy to Joe offended me more than his prognosis. It scored across my nerves and made me wince. Joe remained oblivious.

'Fuck off, Mac,' I snarled, the words snaking from my mouth. 'Just fuck off out of it.'

His eyes narrowed, half closing, 'Sorry, Cub, but it's obvious...'

'Fuck off!' I screamed, springing to my feet and taking one step towards him. I would not hear it. Mac stared at me, at my disintegration, and then shrugging, left us both alone.

Later, in the afternoon, Fraser came to see how Joe was doing. He bobbed down next to me. For a while, he didn't speak. He just squatted by me, watching the tremors rack Joe's body and listening to the cadence of his ramblings. 'He's in bad shape,' he said eventually.

'But he didn't drink the sea water!' Somehow I felt it necessary to leap to Joe's defence, as if by denying his culpability for the sickness, it would acquit him from a sentence as miserable as Murack's. 'It's just a fever. He'll be OK.' I needed to believe it but my voice belied the assurance of the words. It came out high and plaintive, betraying the appalling, hovering sense of dread that threatened, swift and dark, to overwhelm me.

Fraser shook his head, 'Maybe it wasn't sea water that took Murack. Moses didn't take it either and he can't have been right in the head the other night.' Fraser gazed down at Joe again and started to tease a piece of flaking skin from his top lip with his teeth. It began to bleed. 'Joe is big. Bigger than most. Maybe he needed that bit more. More water maybe. Could he eat?'

I rubbed my hand over my face, pinching my thumb and fingers together at the bridge of my nose. 'No more than me. Maybe less. He tried.' Fraser, still crouching, his elbows on his knees, let his head fall low so that his chin rested on his chest. There was no helping it. We did not know why and it didn't seem that there was anything left to say.

Most of what Joe muttered was unintelligible. I heard Maggie's name a couple of times. My own. He called to Moley that he'd never make it and in more frenzied, frantic moments he wrestled and writhed in the seeping water, struggling breathlessly to take in air and cried out that he was drowning. I tried to soothe him, to keep him still and cool him but he did not seem to know that I was there. Almost imperceptibly, he began to quieten. His mumblings became less audible and for longer intervals, his lips stopped moving altogether. The muscles in his face, around his eyes and mouth, slackened and his body slowly ceased to strain. This peacefulness, stealing softly through his being, I told myself, was heartening. A revocation of the fever; sleep would be restorative. But in the stricken hollow of my heart, I knew that he was dying.

As the sun began to dip and melt, powdering the sky with a gentler palate of softer hues, I went up to get his water. No one asked and none sought to catch my eye. By the barrel, Clarie and the skipper were talking of our prospects when we got to land and of the probable need to hydrate slowly. Sickened, I returned to Joe. Inching my hand underneath the side of his head and tilting it slightly, I put the cup up to his pallid lips and tipped it, watching the water trickle purposelessly past them, splashing over and around my wrist beneath. There was nothing more that I could do for him. I knelt down beside him on the floor and heaved his broken body up on to my knees. I put my arms around him and sat there, waiting for him to die. He did not object or fight against me. He lay, head bowed low against my chest, fighting in and out each shallow breath.

Sometime before the end, he had a moment of lucidity. His body, suddenly stiffening, jerked involuntarily away from me, and I grasped at him to stop him sliding. His hand found my wrist and clasped it and I was startled to find him staring up at me, with eyes apparently that understood. I felt his fingers tightening around my forearm, clenching with all the strength he had left in him, and I smelt the stinking breath of death. I could feel the burning heat from his head against my body and I could see the wavering of his eyes as he sought desperately to hold them steady, to stop them rolling. 'Maggie,' he breathed. His eyes were wide and raw and red. They fixed me: I could feel the effort in the tautness of his neck as he willed them straight. He tried to lick his lips, sandpaper over sand.

'Cub...' he struggled. 'You make sure...' He paused to swallow, grimacing with the effort, 'you make sure of Maggie.' He tried to smile, a depth of gaping darkness. Done.

'Joe...' But the sharp glimmer of perception in his eyes, as they began to roll, receded as I watched, to be replaced again by dim opacity. A calm passivity settled across his features, fixing them as they had become and though he still breathed, there was little left of Joe.

I don't know when he actually died. Or why. I only knew that I had never thanked him. With that regret consuming, I held him until I recognised that night had come and both of us were cold. What had he not done for me? He had stood beside me, made me take my chances, preserved me from my own rash choices and, in keeping his, insisted I keep faith with my humanity. I am not particularly religious. I am not superstitious. But from the moment I had met him, he had watched over me. He had fought for me, guarded me, protected me. He had believed in me. There was no reason why he should. A self-appointed older brother. The briefest snapshot of a person who had flashed across my life when I had most need and influenced me more than any other. If I had believed in guardian angels, I would have believed that Joe was mine.

I was nineteen. I was immortal. But when he died, I thought that my immunity from death had been taken too. He had been it. Vulnerable now, alone at the bottom of the boat with his stiffening corpse, as others got on around me, enthralled within the cages of their own separate purgatories, despair unbound me. Despair and rage and fear and pain. For the first time, I saw that I was going to die. There was no point. He and I were never going home.

This inhospitable sea, this wretched boat, which would not make it through the breakers. The tantalising hope of land. God knows what we would find there even if we made it. There was no point. I cried then. For the first time, I cried. The strange, dry, racking crying of youth with nothing left. No tears, no spit, no life. I all but gave it up.

And yet, even while his breath was failing, Joe had given me a point, a reason to endure. He wanted me to get to Maggie. He wanted me to let her go. There was something, something still, that I could salvage from this waste. I knew that he had done all that he could have done for me. I owed him only the same courtesy.

I carved out his notch myself that night. The twentieth notch. And then I went to row.

CHAPTER 10

JOE'S LAND

The boat broke up around us. It bowed and creaked and twisted, threatening to split apart almost as soon as we hit the drawing waters. At the waves' conception, they began to swirl and tug us forwards, our course inexorably set now for the shore. The end. Breath held back in tight anticipation, we felt the menacing power beneath us, its rising fury, building slowly, pushing us ominously on and upwards. With absurdly optimistic forethought, some among us sought frantically to find some useful purchase, grasping at the boat's side, the oars, the mast. But I grabbed on to Joe. Even as the wood began to cleave around us, I clutched him by the shirt at his shoulder with some idea that I could hold him, that I could keep him with me and not surrender his body over to the avaricious tyranny of the sea.

At last our little boat, skewed sideways, was lifted, teetering on the crest of the first enormous wave, to be flung far forwards, wreaked apart before it even fell in shattering pieces on the furious foam. The heavy, lifeless weight I held was wrenched away as soon as I hit the water and my cry of anguish at its loss was drowned out as I was dragged beneath and backwards, only to be cast up again and whipped forward by the next. Time and time again, the great Atlantic's mighty rollers, merciless, hurled me over, thrashing me out in front, to suck me then back under, before I'd even had the time to snatch a gasp at breath. At first I kicked and fought and struggled, thinking I could make some difference, thinking I might have some sway, and my presumption was not unpunished. The harder I sought to keep my head above the water, the more insistent the sea's reproof, pulling me beneath. My body soon exhausted and I gave myself up to the water's greater will.

Finally, it chose to spew me up, smashed and barely conscious, into the shallower waters where my flailing legs floundered on the shifting ground. I stumbled, half crawling, clawing with my hands up towards the shore as far as I could manage and then collapsed onto the fluxing sands. I retched and sucked for air and retched again. Easing slightly, I felt the smaller, tugging waves of the foreshore caressing up against my limp and battered body, and so I crumpled then, down into the gentler rivulets of water. I laid my head upon my arm and closed my eyes. Land.

Darkness started at the corners of my mind to hurry in, encroaching on my consciousness, closing over me, pulling me gently under with promises of quiet and sweet, seductive peace. A blackness without pain or even sense. Without sorrow. It would be so easy.

My eyes flicked open. Joe.

From where I lay with my head upon the sand, I became aware of other bodies being washed up around me. Some lay, half-prone and spluttering, a little further up the beach. A few were sitting up and heads in hands were struggling to bend their minds to understanding, to grasp the realisation that it was done. One or two were even trying to stumble to their feet but fell, unable to make their legs believe that the ground was flat and stable, that they should forget now to accommodate the constant swaying of the lifeboat that had become their natural stage.

One, within my line of sight, lay twenty yards or so up from me along the sands. His clothing moved with the ebb and flow of water, his shirt at the shoulder fluttered lightly in the breeze, but otherwise, he lay quite still. Even from this distance and this angle, I could see his crazy hair being fanned up and outwards, splayed upon the small, insistent fingers of the waves. It stood on end and then washed down repeatedly to cling about his face.

Bits of wood and planking from our boat nudged towards the shore around us, until the waters, finally deciding where to dump them, snagged them up on arbitrarily prominent creases in the sand. Our water barrel bumbled in and broke apart, the last of our fresh water seeping eagerly away, inseparable from its salty origin. The remnants of our temporary home, half the mast, tarpaulin, bits of sail, locker doors and canisters thrashed in and were settled here and there down the beach for as far as I could see.

I thought I could hear shouting. I raised my head and, ignoring the popping colours behind my eyes, I strained to focus. Squinting up the beach, blinded by the sunlight, I could make out someone, maybe Mick, kneeling down, with his back to me. His arms were held aloft. The thickness of the heat made his outline hazy but I could see others now, wavering down the beach to join him. I propped myself up on one elbow and wiped my other arm across my eyes. Adjusting slightly, though stinging raw, my vision sharpened and despite my inability to keep my mind from blurring, I understood then that the shore was barren. The beach, sprawled across the feet of huge, imposing dunes, was wide, but it was bare. I scanned the length of it but could see no end to its featureless monotony. There was no tree, no grass, no vegetation. Scorched and arid, pitted with craggy rock and crooked slabs of stone, the sand looked little more than coarse, grey ash. I knew it meant no water. Apart from us, there was nothing here.

I began to inch my way forwards but also sideways, away from the gathering group of men, to get to Joe. The wet sand gave way beneath me, dragging at my every movement. My hands and knees sank heavily each time I made to haul myself a little further but I fought against it, wriggling and writhing, breathing hard until it occurred to me that I might make more progress if I could get up on my knees. I did not know if I had the strength. My legs shook uncontrollably and my hands went down onto the sucking sand to steady myself time and time again. I had to stop after almost every single, interminable movement to gulp at breath, shaking my head in a constant effort to keep my bearings, to keep my will. I tried to clench my teeth but, despite the blazing heat, they began to chatter and I could not stop them.

By the time I reached him, I knew I could not possibly get him out. I was dizzy and disorientated, and his lifeless form lay curled heavily into the sand. The water swirled around him softly, rocking him slightly this way and that, laying its claim to him still.

I sat back beside him in the shallow channels running out from his embedded frame, and laid my arms across my knees. I had no thought at all that I must do something next. I just sat, as if to keep his company. I sat and watched the ceaseless turning of the waves, understanding no more of their fathomless convolutions than I could hope to understand why it had been him.

After a while, I became aware that the others were calling to me but I did not need to answer. I wondered why they could not just let us be. It was Fraser who splashed up towards us in the end, and he went to stand on the other side of Joe. He let his hands rest one on top of the other at his stomach and waited in silence for me to speak. But there was nothing at all that I could think to say.

'We'll have to bury him,' he said eventually. 'I'll get some of the others.' When he came back, seven or eight of them were with him. Big Sam and Mick. Mac. Clarie. We struggled in the first place to lift him even from the water. The initial hoist caused us to weave and stumble for though his body was half the size it had been, thin and wasted, he was big-boned and he was heavy. Fraser tried to steady us, barking breathlessly short, clipped instructions to keep us straight. Even so, our weakened legs, unaccustomed to walking firmly, could barely support our own, let alone the cumbersome, unwieldy weight of Joe's saturated frame. We staggered apart, lurching one way, then another, stumbling through the water out of step and time, so that Joe's leaden body was pulled and dipped and crushed between us. Straining, almost against one another, we slogged on until we reached the thick, dry sand and started up towards the dunes. Our feet singed and sank into its heat.

The ground gave way at every step, forcing us to bend our knees which, already too vulnerable, could scarcely resist the overriding compulsion to give in and fold. More than once, one or other of us fell or stumbled over, dropping his part of the burden. We had to keep on stopping. It made me want to scream.

About halfway up, two of the others let go at once and Joe's body, at the waist, creased sharply, tipping towards me so that I too, let go and fell backwards on to the burning sand. As I did so, I watched it drop, almost slowly, from his gaping pocket, catching glints of sunlight on its casing as it fell. The small, gold disc. Maggie's compass. I spun on to my knees and scrabbled forward, 'Stop!' I howled, 'Jesus! Stop!' and snatched it up. The others laboured to an unruly halt. 'Wha' the fuck?' Mac swore, exasperated to have his gritted efforts arrested yet again. Trying unsuccessfully to work my mouth, I faltered to my feet and held it out before them, across his body. 'It's Maggie's,' I said, shivering.

'It's 'is compass, isn't it?' Oblivious, the harshness in Mac's voice betrayed his frustration to get on. He spoke over me. 'Might need that.'

'It's his!' I shouted hoarsely, as vehemently as the constriction in my throat would allow. My voice, dropping, cracked into a low, thin whisper. 'It's his.'

Mac shrugged, uncomprehending, impatience written through every line across his face. They watched me as I closed my hand and, struggling with Joe's trouser pocket, shoved the compass as far down as I could inside it. We lumbered on.

We dug a shallow grave up beyond the water line, using bits of wood from our boat as spades. Each feeble effort at scraping out a hollow proved more ineffective than the last, for the sand would slip and slide continuously back around our makeshift tools so that eventually we took to grubbing it out with our hands. We lined it with the longer bits of planking that had been washed up and, wrapping him in a tattered piece of old tarpaulin, we lowered him in.

I did not think that I could bear to watch him covered, so while the others filled it in, I wandered vaguely up and down the beach, weaving in the throbbing heat, and clinging solely to the purpose of finding two small bits of wood so that I could make a cross. I forced my mind to concentrate entirely on that single task, that one distracting exercise, the thought on which might hinge my reason. For numb with pain and guilt and sorrow, I could not look upon what reigned within me nor listen to its long, low, keening cry of grief, which, constant and all-conquering, deprived my own salvation of any sense.

Eventually I picked two pieces that would do and, tying them together with a frayed and knotted piece of rigging, I worked it into the ground at the head of the new, low mound of sand. The rest of them gathered at Fraser's bidding and the captain murmured some old, familiar words of prayer, which brought no ease or comfort.

I moved away then, a little further up the beach, ten yards or so, and fell upon my knees and from there, laid my body on the ground. The sand pulsed beneath me, throbbing with the fervour of the sun, but my skin, scaled and leathered by long exposure, did not flinch from it. I did not close my eyes. Arbitrary and untimely, Joe's death had brought about in me a dislocation that none other of our trials had done: a hard-edged, emotional jarring that resulted altogether in a bleak rebuttal of ordinary feeling. I could hardly care for anything any more. I lay there, blank, exhausted, unconnected, and listened to the others start to argue.

The burial over, they sat about, a couple of yards away from me, in twos and threes, discussing what should now be done. Their words, as though coming from a distance, hung in the thickness of the air around me, slurred and slow. They settled vaguely about the periphery of my understanding, separate and ill-defined.

While half of us had been struggling to retrieve Joe's body, others – Tomas, the captain, Rawlins and his boys – had been making fairly faint-hearted explorations of the immediate vicinity to try and discover if there was any hope of water. Battered and disorientated, they had not managed to get far, but far enough to realise that this land would yield us nothing.

'Got halfway up that bastard.' Billy waved an arm weakly in the direction of one of the massive sand hills behind. 'Couldn't make it any further. Ain't nothing behind 'em anyhow. Just more of the same.' He rubbed his face, passing his hand across his eyes.

'There's no water anyway,' the skipper sighed. 'Dunes behind us. Sea in front. We aren't that much better off.' There was a short silence as the truth of this sank in. The rapturous glee we'd revelled in at the sighting of the land and the heady dreams we'd nurtured of abundant water taunted now, as much foolish as premature.

'Seems to me we should gather what we can, rope and that, and head up that way.' Jerking his head towards the dunes, Mick looked from the captain towards Fraser. 'Get through the dunes. Might come upon some water.'

'More 'n likely not,' Mac growled, his head lowered and eyes fixed on the sand.

'I just told you, you stupid bastard. You can't get up there,' Billy swivelled where he sat, to glare at Mick. 'None of us can.' He threw his hands up in the air. 'Die just bloody tryin'.'

'And besides, if this is Africa, beyond the dunes, there's probably nothing more than miles of desert.' The captain, beyond dispirited, seemed incapable of adding anything at all encouraging. His withered body, heaped on the sand, was not much more than a pile of bones, picked dry.

'Then we're gonna die here!' It was less a statement than a direct plea to prevent it being so. Jack's small and hollow voice broke up somewhere to my right, filtering through my consciousness, resounding with alarm. If Joe were here, the thought danced lightly through my mind, he'd look at Jack and shake his shaggy head assuredly. 'We're not dead yet, Jack the lad,' he would have said.

Sighing heavily, I fought to swallow and then lifted my elbows and pushed my hands down into the sand, fanning out my fingers on the coarse, hot grains. I sat up slowly, closing my eyes and inhaling sharply to resist the blackening dizziness that came with almost any movement now. I squinted at the sharpness of the sunlight but turned my face in the direction of Jack's voice and shook my head, trying to shape my crusted lips in to a smile.

'No,' I rasped. I tried again. 'No, Jack.' My hand wavered out in front of me, towards him. 'No, no, we're not. We've made water once before. We've more wood now. We can do it again. We know it works.'

'For Christsakes, it'll take too long! How the fuck can we do that when we haven't got the frigging kit?' Mac cried. 'I'm with Mick. We should move out!'

But Mick, having once been proved wrong before and eager to believe, was more inclined to put his faith in me, 'Wait, Mac, wait. The boy has done it once before. Can we do it, d'you think we can, Cub? Do you now?'

'If the fuel tank's been washed up and a bit of pipe, we could,' Fraser, catching hold, began to cast about, and started to get up on to his feet. 'We need to scour the beach. Wood, the fuel pipe and the tank. Anything we can burn.' He came across to stand in front of me and offered me his hand to help me up. 'Joe was right about you,' he murmured, as my eyes levelled up with his. 'You are the brains.'

'We can't do it.' Clarie's voice, dull and hoarse, brought us up short. 'If we can't get across the dunes, if there's only desert, we're gonna have to get off this beach somehow.' His skinny throat worked painfully. 'We need to try and rebuild the boat. A raft or something. Try and get further down the coast. We can't stay here.' He looked around, from one dishevelled, wasted face to the next until his eyes came to rest upon the skipper. 'Captain?'

The captain stared at him, raw-eyed and weary, 'Rebuild the boat?' he repeated vaguely. 'Yes. Rebuild the boat... I expect we have to.'

'Jesus Christ,' Billy muttered, 'I can't get up a frigging sand dune, never mind start 'n build a bloody boat...'

'Well, what the fuck d'you suggest we do then? Sit here till we die?' Big Sam's guttural growl cut Billy off. Wincing with the effort, he hauled his heavy bones up to standing. 'Well, I ain't gonna,' he said.

'We must do both,' snapped Fraser, exasperated by the senseless, circular bickering. 'Some of us; me and Cub, Sam, Mick, if you want.' He nodded decisively at each one of us as he said our names, assuming our solidarity. 'We'll try and get the water going.

Find the fuel tank or something else. We'll use the smaller bits of wood we find to burn. Captain. Clarie. You organise the rest. Collect the bigger bits of wood, ropes and rigging, whatever we could use to build a boat.'

As Fraser finished speaking, I became aware that I felt inexplicably unsettled, quietly conscious of a prickling, deep unease rippling stealthily up my back and neck, as though suddenly I was once removed, watching myself and those around me acting out the horrific disintegration of our hopes for survival. A constant feeling of vague disconnection had accompanied me now for days, a kind of secondary mode of being, in which my mind felt itself separate from my body and its surroundings, but I had ascribed that feeling to the nature of my extreme debilitation. This was different. I had an eerie sense, a shadowy misgiving whispering softly that there was something out here somewhere which, while creeping forward, threatening, had so far eluded us.

Some of the others, following Big Sam's cue, started to falter to their feet and Clarie, pushing on one knee, half turned to the captain saying, 'Right then, Captain, shall I…?' but the words died in his throat as his attention was suddenly transfixed on a point somewhere behind me, up in the sand hills beyond. Simultaneously, one or two of the others facing me caught sight of whatever it was that had silenced Clarie and, eyes widening with alarm, they stopped exactly as they were, stricken with a newer, more immediate fear.

Startled by their faces, a blast of cold apprehension swept across me, hollowing and twisting up my guts, spinning me round to scan the mass of dunes behind.

'Cannibals… oh, Jesus, cannibals,' Bob Cunningham, who after several attempts had only just achieved a precarious upright balance, suddenly dropped down heavily onto his knees and, hunching over, covered his face with his hands and began to rock his body slowly back and forth, moaning softly. 'Oh God… oh God, have pity… have pity on us… Jesus…' He began to cry and the dry heaving of his sobs rose uncontrollably, raking across my quivering nerves and infecting all of us with panic. Appalled and frightened by his anguish, fear gave rise to anger.

'For Christsakes, Bob, pull yourself together,' snapped Mick, unable to endure the naked abandon in Cunningham's collapse. 'Jesus! Pack it in. 'Course they won't be fucking cannibals…'

But the quiver in his voice belied his scepticism and he glanced across hopefully towards Fraser, then to the captain, for reassurance. But neither one of them was listening nor would take their eyes away from the gathering company on the hills. Cunningham continued to keen and rock, jamming his fist up into his mouth as if he might by that means stop up the outpouring of his terror.

'People. Least it means there must be water about here somewhere,' murmured Fraser, out of the side of his mouth to me. 'How many, d'you reckon?'

I could not tell. I could make out maybe twenty-five or thirty, tall, silent figures standing on the dune tops. The light breeze tugged gently at their long, loose robes, which billowed out around them, but each stood absolutely still. Staring. Though their heads were covered with large, swathing turbans that also framed and partially concealed their faces, there was no mistaking the distrustful hostility of their attitude. The thickness of their beards served only to accentuate the dark ferocity of their features, furrowed with malign suspicion. Some held sticks before them in two hands, while others, chins on their folded arms, used theirs to lean on, bowing them slightly with the weight. From where we stood, I could make out the knots at intervals down each length, the heavy flexibility of their sinew, a strength that surely could be used to deliver a beating so severe that none among us would survive. Our arms and legs were now as thin as the thickest one of them.

And still they stared.

'Thirty. Maybe more,' I worked my mouth to speak, trying hard to swallow. My voice came cracked and thin. 'We're no match for them.' I tried to swipe my hair from across my eyes but my hands were shaking with a violence I could not control. I found that I could barely focus. The outlines of the brightly dressed figures before us shimmered and shifted before my eyes. I had to screw my face up to make them still. The sandy wasteland between them and me kept up a constant swaying motion, lurching, tilting; it was all that I could do to keep myself from falling.

'What d'you think they want?' hissed Clarie, his eyes darting from them back to Fraser anxiously. For some irrational reason, movement and speech instinctively seemed risky. Surely it was better to keep silent and keep still, as if any sudden gesture or noise from one of us might precipitate a swift and unwarranted reaction. 'D'you think they're gonna kill us?'

No one answered. We stood, both groups of men transfixed, apparently incapable of action, in the heavy timelessness of impasse. The sun glared down between us, the density of its heat throbbing visibly, silencing the very air.

'Well, there's only one way to find out,' Fraser said eventually, drawing himself up. It was typical of his impatience for indecision. If he was to die, he would rather get it over with. 'Captain Edwards. Clarie. Shall we?'

'We should all go. Approach them friendly like. Hands up in the air,' Mick gabbled quickly, apparently just as anxious at being left behind as he was at the prospect of an approach.

'Might look more threatening if we all go at them,' I whispered.

'What's the difference anyway?' the skipper said, shrugging resignedly. 'If they're gonna kill us, they're gonna bloody kill us. Let's get on with it.'

He broke away from us, taking a couple of steps forward and then looked back at Fraser, who stepped up immediately to join him. The rest of us began to shamble after them. Twenty yards now from the nearest. They did not flinch but watched us, giving away nothing. Stragglers allowed themselves to drop a little way behind, Mac and Cunningham, taut with fear, ready at any moment to turn and run. Fifteen yards from the bottom of the dunes. We squinted up towards our audience, shying painfully before the sun behind them which, blindingly belligerent, blackened and enlarged their coloured garments.

'Put your hands out. Show 'em we don't mean 'em any harm,' Mick breathed tentatively, slowing up a little, and the rest of us, despite ourselves, slackened pace. Ten yards.

There was a sudden, startling shout of something unintelligible from one of the men on the hill in front of us. He whipped his stick up, out in front of his body horizontally, as if to bar against our further progress. We froze.

I heard Billy swear and Cunningham moan. Even Fraser flinched, turning slightly sideways and raising and bending one arm across his head, as if to protect himself against an unexpected missile. The figure who had arrested our approach started speaking down to us in a fast and furious flow of incomprehensible language. He'd pause abruptly, apparently waiting for an answer and then, impatient, rattle on, firing us, or so it seemed, with a torrent of aggressive questions. The dark blue garments he wore flowed and flapped around him as he gave vent to his displeasure and alarm.

We waited, swaying with the strain and eventually, Fraser, taking advantage of a short hiatus, cleared his throat. 'Do you speak English?' Even to me, his words, his very voice, sounded preposterously out of place in this heat, on this dusty shore, to these native men.

There was a silence as our inquisitor digested this and then, he turned and signalled to the men around him, beckoning them in. He took one or two steps down the dune towards us and the others, from their various vantage points around the hills, made strides across to join him.

'English?' Fraser tried to lick his lips, fending off his fear at their approach.

The gathering of them up in front of us remained formidable but somehow, with the attempt at communication, their attitude seemed to have softened slightly, as if the sound of another human voice, querulous and desperate, had struck a common chord. As they began a slow and rather tentative descent, their sticks became more clearly now supports, no longer vicious weapons. And although physically so much stronger and exceeding us by far in number, they did not look, as they got nearer, quite so threatening, but appeared, more prevalently, perplexed.

As they reached our level at the base of the dunes, they spread out a little, craning round one another to get a better look. There must have been more than thirty of them and they formed a loose semicircle as their cluster thinned around us. We inched more closely together, huddling in defence.

'English?' Fraser tried again. 'Water,' he said. 'We need water.'

The men regarded us quietly, though there was some nudging and a few low darts of speech between them.

'Let Tomas try!' urged Clarie, spinning round to face the rest of us as it suddenly occurred to him that there might be some advantage to be gained from a change of tack. Tomas' head started up, registering both surprise and fear, as we all looked towards him but he made no move to push himself forward, out from safety to the frontline of our number.

'They ain't gonna know Portuguese any more than they understand bloody English,' muttered Billy, as those of us shielding Tomas edged aside, leaving him no alternative but to step forward.

'I will try Spanish,' he said anxiously, glancing across Clarie, to the captain. 'More likely they know Spanish?'

The skipper nodded. 'Worth a try.'

Reluctantly, Tomas took two more steps until he drew parallel with Fraser, and his voice when it came trembled uncontrollably, '*Español? Hablais español? El agua.*' He cupped his hands and brought them to his mouth before bringing them, palms upturned, beseeching, out again in front of his body. '*Por favor, el agua!*'

There was no response. The dark faces before us continued to stare at us impassively, blinking slowly in the white-hot heat, as though inclined to wait for as long as they might choose, unmoved as equally by our obvious desperation as by the raking inhospitality of the sun. Our close-knit group, by contrast, seethed with fear and with frustration; shuffling, scratching and shivering on the ragged edges of despair.

'*L'eau,*' muttered Fraser suddenly, and then looking up at the tribesmen, he tried again more loudly. '*L'eau. S'il vous plaît. Nous avons besoin de l'eau.*'

Immediately, several of them nodded and turned to each other, as if relieved at having finally made some headway and their blue-robed spokesman puffed out his cheeks and exhaled deeply. He put his head on one side as though summing up the situation and began to nod thoughtfully. He moved a little closer, keeping his eyes fixed all the time on Fraser, his face now flickering into interest.

'Jesus! What the fuck was that?' Mac muttered behind me, as the others among them visibly relaxed and started talking, jabbering quickly to each other and then gesturing at our dry and brittle bodies.

'French, wasn't it, Fraser?' asked the captain, 'It's lucky that you speak it.'

'I don't,' Fraser shook his head, 'only bits I've picked up. Not enough to hold much of a conversation.'

'Well, it's enough for them to understand. You asked for water?'

Fraser nodded, and looking directly at the eyes of the blue-robed man who was now perhaps three yards in front of him, he put his hands together, fingers interlaced, as if in fervent prayer. '*L'eau, s'il vous plaît. L'eau,*' he breathed.

Their intermediary stopped abruptly. He was an ageing, spindly man whose every year was marked in minute detail by the myriad of crevices fanning across his weathered face, but his body looked bulky in comparison to the wasted frame of Fraser. He nodded and then turning to one side he put out an arm, the furthest one from us, to indicate our direction and with his other hand he waved us onwards. '*Oui,*' he said, '*l'eau.*'

We followed him and Fraser and the captain, flanked on every side by dark, inquisitive eyes. I was not far behind them so I could hear the quick, interrogative tones of their leader and Fraser's long and faltering pauses as he tried to summon up words enough to explain how we came to be among them. Often, he stopped, reduced to gesturing and mime but the incredulity of his audience, particularly as he held up his hands and counted twenty-one out with his fingers, was singularly apparent.

We made slow and laborious progress. Our disaccustomed legs struggled to keep walking on the sinking sands and our extreme exhaustion and physical fragility precluded any speed. We stumbled and we weaved, unsure of every footing, surrounded by our new companions who stopped at intervals, waiting, patient and unhurried. Heads down, we trudged on and on, our scrambled senses nullified before the blinding starkness of the sun. The cool of promised water, which in the mind's eye of every one of us shone and glistened with its promise, tantalised, shifting and shimmering just beyond the next dune and the next, sliding slightly further off with the drudgery of every arduous step.

Mac, two or three paces behind me, kept up an interminable invective as he fought to keep his legs from folding. 'Why the fuck should we trust 'em?... Could be taking us anywhere... leading to the fucking desert... leading us to die there . . . probably their next meal... Jesus... fucking cannibals.' He stumbled then into Jack, who fell on to his knees, groaning with the pain of it. We stopped again. Jack put his hands into the sand in front of him, shaking his head to rid his eyes of blackness, breathing hard and trying to muster up a single scrap of strength from the void of his resources to get himself back up on to his feet.

'Jesus, Jack... gerrup,' Mac swayed heavily beside him. 'Bastard... gerrup, for Christsakes... Ah, wha' the fuck. Bloody stay there.' He tottered to one side and then staggered on.

I thought of Joe. For an instant, I saw his crazy hair sticking up at every angle in the moonlight. I thought of all his irritation at Mac's mean-spirited malice and his general impatience of rank unkindness. Joe would not have borne the selfishness apparent in Mac's mindless wittering, which disregarded utterly the fears of those around him. And more than that, he would not have allowed for any one of us to be left behind.

Despite the dizziness that menaced in the darkness at the corners of my eyes, I bent, putting one hand on one quivering knee and the other on Jack's arm, just beneath the armpit. I could not pull him but I tugged his skinny arm as fiercely as I could manage. 'Jack,' I croaked, 'Jack.' He nodded his head weakly in acknowledgement and, moaning with the effort, he hauled himself up off the ground.

The tribesman took us some distance down the beach, and then up between two apparently insurmountable sand hills before leading our descent, on stones and sliding sand, into a lower-lying basin where, evidently, they lived. Three large tents, constructed out of cloth and wood and spaced perhaps a couple of yards apart, occupied almost entirely the small, flat area at the base of several high surrounding dunes. The middle tent was circular and the other two, long and lower, flanked it either side.

There was silence from the women, children and crooked elders who stood about in small groups, some at the gaping mouths of the tents, some lining the slow and pitiful path we trod, until our leader stopped abruptly and turned to face us. The rest of the community, emerging soundlessly from various directions and from beneath the skirts of their accommodation, followed us in and then gathered round us where we stopped, murmuring and curious. The man in blue motioned to us to sit, and gratefully, with every nerve and sinew thrumming out desperate relief at the promised imminence of water, we sank onto the ground.

He called then to two or three men within the crowd, in a rapid, unintelligible tongue, and in response they slowly made their way towards a group of several camels that were tethered on the incline, a little way beyond the tents. They did not hurry. They moved with all the indifferent languor of men who permanently live beneath the glare of an unforgiving sun. They mounted and began to make their way up a massive sand hill, opposite the one we had just struggled to descend.

'Ask him where's the water,' Clarie, bewildered by the unexpected wait, hissed at Fraser.

'Probably isn't any fucking water,' Mac snarled across him. 'Gone to get their fucking spears.'

Fraser pushed himself with great difficulty back up onto his knees and then spreading his arms apart, he shrugged questioningly at their spokesman. '*L'eau?*'

The reply came quick and calm, '*Il faut aller la chercher à l'oasis. Faut l'attendre.*'

Fraser clearly strained to understand. He winced with effort as he sought to clear his head and separate out the words. His knowledge of French was remote and faded, and the lucidity of his mind befuddled by physical weakness. He had no hope of keeping up. Eventually, he shook his head. '*L'eau assis? Qu'est-ce que c'est? L'attendre – pourquoi?*'

'*L'oasis? L'oasis,*' the tribesman looked at him coolly but Fraser shook his head, uncomprehending, until, taking his stick in both hands, the man drew a circle in the sand, a few lines at its edges to denote some trees and then stabbed it at its centre with the staff. '*L'eau,*' he said, clearly satisfied.

'Oasis,' the skipper pointed out, finally grasping it. 'They've gone to get it.'

'Ah, for fuck's sake!' Big Sam cried. 'How long they gonna be?' Desperate at the prospect of further unforeseen delay, he toppled forward, writhing, onto the sand. To be brought to such a pitch of feverish expectation and then to be denied was enough to break a man apart.

Fraser looked beseechingly up at the tribesman, who regarded our consternation placidly.

'*Combien de temps?*' asked Fraser flatly, but the man just shrugged his answer.

The crowd around us began to thin and peter out. The children, losing interest in the pathetic group of skeletal foreigners who lay whimpering but otherwise motionless upon the stony sand, took up their games again, calling more confidently to one another across our carcasses. The women, too, presumably had better things to do than watch our suffering and so they wandered away, drifting back to work. Some of the men though, stood on by us, wary still and wondering.

The heat, trapped and concentrated by the high rising walls of dune around us, bubbled at ground level in the dell. We waited, bodily annihilated, quietly disintegrating into the dust. Entirely at the mercy of the sun, she sought once and for all, vindictive and omnipotent, to unburden us of our senses, of ourselves. We waited. Slowly, slowly, the weight of time settled silently around us. The humming of the heat blanketed our bodies, subdued our spirits and reduced our minds to stupor, so that waiting became a final state of being, scarcely affording realisation that there was purpose to it. Time without an end.

My eyes returned time and time again to the gaping hole, dark at the entrance to the circular tent before us. Black and hollow, it beckoned to me, promising me cool and shelter. Infinite peace. And yet every time I felt my mind begin to slide towards it, I was brought up short, my attention snagging on something just beyond the periphery of my vision. To my right, there, up on the crest of the sand hill. A snatched glimpse of a person, shaggy-haired and huge, arms folded and whistling. But when I turned my head towards him, he turned away, dark against the brightness of the sun and walked over the top, disappearing down behind the other side.

At last, our blue-robed guide, who had stationed himself within the shadows at the doorway of one of the smaller tents, roused us with a cry. Blinking and disorientated, I could not, at first, train my eyes to follow in the direction of his outstretched arm but squinting painfully upwards to scan the hills, I eventually found one, two, then three blackened, shifting shapes broadening into view. The water bearers had emerged at the top of the steepest dune, their backing the dazzling whiteness of the sun's full force. Their silhouetted forms and those of their camels wavered on the skyline briefly before they began their snaking descent towards the settlement.

Our interpreter went to meet them and taking a bulging goatskin from the first to dismount, he came back to stand before us. He held it out to Billy who happened to be the nearest to him. Billy lurched towards it hastily, both hands outstretched but incredibly, unimaginably, the tribesman then drew it back. Putting out his other hand, palm up, he twitched his fingers expectantly up and down, 'Faut quelque chose en échange.'

'Wha'?' Billy, utterly confounded for an instant, gaped and turned to Fraser for explanation. Fraser was on his feet and he tottered towards them, his face contorted in horrified disbelief. 'Comment?' he gasped.

Billy looked from one to the other of them and then anger, suddenly replacing his bewilderment, flushed across his features.

'Give it here, you fucking bastard!' he spat. 'Give it to me.' He made a quick, threatening gesture with one arm as if to strike at his tormentor but as he did so, two or three of the other tribesmen stepped up beside their spokesman, implying force. So Billy turned furiously on Fraser. 'What the fuck did he say? Why won't he give me it?'

Fraser stared at the tribesman, who regarded him calmly in return.

'*Faut échanger,*' he said again, bringing the goatskin forward and then moving it back once more, putting out his other hand as he did so, to simulate the action he required.

'We have to give them something for it,' cried Fraser incredulously. 'Jesus Christ!'

'I don't believe it,' the skipper, behind Fraser, shook his head. 'I don't bloody believe it. That can't be it.'

'It is. I'm bloody telling you. They want something in return.'

By this time, the other water bearers had made their way to join us and we could plainly hear the water sloshing in the four goatskin bags they held before us.

'I got this,' Mick suddenly pushed his way through, barging in between Fraser and Billy, and presented himself, eyes fixed on the goatskin, before the tribesmen. In his open palm, which he held out for them to see, he held a small, black, plastic comb.

There was scarcely a flicker from the haggler. He picked up the comb from Mick's hand and looked it over carefully. Then he nodded quickly and handed Mick the goatskin. Mick snatched it up to his mouth, threw back his head and glugged, his eyes widening with the effort. Thick, brown liquid slid down at the sides of his mouth, over his beard and down into the creases at his scrawny neck.

'Mick! Not much!' shouted Clarie at him hoarsely. 'Not so much at once. Your body isn't used to it. A bit at a time!'

Mick pulled back and breathing hard, he looked from one of us to the next. 'Sandy,' he grinned, clicking his tongue, 'but it's fresh!' His face transfigured into pure delight.

There was sudden scrabbling all around as men searched their pockets and their bodies, desperate for something which might do to trade. Belts, most too big now to be much use to us, were accepted impassively, though rings and bits of jewellery went down with slightly more enthusiasm. Even crumpled up pound notes were nodded at and tucked away. We crowded in around the water bearers, offering the very last of what we had in terms of personal property, giving up the remnants of what had tied us to a previous life without a second thought. Water. It was all.

I got pushed back a little, jostled by the fray of men who clamoured around the four tribesmen with the goatskins. Clarie, having already bartered off his wedding ring, was bleating vainly at the buzzing groups about rehydrating slowly, about it being dangerous to take too much at once. I had absolutely nothing of any value on me and so I was struggling to unloose the cord which tied at the front of my pyjama bottoms, hoping that it might do to trade and thus gain me access to the relief some of the others were already celebrating. Fraser called to me, 'Cub, come on!' and as I looked across to answer him, I caught a glimpse of it by chance, glinting in the palm of Mac's upturned hand, just as the tribesman lent in to take it from him.

I stumbled at him, my arms flailing out in front of me, though I did not recognise at first that the unholy cry of agony that I could hear, high-pitched and stupefying, was coming from my own throat. I grabbed him at the shoulder, spinning him round to face me. He wobbled drunkenly at the force with which I had thrown myself towards him and he staggered back a little.

'You filthy, thieving bastard,' I shouted, 'haven't you any respect? Any fucking respect at all?' and then I hit him with all the might I had left in me, catching him just shy of his nose on the left cheek. Given my weakness, it wasn't much of a punch but Mac, also stripped of strength, sprawled backwards, landing on his backside in the sand.

The buzz of the bartering, which had been going on around us, suddenly ceased. The tribesmen fell silent, their transactions halting abruptly and the crowd, which had swelled again to view the bargaining, fell back a few steps as though fearing that this sudden aggression among our company might escalate and that we might well, after all, turn on them.

I must have looked wild enough to throw myself on top of him and meant to, but the severity of Fraser's tone brought me up,

'Cub!' He grabbed my arm and yanked me back, holding me away from Mac, who sat on, shaking his head in disingenuous wonder and wiping the sand off the side of his arm. The skipper signalled to Clarie to help him up.

I passed my arm across my eyes, and stood swaying a little, quivering at the horror of Mac's indifference for the dead. My dead.

'Joe's compass,' I said, pointing at the tribesman who held it now before him, at arm's length in the palm of his hand, as if fearful suddenly of its importance and the violence it had wrought.

Fraser dropped his gaze from my face a moment. He blew the air out of his cheeks, letting it go slowly through his gritted teeth and then, putting a hand up to the back of his neck, he rubbed it thoughtfully. We both stared down at his burnt and calloused feet, blackened and livid against the dusty colourlessness of the sand.

When I looked back up, he was waiting, watching me. It was not just sorrow that I read within the dark hollows of his eyes then, but also, it seemed, profound and aching shame. Shame for all that we had been forced to witness upon the boat, shame for the limitless and overriding capacity for self-servitude in humankind which had been so undeniably exposed, and shame for what he was now about to do.

He put a hand upon my arm and shook it gently. 'He's no use for it now, Cub.' He stopped me with another scarcely perceptible shake as I opened my mouth to protest against the prosaic victory of grasping need. 'Look at us.' He cast one arm wide, encompassing the sorry crew of bearded, broken men, in tatters, who stood in twos and threes, regarding us. 'We need the water.'

I looked around at the silent faces watching me. Most of them, scarcely more than bone and sinew, would possibly have sold their souls for water, given half the chance.

I could not blame them for it. Tormented as entirely as ever Tantalus had been, we had journeyed through the scalding fires of hell surrounded on all sides by water; water which, shimmering, beckoning, taunting, relinquished no relief. And I could not think of any personal possession I would not eagerly have parted with at that moment without a second's hesitation. But Joe's compass? Scored by guilt and grief, I alone knew how much it would have cost him to have had to give it up. And yet I knew he would have done so. I was not in any position to vouch for my compunction and some – Billy in particular and even the skipper – looked annoyed by it.

I nodded and turned away but the man beneath whose robes the compass had now vanished called out to me. I did not, at first, understand whom he was addressing until he stepped towards me, putting out a staying hand and touching me lightly on the arm. Neither did I know what it was that he was saying, but when I turned to look at him, he held the goatskin out, nodding at me encouragingly. His brow was furrowed but his eyes were light with sympathy.

And so I took it and I drank.

CHAPTER 11

ENLÈVEMENT

'Why ain't you eatin'?' Big Sam's greasy lips, glistening with moisture and patchy red with stinging salt, stopped, for a moment, their feverish endeavours to suck the salted fish completely dry, before continuing to devour the rest of its flesh with smacking relish. He wiped his arm across his mouth, a piece of fish grasped in either hand, and looked at me incredulously.

We had had to trade for food. The men who had provided it, though not apparently ungenerous, clearly had a sense of cultural order that could not be cast aside. The extreme severity of the conditions in which they lived would not concede exception for the hardship we had suffered. They knew what hardship was, for they lived by it, and ours appeared perhaps no worse than they, at some time or another, had had to endure.

Washed-up hurry bags and their random contents had yielded us a little more in terms of bargaining material, but as each new goatskin was produced and as, under Clarie's fastidious instruction, we had to drink only small quantities at a time, we were quickly running out. The actual bags had been accepted, knives, a couple of saturated – and therefore useless – torches, and the skipper, in desperation, had resorted to handing over his false teeth.

In return, that evening, they gave us salted fish. We cooked it over a fire set with driftwood, which some of us, strengthened marginally by the water, its restorative promise and the enticement of a return of the capacity to eat, had limped about the beach to collect. Some of the smaller children ran to help us, wheeling about the sands, shouting, full of energy and light-hearted laughter. Thinking it a game.

The sight of the fish, sizzling softly, charring, and its smoky redolence, was maddening: too tantalising. My eyes stung as I crouched low over the fire and my mouth strained and twitched involuntarily in fervid anticipation. Eventually, sliding the fish down off my blackened stick with juggling, burning fingers, it broke apart between them, thick slivers of dense, glossy flesh, running with juice and salty succulence. I shoved it between my lips, which numbed immediately in an ecstasy of tingling pain, and then revelled in the glorious reawakening of every shrivelled, dried-up nerve within my mouth, as each one, responding to the fish's sharp asperity, exploded into re-existence. The pleasure, so eagerly and long-awaited, so exquisite, far outstripped the pain.

But, despite my desire, I found that after two mouthfuls, I could barely swallow. The familiar, crouching nausea that had settled so heavily in my stomach but which had become so inseparable from my overall debilitation, suddenly unfurled its protest, roaring up into my throat, bubbling at the back of my mouth and threatening forcibly to reject any further attempt to push food across its threshold. Horrified, I clamped my lips together tightly, and tearing my eyes away from the glistening flesh between my fingers, I glanced around at the intense concentration illuminated on the faces of my companions around the fire. The reluctance of my stomach to countenance the food set me apart. The sound of smacking, drawing mouths and sucking lips was punctuated only by the spit and hiss of the flames. There was no talk, no consciousness afforded beyond what each man held within his hands and on the single-minded objective of assuaging appetite, all eyes, all thought, were bent.

Pent-up voraciousness, induced by three weeks' protracted starvation, had finally been given rein and, inflamed by the assault on every sense, would brook neither company nor interruption until primal need had been appeased. It would not take long though, for craving far outstripped capacity for shrunken, unaccustomed stomachs to take their fill, and though having dreamt obsessively for days on days of bountiful provisions, a small salted fish would prove more than adequate.

Apart from me, only Mick and Bob Cunningham were not eating. Having ignored Clarie's repeated warnings to rehydrate more slowly, the two of them had guzzled the water, determined at a single sitting to gain definitive relief from the torment of their thirst. The consequences were now all too apparent, as Mick sat almost on the fire, shivering and groaning at the spasms of pain that ripped across his abdomen, while Cunningham lay curled up on the sand on the edge of the darkness, semi-conscious and clutching at his stomach.

Big Sam, fully sated, wiped his arm across his mouth and eyed the fish, barely started, which I held between my trembling hands. 'What's up with you?'

'He's gone and done the same as Bob and Mick, ain't he.' Less a question than a statement of fact, Mac's voice came out muffled as he spoke without looking up from his efforts to fill his mouth as quickly and as fully as he could manage. 'Drank too much too quick, didn't he.'

'I told you, Cub,' Clarie looked up across the fire and shook his head briefly at me, 'gotta take it slow with the water. Your body isn't used to it.'

'It isn't that,' I muttered, stung suddenly by the implication that I had disregarded their collective prudence. 'I drank about the same as you all did.'

'What's up with you then? Too salty for you? Officer boys mebbe only take their fish with lemon!' Mac snorted scornfully and then began to cough, spraying the fire with bits of fish. It fizzled and snapped its protest.

I became aware that Fraser had stopped eating and was staring sidelong at me with dark concern. 'Eat it, Cub. Be needing your help tomorrow.' He sniffed noisily, as though vaguely embarrassed by his admission. 'Need to try and build the water purifier back up again.' He nodded at me curtly, before tearing off another mouthful from his own piece of fish.

I got stiffly to my feet, lurching with the effort at not putting my hands down on the sand. Though perversely my body would not take it, it was unthinkable that I should therefore cast aside the food which, appallingly, I could not consume. And the brunt of their attention, either solicitous or sneering, was more than I could bear. I shrugged and turned away, stumbling off towards the beach, into the darkness and away from the flickering circle of the fire's light.

I got about ten yards before Fraser caught me by the arm.

'You mustn't give up now,' he said gruffly. He paused and put his head on one side. 'Joe wouldn't've had it.'

'It isn't that,' I blurted out, too loudly.

'What then?'

'I'm all backed up.' He did not understand me and I could sense, rather than see, the enquiry on his face. He waited. 'I can't go... I can't eat. I haven't been... God, with everybody watching... I just couldn't go. And now I'm gagging... when I try to eat... I can't swallow...' my voice, rising in panic, cracked as it all came out in a rush, surprising me.

'Since when?'

I hesitated, though I knew full well. 'Since we set out.'

'Since we set out? On the lifeboat? These last three weeks?'

I looked away, down the beach, into the darkness, and Fraser continued to stare at me incredulously. Eventually, he looked down, exhaling slowly. His hand went up to behind the back of his neck and he rubbed it slowly. There was a moment's silence and I crossed my arms, putting my hands up beneath my armpits. Suddenly cold. I realised that I was rocking slightly, from my heels to the balls of my feet and back again, and that I had clenched my teeth together, determined to stop them as they began to chatter, perhaps as much in fearful anticipation of his measured prognosis, as by my lack of insulation.

'You're gonna have to get it out.' His voice was harsh but somehow, the grim resolve behind it was reassuring, as if by offering a solution, he was confident that there was a cure. He waited for me to speak, to show that I knew what he meant, but I could do nothing more than stand in front of him, cowed and shivering, as the slow subsiding panic that had gripped my body was rapidly replaced by a sharp stab of terror at the thought of what his suggestion might entail. My mind, shot and quivering, resolutely recoiled from trying to piece together the slightest picture of how it could be done. So I did not reply.

When he spoke again, his tone was gentler, patient. 'You'll have to get yourself a shell. Flat-edged. You're gonna have to scrape it out. Go down the beach, into the shallows.' He put his hands, palms up, between us. 'Be bastard painful but you're gonna have to relieve it somehow.'

The pain was excruciating. Cowering from it, alone and in the darkness, I crouched on the sand, pushing the shrieking rebellion of my mind towards it. Afraid of dipping in and out of consciousness, I had hunkered down by the water's edge, fearful of collapsing, and perhaps drowning, in so humiliating an occupation, so I hovered on the foreshore in the thinning, spittled covering of receding foam. The nails on my free hand tore into the bony narrowness of my buttock and I dared myself to do it, my other hand wavering, shaking uncontrollably, and blenching at the task. Heat prickled across my body and convulsing with the pain of it, I screamed out low, ragged groans of agonised effort, grating and grinding my teeth, gasping hoarsely at the bitterness of having to endure. My body, fraught and fragile, spasmed, every weakened muscle repulsed by so harrowing an intrusion, and the ground swam up before me. I fell forwards, whimpering, into the water, time and time again. Once unstopped and relieved of the solid, heavy clagging in my bowels, the flow of excrement and blood was constant. I sat in the shallows, moaning softly, as the salty water bathed me, stinging an unsoothing sympathy, until I realised that shock had exempted all other feeling and now I could barely move from cold.

Still hampered by my body's bloody effluence, I staggered, lamed and limping, up the beach and found the others huddling under various bits of canvas that had been salvaged from the remnants of our sail. They lay bunched, as close as they could get to the dying embers of the fire and despite themselves, had resorted to shuddering up together to try to generate some warmth. I crept down and found a place by Slim, thankful for the cover of the darkness and the inevitable self-concern of exhausted men, struggling to sleep in the extreme discomfort of implacable cold.

Bare-boned and wet, I trembled at the contact with the chill severity of the sand, flinching against every movement as my wounds continued still to ooze their fluid. I clenched my teeth. McGrath had been wrong, I told myself. I had lasted out the ocean. This hideous physical anguish, this too, would pass. The barren land, it would not be the last place on earth my eyes encountered and the faces of these men around me, so intolerably familiar, not the last that I would ever look upon. For somewhere yet, low and distant, echoing within labyrinths of grey delirium that laid its constant siege to my rational mind, I still could hear Joe whistling. He was still here.

I would get back. I had a debt to honour. I squeezed my eyes tightly closed, grimacing at the pain, and summoning the little control I had left on the restless disquiet of my mind, I deliberately directed all the sentience of my being inwards, down beneath the layers of grief, of agony, of horror, to safeguard in the solace of his memory, the resolution he had come to represent.

I could not risk going near the thought of him as dead. That I had buried him. I could not believe in it. I would not. His became a nebulous presence, a finite absence, an indispensable influence who was simply, physically, somewhere else. Whose connection with me I would not accept as done. And rather than gaze upon the empty blackness of his non-existence, I closed my mind to the loss of him, to the small responsibility I feared I bore for it, and in doing so, I severed my emotional being from my consciousness: smothering it, denying it a life.

From that point on, I did not go near his grave. I began to live by rote. I catered for my physical needs. I concentrated on my daily occupation. I forgot to speak. Fought not to think. And I got by.

Slowly, very slowly, I learned to eat again. The lacerations to my backside began to heal, though the damage I had caused to the muscles there rendered them completely ineffectual and I was plagued by the constancy of rank and trickling secretions.

As each blistering day followed the bleak coldness of the nights, I gained marginally, as did we all, in physical strength. And with the provision of water and with food, we calmed and settled to a new and, in contrast, mentally less demanding existence. And while we did so, the sun's keen and constant pounding beat time into irrelevance. I lost track of it, of the hours, of the passing of the days. We spent them, for the most part, seeking out whatever shade the dunes and rocks afforded. Dozing. Watching the horizon. And the horrors of one night's fetid dreams saturating fretful, shivery sleep were the same as the next. And the next. The perfect arc of Moses' body, etched into the moon; the gentle undulation of a boat with nothing on it save for the gaping skulls of men; and a small, gold compass, glinting momentarily, as it slipped from between the fingers of a large, clenched up hand.

For those first few abstract days of hazy scepticism as to the reality of our relief, the only matter of any consequence was that we now had reliable, if not entirely free-flowing, access to that which we had been so gruesomely denied. Water. For the moment, it was enough. Water. The want of it had taken each one of us by the neck and forced us through the vale of death. And there, the garbs of social conscience, of sanity, of our fragile humanity, like the flesh about our bones, had dropped away. Water. Now, its slow sustaining influence wrought an uneasy restoration, a gradual reawakening to the consciousness each of us had once presented to the world as personality. The inhibitions of social behaviour revived as water crept its way once more across our bodies' fibre, engendering life and energy, relieving the vicious concentrate that had so reduced blood and muscle, mind and heart.

In our new environment, provided with this most fundamental of panaceas, we fought to shut away what we had seen and heard on the boat. What had been said and what had been done. It could be ignored. We began to busy ourselves. There were things we could be doing. But it could not be undone and it could not be forgotten. Though it began to take on an abstract unreality as time quietly gave it distance, each one among us carried the guilt of complicity in the hideous unfolding of the trauma which had so exposed us, and the bearing of none would stand up to close examination. Except, I thought, for Joe. And so we looked upon each other with scaleless eyes and maintained a civil distance.

The all-consuming obsession for water slowly began to fade and though still a luxury in the desert heat, the drinking of it again became an easy habit. Clarie stopped hounding us about taking our rehydration slowly. Some among us were even confident enough now in its existence and our right to it to complain about its quality, for the liquid that the tribesmen poured into our salvaged tins and cups was black and silty, grained with sand. Fraser was petitioned constantly by Clarie and by Billy to ask the tribesmen where the oasis actually was, so that we might go ourselves and skim away a more palatable top water, and when the captain's voice was added to the clamour, he was eventually persuaded to try. Reluctantly and in his laborious tongue, Fraser tried to question our blue-robed intermediary, but the latter's stony face and defensive eyes reflected a suspicious unwillingness to show any understanding.

Consequently, Fraser became more determined to try to reconstruct our water distillery device with the bits and pieces from the boat that had been washed up on the shore. We had found the fuel tank but the length of piping screwed on to it had snapped along the shaft and there was scarcely enough of it left to make a spout. Steam escaped too readily as the cooling mechanism was reduced, and the irregular splashes of water that did drop into the waiting tin proved inconsequential. Besides, we needed an abundance of driftwood to get a good fire blazing and there was little to be found along the wastes of barren beach. What we did collect was all too precious, for the nights brought bitter cold and a meagre fire remained our only source of comfort. And to the further puzzlement of our hosts, we needed it to continue to cook the fish we bartered for, while they looked on, bemused at what they must have considered an unnecessary nicety of custom.

Clarie remained almost equally committed to the idea that we should try to rebuild our boat, or at least some kind of vessel that might get us off the beach and further down the coast, in the hope of finding further signs of civilisation. He enlisted the support of the skipper and of Tomas, and argued with all-comers as to the necessity of not burning up the larger planks of washed up wood from the lifeboat. The younger and more credulous ones among us, Tomas, Wallace, Jack and me, took advantage of the cooler hours at first light and in the evening to help him comb the beach for bits of rigging and lengths of rope and painter that we might use to tie the shafts together. But our explorations were limited by our lassitude and our discoveries therefore few and far between. The frayed and knotted pieces spewed up by the ungracious ocean proved anyway to be of little use.

Hot, and finally frustrated by the lack of suitable material, after many slow and heavy days of tedious trial and error, we were forced to concede that the chances of making any real progress with either project remained proportionately slim. And yet the efforts we expended, almost certainly for Fraser and definitely for me, had been necessary for the preservation of our sanity and the fragile optimism that making land had lent us. We toiled to keep alive the theory that this relatively safe haven was merely another interval, another episodic part in a voyage of misfortune that surely, would eventually conclude in our repatriation. In the short term, we were alive. We were safe. There was water and there was food. There was far worse than this. And yet every day, all the days, the eyes of every man among us restlessly returned, time and time again, to the horizon, scanning, scouring for the slightest sign of hope that we were not, would not be, forgotten. But none came.

For the time being at least, it seemed that our new companions would have to share their home. Their community, which consisted of about eighty men, women and children in total, accepted our presence alongside them with gradually lessening wariness. We gave them all we had in return for our keep and, as we quickly ran out of actual objects to exchange for their enforced hospitality, we offered them instead piecemeal and at first pathetic attempts to help them with their labours.

Their primary concern lay with fishing, and though their methods were apparently unsophisticated, they had what appeared to be a satisfactory rate of success. At each low tide, they staked out their nets to form a set of squares. One side of each square they left incomplete thereby trapping, with the flow and ebb of the following tide, a sizeable quota of their daily catch. The fish were then gutted and liberally salted to be eaten raw or to be stored in salt-lined holes dug deep in to the desert sand, a sand that stretched away endlessly beyond the dunes: an empty, soulless nullity of colourless, lifeless sand.

With the revival of a little strength and eager to show willing in recompense for their stilted generosity, we offered help, worthless as it was, with both the fishing and the digging of the pits. Patient and impassive, they let us try, grinning between themselves a quiet amusement at our unschooled incompetence.

But that they were so determined to catch and store so many fish, much more than was apparently necessary to feed their number, as we became more conscious of it, perplexed us. It did not appear that such an occupation could be seasonal, and their settlement, with its wooden frames and established structures, had an air of semi-permanence. It was not then, that they moved inland and used this place as a base for fresh supplies. Fraser's limited French scarcely lent itself to in-depth questioning and the vast amount of conversation that took place between the members of the two parties had quickly been reduced to a series of implicit grunts, exaggerated facial expressions and often exasperated gesture.

His repeated efforts with '*Pourquoi tant de poissons?*' were met with an eyebrow barely raised and a dismissive shrug. But one night, two, maybe three weeks after our arrival, Fraser, who had been working with the tribe at the nets to gather up their haul, joined the rest of us at our paltry fire with eyes of kindling hope.

'They keep talking about an *enlèvement*. All day. I keep hearing it. *Enlèvement*. I think it means collection. *Des poissons*. I think they fish for someone else.'

'Did you ask 'em? What they meant?' Billy looked up at him sharply.

'Tried,' Fraser shook his head and crouched down to take up one of the sticks we'd laid aside to spike and cook our fish on. 'They speak so quickly. I thought he said something about the French. I couldn't make it out.'

'It would explain why they store most of their catch,' I said, eager to give the information credence. 'Did it sound like they thought it would be soon?'

'I dunno,' Fraser sighed. 'Couldn't tell. But if they're talking about it now, they must be expecting something.'

We watched with a heightened sense of awareness the following day, and the day after that, for the slightest shift in the tribe's general routine, for some hint that they might be expecting change. But nothing seemed unusual and Fraser was just beginning to dismiss the reliability of his understanding when, on the third evening, we were astonished and then exultant to hear, more loudly and more clearly by the minute, the sound of a motor engine chugging close, then closer still until, as we rushed from our various positions, shouting and calling down onto the beach, a large motor launch hove into view, its prow aimed purposefully at our particular stretch of the shore.

As our cries of encouragement turned to hoots of joy, it chuntered on steadily towards us, ploughing resolutely through the breakers and scything up the beach to run to ground finally on the sludgy foreshore. We crowded round her, jubilant and excited, and were joined almost immediately by a slender, dark-haired man of about thirty-five, who leapt down lightly from her deck to stand before us. With his hands upon his hips and wearing an expression of exaggerated puzzlement, his quick, bright eyes darted from one man to the next, growing larger and more incredulous by the second, as he wrestled with the swift gamut of emotions that played out almost comically across his bewildered face. His thick, black eyebrows shot so far and so enthusiastically up towards the top of his head that for a moment, it looked as though they might leave it altogether.

Astonishment at our presence there at all, enquiry as to how and why, horror at our bodies' evident degeneration, and shock at the ragged desperation in our appearance, were quickly overtaken by a frown of resolution, which was soon replaced again, finally, by sheer delight as he realised that he was so obviously the cause of our wild and rapturous celebration. One distinct sentiment after another swept across his boyish features as he struggled to find the words to begin.

'*Guillaume. Je m'appelle Guillaume. Au nom de Dieu, qui êtes-vous?*' Then, with the instinctive understanding that we quickly came to recognise as one of his many qualities, he saw, in a split second, our dismayed incomprehension. 'English? I am Guillaume. What, for God's sake, are you doing here?'

'Where exactly, is here?' Clarie, typically fastidious, wanted to know, but his question was drowned out by the clamour of other voices, rising to be heard.

'Can you get us out?'

'Have you any water with you? Any food?'

'On a lifeboat. We were torpedoed. Three weeks in a fucking lifeboat, two or more on this godforsaken beach.'

'Living on stagnant water and salted fish. Next to nothing before that. Fucking starving.'

'You've got to take us with you. Surely you can get us in.'

'We're the ones who made it,' I said.

Guillaume's attention shot from man to man as he strove to keep up, to glean a basic understanding from the avalanche of foreign words his question had precipitated.

Some particular phrases he caught hold of readily and he repeated them with wide-eyed wonder, shaking his head and throwing up his hands at various intervals. '*Trois semaines? Merde, alors. C'est impossible!*… Food? *Mais oui.* Of course. I have plenty. You must eat, *bien sûr*, you must all eat!… Return with me? Of course, we must try…' As I had been one of the first to reach his boat, I stood quite close to him and so he turned his head towards me at my voice, tilting it on one side and looking carefully into my face. Lowering his voice, he smiled at me very gently. 'There are good friends then, who did not.' He did not require an answer but for the first time since Moley Wells had been abandoned, water suddenly gathered at the corners of my eyes and my vision blurred. I could not speak. Guillaume put an arm around my scrawny shoulders and, directing me towards his boat, he said then, 'You must help me get them down some food.'

Guillaume was not a man to skimp on anything and evidently he prided himself on travelling in style. I stood by the prow of his launch while he handed down to me an extraordinary array of provisions, some verging on the luxurious, but all, to our famished eyes, miraculous. He seemed to have an inordinately plentiful supply: tins of meat, of bread, crackers, biscuits, chocolate and coffee. He even produced a couple of tins of foie gras and then two bottles of red wine.

All the while he darted about the deck, opening and closing cupboards, slapping his forehead and exclaiming in enthusiastic affirmation at the plain necessity of the next discovery, before appearing again suddenly with another packet or tin held cheerfully aloft. Out of deference to his particular kindness, I wrestled with all my will against the frantic urge to abandon my post and join my ravenous companions, whose awaiting hands wrested each piece of manna from me eagerly as I passed one after another back, grappling to hold as much as they could manage before making off, a little further up the beach, to make an exuberant start.

Guillaume sat with us on the sand and talked at us while we ate. He worked for a French canning company in Villa Cisneros, a town in Rio de Oro, three days north of our present location, which turned out to be Cape Tamarisk on the coast of Mauritania. He made regular trips to settlements that were dotted at various intervals down the coast, collecting in the fish, paying the villagers for their labours and providing them with salt for the preservation of their catches until he next returned. He reckoned he could get us all on to the launch and take us back with him. If we could put up with the squeeze during the day, we could sleep ashore by night, and he felt sure that he had food and drink enough to provide for us quite adequately until we got there. Having fully appeased our stomachs now, and so gratefully, we assured him that we had suffered so much worse.

He listened then, appalled and astounded, to Mick and Clarie, who, aided by a series of bald interjections from Mac and toothless lispings from the skipper, recounted the bare facts of our horrific journey. The expressions on Guillaume's face lurched between disbelief and astonishment, from consternation to naked admiration and back again, as his inability to contain the ferocity of his feelings became increasingly evident. His frequent but very genuine exclamations of amazement and alarm were interspersed liberally throughout the telling of the tale. Several times he leapt up onto his feet, staring around at our upturned faces as if hoping to hear, at any moment, one of us refute the truth of it.

They told him of the sinking of the ship, and the ensuing catalogue of disasters we had had to bear: the other lifeboat and the broken mast, the half-empty water tanks, the elusive Canaries. Of how we had managed to make seven gallons of water, at which point he leapt again onto his feet and rushed to shake the hand of a slightly startled Fraser and clap me heartily on the back with such a force that it made my ribcage rattle. He sat again to hear how we had burned the life jackets and half the boat. How we had been lucky with the constancy of good weather and the consequent relative calmness of the sea. They told him of painful, strenuous nightly rowing, of our thirst and of starvation and of our landing here and the unsympathetic nature of our welcome.

But they did not talk of feral, primal fighting, of the gradual disintegration of civilised awareness, of knives at throats and threatened murder. They did not tell of overriding self-concern. Not of hatred, prejudice or greed. Of solicitude resigned nor the abdication of humanity. They did not mention, by name at any rate, Moley Wells and Moses, Murack and Fred Watson. Joe. Their voices and their eyes were once again those belonging to reasonable men and there was little in what they presented to Guillaume to betray that it had ever not been so. Replete, and confident now in our salvation, they talked until our shadows grew long and pointed on the sand and the sun began to ravel in her dusky warmth.

In the morning, Guillaume, who had been outraged to discover that the tribesmen had refused, on our arrival, to give us water and then food unless we could offer something in return, marched into their settlement and in a voice of rousing and incredulous fury, yelled at their assembled group. Some of them slunk off into their tents reluctantly, to return in dribs and drabs, bearing the various sorry items they had taken from us. I picked up Joe's compass, which was thrown on to the sand at Guillaume's feet, along with a few paltry plastic combs, some belts, a couple of canvas bags and the few bits of jewellery we had been forced to part with. His anger was only heightened by their apparently casual impenitence, though the sight of Captain Edwards' false teeth landing in the pile was so unexpected that he could not repress a burst of laughter. The atmosphere immediately lightened and though most of the jewellery was returned to its rightful owners and some of the belts snatched up for immediate service, we left them to the rest of it, if not in recompense for their inconvenience, then to serve as souvenirs.

We spent the day helping Guillaume load the community's fish on to the launch. We ate with him and though he was more than eager to share his food supplies, we agreed that it would be sensible to ration them. His provisions were plentiful and varied, but he had not been expecting to escort fifteen starving men up the coast for the next three days.

That night, knowing that we would be leaving in the morning and without having made any conscious decision to do so, I went to where Joe lay. The rudimentary cross I'd made leant drunkenly on one side and so, tutting and rolling my eyes at him, I put it straight and sat down.

I couldn't think of anything to say. From here, when I looked down along the beach, I could see the rest of the crew sitting around the fire with Guillaume. They were all listening to him in attitudes that I could see even from this distance denoted expectation, and I knew as well as they did that he was telling them some great yarn that would end in great guffaws of laughter. Joe would have thought him marvellous.

I rested my arms loosely around my knees and stopped to listen for a while to the sounds of the shore, which were now so embedded in my consciousness that I no longer noticed them. I listened. I listened to the steady, surging constancy of the waves' approach and the recurrent, drawling answer of their infinite retreat. To the insistent scuffling of some small animal in the cavernous darkness of the dunes behind and to the enormity of silent stillness in the skies above, from where the stars watched all with pitiless impassivity. Soothed, for the first time, by such strange and simple beauty, my mind's restraint gave way momentarily to deeper understanding and I caught a fleeting glimpse of what it meant to live. To have known and to have loved. I would remember.

The flaccid skin along my arms began to pucker in the chill of the night air. I took his compass from my pocket and looked at it in my hand, as I passed my fingers and thumb slowly across it.

Then, making a small well in the sand on the shrunken mound at the foot of the little cross, I put it carefully inside and covered it over, pressing it down with my palm. 'I'll do it when I get home,' I said.

CHAPTER 12

INTENT ON TRUTH

'*Merde! Regardez-les! Ils sont à demi morts. Abaissez les armes!*' Guillaume stood squarely in the middle of the deck, squinting up the harbour wall at the line of Mauritanian soldiers, whose glinting rifles pointed down, moving slowly from one wide-eyed prospective captive to the next. Impatiently, throwing up his hands, Guillaume tutted his disgust. '*Allons-y,*' he muttered, '*Alors,* let's get this over with.'

One by one and shakily, we scrambled up the quayside until we stood pathetically, huddled and trembling in the glorious sunshine, before the guns. No one spoke. The eyes of the soldiers passed silently over our emaciated bodies, our tired and filthy faces, half concealed by wild and matted hair, and the tattered remnants of our clothes. None of us had shoes. And one by one, they let their weapons fall.

Guillaume, apologising vehemently, had had to radio ahead to alert the authorities in Villa Cisneros to the fact that we were with him. To a Frenchman working for the Vichy French, technically, we were the enemy, and whether he wanted to or not, he was duty bound to turn us in. He had hoped, however, that we would be well cared for, and as we were herded into the back of an awaiting truck, I could hear him still, busily firing questions and instructions at the soldiers at its side.

As two of them closed and bolted up the tailgate at the back of the truck, he appeared again beside them, grinning widely. 'They are taking you up to the hospital. For examination and for treatment. You will be all right. I have told them, eh? You will be all right.'

One of the last ones in, I had taken one of the seats nearest to him and Captain Edwards, wincing, leaned across me to offer Guillaume an extended hand, which he took and shook warmly. 'Thank you, Guillaume, for everything you have done.'

'*Euh! Je vous en prie! C'est rien, monsieur,*' he raised his shoulders so that his neck disappeared completely and, holding them there, he shook his head with typically natural deprecation. 'It was the least I could have done.'

As the engine started up, engulfing us all in billows of filthy smoke, he turned to me and reaching into his trouser pocket, produced an unopened packet of cigarettes. Raising one eyebrow and holding them briefly aloft for me to get ready for the catch, he tossed them over the tailgate, aiming for my hands. 'And you, *mon ami affligé,* you will be all right?' he shouted.

I smiled at him and nodded. 'Is there anything I can get to you, when I get back?' I yelled over the revving of the engine, which, due either to the decrepitude of the truck or to the gross incompetence of the driver, was building to a deafening crescendo. He looked thoughtful for a moment and then, as the truck began to lurch away, his face lit up with joy.

'Shakespeare!' he cried. 'One book. All the…' He struggled vainly for the word and failing to find it, threw up his arms and laughed. '*Pièces.* I lost mine. You send me that!' He put both hands high above his head then and waved. I watched his figure receding as we drew off, up the hill through the town and away from the harbour. And he kept on waving until we reached a bend and swung out of sight.

The hospital was, in fact, a small, low, mud hut on the other side of town. We were ushered from the truck by our guards to be greeted by a thin-faced, young French doctor, the only one to work there, whose spectacles, bending wonkily across his face, were held together at the rim by a dirty fold of medical tape. He was sent immediately into a frenzy of activity by our appearance, scurrying about and squawking instructions at a couple of desultory and unruffled native nurses. Edging us fussily towards the eight tightly spaced beds, he rushed around, gathering together a motley and ancient-looking selection of implements, so that he might properly commence his examinations. We sat in twos and threes along the bedsides and waited, as he gazed and prodded and manipulated, considering each one of us carefully and in turn, and accompanying all his deliberations with a series of little hums and hahs of gratified appraisal. Some of us were presumably in better shape than others for, having applied dressings to the most infected open sores and instructed the nurses to dispense quinine to us all, he dispatched one of them to take Clarie and Tomas, Big Sam and four of the others, '*à la maison.*'

'Fraser?' Clarie wavered before he would obey the airy hand that waved him after the retreating nurse.

'House.' Fraser shrugged and then nodding him on, added, 'It'll be OK.'

The doctor shook his head at me and mummed his disapproval, after looking in my mouth. My tongue, he said, in faltering English and holding up three fingers, had split into three parts. Too dry, he told me and though I had felt it strangely unresponsive for weeks, I had not appreciated quite the extent of the damage. 'Cognac,' he said. 'You stay for cognac.' I had no idea why a shot of cognac would be the answer to the problem with my tongue and it ripped across the rawness of my throat until my neck and ears burned red and my eyes stung, but as the doctor pushed me towards a bed in the corner with rusted steads and greying sheets blotted with stains of mottled brown, I sank on to it with heavy relief. A bed, any bed, was infinitely preferable to damp, unyielding wood that chafed and creaked with every movement or to the pervasive chill of dank, intrusive sand.

Mick apparently had the same diagnosis and he too, was instructed to remain, along with the skipper, whose shrunken frame and evident reluctance to move reflected the extreme fragility of his body. The salt water ulcers on his legs and feet had become infected. They were black and swollen and prevented him from walking any distance without obvious striking pain. The others who were allotted beds alongside us had similar complaints or had just appeared to the doctor to be suffering most in terms of physical disintegration.

And so for hours, our restless bodies bucked and twitched on filthy beds in sweltering heat, tormented by the noise and relentless persecution of the thick, black hordes of flies. They kept up a constant, buzzing vigil for any opportunity to intrude upon the sweat-soaked creases on our ravaged carcasses and invade every grimy orifice. The tight, mesh nets the nurses draped about our beds were no obstruction to them, for the dark, mutating swarms swept up and down the room and flies, in their legion, crawled at every crevice, crowded in to feed on every open wound at each redressing, and snatched greedily at the chance to gorge on the goat's meat and rice we were given, even as we sought to get them up into our mouths.

I lay curled upon my side, seeking not to think, my hands pressed between my knees, and my eyes, undirected, followed the dark profusion. The throbbing mass seemed at times to form itself, to my prickling horror, into a series of terrifying shifting shapes, a parade of grotesque images from my recent memory: contorted features on anguished faces, black, cavernous mouths, screaming, screaming, and eyes pinned wide in naked fear. I closed my own, determined that my consciousness should not fragment, but I could no more block out the hypnotic thrumming of the flies than I could the disquiet of my mind.

And yet, despite the primitive and unsanitary conditions, slowly, surely, our bodies at least began to mend. The doctor attended to each one of us conscientiously and the basic medical care he gave us, coupled with better food and unlimited water, breathed life back into our withered husks. And so when our guards returned to herd us all back on to the truck four days later, we saw our own improvements reflected in the brighter-eyed, smooth-lipped exclamations of those who had been taken to the house. Theirs had apparently been a similar experience. They had been cared for by the nurses and, although they had not had the dubious comfort of an iron bed, they were not envious, for their accommodation had apparently been relatively free of flies.

And though we had been left unguarded at the hospital, the return of the soldiers and their guns, coupled with their perfunctory disinclination to answer any of our questions, assured us unnervingly of our status now as prisoners of war. It became all the more apparent when they returned us to the harbour and marshalled us aboard a small French sloop, the *Dumont D'Urville*, bound, we were informed by her cheerful little captain, for Dakar.

'And Dakar would be…?' Mac raised his eyebrows and shrugged his ignorance, looking from the commanding officer on the bridge, who could barely stop himself from bidding us all most welcome in his enthusiastic if imperfect English, to our skipper who stood among us on the well deck. The sun was high and hot, and the harbour walls of Villa Cisneros receding fast behind us.

'It's a port,' Captain Edwards murmured. 'Down the coast from here. In Senegal.'

'I've been there,' said Big Sam, slowly remembering. 'Mebbe six, seven years ago. It's a big port, isn't it? There's a huge old harbour there.'

'Be Jerrys there? Or French?' Jack broke out, loud enough for his apprehension to be evident even to our diminutive host, who started, and then began to beetle his way along the bridge to come down and join us. Jack continued anxiously, 'Will they be waiting for us, d'you think? D'you think they'll send us home? We're civilian, ain't we? Not fighting forces.'

'Send us home?' snorted Billy roughly, folding his arms. 'Put us in some flaming camp, more like.'

'If we're lucky,' Cunningham added wryly.

'Given that this ship was waiting back there to bring us in, I should say that someone will be waiting for us, yes.' Shooting Cunningham a withering glance, Fraser's voice came calm and measured in an effort to give Jack, and perhaps the rest of us, some meagre reassurance, but he could not pretend that he believed our situation to be less serious than he thought. 'But I doubt they'll send us home. We'll be on enemy territory.'

'On my ship, *non!*' The voice of the sloop's captain from within our number startled us. Having approached behind Big Sam and Tomas, he was now squeezing himself between them, for he had quietly made his way, unperceived by most of us due to the modesty of his stature, into the centre of the group. Big Sam could have rested his elbow quite comfortably on his head. 'The Germans, yes, yes. They wait for you in Dakar. I am sure they ask the question, for to listen your... *disastre*. But not to damage. *Non*.' He grinned widely then at Jack, nodding his encouragement.

'What's he on about?' Slim, looking flummoxed, nudged me in the ribs.

'Fuck knows,' hissed Billy, across me. 'But the Jerries are in Dakar, waiting for us.'

'How long will the journey take?' asked Clarie, trying politely to divert the attention of our new and somewhat overeager ally from the disgruntled mumblings.

'Four days we arrive. Until this time, on my ship, we are the friends.' He spread his arms out wide, swivelling his upper body from right to left and back again in an effort to impress on all of us the sincerity of his statement. 'My men give to you the assistance.'

'And lots of food, I hope,' muttered Mac gruffly, purposefully loud enough for everyone to hear.

'Thank you, Captain,' Captain Edwards spoke quickly over him. 'We appreciate it.' And our new patron, nodding and smiling at each one of us as he passed, scuttled back up towards the bridge. There was a short pause as we digested this information and then, sighing, Clarie concluded flatly, 'He meant that the Germans are waiting to question us.'

'Interrogate.' Quietly, almost to himself, Slim corrected him, 'Interrogate's the word.'

'Then what?' asked Jack, the rising alarm plain in the tight constriction of his voice. Again, there was an ominous silence as we all considered the worst that could possibly await us. Swallowing,

I looked down at what was left of my sagging pyjama bottoms. Blanched and worn in places into threadbare non-existence, torn, bedraggled, faded. Fit for nothing. All this way to die. I did not think so.

'Fuck knows.' Billy sniffed once again. 'But we better get our bloody stories straight, make sure we tell it all the same, or there'll be fucking hell to pay.'

'Just tell the bloody truth,' snapped Mick suddenly. He elbowed his way past me and Slim and, stopping in front of the captain and Clarie, he put his hands upon his hips and looked at Billy. 'We don't need a bleedin' story. There's nothing we got to hide. Just tell it like it was.'

'What about the convoy? The cargo?' Clarie asked him, apparently oddly nettled by the idea that anything we had to say would be of minimal importance to the Germans. 'What about trying not to give over any information to the enemy?'

'The Jerries aren't interested in a load of bloody coal. We don't even know what we were gonna be bringing back.' Mick rolled his eyes and turned to address the rest of his frustration directly at the captain. 'They know damn well where and how they sunk us. And any of them other ships of ours will bloody well be almost home again by now. We can't tell 'em anything that'll be much use to 'em. Eh, now, Captain, can we?'

Captain Edwards nodded his agreement slowly. 'Just tell them what they want to know,' he said.

The captain of the *Dumont* was as good as his word, as were his crew. They seemed keen to feed us well, the incentive perhaps their own discomfort at having to look so closely upon the unsightly disfigurement that dehydration and starvation had wrought upon our shrivelled bodies. They were both horrified and impressed by the version of our story, or as much of it as they could glean, from Fraser's patchy attempts at translation and from the undoubtedly quite comical series of gesticulatory re-enactments to which the rest of us could treat them. And though we took comfort from their friendly hospitality, none of us could quite throw off the fearful apprehension that grew steadily more unnerving as we approached Dakar.

Big Sam was right. The harbour there was huge and it was teeming. All the hardcore vessels of the German navy and the French, it seemed, must have been using it as a refuelling and re-fitment base, for wall-to-wall, line on line of basking submarines barred our entry. Their compact order was only broken by the presence of several enormous Q-boats. The glorious morning sun sparkled playfully on the narrow gaps of water, which slapped and bobbed between the dark sleekness of their glistening hulls, its blinding glare bouncing sharply back from the shiny metals of their mounted armoury.

Tethered and tame, as tightly packed as stepping stones from one side of the harbour to the other, and submitting calmly to the ministrations of countless busy crews crawling all over them, they appeared unthreatening, entirely unconnected to the prowling, stealthy author of our destruction and subsequent misery.

'Jesus!' Mick breathed, struck with sudden wonder at the impressive display of German might, and overawed the more so perhaps, having become so unaccustomed to both noise and population. 'Wonder if the bastard who did for us is here.'

'Would you know 'im if you saw 'im?' asked Wallace, and not waiting for an answer, he shook his head and pursing his lips, glowered, 'I wouldn't. More's the pity.'

'Why?' Billy sneered sarcastically, irritated by Wallace's speculative bravado, 'What'd you do if you did? He'd be real scared, wouldn't he? Tremblin' in his boots at the sight of you.' Butler sniggered and turned away, but Wallace, either too agitated by our imminent arrival or only too conscious of the truth of his utter disempowerment, merely shrugged and answered, 'I'd've had a bloody good go at pissing down his fucking conning-tower.'

Our sloop eventually found a berth, forced alongside one of the outer-lying U-boats and, led by the jovial captain and flanked before and after by his crew, we were trooped across the duckboard walkways, which lay across the hulls of the submarines to grant their crews easy access to the harbour walls.

A posse of German soldiers watched our progress from the quay and as we got nearer, to a sharp command, two or three of them raised their rifles. One of the officers stepped forward to greet his French counterpart who, I noticed, did not return the German's starched salute. As we were surrounded to be led away, the *Dumont*'s captain, nodding and smiling still, made a series of little bows to each small group of us that passed him. 'Good chance!' he offered encouragingly. 'I wish you safe return.'

We were taken to an enormous red-brick warehouse by the docks, at one end of which we huddled silently, shivering at its hollow coolness and at the empty echoes of German boots and scraping chairs that resounded from various recessed areas down the length of the cavernous hangar. I became aware as I stood with my arms folded and each hand clenched tightly up beneath my armpits that my feet, still bare and cold on the rough-hewn tiles, were suddenly warmly wet and stinging. I looked down quickly and following the small pool of rapidly spreading water to its origin, found that Jack, beside me, was still completely unaware that his trousers at the front and down one leg were now soaking wet and that he was standing in a pool of his own urine.

I was about to exclaim but caught, in time, the look of frantic fear slashed across his face. Every single muscle from his furrowed forehead to the clenching of his jaw was taut, rigid with a horror-stricken apprehension that set his face into a stiff, uncompromising grimace, a petrified mask that reflected almost physical pain. His eyes, wide and restless, darted uneasily back and forth between the two soldiers who'd been left to guard us, as if convinced at any moment that one of them was bound to shoot. I glanced towards them. Though their guns were still trained in our direction, their eyes, which had had by now plenty of opportunity to gauge the depth of our destitution, conveyed far less aggression than what appeared to me to be more like sympathetic respect. I did not think that we were in the kind of danger Jack was clearly imagining.

Besides, I was in no position to vouch for the reliability of my own body's accurate function since its painstaking and faltering return from the brink of almost total collapse. I could hardly take exception to Jack's involuntary lapse of muscular control induced by such evident, if what I thought might be misguided, terror.

'Jack,' I whispered. 'Jack!' He barely heard me but at my third, fairly loud attempt, he tore his eyes away and glanced at me. 'Mmnn?'

'They're gonna question us. Not kill us.'

'How d'you know?'

'Look at us! We're not armed. We're skeletons. Jesus, I'm wearing bloody pyjamas! We hardly pose a threat. 'Sides, we're civilians.'

'They don't know that.'

'Course they do. They'll know what ship we're from by now. Don't give 'em the satisfaction, eh Jack? Of knowing that you're scared.' I raised an eyebrow and taking him by his scraggy shirt-sleeve, guided him gently forwards so that he stepped away and out of his own water.

I could not explain it. Sometime, since the night I had sat beside Joe's grave in the darkness, knowing that the morning after, we would be leaving with Guillaume, I had ceased somehow to be afraid. I knew now that I would make it. I had to. If not for my own sake, then certainly for Joe's. It could have been that the gradual resuscitation of my body, revived by food and water, had in turn restored my ability to think more rationally. Or it may have been that the irrepressible hopefulness natural to youth never could entirely concede defeat and die. Or perhaps it was just that, without making any conscious admissions, I had opted to protect myself. Fragile, having been unravelled once, I could not again afford the risk of caring so much when I lost all.

Consequently, I had begun to feel a strange, voyeuristic dis-association from my fate, which, inextricably bound up with that of the others, unfolded as I, with almost dispassionate curiosity, looked on. I saw myself less as a participant in our trials than as an impervious witness. It was not that I had ceased to care but that I did not need to. The question of my own survival was no longer pertinent, for sheltering beneath the quiescent shadow of Joe's death and the unwilling promise I had made to his appeal, once again, I had become invulnerable.

And so we waited. The only disturbance to the enormity of silence that began to settle uncomfortably around us lay in the sounds of the busy, bustling quay outside, which came muffled through the wooden heaviness of four or five great, musty, double doors, spaced about fifteen yards apart down the harbour side of the building. Their dark density held back an importunate sunlight that spilled determinedly through every crack and splinter, entreating but denied admittance. Its spangled shafts of yellow light traced perfectly the small rectangles of the high windows onto the floor, banishing from the confines of each flawless imprint the dank and murky shadows. And the dust, caught in their cast, danced and swirled and spun, directionless, on the luminous waver of the air. And still we waited.

Eventually, with the appearance, and subsequent repeated reappearance, of a tall, sallow-faced young officer, we were pointed at and beckoned forward, one by one. In turn, we scurried barefoot after the heavy clipping of his boots across the uneven tiles, almost to the farthest corner of the massive space, where we were finally delivered before one of two tables. Positioned opposite one another but separated by the enormous width of the room, both were set back behind a couple of carefully positioned stacks of wooden crates, and were therefore hidden from the rest of our company. Two officers were seated on the other side of the table to which I was taken and the pair of them were still chatting genially to one another as I came to a standstill a yard or so before them.

After what can only have been a matter of minutes, the older one, a man of about fifty whom I took to be the commander, looked up at me. His heavily greased white hair fell in thick, solid swathes across his forehead, disturbing the wiry profusion of his greying eyebrows and the spectacles that perched before them. Shoving his glasses back up to the bridge of his nose carefully, he took in my tattered appearance with one swift, dismissive glance and then folding his arms, he leant them on the table. The other officer, a younger, thinner man cleared his throat and, shuffling his papers, took up his pen. Eyeing me civilly, he told me to sit down.

'Name please?' he said, after I had done as I was told.

'Cubby Clarke,' I answered without thinking and then immediately corrected myself: 'No, no, I mean, Brian. Brian

Clarke.' And then suddenly, as much to their consternation as to my own, I couldn't stop myself from grinning widely, inadvertently allowing a ridiculous guffaw of unexpected laughter to leave my lips. That I could not even give them a nickname, however unconsciously done, without immediately feeling it necessary to disabuse them, would have amused Joe no end. His crinkly-eyed, sun-baked face had suddenly swum up before my eyes, as he shook his shaggy mane and laughed at me with easy humour. 'Don't ask Cub. He'll tell you,' I heard him say. I could not help but smile.

Again, the commander pushed back his glasses and peered at me more closely. It was quite possible that the one he had before him now, given the circumstances, had lost his mind. There was a short pause as they waited for me to regain my composure and then, as though slightly disconcerted by my strange behaviour and eager to ignore it, the younger officer, sniffing, resumed his questioning. They wanted to know about the old *Sithonia*, our cargo and the convoy. Where we had been bound and where we had been sunk. If I thought they could be expected to believe that we had spent three weeks on a lifeboat without water and, from the coordinates I'd given them, ended up where we had in Africa. And as I answered them, having begun the interview on such an inauspicious note of nervous hilarity, I found myself continually having to fight to hold down at the back of my throat, in my armpits and behind my ears, the alarmingly inappropriate desire to laugh. At the mention of the *Sithonia*, Joe's voice, laden with laughter, echoed 'Snithers' in my ear and when I mentioned South America, all I saw was Clarie glumly handing over cigarettes.

The commander, elbows on the table and fingers playing ceaselessly up by the corners of his spectacles, watched my efforts and increasing discomfort with solemn perplexity. Finally, apparently concluding that my disorder must be due to the extremity of my mental disintegration, he cleared his throat and brought the interview to a close at that. Shaking his head somewhat sorrowfully at his companion, he sent me off to join those among my crew who had already been questioned, and who were now being made to form a line in front of a long, low trestle table set up against the back wall of the warehouse.

On it lay piles of shirts and shorts, each item clearly displaying the six-inch white circle denoting prisoner status. Old army boots, in various sizes and tied together by the laces, were piled up at one end and at the other, towels and toiletries. We were each issued with a couple of shirts, two pairs of shorts, a towel, a razor and a toothbrush and though not ungrateful, it struck me that the latter was fairly superfluous without the accompaniment of toothpaste, and one safety razor each would soon pale into insignificance before the wiry thickness of dirty, tangled hair that ran riot over every face.

The officer dishing out the boots began to chew his lips and rifle through the pile uncertainly when he came to look at my feet, which, big anyway, were still discoloured and swollen with salt-water ulcers. He threw down a pair of size tens into which I duly tried to force the balls of my feet, but I could not get my heels to follow. I tossed them back up onto the pile and told him that I needed a size twelve. Jerking a thumb in the direction of Big Sam, already shod and waiting by the wall, he shrugged down at me, unconcerned, 'Your friend has got the biggest boots. There are none bigger,' he said. 'You take those or nothing.'

'Nothing, then,' I answered, unable to contemplate even the thought of having my ulcerated feet chafed raw to bleed and ooze again, by the hardened, biting leather of a dead man's boots. When the far double doors were finally flung open and we were led out, blinking into the blinding brightness of the midday sunshine, I was the only one who still went barefoot.

CHAPTER 13

BETTER THERE THAN HERE

'Where they taking us?' Jack stopped in his tracks just in front of me, a few feet beyond the doorway and before my eyes could adjust to the biting brilliance of the sudden sunlight, I smelt the air, thick with the heavy fumes of running engines. 'Where are we being taken?' he babbled to no one in particular. 'Where we going now?'

My feet began to seethe at the sudden contrast between the coldness of the tiles in the warehouse and the burning heat of gritty, sun-baked sand. 'It's all right, Jack. Keep your hair on. They've given us clothes… It'll be some kind of camp,' I murmured, nudging past him.

Two trucks had been reversed to within ten yards of the warehouse exit and the German soldiers coming out behind us began to usher us towards their open tailgates.

'I'm not getting in any truck till some fucker tells me where the fuck it is we're going now!' Mac cried, clutching his towel and toothbrush to his chest and casting around defiantly in search of some kind of explanation. His bluster soon evaporated though, when one of the officers to his right lifted his rifle slightly and inclined it gently into the small of Mac's back to move him on.

'Could you tell us where we are being taken?' Clarie asked, appealing to the younger officer who had questioned me.

'Sebikotane,' he replied politely, and Clarie, as though this answer were enough to allay all qualms, nodding and thanking him, pulled himself up into the truck.

As we left the city at what felt like reckless speed, the quality of the roads deteriorated rapidly and to such an extent that soon a slightly raised promontory of rocks strewn with tufts of spiny grasses, running along the centre of a barely visible dusty track, was all there was in terms of demarcation. Rutted and pitted with enormous potholes, these grooves ran seemingly across the vast tracts of surrounding scrubland into nothing, though on reaching their apparent end, the bouncing truck would suddenly swing round again to plunge into a new direction through the next few miles of arid waste. Thickets of spindly bush grew up between the rocks and banks of boulders, and dust flew up in vast, suffocating clouds as our trucks smashed through, disturbing it. Flung from side to side and seeking desperately to clench our thighs against the wooden side seats and gain purchase by pressing our feet hard on to the floor, we choked and coughed as the grit and dust spattered across our faces, slashing at our eyes and forcing stinging entry into our mouths and ears and noses.

We jolted and jerked through disparate gatherings of cattle and of goats, their tinny bells clanking skittish alarm at our approach as they fled to scatter about the scrub, while their herdsmen, hands on staffs, gazed on in groups of twos and threes, and chatted unconcerned. We sprayed up dust at women in brightly coloured robes on the roadside, who waded in slow motion through the heat, carrying their bundled burdens on their heads. We swayed bumpily through villages, catching just the briefest glimpse of barely clad children playing by the dusty, dried-up water holes and their mothers, who sat in the shade at the doorways of their huts, pounding at the bowls in front of them and waving away with languid hands the persistent flies that plagued them. The journey seemed interminable.

And finally, as the shadows of the scanty vegetation began to slim and lengthen, and the molten colours of the evening sun, casting their more sympathetic influence, began to redefine the landscape's stark severity with the softer browns of dusk, the trucks swerved suddenly from the beaten track and began to lumber and spin their way across the scrub towards a small cluster of concrete buildings lying low against the skyline. As we reached them and skidded round the dusty outbuildings, groups of native soldiers, who seemed to be standing about not doing very much at all, turned casually to watch our progress. We swung on regardless through the compound, impeded neither by gate nor surrounding fence, until we came upon a large, dusty, open square where we lurched emphatically to a shuddering halt.

With every bone in my body reverberating and still clutching at my new belongings with both hands, I jumped down from the truck. My knees immediately buckled beneath me and, unable to help myself, I scrabbled forwards, sliding in the dust and almost knocking into the immaculately groomed middle-aged man who had emerged at our arrival from one of the flat, grey buildings that enclosed the square. His uniform, pressed and spotless, gleamed reprovingly as our tattered group descended, shaken and exhausted, to form a filthy, bedraggled huddle just in front of him. His attitude of disdain, compounded by small, beady eyes and a thin beaked nose, added to the overall impression of the neatness of his person. Nevertheless, as I skimmed to a stop almost at his shoulder, I suddenly became aware that here was a man who clearly, if mistakenly, believed that the most effective combatant to body odour was the over-liberal application of talcum powder.

He turned on his heel without a word and stalked over to a small, wooden rostrum about ten yards away. He mounted it and then, nodding impatiently at his sergeant, a much bigger man who had been loitering in a nearby doorway, waited for him to realise that he was expected to come out and herd us in to the kind of order that might denote appropriate attention. At the sergeant's sheepish bidding and with some puzzled prodding from our German escorts, we shambled over to form a half-hearted line and stood, grumbling to one another before his rickety podium.

'Jesus, got a right one, here,' Mick muttered in my ear as the petulant official cleared his throat extravagantly. Obviously relishing the height advantage the two steps up the rostrum lent him, he had placed his hands neatly behind his back and, taking care to position his feet precisely two lengths apart, he now drew himself up, sufficiently prepared for oratory.

'Welcome to Sebikotane,' he began imperiously, as if the square were full.

'To where? That wasn't what the guard said, was it?' I heard Clarie whisper frantically, from somewhere further up the line.

'As you can see, this is not a prison camp. This is an army barracks,' he continued, effortlessly fluent, though the rapidity of his speech and the peculiarity of inflection his native French ascribed it made him difficult to follow.

'I am the Commandant and you will address me accordingly. We have no fences here, no barriers. But you will not escape, for where...' he paused and raised his arm, before sweeping it emphatically at the endless, barren landscape that lay, at every turn, beyond the buildings, '... where would you go?' He allowed himself the luxury of a small, thin smile and then threw both hands up dismissively. 'Pah! You would die like dogs in the desert. Here, you will have food. You will have accommodation. You will work hard. You will cause me not a moment's trouble.' He paused again, this time presumably to give us the chance to appreciate more fully the threat behind his precepts.

'Is this understood?' Clearly, one or two vague murmurings of assent from a reluctant audience were unacceptable, for, instantly enraged by our apathy, his hands sprang to his hips and, eyes wide with sudden fury, he bawled into the dusky silence, 'Is this understood?' It took us two or three lacklustre attempts to respond volubly enough for his satisfaction, before he dismissed us, snapping angrily at his lumpish sergeant, 'Show these men their quarters.'

We shambled slowly off behind the drooping figure of the sergeant, conscious that the Commandant remained stiffly attentive on his little rostrum, staring beadily after us, as if eager to impress upon our scrawny shoulders the understanding that each one of us had been duly and unfavourably noted. Fraser caught me up. 'Jesus, has he been stuck out here too long,' he muttered as he fell into step beside me. 'Mad, and in the middle of bloody nowhere.'

'Well, it's not as if we've not been there before,' I answered grimly, without looking up.

The sergeant, posting two Senegalese soldiers outside the door, left us in a long, low room at the back of the barracks. It was bare, save for a heap of brownish, heavy-looking mattresses that had been thrown into a pile against a wall in one corner, and it took us more than half an hour to lug them down and drag them into spaces on the cold, concrete floor. The one electric light bulb, which hung disconsolately down close by the door, illuminated little but a small circle beneath its pallid glow, so we laboured in the semi-darkness, heaving one mattress after another down and across the floor. A startled yelp from Slim, who had returned to the corner to help Tomas and Big Sam work the eight or ninth mattress down from the pile, stopped us all.

'Fuck! Fuck!' he leapt backwards, dropping the corner of his burden as if it had just stung him. 'Jesus, what the fuck is that?'

Big Sam whipped his hands away from the middle of the mattress. 'What?'

'That! There! There! It's fucking huge!' he pointed, shaking his hand frantically at a dark, shadowy area against the wall. 'It fell out from in between when we pulled this one off.' The rest of us, dropping what we were doing, went over to investigate.

'Where?'

'Wait… there! See 'im?'

'Jesus, you can't bloody miss 'im. What the fuck is that?' gasped Mac. As he spoke, a black form, easily over half a foot in length, suddenly unfurled itself from the cover of the darkness and began to scuttle quickly along the side of the wall. Wider at the front and clawed, its back end narrowed off and, when the creature stopped just as abruptly, its tail flicked round, curling up back over its own body.

'Scorpion,' the skipper frowned. 'Better kill it.'

'Scorpion? They'll kill you, won't they? If they sting you?' Jack flinched.

''S why we better kill it,' the skipper replied evenly.

'Have to stamp on it. There's nothin' else to do it with,' Big Sam said. 'Don't look at me! I'm not going near it,' he added, shaking his head and taking a couple of steps backwards. 'And I'm not sleepin' on the fucking floor either, with them about.'

'Where the fuck else you gonna sleep?' Billy sneered across at him. 'Ain't exactly got much fucking choice.'

We showered the scorpion with boots, though it managed to scrabble its way round to the middle of the next wall before it finally stopped moving. And when Mick thought it safe enough, he went gingerly forward, boot poised in hand, to smash its body into pieces with the heavy heel.

Having arranged our beds, we sat about until the sergeant suddenly reappeared, this time with three soldiers, two of whom wore greasy, splattered aprons and bore between them an enormous pan of wet and slithering macaroni. They dispensed it sloppily into the tins handed out among us by the third and then they left us to it. Macaroni. It was lukewarm and it was slimy but having eaten nothing since we'd breakfasted on the *Dumont* early that morning, it was very welcome.

We lay down eventually, unwilling to sleep for, though weak and therefore still permanently fatigued, it was not only now the prospect of abhorrent dreams that fuelled our reluctance to surrender to the night. The thought of sharing floor space with whatever else might be lurking in the concrete crevices was almost equally horrifying.

In the unnerving, palpable silence of the big, cold room, I lay with my eyes wide open and watched: watched the heavy darkness closing in and watched the livid, shrieking memories of the other men, who lay awake and watched mine. I wondered if it would always be the same. When we got home, when we disbanded and I could live a separate life, a life in which I knew I could not afford for any one of them to figure, would I, would each one of us, as we lay down at night to sleep, be forever bound by the horrors of our collective memory?

Slowly, unexpectedly, sleep began to smooth at the edges of my mind and as I let her soothe, I felt again my body floating, rising and falling at the gentle undulation of the waves and heard the waters' soft welter of disturbance at the slow and rhythmic digging of the oars.

'Cub!' Jack, who had taken the mattress on the floor next to me, slapped my arm and stage whispered me awake. 'Hear that?'

'The water? Joe?' I could barely form the words, fear closing in my throat, smothering them down, as the sickening terror that I had woken in the lifeboat struck and then slowly subsided.

'Wha'? It's me, Jack. D'you hear that scuffing sound? What is it? Like something creeping... close... Jesus Christ!' he shot up, 'something ran over my arm! Turn the light on! Turn the fucking light on!' he screamed.

The door flew open and the guard, who had been posted outside purely for the sake of form, snapped on the light. He had clearly been asleep, for squinting and shading his eyes at the sudden contrast, he stumbled his way down the centre of the room to where Jack, white and wide-eyed, stood in the middle of his mattress, shaking and squawking about a furry animal having leapt on him. The guard tutted and kicked around at the sides of Jack's makeshift bed before grinning slowly. Leaning down, he grasped at and then held up by one of its thick, hairy legs, an enormous, dark coloured spider, easily the size of his own fist. Chuckling softly, he bobbed it cursorily in Jack's direction before turning, with the dangling creature held out in front of him, to make his way back towards the door. He switched off the light as he went out.

The following morning and every subsequent one thereafter, we were escorted by whichever guard it was who had slept the night outside our door back to the square. There, day after day, we queued to breakfast on tepid, viscous macaroni and then, by order of the Commandant, ever pristine and waiting impatiently on his rostrum, were made to stand for the Marseillaise. Invariably, the trumpeter assigned the task of playing it, as the Tricolore rose above the Commandant's quarters, squeaked and blared his way through his rendition while the Commandant cringed and glared at him an increasingly furious disapproval. The Senegalese soldiers served only to infuriate him further by undertaking then to perform an extravagant display of unqualified incompetence in their perfunctory efforts to complete their daily drill. Screaming orders and frustration from his podium, he would berate them wildly, as, out of time and out of step, they marched into and turned back upon each other, succeeding, every single morning, in effecting utter disarray. The Commandant, speechless by this time with apoplectic rage, would signal to his officers who, divesting themselves of any responsibility for the ridiculous charade, would rush in from the sidelines, beating sticks held high, and proceed to thrash the worst offenders to the ground, battering them until their bodies crumpled and slowly stilled.

That first morning, weak and insignificant, I cried out pathetically in protest, prickling in alarm at what was taking place before our eyes, but unsure of what could possibly be done to prevent it. The rest of the crew stood around, appalled into silence, but it did not occur to me to appeal to any man among them for action. I had, albeit unconsciously, ceased long ago to refer to any one of them as a point of reference, for having all too bitterly been exposed to the expendable brand of brotherhood espoused by their majority, I found it only made me cling more desperately to Joe's.

And I realised that I felt not only fear and anguish for the soldier on the floor, but beneath that, a hard, impetuous and resentful rage. Rage at my own impotence. Rage at the hypocritical disgust of my companions, some of whom would readily have delivered such a vicious beating, or worse, upon the lifeboat. Even rage at Joe. Not for the first time, I wondered what he, had he been with me, and given his propensity to rush in for the underdog, would have done. Would he have risked his neck and taken on the Commandant? Would he have tried, no matter how worn and enfeebled, to stay the sticks of the assailants or would he have recognised the futility of interference and suffered with the pain of it? I did not know and I raged at him for leaving me alone and unanswered.

The suspicion that he would have acted, that he could not have stood by and watched such brutal violence and injustice without trying, at least, to deflect it, spurred me on. I started from my line, arms held up to show surrender, but calling out my quavering objection. Startled by the unprecedented interruption and momentarily distracted, the officers stopped abruptly and turned to look at me, their sticks held high behind their heads, hesitant. I came to a standstill, ten feet away, afraid. And to my complete astonishment, the soldier on the floor who I was certain was surely severely wounded, if not dead already, took advantage of the sudden hiatus and, leaping to his feet, ran quickly off to join his company. Their noisy cheers and laughter at his return, as they clapped him cheerfully on the back, resounded round the square. Aware that his narrow eyes were now upon me, I looked across at the Commandant. His arms were folded and the gleaming buttons on his perfect uniform winked as he leaned forward. 'You are a fool. You do not understand these things,' he spat. 'None of you will eat today.'

It soon became apparent that the beatings, and the manifest indifference of the soldiers to them, were, in fact, a daily ritual. I need not have, after all, had to endure the cold-eyed, bitter scorn of most of my companions for having deprived them of their food and the resentment that in some cases did not wane for several days.

I did not care. I had decided how it was that I was meant to live. I had once been taken to the brink of death with a man whose generosity was natural, who had tried, in the worst extremities of experience, against all odds, to keep his faith in sympathy and in kindness and who had, in eschewing the hatred and selfishness borne out of fear, shown me what it was to try to live with grace. How could I not even try? I had at least been given the chance. He had not. What would Joe have done? There have been so many times in my life since then when I have thought it. And so often it has made me act, bringing out in me the better man.

We were put to work clearing scrub. Every day, beneath the unflinching desert sun, a couple of disinterested guards accompanied us beyond the buildings, to any point in the vicinity they cared to sit, and there, they watched us toil against the undergrowth, slicing our hands, and in my case, feet, on the spiny weeds and grasses. It was a pointless exercise designed purely to keep us occupied, for the incorrigible bush reinvaded almost as soon as we had cleared it. Besides, the following day, we would be taken out to begin again in an entirely different place.

The monotony of our labours was relieved from time to time with the discovery of one in any number of a wide variety of massive snakes, which slithered suddenly out from beneath the undergrowth. Startled cries of alarm from whichever poor unfortunate had inadvertently disturbed its rest would compel even the slow blinking guards to action and, getting up wearily to investigate, more often than not they would conclude that the snake was dangerous, and so proceed to batter it to death with the butt end of their guns.

If nothing else, our limited excursions into the wilderness, the vast endlessness of which reduced the compound to a tiny blot of insignificance on the landscape, convinced us of the truth in the Commandant's assertion that escape was hardly possible. Standing up straight to crick our aching backs and wipe away persistent sweat, we gazed into the distance, in all directions, at mile on mile of savage wasteland, dry and hard and unforgiving. Any attempt to slip away would surely result in a slow, burning death somewhere out there in sun-baked scrub, while the prospect of voluntary return or recapture brought with it images of beatings equal to those we witnessed almost every morning. Our bodies, emaciated and already broken, could not long have borne either.

The difference between one interminable day and the next, from each yawning week to the one that followed as they rolled unvaryingly towards a month, then nearly two, might not have been discernible had it not been for the arrival, one morning, of a Mr Latimer from the American Consulate in Dakar. It was heralded by the appearance of a boiled egg, with the macaroni, in our breakfast tins. The Commandant was apparently eager to show his American visitor that the prisoners in his camp were being well treated, and though Latimer's presence was clearly inconvenient, the Commandant seemed keen to demonstrate his prowess as officer in charge.

The long-suffering Mr Latimer stood politely by the Commandant's podium and watched the Senegalese perform their morning pantomime while the Commandant, in his turn, refrained from displaying quite his usual range of furious agitation. The beatings were dispensed with that particular morning.

Afterwards, Latimer made his way across the dusty square to greet us, arms out wide and face positively glowing not just with curiosity, but more patently, with frank and cheerful admiration. The Commandant stuck by his shoulder, nipping along neatly beside the American's generous strides.

'Well, you boys've certainly been through the wringer! Jeez, you look like a bunch of skeletons! Betcha thought for a while there that you'd never make it.' He stuck out one hand well before he'd reached us. 'Harold J Latimer. Clerk to the American Consul. Based at the British Residence in Dakar.'

He grabbed Big Sam's hand, taking it between both of his and pumped it up and down enthusiastically. 'Good to see you, good to see you.' By the time he'd shaken hands with every one of us, the Commandant was already beginning to huff and stamp his heels impatiently.

'Got word through you'd been sent up here. Doin' what we can to look out for British prisoners who get picked up and dumped in camps from Dakar. Heard about your lifeboat landing. One helluva lucky break, I'd say.'

'I'd've said it was a lot of things,' Fraser muttered grimly, 'but lucky wouldn't've been one of 'em.'

'Ah, I'd say it was lucky,' said Latimer, glancing quickly across at him, before suddenly squatting down in the dust and opening up his briefcase. 'If you'd've hit the coast a mile or two further up or down, might not have come across anyone. Nothing but desert for miles that stretch of coast.' His eyes flicked from Fraser to the skipper, before coming to rest on me as he added wryly, 'And by the look of you, you wouldn't've lasted long.'

He began to rummage within his case, finally coming up with a wad of papers and half a dozen pens. Bobbing up again, he thrust them all into the skipper's hands. 'I've come to take your names, details… get word home that you're alive. Brought you pens and paper so you all could write. I'll take your mail back with me. Get it to them.'

'Why ain't it a British Consul then, lookin' after the British here?' Billy asked him, moving in to take paper from the captain.

'Mmm… ahh. Hasn't been one down here for a couple of years now. We're all the eyes and ears you guys have got down here. Still, mayn't be for long. Hopin' Boisson'll maybe change his tune when the Allies reach North Africa.'

'Who?'

'Boisson. Governor General of French West Africa. If he'd come over to de Gaulle, shouldn't be too long before they start sendin' all you fellas on home.'

'All?' queried Clarie.

'Must have about four hundred of you guys on record now. Most are picked up in the ocean by the French. Put in camps all over.' Latimer shrugged. 'Like I said, we're doin' what we can.'

'Mr Latimer.' The Commandant, clearly irritated by his exclusion, suddenly rapped his guest officiously on the shoulder. 'We have business to attend to. Time is getting on.' He tapped at his watch lightly and then put out an open palm to indicate the way back towards his office. The easy smile faded from Latimer's eyes.

'If you don't mind, Commandant, I'd like to take some time to talk with these boys, ah, alone. Find out how they're doing. Might not feel so free to talk while you're… you understand? You go on. I'll be along in just a couple of minutes. Just need their names, a few details… so we can inform their families. Let them know just how're they're getting along, that they're being treated well, that sort of thing. You won't mind?' The reassuring complicity of his tone suggested to the Commandant that both of them were reasonable and moderate men, and seemed halfway to persuading him that there could be no possible harm in the request.

'I am sure you have so many things to do. You must be a very busy man. You go on. I'll be fine.' Having wavered, the Commandant was instantly won over by the American's flagrant flattery. Nodding a taciturn assent, more in agreement perhaps with the reference to his assiduity than with Latimer's appeal, he turned on his heel and headed back across the square.

Latimer watched him go and then turned back to us. 'So. You guys look pretty rough. You been here what? A month already?'

'Thereabouts. You think we're looking bad just now. You should've seen us when we landed up the coast,' Mick told him. 'Least we got water here. And food.'

'I was gonna ask you that. You boys doin' all right? For food?' His hand hovered, perhaps for unconscious reassurance, about his own fairly ample girth. 'They lookin' after you?'

'All right if you don't mind macaroni every single meal. And sleeping with scorpions and spiders. We're not so bad.'

'Not so bad! Jesus Christ!' Mac shook his head and spat into the dust.

'So, anyway,' Mr Latimer continued, ignoring him, 'the word is, you boys are being moved up country. To Timbuktu. There's a POW camp up there. Quite a big one. Thing is...' he leaned down and, turning his back quite deliberately on the direction of the Commandant's office, picked up his briefcase. He snapped it open once again, but this time half pulled out a large, green, folded piece of paper, far enough so that we all could see quite clearly what was on it.

'Train you're goin' on, it's pretty slow up the hills. If someone were to know the area, and had a mind to it, train's slow enough to jump off in places. If a guy were to have a map, got some provisions ready, well, it might be quite an easy thing to do.' He looked at the captain and then at Mick meaningfully. 'Escape, I mean.'

He cleared his throat and then putting the briefcase back down on the ground, left it open with the folded map still protruding. He began to walk backwards away from us.

'You write them letters now, for home. I'll take 'em with me. Be here till after lunch. Now, I expect the Commandant is waiting.' He turned abruptly then and strode quickly back across the square.

We studied the map carefully that evening when the guard had left us. Mick had shoved it up beneath his shirt and Latimer, having rejoined us in the square for an unprecedented lunch of goat's meat and macaroni, had taken back his briefcase and, winking, wished us luck. He had marked the map in various places on the railway line up country, highlighting obvious areas where the inclines were the steepest and which therefore provided the greatest opportunity for escape.

'We can't all go,' Mick said, glancing up across the map at Fraser. He had laid it on the floor directly beneath the cheerless cone of light cast by the meagre bulb in our room and as the captain, he and Clarie knelt to pore over it, the rest of us stood about, unable to see and restless, waiting for their verdict. 'We'll have to decide who's got a real chance of making it. Who's fit for it. Won't be easy.'

'He'll have to go,' Clarie jerked his head up in Fraser's direction. 'He's the only one who can speak any French.'

'I can try it,' Fraser said, putting a hand up to his chin and rubbing thoughtfully. 'With a couple of others. Big Sam? You strong enough? You and Wallace fit in well enough out here.'

'Yeah, I'll go,' replied Big Sam slowly, nodding a relatively cautious assent, though Wallace threw up his hands, shooting Fraser a look that twitched with blatant fear. 'I'm not jumpin' off a bloody train. No fucking way. Get caught, you bloody well get shot. You try it if you want to but count me bloody out.'

'I'll go,' I said. All eyes in the room swung round to me. I meant it. An escape attempt might well be dangerous, and given our physical condition and the uncompromising nature of the desert, even foolhardy. But the chance to take some action, to reassert my own sense of control, however insignificant, on the outcome of my fate, was one I had learned through pained experience should not be passed up. The reluctance to countenance change, no matter how risky the attendant consequences might seem, simply to avoid having to make a choice, felt somehow acquiescent. On the lifeboat, to have lain down and waited for the passing of ineluctable time to provide some let-out, would, as it had turned out, have proved fatal. In insisting on throwing out the engine, in carving up the boat, Fraser, Joe and I had fought against the acceptance of inevitable circumstance. We had chosen action and I had learnt then, when I had taken momentary pride in Joe's admiration for my part in it, the hard-won self-respect that comes of being strong enough to act.

But to my surprise and annoyance, Fraser shook his head. 'You're not fit for it, Cub. Look at you. You've hardly put on weight. You don't sleep well. Besides,' he offered as consolation, 'we'll need some people on the train to distract the guards while we make the break.' Though I was standing in the dim periphery of the light, he must have seen the frustration flush across my face for he cut me off quickly as I opened my mouth to protest and, depriving me of the chance to argue further, turned to Tomas and enlisted him, along with Slim, on the grounds of their willingness and more obvious physical rehabilitation. Later, when I approached to tax him again in private, he waved me off, saying quietly, 'I know that you are brave, Cub, but you know that I am right.'

In preparation, we began to steal the tin water bottles the soldiers left on the ground after morning parade, and to pick up the odd pieces of useful clothing they left lying about the compound. Being so loosely guarded, we took turns to keep watch as Big Sam, who had been transferred to work in the kitchens after the Commandant had discovered his trade, passed out rice and tins of meat he purloined from the stores. We stored our ill-gotten gains in a pit in the undergrowth at the back of our dormitory and settled down to bide the time until the orders came through for us to go up country.

The blank monotony of the endless hours, which gradually effaced the passing of the days, was interrupted late one hot and heavy afternoon when a cry from our guard startled us up from our struggles against the scratchy undergrowth. He pointed across the vast, browning listlessness of the landscape at a cloud of dust travelling quickly through the scrub. As Latimer had been the only visitor we had seen at any time in the camp during our confinement, we presumed that he was now returning, possibly with some news from home. Ignoring the cries of protest from the guard, we dropped what we were doing and rushed with rising hope towards the square. We arrived in time to see a truck swing in and shudder to an abrupt halt, as ours had done only a couple of months before.

Six RAF men, looking dazed and shaken, dropped down from the back of it into the dust, and the Commandant, after treating them to the same address as he had given us, called Captain Edwards over to entrust him with the responsibility for their conduct. They'd ditched their Catalina somewhere off the coast near Dakar and had been picked up three days ago. They were to room with us, work with us, attend breakfast and parade with us. They would not be with us long. They would be transferred to the camp at Timbuktu within the next few days but while they were in his compound, Captain Edwards would please see to it, they would cause the Commandant not a moment's trouble.

That night, beneath the dingy glow of our solitary bulb, we pulled out Latimer's map from beneath the skipper's mattress, to show them how we'd planned escape and told them of the cache of stolen rations we'd hidden away for our chosen four.

'We're still waiting for the order to move us up country,' Mick finished restlessly, pacing about in front of them. 'Been waiting near a month. Even Latimer couldn't tell us when.'

'So who's going?' their Flight Lieutenant asked, casting a doubtful eye over the motley crew of thin and ravaged figures, who stood about, shrouded in the dim half-light of the shadows.

'I am,' Fraser said, stepping forward. 'Big Sam. Tomas, over there. Slim.' The others nodded their commitment as Fraser pointed each one out, but the Flight Lieutenant, a young, muscular-looking man named Taylor, had already begun to shake his head.

'It's madness! You know it is,' he said, staring incredulously from one straining, hollowed face to the next. He got up from the mattress where he'd been sitting and moved confidently to stand directly beneath the light bulb and, with one hand on his hip and the other held out in conciliatory appeal, he proceeded to point out the most obvious flaws in our carefully constructed plan. 'With all due respect, none of you look as though you wouldn't break in two with the jump, never mind the days of hard travel, rationing, hiding out in the desert. You just don't really look as if you're strong enough. Any of you.' When no one made to contradict him, he tutted into the silence, 'Well, to be honest, are you?'

'We've not been doin' so bad,' Big Sam mumbled down into his chest.

'But not really doing so bad isn't really good enough for the kind of journey you're proposing. Do any of you even speak a bit of French?'

'Fraser does,' Clarie put in defensively.

'Only a little,' admitted Fraser, looking wryly in the Lieutenant's direction. He put his hand up to the back of his neck as I'd seen him do, in uncertainty, so many times before and shifted uncomfortably on his feet.

Taylor, apparently satisfied, turned to Captain Edwards. 'Look. The way I see it, we were picked up three days ago. We've eaten well, been looked after. We're fit. Wilson there, and Gilbert,' he waved a hand vaguely at two of his men who sat with their companions along one side of the hitherto superfluous pile of mattresses left in the corner, 'both of them speak fluent French. We're going up to Timbuktu within the next few days. Let us take the map. Your supplies. We've got a much better chance, surely, than any of you, of making it.'

'Purh! Fucking cheek!' Billy muttered. He had been sitting cross-legged with his back against the wall, listening to the persuasive tones of Taylor with increasingly belligerent mistrust and as he exclaimed, furious now, at this last suggestion, he leaned forward, shaking his head in scoffing disbelief.

'But we've been planning it for weeks. Stealing. Risking our necks,' Mick cried. 'You can't just come on in here and take our plan. Our boys think as they can do it, don't you, lads?'

'Steady, Mick, steady on,' the skipper said. 'He has a point. They're in good shape.' He nodded towards the aircrew in the corner. 'Our boys are still so thin. Might very well never get through the desert, shape they're in. And we don't even know yet when we might be sent up country, if we're sent at all. We know these fellas are going within the next few days.'

'After all,' Taylor said, smiling, 'we're on the same side, aren't we? Mick, is it?' He moved suddenly in Mick's direction and held out his hand for Mick to shake. 'Doesn't matter who causes the Jerries strife, does it, so long as someone does?'

Cornered by Taylor's courtesy, Mick wavered. 'Well, I suppose not. When you put it like that... Fraser?'

'I think we should give them what we've got,' Fraser said, looking, I thought, quietly relieved.

Taylor and his men left two days later with the map and the prized provisions we had so painstakingly collected, concealed about their bodies. And three weeks after that, the Commandant ordered us at morning parade to return to our dormitory and collect up our belongings. The orders we had been waiting for had finally come through and we were to be taken by truck to the railway station to be transferred to Timbuktu.

Timbuktu. Reputedly, the end of the earth. The nebulous never land that existed just beyond the realms of reality. One place too far. I remembered what Joe had once laughed up at Mick who'd yelled at Tomas for failing to keep the lifeboat's course, bellowing that he'd have us all in bloody Timbuktu if Joe did not get up to guide him with the compass.

'Better there than here,' Joe'd laughed. I hoped that he was right.

CHAPTER 14

LAST PLACE ON EARTH

It took three days. Cramped up, side by side, along the hard, wooden slats running across the dusty, bare compartment, we squirmed against the heat and harsh discomfort, for space. Our skinny backs and buttocks ached and numbed as the train straggled a weary, ragged course up through the barren countryside, which lay endlessly bland and brown and featureless on every side. Our bones, unprotected by any flesh, flinched and rattled with every jolt, as the wood-fed engine creaked and crawled along the unequal camber, unhurried, pushing slowly, relentlessly, on beneath the stark inflexibility of the sun.

And as we reached the various hills that Latimer had marked for us so carefully on his map, we saw that he had been right. The engine laboured up the inclines, slowing to such a speed, that, had we been permitted, we could have walked alongside it without losing any ground. As it was, with one guard lounging listlessly at either exit, we fought with one another to get closer to the slits of open window, praying for a downhill slope that might bring speed enough to pass through a momentary blast of hot and heavy air and afford our sweat-streaked faces some small breath of comfort.

'Wonder if they made it,' Billy yelled back suddenly, raising his voice to be heard over the constant rickety racket of the train in motion, but in doing so, fracturing the isolation of somnolent silence that the rest of us had unconsciously embraced. At one time or another over the long and changeless hours, his thought must have occurred to every one of us. He turned his head away from the window out of which at that moment he could almost have counted the separate blades of spiny grass in every clump we passed. Mac stood up and yawning, tried to stretch.

'Mmnn?'

'Bastard Taylor and his frigging aircrew.'

'Must've. Be bloody easy here.'

'Fuck it, Mac. Watch what you're doin',' Clarie started up, wildly irritated in the sweltering confinement by Mac's flailing arms. 'Where'd you think they'll be, then, by now?'

'Hopefully on some boat. Out of Dakar maybe. Lucky sods,' Mick muttered. 'Should never've let them have our stuff. Fraser? Reckon you could've made it easy here, couldn't you?'

'Don't look too inviting, though. Desert goes on for frigging miles. 'S hard out there,' Big Sam said, almost to himself.

Fraser, leaning his head back against the wall, did not open his eyes to answer. 'Let's hope they've bloody made it and aren't sitting out there, lost, dying of dehydration in the heat. Wouldn't've wanted much to try that twice.'

We slept where we sat, giving over to exhaustion, only to be jerked awake again by the brunt of every stilted lurch and shudder of the train, as, struggling, it fought to make a halting progress across the rough terrain. However, the uncomfortable monotony and the heat-inflicted aggravations of the journey were at least made more bearable by the regular stops that we were granted to be fed. At designated stations, we fell out of the train onto the platforms to be greeted by hoards of clamorous locals who rushed around us, thrusting at us spicy-smelling couscous, fried bananas and baked peanuts in the hope that we would buy them. Having no money, we were herded past them along the platform to some table, where a couple of weary-looking soldiers would slop a spoonful or two of rice into a tin and let us have some water.

The station at Timbuktu, when we finally reached it, was no different. It was bustling with business, though we were quickly hustled through the crowds of importunate and persistent sellers to waiting trucks. We managed just the briefest glimpse of a low and rambling town, where light stone buildings crumbled in the heat and where roofs of corrugated iron glinted, dazzling back its brightness to the sun. They whisked us through it and out into the desert beyond, our destination a much larger camp made up of row on row of concrete buildings, surrounded by a rusty-looking fence, which lay half a mile or so from the town.

Stiff and aching, we shambled down from the trucks and were immediately accosted by a gaunt, weasel-faced officer who barked at us in French a command, as far as we could tell, to follow. He led us along a labyrinth of dusty pathways before ushering us impatiently into a small, grey structure, not much bigger than a hut, which turned out to be the Commandant's office.

Barely glancing up from his desk as we crammed ourselves into the space before it, the Commandant, a heavily moustached Frenchman, asked for our captain to step forward. He tried it first in French and finding that not one among us moved, he looked up properly and repeated his request in a slow but perfect English. Wetting his pencil with his tongue and addressing Captain Edwards only, he proceeded to take down all our names and that of the *Sithonia*, laboriously writing each one down and appealing to the skipper from time to time for clarification with regard to spelling. This done, apparently to his satisfaction, he folded his hands together slowly and, placing them on the paper that lay before him, he tipped backwards slightly on his chair. He was a man of about my father's age, silver-haired and broad-bodied, but it was his eyes that attracted my attention as soon as he sat back. Set wide apart due to the broad nature of his brow, their grey lucidity reflected a prepossessing intelligence, a bright curiosity that somehow implied both sensitivity and candour.

As I watched, he took time to let them wander over the limbs and faces of the dishevelled group of skeletal figures who vaguely swayed in front of him, and as the appalling nature of our condition gradually dawned upon him, his face darkened, furrowing with what appeared to be sincere and grievous sorrow. Finally, looking back up at the captain, he cleared his throat.

'Captain Edwards. I hope that you will not be here for long. I am confident that our Governor General, and I hope, the administration of all French West Africa, will soon see sense and join the Allies. I will then be pleased to inform you of the orders for your release.' He paused, long enough to watch the loosening effect these words had on our strained and tightly watchful faces. 'Until that time, I am afraid that you are prisoners here and I want you to understand, I am very sorry for it.' Shaking his head slowly, he let out a sigh of heavy resignation and dropped his gaze for a moment to his hands and to the sheet of paper that bore our names beneath them.

He then snapped up to his feet so quickly that his chair screaked sharply across the floor, making me flinch. He began to bellow in rapid French at the weasel-faced officer who had brought us in and who had, up until this point, been lolling carelessly against the door frame.

At his superior's sudden change of tone, the weasel started quickly to attention, and nodding abruptly several times at what I assumed were a series of specific commands regarding our incarceration, he opened the door and, jerking his head irritably at Fraser who stood nearest to him, began to lead us out.

As I was one of the last to turn and leave the office, the Commandant got the chance to look at me more closely and as a result, when I reached the door, he let out a cry of furious exasperation. Pointing angrily at my shoeless feet, he suddenly roared from behind me at his officer who was by now ten yards in front, '*Et allez chercher des souliers pour ce gars: il va pieds nus!*'

The weasel marched resentfully in front of us to the far side of the camp, to the stores where an ageing native soldier, oblivious to his officer's scowls, took his time in fetching each of us a blanket and a towel. As he handed the carefully folded items over, his thin, high voice piped time and time again, what he must have been taught by some English-speaking joker was some kind of mantra of encouragement. 'Welcome to Timbuktu,' he chirped, nodding cheerily and grinning wide his toothless gums, 'last place on earth.'

The weasel, scarcely able to contain his impatience at the man's slow, deliberate pace, hurried us away, striding ahead as we bunched dilatorily behind him, a further aggravation that jerked him to a standstill every twenty yards or so to roll his eyes with exaggerated irritation. Our accommodation, it seemed, was in another far distant corner of the camp and, sore-bodied, still suffering from the effects of three solid days crammed together on the train, we struggled reluctantly behind him, wilting with the effort in the unremitting heat.

Eventually, he stopped and flung the door open on an enormous, long, grey hut whose tiny windows were little more than air vents spaced at regular intervals just below the roof line. Inside, as our eyes gradually grew accustomed to the murky darkness of the cavernous interior, we discovered line on line of metal beds, so tightly packed together that there seemed scarcely space enough for a man to stand by his own bedside. At the far end of the room, beyond the beds, there were several wooden tables and around them, clearly having lunch, crowded a noisy gathering of men. All of them were dressed as we were and all, it turned out, were the survivors of other torpedoed ships and prisoners from the armed forces who had been taken in the area.

Having shown us to our beds, the weasel, waving a dismissive arm in the direction of the queue for macaroni, left us to it and so, dumping our belongings, ever hungry, we made our way up to the top end of the room. As we approached, Billy, with a sudden cry, pointed to a small cluster of men already eating at one of the tables we had to pass to join the back end of the line.

'Well, well, well.' He stopped in front of them and, smirking complacently, folded his arms. 'Would you look at just who we got here. If it ain't Flight Lieutenant Taylor and his troop of merry men!'

Hearing his name, Taylor looked up quickly from his tin, his fork poised midway to his mouth and, recognising Billy and then the skipper, he put it down again and stood up. Smiling sheepishly, he paused and then started round the table to offer Captain Edwards his outstretched hand.

'You didn't make it then?' the skipper said, taking the hand and shaking it.

'Didn't really get the chance,' Taylor admitted flatly. 'Opportunity never came. Too heavily guarded most of the time.' He put his hands upon his hips and shook his head. 'Sorry,' he shrugged ruefully.

'Too heavily guarded?' Billy snorted, looking towards Mac and Cunningham in front of him for sly support. 'Call two sleepy Senegalese at either end of the carriage heavily guarded? Hey, Mick... Mick! For once, you got it right. Should never've let 'em have the friggin' map for all the use they bloody made of it.'

'Three guards we had,' Taylor eyed him coolly, 'and there's only six of us. Seems they guard prisoners from the armed forces a bit more closely. You are civilians, after all.' Disarmed by the deliberate moderation in Taylor's voice but suspecting him of that insolent brand of superiority with which some servicemen occasionally regard others, Billy's eyes narrowed and he dropped his contemptuous smile.

'So where's our stuff? All that stuff that we collected?'

Taylor addressed his answer to Captain Edwards. 'Shared it out. Thought it best. Fifty-one of us eat and sleep in here – all of us, always bloody hungry.'

'Sixty-six of us now,' said Fraser dryly, as he put a hand up to the captain's arm to guide him on towards the lunch queue. Billy was still muttering about how there were hardly any guards in here now and how it couldn't have been that bloody difficult, train went so slow, to have even tried to make a break for it, when I left him at the serving table and went off gratefully to try to find a seat.

Taylor's explanation for failing to attempt escape did lose some credibility in light of the fact that, as far as we could see, we were all to be fairly loosely guarded from the outset. The camp was huge and several other accommodation blocks, almost as big as ours, were already full. The French guards, few in number, and their West African counterparts, seemed overstretched and as incapable as the rest of us of shaking off the shiftlessness induced by the aggravating temperatures. They were plagued by the same torments as their prisoners: boredom, broiling heat, and the all-consuming constancy of pernicious hunger. Consequently, they shirked their duties where they could and troubled to monitor our movements scarcely at all if they were able to avoid it.

For the sake of form, they kept us to a perfunctory schedule. Two of them arrived in our hut with one of the cooks and the pans of macaroni at dawn, and after breakfast, they would accompany us listlessly along the half-mile trail down to the primitive and very public shower block. Without ever bothering to count us either in or out, they would take us then beyond the fence where, seeking out some sliver of shade, they sat back to rest, while we stood about, enervated by the brash morning sun and vaguely poking at the undergrowth, waiting. Waiting. Waiting for the call to come for lunch so that we could return, exhausted, to the cool and darkness of our hut for macaroni and brief but coveted respite.

The afternoon hours, which mirrored almost exactly those of the morning, crawled by as agonisingly slowly, and as those hours stole into days and the days crept towards becoming weeks, it began to seem impossible that the time would ever end.

One morning, though, having been called up as usual for our ablutions and been among the crowd who started out, I realised within a hundred yards that I had forgotten my towel, and so I returned to the dormitory to get it. Having picked it up, I reached the door to set off again, only to find Mick and Tomas with Big Sam and the third mate of the *Oronsay* outside, fighting over one another to get back in.

'Hey, Cub, just stand out here for a minute for us, will you?' Mick hissed, grabbing me by the arm and pulling me back as I made to pass them. 'Shout if you see anyone coming.'

The four of them disappeared into the dormitory, shoving each other and snorting to suppress their laughter. Uncertain of quite what to do but unwilling to lay them open to getting caught in whatever clearly illicit activity they were engaged, I hung about indecisively, scuffing at the small stones in the dust and finally opting to lean back against the wall with as much nonchalance as I could muster. No one came and eventually Mick's head appeared around the side of the door, which he seemed to be struggling to hold open with the back of his left shoulder. He glanced at me and then checking furtively right and left, shoved the door more fully open.

'Here, Cub, cop hold of these, would you?' He thrust a pile of folded blankets into my arms before disappearing momentarily to come out again with the other three all similarly encumbered.

'C'mon!' he grinned in explanation, jerking his head to beckon me after them as Big Sam, followed by the other two, began to creep his way along the side wall of the building. 'We're gonna sell 'em!'

'You can't sell these,' I cried, a bit too loudly, for all four of them turned to shush me fiercely. 'They'll have your bloody guts for garters!' I said, lowering my voice.

'They'll never know,' Mick replied, pressing himself up against the wall and pausing to look back at me. 'Or at least not before it's too late to stop us.'

'Of course they'll bloody know. Be bleedin' obvious there's blankets missing as soon as they inspect the dorm.'

'Nah. We cut 'em exactly in two halves. Laid the other half back on all the beds we took 'em off. You'd never know, looking at 'em.'

'They'll know tonight when it's bloody cold.'

We'd reached the end of the wall and bunching up again, the four of them crouched down and over one another to scan the open space between ours and the next row of accommodation blocks. Tomas nodded and the third mate of the *Oronsay*, a bloke called Jed who Mick apparently knew from home, suddenly bolted, sprinting wildly across the open alley to fling himself down by the side of the next long, low building twenty yards away. We all held our breath as we watched, dreading, half expecting to hear at any moment a barked command to stop. Despite myself, my heart began to pound within my chest as the thrill of the escapade took hold.

'C'mon, Cub,' Mick coaxed. 'We're gonna sell 'em and then we're gonna go and eat! Think of it. Real meat, bread, wine. Pastry mebbe. There's no harm in it. And anyway, you gotta come with us now,' he whispered finally, putting an end to my objections by raising an errant eyebrow at me as he prepared to make the dash himself, ''cause I cut up the blanket on your bed too.' And with that, he shot away.

Old and badly maintained, the six-foot fence around the compound was an ineffectual deterrent. Many of the rusted, sun-worn stakes that held it up had buckled, creasing up the browned and brittle mesh between them, so that it was possible in some places to walk it down, crushing it with minimum effort onto the ground. Jed had already discovered a discreet and crooked stretch behind the guard's ablution block that proved easy to trample underfoot, and from there, the town, it turned out, was less than half a mile away.

We crept towards it, sliding in between the low, stone buildings, keeping to the crumbling walls and corrugated doorways, and darting from one dusty side street to the next, aware that our clothes, emblazoned with the white, tell-tale patches of the prisoner, announced our standing at the very first glance. We need not have worried. As we approached the centre of the town, we paled gratefully into insignificance amid the tumultuous chaos that clearly throbbed at the heart of its daily life.

Unnoticed and unchallenged, we jostled our way down the crowded, bustling thoroughfares that led towards the railway station, with Mick assuring us as we battled on, hugging our blankets to our chests, that he'd noticed, on our arrival, a busy, thriving marketplace close by it.

He was right and it was heaving. Stalls upon stalls, so closely packed together there was barely room to get in among them, were piled high with local produce, as the vendor's voices rose in shrill and constant contest to undercut their neighbour's millet and maize, rice, cassava. Craftsmen, crying out for custom as they worked, bent low over their silver filigree, their intricately embossed leatherwork and carved enamels. With one sly eye kept all the while on the close-quartered competition, they called across each other's stalls in their efforts to best one another in quality and price. Frantic flies swarmed to drying, shrivelled hunks of meat that swung head-high alongside swathes of brightly coloured fabrics, while on the ground, chickens in makeshift cages scrabbled their futile protest and goats, loose and bleating, skittered about among the pots and pans and baskets laid out for display.

The air was pungent, thick with the stench of heat and human interaction, though the beguiling smell of baking bread from somewhere, waxing and waning on the hot and heavy air, went some way to relieving it. My every nerve end, deadened by long and lonely isolation, reverberated with the general hubbub, though, as I stood, hesitating on the periphery, some small part of me could not help but marvel at the persistent optimism in so vital a society. People thronged from all directions: shouting and laughing, arguing, pushing, bartering, all engaged in one form or another of frenetic and vociferous activity and all caught up in the endless, inexhaustible motion of the necessity of their own existence.

Where the stalls ran out, business had overflowed onto the ground beyond, and as Mick pushed through, we wound our way behind him until he stopped, claiming a small space by the roadside as our own. Hardly had we time to put down our piles of blankets before people were upon us, clamouring for the price and then inevitably, with clicking tongues and shaking heads, were keen to buy only after the obligatory round, and more, of haggling. Our lack of common language proved no barrier, a series of nods and gestures being adequate to our purpose and, where they failed, we squatted on the floor with prospective clients and wrote figures in the dust.

We had sold out within the hour and, waving away the requests for more, enlivened by success, we headed back towards the camp.

Dodging the listless and incurious patrol, we made it back to our accommodation block in time for lunch. It seemed that our absence had gone unnoticed by the guards, if not by Billy Rawlins who, I noticed, nudged Butler as we entered and, smirking knowingly, inclined his head in our direction. We joined the queue for rice and began to dream of nightfall and the opening of the railway station's restaurant, which Jed had reckoned was the best place to splurge our morning's takings.

Dusk found us sneaking back across the broken fence and spurred on by constant, clawing hunger, made all the more desperate by the prospect of a feast, we hurried back into the town. We fell onto the food scarcely before the waiter had time to place the plates upon the table. Chicken, warm and smoky, fell off the bone, soaking up the richness of its creamy sauce, which made it softer, lusciously more tender. The burnished casing of the large, salted *pommes frites* hid a snowy white interior which, deliciously dense and floury, melted away across my riven tongue while the steaming beans, fat and split and green, came bathed in buttery luxury. The wine was red and rough, burning down the length of my chapped and shrivelled throat but was all the more satisfying for it, while the *tarte aux pommes*, glistening with sugared glossiness, stung sharp its sweet asperity. I have never, before or since, tasted food more glorious.

But as our stomachs filled and the speed with which we ate gradually began to slow, I became more and more conscious that Big Sam, sitting across from me, kept stopping and looking over. Several times, out of the corner of my eye, I saw him swallow and then glance across as if to engage with me, as if on the verge of speaking and then, taking in another mouthful, deferring the moment, unsure of how best he might begin. When I looked back up at him, he quickly looked away.

Since I had stood up by Joe the night that Moses had thrown himself into the water, Big Sam and I had barely exchanged a word. In his renunciation of Joe's friendship, he had also revoked mine. He had never said anything to me about it and he never did speak to Joe again, but I got the impression from him after Joe had died that somehow he was sorry. He had, I knew, come silently down the beach with Fraser to help carry Joe's body back up from the sea. As the rawness of his anger at Mac had turned to justified disgust, he had perhaps realised the truth in Joe's assertion that Mac's murder would have resulted in his own. And now, with his health slowly returning and his rational mind restored, Big Sam had recognised that Joe indeed had been his friend and had, as Joe had argued, been trying only to protect him.

After the fifth or sixth time I caught him looking, I put down my spoon and stared directly across at him. 'Sam, what? What is your problem?'

'Eh?' said Mick, starting up and spraying my plate and half the tablecloth with flecks of apple pastry.

'Nothing. It's nothing.' Big Sam shook his head then and lowering his large, heavy lids, shifted uncomfortably in his chair. I shrugged and made to pick up my spoon again, but he suddenly folded his arms and leant forward, resting his elbows on the table.

'It's just that I was thinking...' he began slowly, staring at a fixed point on the cloth just in front of him. 'I was just thinking that Joe wouldn't half have enjoyed this, Cub. Wouldn't he, eh? The whole damn thing.' He looked up at me then, and as I nodded, fighting down the sudden pain that clamped around my chest, I saw the guilty sorrow in the darkness of his eyes. 'I would have liked to have seen him here with us, Cub. That's all,' he added quietly.

As he finished speaking, the outlines of his features slowly began to merge and dim and, blinking quickly, I had to look away.

'Bloody 'ell – get down!' Mick suddenly lurched sideways in his seat, bending low and making a grab at the menu from the middle of the table, flicking it upright in front of his face in an inane attempt to hide. 'Jesus, we're fucking for it now!'

In reflex, we all flinched down without yet knowing why, but as we looked at Mick to track the cause of his wide-eyed alarm, we saw that the Commandant and his wife, accompanied by another couple, had just come in and were being shown to the corner of the room to take their table.

'He has seen us?' Tomas hissed at me, sliding so low down in his seat that his shoulders became almost level with the table. He scarcely dared to turn his head to look, for fear of drawing attention to himself with the movement, and the five of us sat motionless for what felt like several minutes, hardly daring to breathe while our minds scrabbled wildly for the best exit strategy.

'He must have bloody seen us. Can't bloody miss us in these friggin' clothes,' breathed Jed. It was true. The restaurant was hardly full and though our table was almost at the other side of the room from the one at which the Commandant's party were now seated, it was central. I risked a recce over the top of the menu that I had snatched up to shield my face and saw the Commandant deep in conversation with one of his companions, but just as he had finished speaking, his eyes swept up and across the room, catching mine for just a sliver of a second. I darted down behind my barricade.

'Seen us,' I said. 'Fuck it.'

'Wanna run for it?' Big Sam, whose body was still not one that could be missed nor easily mistaken, half rose in readiness.

'Too late.' I let the menu flop down before me on to the table, steeling myself for the Commandant's approach but as I looked again towards his table, I found, to my surprise, that he had not moved. He was drinking wine and listening attentively to the woman on his right.

'Let's get outta here.' Still crouching and keeping my head down low, I glanced at Mick who had ducked off his seat and was more or less underneath the table. 'Let's just leave the money here.'

'What? All of it?'

'Yes, bloody all of it,' Jed snapped. 'Let's go! That way.' He nodded at the double doors leading to the kitchens but which, unlike the restaurant's entrance, were in the opposite direction to the Commandant's table. Without daring to look behind, we scuttled from our seats and, hearts pounding, scrambled for their cover.

Still pulsing with adrenalin and wondering what exactly we might have got away with, though for the first time in many months, adequately fed, we snuck silently back into the camp and were still lying wide awake on our beds when the lights snapped on at midnight and the Commandant, with the weasel and one other officer, marched in. Making a beeline for the foot of Captain

Edwards' bed, the Commandant strode purposefully down the room and stopping abruptly, called his name. Only a few white tufts of hair were visible from beneath the blanket at first, but when called again, the skipper's sleepy face appeared, wincing and disorientated by the sudden light.

'Captain Edwards,' the Commandant began evenly, but loud enough for the whole room to hear. 'I have just seen five of your men sitting in a restaurant in the town. I would recognise each one of them.' He paused deliberately and looked around the room. 'You will report with them to my office in the morning before breakfast. We will decide together then, on the consequence.' He waited for Captain Edwards to nod his hesitant agreement and then turned on his heel. 'Good night.'

As soon as the door had closed behind them, Billy's voice rang out across the darkness, laced with smug and eager satisfaction. 'It was Mick. Sam was with him. Tomas and Cubby Clarke. Thievin' bastards. Saw them coming in this morning. With some other bloke. Knew that they were up to something but if I'd've known they were takin' blankets off my bed, I'd've bloody had them for it then.'

I heard the skipper heave a sigh as, turning his back on Billy's malice, he tried again to settle down to sleep. 'I know full well who it was, thank you, Billy,' he said forbearingly. 'Just wish they'd had the bloody sense not to get caught.'

The following morning, we shuffled into the Commandant's office behind the skipper without Jed. The captain had asked us once for his name and, greeted by downcast eyes and silence, had shaken his head indulgently and muttered, 'Perhaps he'll even see some merit in it.'

I brought up the rear, fixing my eyes firmly on the dusty toe-caps of the size fourteen boots that the weasel had rooted out for me. They were too big and my feet slid about inside them but they did not hurt. I was surprised into looking up though, by the friendliness in the Commandant's voice when he asked if I would shut the door behind me. He was standing behind his desk, with his face half-turned towards the open window and in the reflected light cast by the bright morning sun, his grey eyes shone.

'Well, gentlemen,' he began courteously. 'I hope that you ate well last night?'

We shuffled no reply but as I looked up at him and his eye caught mine, I saw his huge moustache begin to twitch slightly, as if to suppress the inconvenience of a smile.

'I did. Very good, the food at that restaurant. You could not have chosen any better. You also could not have chosen a more perfect moment for your break-out.' Clearly enjoying the confusion that must have registered on our faces, he threw up his arms and smiling broadly, came around the side of his desk, to extend his hand to Captain Edwards. The skipper, not knowing quite what else to do, took it and looked up in bewilderment at the delight exuding from the Commandant's face.

'Well, my friend, it appears that the Allies have landed in North Africa!' He pumped the captain's hand up and down excitedly, shaking the skipper's fragile, little frame almost off the floor. 'Governor General Boisson has finally gone over to your side. All of French West Africa has. Do you understand me? You and I, we are no longer really enemies.' He turned enthusiastically towards the rest of us, 'You saw me out last night with friends. We went out to celebrate!'

'Then we're going home!' Mick, incredulous, looked joyfully at me and then back at the Commandant for confirmation. 'You're releasing us?'

But the smile on the Commandant's face faded slightly. 'Ah, no, not yet,' he cleared his throat. 'No, not quite yet, I am afraid. At the moment, it is still rumour. Wait, wait! But it is true,' he added hastily, keen to allay our evident disappointment. 'And I must await my orders. But in the meantime, I do not see why you should be kept so much as prisoners.'

He went back around to the other side of his desk and taking a piece of paper and a pencil from the top right-hand drawer, he sat down. Again, wetting the pencil with his tongue, he took it to the top of the paper and looked up at us expectantly, 'What can I do then, to make your stay here more agreeable?'

By the time we left his office half an hour later, he had agreed that all prisoners should be granted passes to allow them into town on a rota basis and that instead of feeding us in the evening, he would provide us with a small allowance, that we might buy our own meat and vegetables from the marketplace and have Big Sam prepare them for us. Guards would no longer accompany prisoners around the camp and the pointless, exhausting hours spent standing out under the devastating desert sun, pretending to try to clear away ubiquitous and unconquerable scrub, were at an end.

True to his word, the Commandant saw to it that these privileges were implemented immediately, and they went some way to alleviating both the monotony and our misery. Though still weak and desperately underweight, the access to a more varied diet meant that the long and laborious road to physical recovery could at least begin.

But it was January before he was finally able to release us. The British Consul General had just returned to Dakar and it was he who apparently arranged for our transferral by train and then by ferry on to Freetown. The trip away from Timbuktu, though as uncomfortable and protracted as the journey up, proved far less onerous. The locals, eager now to embrace us as their allies, could scarcely have been more solicitous, pressing food and drink upon us at each station and hailing us with joyful solidarity as we passed through. Besides, we were girded by the knowledge that it was over and we were going home.

In Freetown, we were allocated berths on the *Johan van Olden Barneveldt*, which was there on the quayside awaiting our arrival and, clenching my fingers around the guiding ropes on either side of her gangway, I reached her deck and did not once look back.

There was an icy wind the day we docked in Barrow-in-Furness, and though it was not raining, a bleak, dispiriting dankness clothed the town in grey.

Fraser stopped me in the companionway outside my cabin and offered me his hand. I took it and we regarded one another silently for the few moments it took to shake and then, as I made to pull my hand away, he held me back.

'You were brave,' he said quietly. 'Hold on to that.' He spoke so softly that I wondered, after he had left me, if I had really heard him say anything at all.

By the time I had made it to the top of the gangplank, Billy was already on the quay. Shouldering his scant possessions in a kit bag filched from somewhere on the *Barneveldt*, he ducked his head down onto his chest as he turned into the wind, vainly seeking to protect his bony body from its bitter edge.

'Hey, Billy... Billy!' Butler, who had come up behind me, suddenly eager, pushed past and, stopping on the threshold of the doorway, shouted down. But the wind whipped away his cries and Billy, striding by below, did not seem to hear.

'Billy! Hey... Rawlins!' Butler bellowed.

Billy finally looked up and turning one shoulder in against the gale, he put up a hand to shield his face and nodded up his answer.

'Friday. The Old Roan?' Butler yelled.

Billy, looking slightly irritated, nodded a couple of times more emphatically and, turning back abruptly into the wind, began to walk away.

My legs were shaking slightly and at the bottom of the gangway, I had to stop for a moment to summon strength. Squalls, icy and intermittent, swirled up the dockside's rubbish and bit into my bones. I had been given a lightweight jacket by one of the *Barneveldt*'s sympathetic crew and I drew it more tightly around my body, but my knees, still exposed, and my sockless feet seemed to seize at the wind's assault.

I shivered and dipping my head, started to make my way across the quay.

'Cub, wait!' It was Jack. I stopped and turned to find him jogging towards me, one hand held up to delay my leaving.

He caught me up and stood breathlessly before me for a moment, his eyes bright and watery, and I waited. 'I wanted to say thank you. You helped me...' he looked down for a second, at the mottled blotches on the concrete, which merging now, glistened with a thin, fine sheen of moisture. 'A couple of times, you helped me... when I needed it.'

Without warning, I felt a lump rise up at the back of my throat and I fought to hold it down, swallowing with pain. Water sprang up at the corners of my eyes and pooled, disconcertingly close to falling, along my lower lids. It was a particularly biting wind. What, had it been Joe and I who were parting now, would I have tried to say to him? Confident in the knowledge that his friendship had been one that would have lasted out my lifetime, it was not the arrangement of our prospective lives and each other's role within them that would have troubled me. It was how, at this juncture, at the end of so horrific a journey, would I ever even have begun to thank him. For his protection, for his friendship, for his unfailing belief in the goodness of my heart and for never once allowing me to give it up. By being who he was, he had soldered up the raw material of my soul and had shown me how to be the man I had become. And I had never even thanked him.

It would have been so different, this homecoming, had he been with me. I would have been like Jack, filled with hopes and happy expectation. As it was, though giddy relief flooded through my veins and I yearned for the love and familiarity of home, my return was marred by his absence, my joy remote and hollow.

'I thought perhaps I'd be seein' you around? Mebbe we could get together, have a drink or somethin'?' Jack said blithely, stamping his feet and rubbing his hands together rapidly in an attempt to get up some warmth.

I looked into his face and read an eagerness to make it right, to lose in the creation of new memories, the old; to take the chance to recreate ourselves as civilised and reasonable men in each other's minds. Had he been Joe, there would have been no need.

'I don't think so, Jack,' I said as gently as I could. 'There are some things that are better left behind and this, I think, is one of them.' The quiet resolution in my voice surprised us both. He looked startled, even slightly offended, as if by refusing such a friendly invitation, I had contravened some unwritten law of polite and social practice, a law that had been summarily reinstated as soon as we had set foot back on our native soil.

'I'm sorry. The memory's hard enough.' I tried to smile. 'Goodbye Jack,' I said, as I offered him my hand.

I turned low to spin away from him, my head down against the wind, eager to be gone, but as I did so, I jostled into a woman who stood alone on the quayside a couple of yards behind me. I had not noticed her before. That she made no attempt to move as I swung around, gave me, in that split second, a strong impression of her vague, corporeal inattention. Her mind, like mine, was somewhere else.

I barely looked at her but registered only that she wore a dark coloured coat and tendrils of her long, dark hair, beaded silver in the mist, splayed out wildly about her shoulders, blown forwards by the wind behind, to cling across her face. One hand hovered up about her forehead, presumably to pull away the obstructive swathes, and her small, thin shoulders crumpled inwards in defence against the onslaught of the weather. And though her general aspect denoted an intrinsic sadness, it did not occur to me that she was there for any other reason than some kind of official business or more possibly, to meet one of the crew who worked the *Barneveldt*. I knew that for the preservation of wartime secrecy, my own family and those of my companions would not have been informed as to the vessel nor the date of our arrival. They would know only that we were coming home.

I bumbled into her, my shoulder taking hers along with such momentum that she buckled backwards, swaying away so that my arms, which had automatically sprung out to try and steady us both, failed to reach her. Murmuring my apologies, I barely even glanced at her before turning away to hurry on. But she put out her hand to stop me.

'Wait! I'm sorry. Please. Can you spare me just a minute?' Turning to one side against the wind that she might gain a greater purchase on my arm, she was immediately disordered by the wild intrusion of her hair which, tangled and unruly, swept again more determinedly across the lower part of her face so that she was forced at once to let me go. I waited as she struggled to disentangle her nose and mouth from its damp, persistent clasp. Pushing it up and aside in obvious frustration, she lifted her head then and put her face directly into the wind so that the volume of her hair flew out behind her. She was much younger than the curvature of her back and shoulders had at first suggested. She turned back to me but no sooner had she done so, than her face was partially enveloped once again.

'You're one of the survivors? From the *Sithonia*?' Although there was little more than a foot between us, I could barely hear her voice above the wind. The fine, grey dampness in the air had finally decided and turned more definitively to rain.

I leaned in towards her, straining to understand and, with what was unquestionably an effort, she raised her voice again. 'The *Sithonia*? You're a survivor?'

I nodded quickly, closing my eyes and wrapping my arms tightly around my chest. I began to lift my feet alternately, in a vain attempt to keep the blood in my toes, in my ankles and in my knees from freezing altogether. I prayed that she would have the wherewithal to appreciate my impatience to be gone and, taking the inadequacy of my clothing into account, keep her enquiries literally to the minute she had proposed.

'Joe. Joe Green. Do you know him?' Again her hand sought my arm and as her fingers reached and clasped my elbow, I heard the sharp incision of his name. My feet stopped moving. The cold, the wind, the grey, depressing rain receded and abruptly ceased. There was nothing else except this woman, removed, alone and undisturbed by the raging clamour of the elements around.

'Do you know him? Joe Green.' She held on to me and as she asked again, I felt her pull my arm slightly as if to bring me to.

I could not reply. I just stood there, staring at her hand upon my elbow with the slow burning realisation of who it was that stood before me rising up from beneath my stomach and blasting my body with its sickening truth.

'Um, I'm sorry. He's not... I don't think I should...' Oh God, what was she doing here? She must know that he is dead. Didn't Latimer get word home? Why doesn't she know?

'Who are you?' I blurted finally, although there really was no need for her to answer.

'Maggie. My name is Maggie. I'm sorry. I am his... you know him then?'

'He didn't... Joe's not...'

'I know. I know that.' She took her hand suddenly off my sleeve and, grasping the edges of her coat, she wrapped it more vehemently about her body. Again, she pulled her hair back away from her mouth as though its obstruction alone might well explain her inability to form the words that could no longer be avoided. She drew herself up and made an attempt to lick her lips.

'He is dead. I know.' She stopped and looked down, arrested momentarily by the stark finality of her admission, an admission that implied a level of acceptance she had not before realised she was capable of acknowledging. The words hung between us and neither of us moved.

'It's not that... it's just that I wanted someone who knows... who knew him.'

Oh God, no. Not here. Not now. I am not strong enough. I cannot do it. It can't be right. He could not, surely, have expected me to stand before this girl, this girl he'd loved, and tell her now that her heart had been mistaken. It was one thing, in heat and pain and fear, scrabbling backwards from the approaching face of death, to promise a desperate and devoted man that I would do it. It was quite another to stand in the cold, grey light of this cold, grey land, before this total stranger and tell her that the foundations of her hope had been built upon untruth. To expect her to believe that Joe, the Joe whom we both had known, had been unkind. Ungenerous. And unfaithful. And in so saying, to deliberately grind her dreams to dust. She would not believe me. I could not do it.

'Did you know him? You must have known him!' Seeing something in my face, her voice, importunate now and urgent, sharpened and she stepped towards me. 'There must be something you can tell me!'

'No, I... he was in the lifeboat. He was...' I could barely get the words out. My teeth, my jaws had become so tightly clenched together that I could not seem to get them moving. 'What was it that you wanted? What is it that you want to know?'

She turned slightly and inclining her head, her whole body, in the direction of the town, she put out a hand again towards my arm in an effort to guide me into moving forward but still, I could not move.

'Could you come with me? Could we talk?' she coaxed, more gently now. 'There's a place nearby. A café. I just want to talk... to hear about...'

The sorrow, the empty, aching sorrow that no amount of talking could assuage and which was so evident in her request, made only that she might keep him near, prevented her from finishing. It made me want to weep.

I should go with her and just blurt out the truth. I could just tell her that she had been loved and loved so deeply that Joe, at any cost, would reduce her suffering. I could just tell the truth. I could. I could renege. I could choose to imagine his had been the befuddled wishes of a confused and dying man. Pretend it would not matter because I pitied her, pitied her more keenly than she would ever know.

But in choosing so, I would renounce all the faith that he had placed in me, the very faith that saw me standing here, the faith that undeniably had kept me alive and that had, in part, been responsible for his death. I would betray him and in doing so, betray the fundamental hope for her release to which he had clung, which he had made me swear I would uphold. And he had done it because he had understood how it was that she had loved him. He had known her. I did not. I only knew that at the most crucial moments of his life, of my own, he had put his faith in me. And though it sickened me to the core, I knew that he had meant for me to do it. And I knew why. He had loved her. If he had to die, then so assured of the endurance of her constancy, now ever destined to be unfulfilled, he had wanted to provide her with such an unconditional reprieve that she might go on to live her life with no regret. Live her life unhampered by a hallowed image. To love and be loved by some better man. I knew what he had wanted me to do and I had seen first-hand, time and time again, the self-effacing generosity that had motivated his request.

And yet the thought of such an interview appalled me. I baulked at it. The thought of actually having to say the words and then sit by and watch the blight of their effect, to inflict such striking pain on one whose pain was already so apparent would require a level of detachment I was scarcely capable of imagining.

Regardless of my commitment to Joe's conviction in her long-term relief, it horrified me. Besides, she would not believe me. She would see it in my face. I could not go with her.

'No. Look, sorry.' I pulled away, so that her hand, which had not quite reached me, wavered in the wider space between us, stranded. 'I don't think I can help you. There's nothing I can say to you that's going to help. I'm sorry.' I watched her hand drop flat against her side.

It would be better like this. That she should never know. I could not do it. Trembling, broken, sick at heart, I could not face the choice. The truth or all that I held most true? Either way would mean betrayal. It was more than I could bear.

I left her there, standing on the quayside, watching me walk away. Putting my head down, I kept on walking, knowing that she watched me go, knowing that every single step I took away from her denied her knowledge and took me further still away from Joe.

I buried my mouth into the collar of my jacket, seeking comfort in the muggy warmth generated by my breath against it. I tried to bend my mind away, to think of something else. Of what awaited me at home, my mother's food and her embrace, the glittering relief dancing in my father's eyes. To consider how, stripped of valuables, belongings and identity, I might logistically begin to make my way there. And that having arrived, how I must make sure that Guillaume got his book. I owed him that much.

I made it to the street and stopped, sagging in against the wall. The back of my head fell heavily against it and, working from side to side, kneaded in. I closed my eyes and, curving my face away from the busy pavement, forced my cheek up against the sharp-grained, gritty edges of the brickwork, seeking external feeling, external pain. And the tears that formed and swelled beneath my eyelids, inexorable and unchecked, broke from their corners, to fall and be immediately lost on the rough-hewn surface, already damp and darkened by the rain.

I do not know how long it was before I became aware of it. The familiarity of it, its calm insistence, snagging on the verges of my consciousness, calling me back. Unable quite to register what it was but slowly comprehending that something in me recognised significance, I looked up, confused, barely understanding but seeking out a source.

The man was old. Small and narrow-shouldered: physically nothing like him. He was tending the newspaper stand on the corner of the street and he had his back to me. But I could hear him. Stooping slightly, he stood with his hands in pockets and, in spite of all the insult in the weather, he was whistling cheerfully, whistling as if he had not one single care in all the world.

Joe.

I had told him twice that I would do it. The only care, the last, I had ever known him have, had been for her. And he had entrusted that to me. What had he not done for me? He had never once lost faith. Every single time he'd had a choice, he had chosen me. It left me with no other.

But by the time I had stumbled back on to the dockside, the quay was already more or less deserted.

CHAPTER 15

THE MEETING

I think, looking back, that I had always known that it was not over. How could it have been over? I had felt, even then, as she had walked away from me all those years ago, that I had done neither one of them the justice they deserved. When it had come to it, I had not had the courage to carry out what Joe had asked of me nor the courage to disregard it. He had sent me to relieve her suffering and I felt, I had always felt, that in falling short of pushing home his cause, I had succeeded only in compounding it. I told myself that I had tried to do only what was loyal, what I had been asked, in the most horrifying of ways, to do, but in more than sixty years, my conscience had never been entirely able to rest easy; my heart had never ceased to struggle with the knowledge that somehow I had failed them both.

And so when her letter arrived, only the second and the last that I would receive from her, I found that the weightless fear, crushing and reductive, which caught at my insides and compressed them while I clutched at breath, was accompanied by something smaller, calmer, something that felt almost like relief. She was calling time and it offered me at least, the opportunity for release.

I had not at first recognised her name but when I turned the letter back over and began to read, I saw Joe's and realised who she was. The thin blue sheet of paper I held in my hand began to shake and the words, which jumped and blurred before my eyes, renounced all claim to meaning.

Guilt, responsibility and shame that had lain for so many years, dusty and unrecoverable, next to the more horrific memories of the lifeboat, had roused and, having woken, disturbed all the unreconciled emotions around them. Now as one, they surged up and unrestrained, broke loose across my being. The fragile framework of my ordinary existence, the carefully constructed edifice of my calm and reasonable mind, quailed at their approach and crumbled into dust. My hand sought my mouth and I felt again the hot and prickling horror of the loss of all control.

I reached out towards the table and steadying myself, sat down.

Over sixty years since the last time and I had told myself that I would never have to see her again. I had not wanted to. However I had tried to think of it, of our last encounter, it broke me apart: what it must have done to her, how I must have caused her pain. From the warm, safe ledge of hindsight, I could see so much more clearly now how frightened I had been, frightened at a time when I thought that fear could no longer touch me and in my fear, I had behaved more harshly than I ever thought I could. I had been afraid, not only of her but of what I felt I had been duty bound to undertake, and fear, no matter how justified, comes hand in hand with shame. At that time, on the back of all that pain, it had pained me just as much.

And yet still, still, I would not have it undone. I would not even now. For there was Joe. He and I had been taken to the gates of hell and he alone had ensured that I had made it back. Despite the hideous responsibility I knew I bore for Maggie's suffering, I could not, would not renounce my loyalty to Joe. It lay with him still, on the barely floating carcass of a lifeboat, on the scorched and arid beach where we had buried him. It did not matter whether or not his premise for the preservation of Maggie's wellbeing had been mistaken or if I had been too cruel in attempting to relay it, for I had been and was ever still, bound by a loyalty I could not forswear because it lay at the foundations of my life and he remained, with all his broad-shouldered strength, a cornerstone of my consciousness. I would have tried to do the same again tomorrow. I would have tried to lie to her. For him. I know that even now.

And yet old age has not, after all, lent me the clarity nor the deeper understanding that I had assumed my vain but constant efforts to unravel the tangled threads of life would automatically bestow: rather her complexities have intensified and her ambiguities only deepened. I have not found that there are any answers. I have lost the surety I once had and have found the world no longer staged in black and white. There are so many blurry shades of grey and Maggie has ever stood, a shadowy figure, within the dusky half-light.

It was not as if I had not wrestled with it. In the dark hours I had fought against the crushing purgatory of the thought that Joe could not possibly have meant it. That his mental capabilities, so ravaged by the sickness that had racked his body, had not been reliable. That shrinking before the blank, cold face of bleak oblivion, he had been hallucinating and had simply snatched at the solace to be had from an illusion, from an impractical ideal that could do nothing but deface his epitaph and undermine the prospect of her peace. And had I not then, in attempting to relay such an impulsive and impromptu message, only granted that the ramblings of his unequal mind dictate a ruinous course? Or had my own misgivings merely been a disingenuous excuse, an explanation that qualified my own reluctance to bear the burden of so pitiless a task? Tormenting and recurring, these thoughts had plagued me, plagued me still. And yet in fleeing them, I had ever taken refuge in the safeguard of my most insistent memory and found again his eyes. The way that he had looked at me. Straining to hold off, for precious seconds longer, the invading darkness of perseverant death, surely they had conveyed more purely than words ever could his absolute conviction. In the bright, liberating light of my better days, I knew that he had meant for me to do it.

And yet even the certainty that, though I had faltered at the brink, I had actually achieved Joe's purpose, has, over the passing of the years, gradually loosed its hold and faded. Perhaps, after all, she did not believe me and as time and unreliable memory have taken me further from the horror of our interview, as I have grown old, I have allowed myself the secret hope that maybe she did not. His love for her had been so purely selfless: he had, quite simply, loved her more than he had cared about his reputation in her eyes, about how she, the one person in the world whose esteem he had most craved, would remember him. I have seen enough of life to know that such unselfish love is rare. It could only be a travesty to have been so loved and by such a person, and yet not have been allowed to know it. And that I should have been the one to have robbed her of that understanding. It was unforgivable.

And yet, despite my guilt, despite my knowledge, I had never once been moved to seek her out. To try to put it right. Dissuaded always by the desire to remain, above all else, loyal to Joe and to repay unswervingly the debt I owed him, I had staked my all on the belief that his effort had succeeded, that Maggie had been released from the shackles of life-lasting grief and had better found fulfilment in some other life. I could not have sought her out. If it did not disturb the peace that Joe had hoped she'd find, then might it not have raised the cry that he had been mistaken? Might I have found that she, embittered by betrayal, had somehow been reduced by his generosity? It was not a possibility I was capable of bearing.

But now. All my lifetime to prepare and yet still, I was unprepared. And if I did not choose to answer her, I would never know what I, what he, had done. His legacy of love, all that which had kept me alive, all that I had sought to live by since, would go with me to my grave. I had more courage than that. Joe had seen to it. I looked down at the letter lying on the table and my eye, scanning quickly down the page, sought out and held Joe's name. His name. Beneath the smouldering indifference of an omnipotent sun, in the lonely, nullifying blackness of the night and before the burnt out, wasted hearts of broken men, it had been etched upon my soul. I recognised its call. He had asked me to make sure. It was not finished.

Edie offered to come with me but she doesn't see so well now and the town is difficult for her. Fuzzy outlines of people looming up suddenly before her. She doesn't like it. If I had wanted her to come she would have, and although she did not say so, I knew she would rather not. So I did not ask.

Edie. She had crept into my heart and settled herself in without my realising. I knew her when I was a kid and when I got back, she was what I needed. She was all that was light and air and laughter while I, I was fraying from the inside out. Slowly, softly, she loved me back to life, dancing me carefully towards the light. And with her came sleep.

She and I are opposites still. She laughs. She has laughed her way through our life together and the laughter lines around her eyes and mouth are testimony to her unfailing good grace. Moreover, she is wiser than I, she recognises her contentment and chooses what will make us happy. And at that time, she took me calmly by the hand and told me how glad she was that I was home.

I hope that I die before she does. I know that sounds selfish but now, the loss of her would be like waking again to the nudging waves around the boat. Eagerly scanning the horizons. Finding only sea.

I took the bus. Edie worries when I drive although there is no need. I only find the parking difficult.

It was one of those dark December days when the morning wakes, stretches lazily and, looking at the weather, pulls the covers more tightly round and turns back towards the night. The light never really gets away from the dragging, dull grey of the dawn, and the gloomy clouds hang despondently around the streetlights which needs must be on all day.

A fine drizzle would not let up and as the bus lurched its way up the high street, I watched the Christmas shoppers hurrying between the awnings, battling with umbrellas and too many bags, but no doubt managing to keep their spirits up with reckless overspending. I could not have been further removed from them – their struggles were not mine and I envied them the burden of theirs.

I got off at the Corn Exchange, thinking I could do with the walk, but the shoppers were insistent and ungenerous. Constantly rebuffed by a contraflow of pressing people, I arrived at the café Maggie had suggested feeling battered and disordered. Already bruised.

I need not go in, I thought, wavering in the doorway. I leant my shoulder and then my temple against the cool glass, gathering myself. I might just step back out into the rain and the seamless crowd and let myself be carried back the way I had come. Disappear. She would never know I had come. I could ignore her and any further attempts she might make to point her wrinkled finger and make me justify my loyalty. Avoid her recrimination. Suddenly I felt too tired for this; it was too bleak. At eighty-one, I was probably physically much stronger now than I had been the last time I had seen her, but then I had been young and seared by my conviction: the only thing that mattered had been to keep Joe's faith.

''Scuse me, mate.' A young man hopped up the step into the small porchway behind me. He muscled to get past but paused when he looked into my face. His own, losing its bland expression of internal preoccupation, creased immediately with concern. 'You all right?' He put his hand upon my shoulder, as Joe had done all those years ago, at another far remote but crucial moment of my life.

I nodded and smiled thinly. 'Yes. Thank you. I'm all right.' Barring my way back, he could not get past me. The porchway was too small for two to pass. I could have turned awkwardly and made him step back down but I was touched by his concern. It was kind. It reminded me of who I was and the boy I used to be.

I stood up straight and smiled at him more fully. 'Thank you,' I said again and then I pushed open the inner door and held it open for him to come on in behind me.

I knew she was there as soon as I got inside. I could feel her eyes upon me but I played for time. I was not quite ready yet. I took off my overcoat and made a show of shaking off the rain, brushing it down at the shoulders and then looked about for a place to put it.

It was an old-style café with six or seven tables only and it smelt of bread and coffee and warm, wet clothes. The damp of drying hair and rosy faces added to the steam from the cups and buttered toast, fugging up all the windows. Out of the corner of my eye, I saw her rise from a table near the fireplace and begin to weave her way towards me. I turned away, pretending I had not noticed yet and hung up my scarf.

When I turned back, she was standing there before me.

'Brian,' she said, 'it was good of you to come.' She took my hand and, pulling me forward, kissed me on the cheek.

She was smaller than I remembered and if it were possible, more slight. The insubstantiality of her body, clad in what was obviously a best blue dress, made her somehow vulnerable. It made me want to put an arm around her shoulder and squeeze her cheerily. But then I remembered who she was and why we were here, so I did not. She looked frail, strangely at odds with the brittle, untouchable young woman I had carried in my memory all these years.

She set off back to the table and I followed. Her wavy hair, streaked through with grey and silver now, was pulled back again into a little bun, but as there was so much less of it than before, she had no difficulty in keeping it in check. No strands had been left out.

She sat down and, lashes lowered, she turned her face towards me, 'I saw you trying to decide. Out there. Whether to come in or not.' There was a smile behind her voice.

Her eyes, already creased, crinkled in amusement. Inscrutable. Well-worn lines fanned out and up around her mouth, and as her quiet merriment subsided, those about the rest of her features and around the edges of her face reverted to their customary grooves, as if for years, calm serenity had been her most natural expression.

I looked vaguely back towards the door and then sat down. 'Were you worried I wouldn't come in?'

'No, no,' she said, more serious now, 'I knew you would.'

This was to me, an extraordinary thing to say. I had met this woman briefly only twice before and on those two occasions, neither one of us could have vouched reliably for our reason. And yet here she sat, professing that she was able to predict my actions. I could not really feel affronted, just surprised by her assumption and, eyebrows raised, I must have shown it. Maggie shrugged, smiling softly, 'I think you are a person who will always try to do what you have said you would,' she said, her quiet sincerity disarming me entirely. I stared at her, unblinking, but she would not let me in.

'What would you like?' It was the waitress by my arm but the question, dragging us back up from the deep, confused me momentarily.

'Mmm?' I forced my eyes away from Maggie and glanced up at her, bewildered.

'To eat,' she said, stifling a yawn. 'To drink. What can I get you?'

We ordered coffee and Maggie asked for cake. We sat awhile, waiting, to all other eyes an elderly couple enjoying one another's company and mid-morning brunch. Waiting. I did not want to wait. I did not want to eat or drink. I wanted just to know.

Maggie was not oblivious. She talked about the weather, about the winter, Christmas shoppers but all the time, she looked about her, not at me. She staved me off. The cake arrived and she admired its size and texture, offering half to me and then tucking in without compunction. Had I been her friend, I would no doubt have been amused by her quick and darting conversation, enjoyed her lively interest in all things other than that which lay between us. But as it was, I felt increasingly discomfited. She had not asked me here to talk about the cake.

'Maggie,' I said abruptly. She stopped. She laid her fork down carefully upon her plate next to the half-eaten cake, and she wiped her mouth, scrunching the napkin up in unhurried hands, which then came down to rest, neatly folded one on top of the other, in her lap. She sat back. Finally.

'Maggie. What do you want?' I asked, trying but failing to keep the waver from my voice.

For the first time since we had sat down, she frowned, and the light-hearted animation that had seemed so natural to her person summarily deserted her. It was replaced by a quiescent gravity I had not seen before. She was silent and, acutely aware that I was watching her, waiting, she looked down, casting her eyes about the table, seeking an object, any object on which she might focus the attention she seemed so unwilling or unable to confer on me.

She found it eventually in her hands which, loose-veined and liver-spotted, formed a gnarled and crooked cradle for the discarded napkin that lay beneath them. I continued to wait and for a while, we both became engrossed in the quiet composure of her hands. Suddenly, she moved them and, bringing them up to rest lightly side by side at the table's edge, she slowly smoothed the cloth.

'Billy died,' she said, deciding. 'Billy Rawlins.' She glanced up briefly across at me, as though vaguely hoping this alone might be enough to explain the reason for our being here. 'Did you know?'

'No.' The word, attempted with what I thought might be my ordinary voice, failed to sound. I licked my lips and tried again. 'No, I didn't know. I hadn't heard.' I saw him for one second, his skinny, sunburnt body crouching low on the wooden seat of the boat, his face, blistered and wasted, framed by the glare of glistening blue and his eyes, his narrow, half-closed eyes, slit against the sun. 'When?'

'Two months or so.'

I let my breath out slowly and closed my eyes, as if by doing so, I might shut out his sudden and unwelcome presence. I didn't want to remember. But Maggie had begun.

'When I saw his name – Billy's – in the paper, that he'd died, I felt… well, what it felt like was… relief. Mnnh. It sounds so terrible, doesn't it, to say that out loud? But it was relief – relief, I realised, because it wasn't you.'

She smiled almost apologetically, faintly embarrassed at having to allude at all to the possibility of my demise. I could not help but smile too then, at her scruple, but she did not notice. Hers had vanished and she was too intent now on getting out what she had come to say.

'I thought if I could see you… I thought that if I could just talk to you again, one last time… while I still had the chance, I hoped I think…' She stopped abruptly, her eagerness frustrated by an unfamiliar incoherence she had not expected. She clearly had not considered the possibility that it would be her own inability to communicate that might prove an obstacle to our exchange.

As I watched her shift uncomfortably on her seat, I had to fight the sudden urge to put my hand out to cover hers but, fearing that she should recoil, I did not do it. Instead, I looked away.

'I don't know… maybe it shouldn't matter really, after all this time.' Offering this uncertainly, she hesitated as if to leave me time to take my cue but, finding the contradiction she invited to be unforthcoming, she shook her head quickly and leant forward to whisper urgently, 'But it does still, doesn't it? Surely it does?'

I looked up. 'Matter?'

She nodded slowly. 'Matter. To me, yes, I think it does. I wanted to get things straight. To understand. It just did not seem right. That I – that we – should get so old, that one day, soon perhaps, one of us should die and the other should look back and find then that it's just too late.'

She paused, but as I gave her nothing, she drew up her shoulders and said suddenly, 'You bury things, don't you?' Waving away the startled look that must have registered on my face, she went on quickly, 'I don't mean you, I mean we all do, don't we? Don't we have to? You have to get up and go on and so you keep it down inside you. You let the layers of your life quietly cover it. You don't have to look at it. But it shapes you. It makes you from the inside out into who you really are. And now, I think, I want to know. I want finally to know if the person I've become, if the life I've tried to live…'

She stopped again, flailing for the words that might most accurately encompass it.

Having started to speak as the thought had taken her, she now found herself at the peak of her explanation without the capacity to finish it, for the violence of emotion that had built up behind it seemed to have deprived her once again of her natural coherence. Furrowing her brow, she closed her eyes briefly as though that might help her rid her mind of all the superfluous detail that hampered clarity and bring only to the fore what she wanted most particularly to convey. 'Well… if my life has not after all been based upon untruth,' she finished quietly.

Then, leaning in towards me once again, she tilted her head slightly and continued carefully, 'You see, I have always wondered. All my life I have wondered but did not think I was quite brave enough to know… to know if what I told myself, if what I let myself believe, was true. What if I was wrong? How then could I have put much faith in anything? How could I have believed in anyone any more? No, no, it was safer not to know. It gave me leave to carry on, living… loving. Finding a way. So much of how I tried to live, you see, the person that I've tried to be, was based on what I wanted, needed even, to believe… Joe had really tried to do.'

Her voice, cracking for the first time, dropped away at the mention of his name and the harsh lines of concentration that had buckled the contours of her brow were replaced by a singular softness that stole across her face as she turned towards the familiar, well-worn path of the past. His name hovered in the air between us, the unfathomable connection that had long kept us apart.

'But now… well, I've nothing left to lose. I have been happy. My life's been happy. And I didn't, I realised, want to miss the chance after all. Of knowing. It was Billy's name there in the paper – but it made me think of what it would have felt like had it been yours. You are the only one who knew, you see. Who knows. The only person I could ever ask.'

Though I was listening intently, I could not take my eyes from the efforts of her fingers which, thin and crooked, unable to unbend entirely, were attempting what could be no more than a loose-fitting grasp on the table's rim. It took me some time to realise then that she was waiting and longer still to understand that what she waited for was me.

But I could not reply. I was still not ready to let him go. The elapse of time had not lessened my reluctance to utter the sentiments that he had begged me not to. It seemed no less of a betrayal now than it had seemed then and I clung to it, clung still to the self-imposed commitment to make restitution for his loyalty to me. But she took my silence for encouragement and, lifting her face, forced querulous lips to form the question she had brought me here to answer.

'I wanted to ask if… if, in the end, what I decided to believe was so much closer to the truth.'

'Maggie, I can't!' I burst out, the heightened volume of my voice cutting across the general conversation in the room so that momentarily, all about us, there was silence. People, having glanced our way, looked at their companions meaningfully before turning their thoughts back towards the slipstream of their lives.

'I can't tell you anything any different,' I hissed, when there was noise enough again to speak. As I had begun to feel the safe ground beneath me give and start to shift and slide away, I scrambled desperately for the foothold carved deliberately deep so many years before. 'I can't tell you even now that I should have told you something different. I can't. You must see that. He… he is the only reason I got back. The only reason that I am sitting here. I would not have made it back, if he had not…' I stopped to swallow, to try to ease the familiar, nagging ache that was beginning to rise again at the back of my throat. 'I never felt, I don't feel even now that I had a choice. And I know… I know how much I must have hurt you. I have regretted it. All my life I have regretted it. But I was thinking only of what I had to do for him. I can't undo it, even now, I can't…'

'No, wait. You don't have to. I don't want you to…' Her hands came up and she put them out towards me, beseeching me to stop. Overwhelmed suddenly by the cavernous depth of the impasse that now lay between us, we both fell silent, each at a loss as to how we might retain the precarious equilibrium that at any time, at a single word, while we were in one another's company, might so easily be lost.

'I was always sorry for it,' I said.

'That did not make it any easier to bear.' This came from her quickly and, for the first time, I heard an edge of bitterness in her voice. It was a reflex of a reply that had come out of her mouth before she had even taken time to think, as if old wounds, unexpectedly chafed, had roused in her the dormant resentment that up until now, she had been certain she no longer felt. It had flared up momentarily in the face of an apology that she doubtless recognised as genuine but that offered her nothing more. She saw me flinch and immediately contrite, she scrabbled to retract it, saying quickly, 'I know. I'm sorry. I know you were.' And then smiling suddenly, she added softly, 'It was all there in your face.'

Realising almost as soon as she had spoken that these words would offer me no purposeful enlightenment, she continued eagerly, 'What I mean is there are some things, aren't there, in your life that never do quite leave you? The way something's said, how someone looked. A couple of words. It can be all that you remember sometimes, can't it?'

She tilted her face slightly up towards me, soliciting but not pausing for accord. 'And what I took away with me about you, all that I could ever bring to mind when I thought of you, was that look of sorrow on your face. At the docks. In that café. There was such a lot of pain there in your face. Pain and sympathy. But there was also something else. Fear. Even shame. I saw that it cost you so to say it. What you said to me. I knew it did. You could not even bring yourself to do it at the docks. You might never have told me anything, had I not sought you out. Such appalling sorrow in your face. I have never quite been able to forget it. Whenever I remembered you. And every single time I thought of Joe.'

Taking a long intake of breath, she pulled herself up and went on: 'And seeing Billy's name there in the paper, it made me think again of something that he told me. When I went to see him. Something that I meant to ask you about when I saw you in that café. But then, well – what you told me… it was so shattering. I could see nothing else beyond it for a while. I could not even think…'

My face, my neck and ears, flushed hot and I looked away. I did not want to have to look at it, to even think of it, of the hideous, searing memory of that image, of a distraught young woman crushed. For one sliver of a second, a flash of anger overtook me, anger that she could have brought me here to make me look again at what I had fought so long and so hard to forget. The defensive anger of shame laid bare. It took me every single scrap left of my strength, of my reason, to turn from my instinct that screamed at me to kick back my chair and beat an unqualified retreat. As I gazed across at her though, my anger dissolved as instantly as it had arisen, for I saw that there was no recrimination in her face. She was not even looking at me. Lost in the moment of her own painful recollections, she hardly seemed to be aware that I was there at all.

'I remembered what he'd said to me only after. When I could afford to think. It has always made me wonder. He told me, almost in passing, that you'd attacked a man who tried to trade off Joe's compass for some water. For water. When he was dead already and you were dying of thirst.'

Putting her elbows on the table, she brought her hands forward to rest together out in front of her and leaning towards me, she bowed her head. Her question came not much above a whisper, 'Why would you have done that? When you were dying of thirst?' And the answer, already on her lips, was out before I would have had the chance, had I been able, to summon one.

'Unless you knew what it had meant to him. Unless perhaps you knew that it was mine,' she breathed.

Unprepared and incapable of knowing how I might ever possibly begin to find the words to explain, unsure as to whether she even wanted me to try, the only reply that I could muster seemed obtusely so irrelevant.

'Mac,' I said. 'His name was Mac.'

'What?'

'The man I hit. His name was Mac.'

'Oh.'

Nodding slowly, she turned this piece of information over carefully, as though determined to consider the possibility of its importance. It was at least something. But then I felt her hesitate as, having dismissed my confession of any consequence, she struggled to come up with some kind of appropriate response.

'Well,' she offered eventually. She lifted her head and, sitting up straight, pulled her hands back across the tablecloth towards her body.

'I began to think that there must be something more, something more than just what I had been so desperate to deny. I never wanted to believe you. What you told me. Though I did. For a long time, I did. I thought of nothing else. I was just a girl. I was twenty-five but I was still just a girl who had been thrown over. And I did not understand. I could not have understood. I hated him and I hated you. I was bitter and I thought I would never, never get over it. I was so angry with you: somehow it was your fault. And I thought that I would die with sorrow.'

A smile hovered about her lips again and there was indulgence in her voice as she recalled the tender-hearted girl she had once been.

'But I did not die. I married, a bit later than the others, but I did not die. And I married a man who loved me, who was loving enough to let me find my way.' The smile about her mouth did not fade as the memory of herself was replaced in her mind's eye by another, one which, if not regarded with the same kind of sympathy, was remembered with an equal affection.

'He was a patient man, my husband. Too patient really. And I found that after all, I was able to love him too. Though I don't think that either of us ever quite knew how much until it was too late.'

She stopped briefly as if slightly startled by her readiness to share this unrelated sorrow, a sorrow which, though privately long acknowledged, she had not before been tempted to express.

'Anyway,' she said, coming back. 'That was a different life. Everything was different after... I was different. Then, all those years ago, when I walked into that café, I knew what love felt like – I felt it more desperately than I ever would again. I felt it. But I did not understand what it meant. It has taken me a lifetime to understand. My husband. My own children. What I would not do for them. Grandchildren. The loss of my parents. People I have loved. A lifetime of learning.

'And all it taught me was what I had begun to think Joe already knew. So I stopped believing it. That he hadn't loved me. You cannot feel like that, be loved like that and just stop believing it was ever there at all. I wondered why you would have fought so desperately for his compass and why I'd seen such pained betrayal written on your face. It was so much more than having to relay a difficult and unpleasant truth. You struggled so. It wasn't only my betrayal that caused you such a lot of pain then, was it? It was the betrayal of the truth.'

She paused and though it had all the implications of a question, she did not appear to be expecting any answer and so, still, I did not speak.

'I think, in the end, it was your face that gave you... that gave Joe away. At least, it was that that gave me hope, permission even, to believe that there might have been some other explanation. And I chose the one that I wanted most to be the truth. You see, he had always been so generous, so big-hearted somehow: I had loved that in him. And so it was not so very difficult to believe that he should have tried to extend that generosity to me. Oh, he meant only to be generous, I'm sure of that. It was a sacrifice of sorts. He tried to sacrifice his memory for my happiness. It was love. He truly loved me and he wanted only to spare me a lifetime of disappointment. No one, for me, would have lived up to him and he knew it. He wanted, didn't he, just to finish it for me.'

She regarded me silently for one moment longer, not quite as though she hoped that I would answer but more as if she were waiting for a particular expression to take possession of my face. Then she tutted softly and, wrinkling up her nose, added wryly, 'My children would no doubt have it that he simply had been trying to ensure that I *moved on*.'

I did not reply but instead, jerked my head up once briefly and exhaled, acknowledging our common disaffection for a language that we both had learned to understand but which would never be our own. I did not look up.

'And you,' she went on softly, 'You loved him. You had been through hell together. What else was there for you to do? You were loyal and you were brave. But you were young. And he had asked you, hadn't he? And you thought... he thought that you'd be letting me go.'

She smiled then, a little ruefully, looking up at me from under her lowered lids and then suddenly, she lifted them and looked at me with eyes that in more than half a century, had not changed in either purity or potency. They were as breathtaking as the day that I had first encountered them. They were the eyes of the girl I had met back then, the same girl who lived on the inside of this small old lady. There was something further, more deeply scarred within them now. They had acquired a wisdom, an inviolability, suffered for and learned from, beyond the reach of most of us.

'I cannot, even now, quite thank you for it but I came here because I wanted to make sure. I wanted, I think, to know only if I have understood.'

I opened my mouth to speak but found that the words, so long and closely guarded, so painfully protected but which I recognised now should finally be heard, could not come. I must have made some sound though for, putting out a hand, she stopped me quickly.

'No, no. It's all right,' she said. She reached out across the table and her hand came down to rest just a little short of mine. 'It's all right. You don't have to say it. You don't, in the end, have to say anything at all. Your face has always been enough.'

The light of her eyes, affectionate now, exonerating, danced across the table into mine, conveying her forgiveness. She had never looked more beautiful.

'I have something for you,' was all that I could manage. Taking out the brown paper bag I had been carrying in my trouser pocket, I pushed it across the table towards her.

'Oh,' she said and she opened it slowly, intent. 'Oh!' she gasped, looking up at me, pleasure shining from her eyes that filled as I watched. 'My gloves.'

She picked one up and stroked her fingers along the soft, dark suede. 'Joe,' she said simply. 'Joe Green.' There was a catch of joy in her voice, as though Joe himself had just walked in and presented himself at our table. Joy and acceptance.

We sat for a while in companionable silence: separate in our reveries, connected by Joe's love.

'Thank you,' she said, suddenly matter of fact, as if coming back to the present. 'I missed them.' She got up and, bustling, gathered up her things. Her hat and coat from the back of her chair. The gloves. And then looking down at me, she added, as if an afterthought, 'You have been very kind.'